Also by Doris Betts

SOULS RAISED FROM THE DEAD

SOULS RAISED FROM THE DEAD

A Novel by

DORIS BETTS

ALFRED A. KNOPF   NEW YORK   1994

THIS IS A BORZOI BOOK
PUBLISHED BY ALFRED A. KNOPF, INC.

Grateful acknowledgment is made to the following for per-
mission to reprint previously published material:
The Ecco Press: "With Her" from *The Collected Poems, 1931–
1987* by Czeslaw Milosz, copyright © 1988 by Czeslaw Milosz
Royalties, Inc. Reprinted by permission of The Ecco Press.
University of California Press: Excerpt from "The Eighth El-
egy" from *Rainer Rilke: Duino Elegies,* translated and edited by
C. F. MacIntyre, copyright © 1961 by C. F. MacIntyre.
Reprinted by permission of the University of California Press.

Library of Congress Cataloging-in-Publication Data
Betts, Doris.
    Souls raised from the dead : a novel / by Doris Betts. —
1st ed.
    p.   cm.
    ISBN 0-679-42621-3
    1. Family—Southern States—Fiction.
    2. Children—Death—Fiction.   I. Title.
PS3552.E84S68   1994
813'.54—dc20   93-30900
                                                           CIP

Manufactured in the United States of America
First Edition

AUTHOR'S NOTE

From the stage at the University of North Carolina at Charlotte, before reading aloud an early section where Georgia Broome, palm reader, is visited by Tacey Thompson, I told the audience that this novel-in-progress had no title yet, and that suggestions would be welcome.

After the reading, a note signed "Judy Dorminey" came forward, written on the back of a supermarket price slip. It said:

There was a window in an old part of Atlanta now cleared by urban renewal which said, coincidentally,

KEYS MADE

KNIVES SHARPENED

PALMS READ

SOULS RAISED FROM THE DEAD

So the title is a gift from a stranger in North Carolina. Actual places named are a gift of the geography of North Carolina. Everything else—people, events—is invented.

A reading this Sunday from the Book of Wisdom
About how God has not made death
And does not rejoice in the annihilation of the living.
A reading from the Gospel according to Mark
About a little girl to whom He said: "Talitha, cumi!"
This is for me. To make me rise from the dead
And repeat the hope of those who lived before me.
                              —CZESLAW MILOSZ, "With Her"

SOULS RAISED FROM THE DEAD

S LOWLY AT FIRST, nervous white chickens stepped through their broken cages and tested the muddy slope down which the poultry truck had slid and overturned. It had been carrying 7,500 capons, fed on chemicals, raised for slaughter in houses heated and lit by electric current, and not one of them had ever set foot to ground before their stacked crates shifted on the sharp highway curve.

To the patrolman at roadside, the first escapees seemed to shiver at the unexpected touch of earth. If it were possible, they might have giggled, the sergeant thought, before they took their first odd leaps and tumbles, trying too hard to be the actual birds they almost remembered.

He snapped his head back, called "Keep moving please!" over and over to drivers who wanted to stop and stare at a ravine full of chickens.

Out of the wreckage, several of them flapped into a hackberry thicket and stuck there like windblown scraps.

"Keep moving, I said!" Frank waved more cars past. Some drivers were smiling. As the chickens scattered more widely a few neighbors from houses along the highway, with feed sacks and bags, began to capture lunch and dinner.

To Sergeant Frank Thompson it was one more comic scene. His eleven years with the North Carolina Highway Patrol included moments of bravery, others of dignity; but often he had been required to impose order on a chaos less criminal than ridiculous.

He squinted as the black truck driver waved, then pointed to the chicken thieves with their struggling tow sacks. Frank shrugged.

"Hell," the man said to nobody. He hefted an unbroken crate and rolled it squawking uphill to the patrolman. "Might as well take some yourself." Frank saw he had a knot on one temple and blood strung down his jaw.

"Not me." It was time for support to arrive—where was everybody? "Mister, I told you to sit still."

"I'm not hurt. Put these in your trunk?"

Frank shook his head but made the man sit on the full wooden crate. "Must have been doing fifty, were you?"

"Nawsir, she won't even make fifty down the hill. It takes downhill and a tailwind for forty—no sir! Listen, she was creeping at ten. Fifteen at the most!"

Frank kicked toward the great gouge raked through the road's muddy shoulder. "Forty at the least." A far siren was coming at last; good, a wrecker not far behind.

The blood trail, Frank suddenly saw, was coming not from the driver's swollen temple but out of the left ear. "Oh, Jesus." He leaned forward to see if the man's eye pupils were still the same size. "You lay down here; I mean it, right now. No, not flat." He waved traffic onward while he tipped the noisy crate into a pillow, pressed him down, eased the man's neck against one edge for support. "Be still and never mind the damn chickens. I told you not to move around till the medics checked you."

"I tell you I'm all right. But look how these people be stealing—"

"Don't talk. Your boss can replace chickens better than your wife can replace you." In spite of Frank's moving arm, their little drama had backed up cars, with people leaning out to see exactly where the victim was bleeding and how much. More than anything Frank hated gawkers.

"I ain't married," said the resting man, but softly.

"Stay alive and maybe you will be." He was just getting traffic under way when the driver made a funny noise and wet Frank's uniform leg with vomit. Almost immediately the flashing red ambulance signal came into view. He stopped cars so it could speed to them. As men leaped out with a stretcher Frank called, "Fractured skull?" then stepped to the center line of 15-501 to alternate north- and southbound lanes.

By now chickens were everywhere, screeching as they made low flight against windshields and metal roofs, lurching onto the road under wheels, one even roosting on the blinking blue light of Frank's patrol car. The slower, injured ones were loose with the rest, dragging half-severed legs or bloody wings. Frank was glad when a Chatham deputy's car appeared and the two local officers agreed to detour traffic on both sides during the cleanup.

Still, it was almost five before the truck cab could be lifted and towed away, later when another poultry truck hauled unbroken crates and survivors back to Pittsboro, even later when spilled gasoline had been diverted from the small stream, and very late when Sergeant Frank Thompson had checked by the hospital, talked to mechanics, and finished his accident report.

He let himself into their Carrboro apartment with his key and snapped on the light. Silence. Tension. Frank stood motionless in the foyer and for the ritual moment allowed fear to cover him in flood, since he was constantly fearful, on entry, unreasonably fearful, of discovering that fire, disease, murder, or rape had on this day found his house at last.

"Mary?"

The upstairs toilet flushed and her ridiculous wooden clogs made noise overhead. "You're late, General Franco!"

He waited until his daughter clattered into view, still uninjured, still unviolated. One more day. At sight of her crisp red hair, the faded jeans in which her legs were awkwardly too long for the rest, his skin grew warm. He laid hat and gun belt on the high closet shelf while she was banging down the steps.

"Pew, what's the stink?"

"Man threw up on my pants. What about that math test?"

She pinched the nose that was too long, like his. "Passed it, that's all I wanted."

"You ought to—"

"Want more, I know, did you eat something?"

"I'll make a sandwich after I clean up."

Frowning, she said, "You ought to—"

"Eat better, sure; I'll do that when you ace math." As he passed, he jerked Mary into a hug so quick and hard it must have felt like ambush. The school counselor claimed she needed affection, a need that troubled Frank. Her mother had filled her own need, probably was still trying to fill it, in bed with many men. "You look nice," he said.

Mary gargled with revulsion. She was twelve, and all spring he had been trying to talk to her about menstruation. He had memorized more pamphlets than a damn gynecologist.

In the shower he looked down his body with puzzled detachment: this body that could disappoint one woman but father another; that had once taken a bullet which left small brown puckers, back and front, where it entered him waist-high on one side, drove through flesh but not organs, and flew on; this lean body built for running Indian-style, not meant to be cramped all day in a car seat while machinery chased after other speeding machinery.

To Frank some days this body seemed like one more uniform, now slightly worn and soiled, which he could step out of, could emerge from hairless and new, still a boy planning to grow up and be a doctor or the nation's president.

Mary's voice yelled through the bathroom door.

"What?" He turned off the shower spray.

"*Dandy!* I just talked to Dandy! They're coming over!"

"Now?" His eyes were raw from soapy water. "Tonight?" By feel he found the towel and scrubbed his face dry. "Both of them?"

"Thirty minutes."

"OK." He was in no mood for his parents. He wanted a drink, but if his mother was coming he would have to hurry. Tacey Thompson knew he drank, knew his father drank, suspected *all* men drank; but she refused to be witness. Vodka and tonic she took by choice to be harmless ginger ale, but bourbon smelled too nasty for her to pass off as iced tea.

Quickly Frank dressed in soft old clothes, hurried to the kitchen, and poured a double shot of Jack Daniel's, neat.

"Bad day?" Mary was peeling a tomato. "Found a body in the river?"

Drinking never took the smell of corpse out of his nose or skin. "Just a chicken truck turned over. I won't eat chicken for a year. What about your own supper?"

"The evidence is in the sink, officer." She nodded at soup can, bowl, the cake-smeared plate, and cloudy milk glass. "You saw the mail?" With too much care she unfolded a lettuce leaf and eased it in place as if the bread might break.

Must be a letter from her mother. He drank deep. "I'll get to it. Dandy say anything else?"

"Said he wanted you to take him out home, maybe Saturday."

"Christ!"

"No, just you by yourself," she said with a sniff.

He had promised Mary to give up archaic, religious swearing. In her seventh grade, all the sophisticates said "Shit!"

"Why can't Dandy go by *himself*? Why can't Mama take him?"

"She hates to, you know that. He drives her crazy shouting at other drivers."

"Nobody cares if I hate it. I spend half my life in a damn car." He answered the ringing phone. Mary slid his sandwich plate and a stack of letters into reach. He talked rapidly to the reporter from the *Raleigh News and Observer*. "Just what you saw in the file. No. No, I saw him at U.N.C. Hospital. He cracked his skull, but he'll be all right." Bills, he saw. Magazine offers. He listened to the phone while sorting envelopes down to Christine's large handwriting—curly capitals, little triangles floating over the *i*'s. "No, that's all right," he said, still staring. He hung up and tried the sandwich.

"What does she say?"

"Who?"

Mary gave him a look meant to melt steel.

"One minute, one minute." Frank drained the bourbon and, while his throat was still hot, snatched up Christine's letter and tore the envelope and a ragged border down the sheet inside.

Short. As usual. His eyes scanned before returning to the main point. "As you know, Mary's thirteenth birthday will be coming up in a few more weeks"—today was June 1; Mary had been born in August—"and I hope for her sake you can spare me a hundred dollars. . . ." Frank knew he would, just as he knew Christine would forget the birthday and he would supply the kind of frivolous item Christine would choose: nylons, makeup, exercise dumbbells, the kind of punker spray that would streak hair purple or orange.

With care he said, "She sends you all her love."

"Sure. Do I hear Dandy's car out front?"

"I don't think so." He did not like Mary's automatic half turn away, the duck of her head, her martyr's voice. "Christine's on the move a lot in this new sales job, you know that. Didn't she write to you recently?"

"January fourteenth," said Mary.

"That long. Well. You're right, I think your grandparents have come," he lied. "I'll just finish this sandwich."

Mary escaped to the front door, but no one was knocking. She waited there—waiting was her best skill—while looking across the dark parking lot past another apartment building and downhill into the small, parched park the landlord had built —yellow-bell bushes, one late-blooming crab apple—until at last the Thompson grandparents would arrive. The Thompsons were on her father's side, Broomes on her mother's side—like two teams. Like a war.

But Mary would wait them all out. She had outwaited years of quarrels in her parents' bedroom down the hall. Had waited in the dark till her mother came home late so the argument could start. Had waited up sometimes to swear falsely that Mama had been on the front row at P.T.A. and was now at a movie with Lila Torrido, the old lady from next door. And one long day after school, grade five, she had waited for a lifetime or so while the television flung its pointless shadows into her face, was still waiting half-asleep on the living room rug, when her daddy came home at midnight and found her alone in the apartment.

Since then she had waited to see who would leave her next. She very much feared that Dandy Thompson's high blood pressure, in some Vesuvian effect, would erupt through his brain and take him to Heaven some night, without good-bye.

But not General Franco. Someday she would bring home the right new wife for her father once she was safely in love herself.

In front of the apartment building, Dandy Thompson was getting out of the car with a bound, a man who had rerouted high blood pressure into power jets. He was already across the lot while Grandmother Tacey Thompson worried with turning off the engine and setting the brake.

"Don't you even own a skirt?" he was already calling to Mary. "At least you can't spend much money—in pants that tight you'll never get your wallet out. How many hours were you on the phone this afternoon, anyway? Twenty?"

Behind him, Grandmother Tacey Thompson was waving out the driver's window. Since she could hardly get a word in edgewise, she was always touching, gesturing, letting her facial expression mirror others in the room, leaning back with a shocked hand to her bosom. You could cue her, the way a director must have cued the actresses in a silent movie, while Grandfather Andrew Thompson, known everywhere as Dandy because of her toddler's word, did all the voice-overs.

He hurried ahead up the steps while she was locking the car. "How's everybody? Mary Grace, this is for you; it just came today from the Hidden Word Contest. Next time I'll win first prize—I can feel it." He held out a bracelet, its dull-gray links neither metal nor plastic.

"Will it give me another green arm? I'm hot and tired, that's how I am," Mary answered just to produce her grandmother's weary mimic sag, "but improving," to prod her upright and perky again. They swapped light cheek kisses while Dandy was wrapping the bracelet on her wrist. "We heard from my mother today," Mary said, so she could watch every wrinkle of judgment snap into place around Tacey's mouth.

"How wonderful; maybe the avalanche and plague will be in touch with you next," said Dandy. He lifted her hand and shook it in midair. "Well made, that bracelet is. No doubt your mailbox is full of letters from the Prince of Darkness, maybe thermodynamics is cooling off this very minute—so what else is new and old with this family? Come on in, Tacey. I'm holding the door. Don't flap around, just say something! How are you feeling today, Mary Grace? Try saying that!" He rolled indoors, already talking to chairs and woodwork, letting the screen door slam before his wife could reach it. "And what is Christine selling nowadays, as if I didn't know? Don't make such a face at me, darlin', come on in."

With elaborate shrugs and facial apologies, Tacey rushed behind him, touching Mary, asking rapidly, "Is Frank still eating?"

"Yes."

"And don't kill yourself changing the subject, either. I haven't said a thing wrong because you can't ever tell about Christine, and even if you can—you shouldn't!" When he sat on the chintz couch and Tacey caught up with him at last she rapped him one. "There's no truth to heredity, and Mary Grace' Thompson is living proof, aren't you, darlin'?" he went on. "Francis?" he called. "You home to your aging parents, Francis?"

Mary winced at his loud voice. Nobody else called her father Francis, except—he said once—the church, which had let the sacrament of baptism go to its head. She hurried forward. "He's eating late, there was this chicken truck turned over?"

"It's always something while the banks are getting robbed down the road." In the center of their chintz couch Dandy spread into his natural frog shape. "Life is just one damned thing after—look there how that bracelet hangs off your wrist; you're getting so thin there's not enough of you to itch."

He snapped his head toward Tacey, who commented, "It's that cold and sore throat that hung on so long. Probably left you run-down and anemic."

"I've been over that cold for weeks. Can I get you both some tea? No? Coca-Cola?"

Grandma Thompson sank into a chair, fingering her blue-tint permanent, and smiled that she would have cola, though Dandy was into a new paragraph about how neither one of them ate right, so Mary got to the kitchen fast. "Your turn, General Franco!" Her father was too tired to be the good son. She could see it in his mouth edges.

He put down his second, half-finished sandwich, plain mayonnaise and bread. Seeing the droop of his mouth she spoke softly. "Just don't tell Dandy what you ate for supper. They're waiting."

"I know it, I'm coming, but God! Am I tired!"

Mary hated it when he threw God and Jesus into ordinary weekdays. "Or you can serve drinks while I make the conversation?"

"Where'd you get that bracelet? What's it made of, barbwire?"

"And spray-painted. I guess Grandma wouldn't wear it."

"Wish he'd take up golf." Frank didn't hurry through the dining room. Late on a hard day, he seemed to lose perspective; what he attained, thanks to alcohol, was a sharp foreground vision, which carried him now with painful alertness past the screaming colonial wallpaper and the red draperies Christine had hung three years ago, under the fake-walnut arch, and into the room where his parents, bright-eyed, waited. Under their examination he felt about ten.

His mother showed him the smile he should have been wearing.

"You're not already worn-out in the shank of the evening? Son, you look like a car that drove all day with the brakes on. You need more regular hours and a diet to regulate the body. Tacey is going to have to bring you some soup, aren't you, darlin'? Now, what about Saturday? We can drive out to the homeplace. Mary said on the phone you were off."

"Not this Saturday." It sounded like a prayer. "I spend half my life behind a damn steering wheel."

"Uh-oh, one part tired and four parts cranky—well, I can wait, Francis; I never mean to impose. Naturally I plan to buy your gas whenever you can find the time to go. You like Mary's bracelet? You still got that record album I won for you—the steel-band music?"

This time he matched his mother's smile. "Oh, all right, if it's early."

"How's Christine? I hear she's able to write letters again. What's she want this time?"

Frank was afraid Mary could hear them from the kitchen. "Christine stays busy selling in the eastern part of the state. Asked to be remembered to you both."

"If she's selling it, that's a novelty in itself. Let her ask— I'm forgetting Christine with every breath, that little trash. That product of trash."

Tacey murmured, "A little charity, Andrew."

"Just be quiet," Frank said. He checked to see if Mary had come into earshot—yes.

"Mary Grace knows I never mean her."

He said evenly, "People know what you say, no more. Don't ask Mary to read your mind."

Dandy pointed to the arched doorway where his granddaughter balanced a tray of wet glasses. "All right, Mary Grace? I never mean you. You're a product of the Thompsons, not the Broomes."

"I'm nobody's product." As Mary set their drinks on the coffee table, Frank noticed the turn, her ducked head, the false voice; he saw suddenly that the stubby fingers handing out napkins came from the Broomes; he wondered abruptly if she had pubic hair yet, and if it was red or as dark as Christine's.

Tacey took her drink but with the other hand felt Mary's brow. "No fever but—but you've lost weight. Are you still coughing?"

Dandy got so tickled he was about to spill cola on the couch. "That's what one casket said to another, 'Is that you, coffin?' Fellow worked at the undertaker's used to tell that—what was his name? Peabody? Same one that said he went into the undertaking business because he liked working with people; you remember him, Francis."

"It's not very nice, Andrew, to take a question concerning somebody's health and turn it into an undertaker joke. Here, set that glass down." Tacey got a folded napkin underneath.

"Really. I'm fine, Grandma."

"Mary's fine," said Frank loudly, by saying so making it true, while wondering if nowadays schoolteachers were telling young girls all they should know.

"She's still winter pale, but Francis," Dandy said impatiently, "Mary's stretching out tall and thin, growing up, and soon she'll have boys all over this living room. You can't work those long night hours then. That's one more reason we ought to get one house for the four of us and combine our laundry and heating and cooking—"

At once both Frank and his mother said no.

Vibrating from headshakes, Tacey added, "I love you both, but I can't run a busy house the way I used to. I'm sixty-six!"

"I'm two more and I ain't dead yet. Why I might win an oil well next week. You've got to look ahead. We'd live mostly on sandwiches—you'd never have to go back to all those meats and hot bread, Tacey, and we'd send out the shirts, and Mary Grace here—"

"Mary would be no help at all," said Mary firmly.

It was a discussion three years old, beginning when Christine ran off with the county tax collector at the very time he ran off with part of Orange County's taxes.

"Think I'll get some of that Coke," Frank said, but the glass he carried back from the kitchen was half-bourbon. He heard Mary saying that the only reason Dandy wanted them all living together was to have "two more people to listen to him."

"Better me than rocky-roll music. Sit right here, Francis. Now the reason I want to go to the homeplace is I hear that fool is parking trailers in the bottomland, you know, the old cornfield. I hear he's sticking the richest five acres in the spread full of septic tanks. Well, it'll swamp up on him, of course, but I've got to see for myself he's that dumb."

"Dandy"—Frank's word, Daddy, and Mary's nickname had long since merged—"Dandy, nobody's ever going to farm that land again, you know that, not by that four-lane highway."

"Not now, not without getting the cholera from human waste. And Mary can come with us. It's important to know what roots you come from."

"Sorry, I've got a riding lesson Saturday."

Frank said, "Besides, developers can't put a drainage field like that by a creek anymore."

"Better on Saturday Mary should be having a checkup at the

doctor's." They looked thoughtfully at her; Tacey Thompson could speak up quickly enough when she had to. "And, no, I can't go!" She added in a rush, "I'm having my glasses changed!"

Since Dandy didn't drive, wouldn't drive, claimed the risk made him breathless and shortened his life, that driving a car today was like running an endless gauntlet of dangers between rows of sensory punishments beating his eyes, ears, nervous system, somebody else had to drive him everywhere.

Why didn't the same noise, bad drivers, glare, and monoxide, Frank often asked him, assault a passenger as much as a driver?

"I'm not responsible for safe survival over here, and that unfrays my nerves," he would answer. Truth was, since Dandy could not talk and drive at the same time, he preferred to be chauffeured while insulting other drivers.

On Easter Sunday Tacey, having taken him driving through fast holiday traffic to see the coming of spring to the countryside, had finally cried breathlessly, "Look at all the dogwood! Isn't this beautiful? Aren't you glad to be alive?"

"Glad?" he replied, "I'm amazed."

Until retirement, Andrew Thompson had managed the shoe department at Belk's, one more farm boy who, after the Depression, had come to town to "public" work. He still gloated over how many size nines and tens were under local prom dresses and bridal skirts.

But the homeplace where he had grown up was in northern Orange County, on a dairy farm, much of its acreage now paved highway or paved parking lot, the milking barn replaced by Revco Drugs and a Winn-Dixie Store in a shopping center built so near the creek that it flooded when heavy rains drained too fast into gutters and culverts. He exulted over television news pictures of wading clerks as they relocated grocery items on high shelves. "Look at that!" he would crow, and telephone Frank to turn on his set fast and see how the mud of Happy Creek was getting into the powdered milk to pollute babies.

Above the clustered stores, on a rise, the deserted old Thompson house, built in 1907 where Dandy's father could count his pastured livestock from the porch, had now become too rotted and dangerous even for winos, so honeysuckle and copperheads were coming indoors.

As a boy, Frank had spent many summers on that farm, where his Thompson grandparents still lived in the 1950s. The sloping front meadow then had flung up doves and quail as he walked through. Frank had meant to grow up, grow rich, and reclaim this land, build himself a white-columned house and set purebred dogs to guard each door with purebred horses posed like statues down the hill. Once he had even walked Christine past the family graveyard and deep into a far section of hard-woods and hollies to discuss building at least a vacation cottage there. "At the end of the world? What for?" she'd said.

It depressed Frank to go to the homeplace now and have such a good downhill view of trailer trucks, neon signs, and trash dumpsters.

But before his parents left at 11:00 p.m., he had agreed to pick up Dandy early Saturday so they could go like tourists to view the ruins.

With Mary he stood on the front stoop, waving them off in the dark. "Is your grandmother right? That maybe you don't feel good?"

"I feel good." She waved beside him. Like kin whom Tacey had trained well, both kept flapping at the departing Thompson car growing smaller while they talked. "I'm just preadolescent. Don't you ever read Gesell?"

"He says you should have a big appetite."

"I'm not as bitchy as his book allows me to be, either."

They were gone. "Don't say 'bitchy,' " Frank muttered as he followed her inside, locked and tested the door. He looked down on her springy auburn curls, troubled. "Any headaches?" She said no. He cleared his throat and said, too loud, "It's perfectly natural to grow up and have certain physical changes, of course."

Back turned, Mary was bent at the television set. "For boys, uh, their voices change. They grow beards."

"I know what girls do." Mary snapped the picture from one newscaster to another.

"You do?" Frank sank into his vinyl chair. "All of it? Who?"

"I go to the library a lot."

He knew that; maybe she went too much. Though she wouldn't, by will, make straight A's like the "other parrots," she was always reading.

He swallowed a throatful of air and made himself ask, "Have you already started?"

"No. But I'm ready." When she glanced up, she said, "I mean I've bought my supplies."

Stupidly he asked, "All of them?"

She threw wide her hands. "A belt. A pad. For goodness' sake, can't you ever let me alone?" She hurried from the room and up to bedroom level, taking at last her turn at bitchiness, he thought. He heard the bathroom door slam. Lately he'd been hearing that door too often in the middle of too many nights, had wondered at her insomnia. Now he supposed she might have been checking pajamas for bloodstains.

When other noises told him she was in her room, then creaking springs that she was in bed, Frank called, "You OK?"

After a silence she answered his real question. "I'm not mad at you, General Franco."

"Good," he called back. He waited five minutes by the clock before he called again to her, softly, "Sleep tight." No answer.

For a long time he read the newspaper. Then he wrote Christine a check and addressed the envelope: General Delivery, Jacksonville, NC. Must be with some marine from Camp Lejeune.

He turned on local radio, yawning; then, thinking of Mary asleep upstairs, he unsealed the envelope and wrote slowly on a sheet of stationery:

Mary is not only having a birthday soon (<u>August 12</u>) but will soon mature from girl to <u><u>woman</u></u>.

He underlined the date once and underlined "woman" twice, looked away to think but carefully skipped his glance over Christine's framed photograph, kept on display for Mary's sake. He wrote a second paragraph:

Perhaps a short visit would be good for her at this time. You could stay here and I would stay at Mama's. Or Mary could even come

No. Not that. Frank snapped shut the ballpoint pen and tore the paper over and over again. He stuffed the pieces inside a paper bag and wadded that into a ball for the wastebasket.

Upstairs the toilet flushed. Mary's last checkup had been last fall for basketball tryouts, then she didn't make the team. Too short. Short like the Broomes.

Next week he'd call Dr. Seagroves about another physical. It couldn't hurt.

The midnight news came on. Some of those chickens had wandered from the wreck into the ritzy country-chic development between Chapel Hill and Pittsboro, where retired New Yorkers had probably never before seen poultry outside a butcher shop. Listeners were telephoning the radio talk show with complaints. Some had heard that any loose bird might carry psittacosis or skin mites contagious to humans. Hungry chickens had been scratching up their marigold seeds, and now that it was dark they were roosting in shrubs or on clothesline poles, dropping you-know everywhere. The outraged citizens wanted to know which state agency to call. One woman complained that the sheriff's dispatcher had laughed at her.

Sometimes Frank wondered if savages had really been worse off when there was nobody to answer their problems but the Sun or some carved-wood goddess.

He went to bed, stopping first at Mary's closed, but not

latched, door. At first from the sounds he thought her still awake and touched the door barely inward with his shoe. No, she was sleeping and murmuring in dreams. Though the words made no sense, he saw by her face that she was happy and far away.

"IT'S JUST MY THIRD SATURDAY, and no—I do not want you to watch me ride." Mary Grace Thompson hung into the backseat to reach her black hard hat. "You and Dandy have a good time." Probably she had hurt his feelings—easy to do, she knew, since Mama had run away. "Maybe you can watch a little when you pick me up."

"We'll get back before eleven, then."

She snapped the elastic under her chin and got out. From the beginning Mary had lied about how cheap the lessons were, huntseat equitation, 8:00 to 11:00 a.m., for only ten dollars per session. Actually, her beginner class only rode between ten and eleven; the rest of the time she mucked stalls, oiled leather, or got in the way of grooms trying to do both. She had told Miss Jillian Peters that she had to come to the stables early on Saturdays, dropped off on Daddy's way to work.

"You couldn't come at ten on your bicycle?" Miss Peters had asked.

"Goodness, not *this* far!" Just this year, Mary had become very good at lying. Probably she inherited lying from the Broome side. Probably she would end up running a saloon and fancy house out West someday, so she would certainly need to be a skilled horsewoman.

Now she hurried past the painted sign, CENTAUR RIDING SCHOOL, with its list of boarding fees and training fees, and down the barn's cool center aisle. That aroma of horse with hay, manure, and sawdust should have made an unpleasant mix, but Mary inhaled the smell deep until it made her toes lift in imaginary stirrups.

Before the stall of Gambler's Chance, Mary stopped and called the Arab gelding, who came quickly to suck up sugar cubes from her palm, one by one. Chancy was a dark bay with four white stockings, a flashy mover, but too calm and lazy to make a show horse. He belonged to a doctor. Someday Mary definitely planned to own him, even if she had to become a secret blood donor for pay, even if she shrank to a white string of herself while she was earning his life by siphoning from her own. His black lip barely met her skin with a tickle as he drew in the last sweetness.

"Mary Thompson? Are you here already?"

"Yes, ma'am, Daddy has to work early—I told you." She clung weakly to the stall door, for, outside the family, she loved Myra Jillian Peters almost as much as the bay horse. "Can I do some work? I like to. I won't be in the way."

"Oh, all right, help me bring up the school horses for the first class." Miss Peters, as tall and fair as a Swedish film star, smiled as she handed over a halter and lead line. "I like to know when visitors are in the barn, that's all. Does your mother work Saturdays, too?"

"She's dead."

Not answering, Miss Peters led the way to the second barn. Her very pale hair fell in a long plait down her back, and her very blue eyes had blue cream blended on the lids. She never mucked out a stall in less than full makeup. Mary had never seen her except with those eyes outlined and fringed with long, blackened lashes. Her full mouth was like a child's, but her sooty eyes might have looked across fancy houses of their own. Mary had cut her own hair a week ago because she'd given up on ever growing such an ultimate plait.

Suddenly Miss Peters turned back and laid an arm about Mary's shoulder so they fell into step. "Can you lead Cookie?"

"Sure."

"Then I'll get Ralph, the gray you usually ride. Ralph steps on feet."

"Yes 'um." At Cookie's stall, Mary shook out of the half hug; she didn't much like being touched anymore. This year it was as if her skin felt sore everywhere.

Miss Peters kept watching her face, probably doubting that she could really halter Cookie by herself, so Mary stepped into the stall and got it done.

"How long has your mother been dead?"

"Just before last Christmas," Mary said, because that sounded saddest.

"I'm sorry." She opened the next stall door to lead out the gray. "You have no brothers and sisters? But you must have good friends at school."

"I used to." Mary was not sure how far to carry her maladjustment. "School isn't as good as it used to be." Far enough, she decided. "Is it OK if my daddy watches the last part of our lesson? About eleven o'clock?"

"I thought your father had to be at work."

"He asked off."

"All right, fine." She led Ralph alongside to check that Mary had not wrapped the lead line around her hand and was not dragging one end in the dirt. "Good. You're going to be bored during these other lessons, since there's not much work for you this morning. You oiled all the saddles last week."

"I like to watch the others ride, and I found a book in the tack room on riding."

"It's too soon for you to think much about theory, Mary. You need to master each stage as you go."

"I'm always reading," Mary bragged to see whether Miss Peters was impressed by serious readers. Maybe not. "The teachers make you," she complained quickly.

They hitched both horses to the rail. By then the first students were arriving, some already tacking up ponies their families owned, others waiting with school saddles to see which mount they'd be assigned. The small child coming to Ralph was dragging a stirrup in the dust.

"Don't get that dirty," Mary ordered. "You know how long it takes to clean leather?" It was no honor, Mary knew, to be put on Ralph—the slowest, laziest, safest animal on the place. Probably he knew it, too, and embarrassment slowed him even further. Mary stopped to scratch in the bony groove under Ralph's chin. "You be nice to him," she instructed the small rider.

But Miss Peters didn't introduce her as an assistant or anything. In fact, Miss Peters was lost to her now, claimed by these beginners who could not reach the horse's poll nor mount without a lift up. Mary waited to one side until all eight riders were circling the ring at a stiff walk. She was sure she looked more relaxed and natural on a horse than any of them did.

In the tack room, she borrowed Miss Peters's book off a shelf.

Just as during the first week of every school year she would read through most of her textbooks and then lose interest, Mary skipped quickly past the present level of her own riding lessons. She wanted instantly to be an intermediate or advanced rider, to understand the pattern of the hand gallop and which hoof moved first; she wanted to know all the theory about jumping, side passes, double bridles. Her mind was ready to ride to hounds or in sheriff's posses. In the first two lessons her class had only walked, with an occasional, miserable sitting trot. Miss Peters would not let her students post until after they had "acquired a seat."

Much more banging on the saddle and Mary would be willing to give her "seat" away. Besides, posting sounded so easy in the book.

Better yet, Mary wanted to canter, to go with the motion, to wipe the seat of her saddle with her breeches as Ralph—recognizing her innate authority at once—took instantly the proper lead at her invisible, deft command. In a chair, Mary looked at the photographs and then practiced the shift of invisible reins that would incline Ralph slightly toward the fence, one foot on girth, one behind—how lightly he would spring into the gait, how relieved to be free of amateurs! Mary hummed; she could already sense the fast waltz tempo of their canter. *Tales from the Vienna Woods.* She and Ralph would be a study in three-quarter rhythm. "Guess my middle name?" she would call to Jillian Peters. "It's Grace! Mary Grace!"

"I'm not surprised," Miss Peters would answer, smiling.

Almost two hours later, when she herself was riding Ralph at an amateur's walk in line around the boring circle, Mary glimpsed her father walking toward the riding ring. Her ankles and knees tensed. Farther behind, Dandy stepped from the car and shaded his eyes to watch her pass no faster than an invalid on a wooden sawhorse.

It was *so* embarrassing!

Mary could not help what happened next. Really, she never stopped to decide. She was not even considering what to do. One foot slid forward by itself; the other suddenly half kicked until Ralph leaped toward the fence into a tentative bumpy trot. Though Mary had already begun to thud awkwardly against the saddle, her body again gave the aids more strongly. Suddenly Ralph was cantering, cantering fast, cantering out from under her! She leaned back precariously, then bounced, then jerked the reins, which had become very long and loose. Her balance shifted aside. One of the stirrups flew off her shoe. Every fence post whizzing by had the shape of a sharpened stake.

Then something hit her hard. For one flash she thought Dandy had taken the wheel at last and had driven the car straight through the fence into Ralph and her and broken all their legs.

STILL WEARING JODHPURS and high boots, Jill Peters hurried into the hospital waiting room. "How is she, Mr. Thompson?"

Frank would not stop pacing long enough to answer, so Tacey said Mary was still in X ray. Though Dandy immediately opened his mouth to speak, she—who had left the optometrist's with her eyes still dilated and come in a cab—made a face and shook her head.

"Conscious?"

"Not fully." Frank stopped to frown at this pretty, frivolous young woman. "Kept begging us not to shoot Ralph. Not that I'd mind shooting any horse that would—Miss Peters, I find it hard to believe you'd mount a beginner on anything that would run away like that."

"Now just a minute, Mr. Thompson. Ralph is no runaway. Mary must have . . ." She trailed off as Frank paced away from her muttering that he should have insisted on different kinds of lessons, art perhaps. Sewing.

Every time he closed his eyes he could still see Mary fly over the gray's shoulder and strike the fence with a terrible breaking noise, then fold somehow over the top rail and drop outside the ring.

Jill Peters shook hands with the grandparents and introduced herself. "I'm sorry I couldn't come with the rescue squad, but I had to wait until a parent picked up the last child."

Sure you did, Frank thought. Responsible to the end.

"She'll be fine; why, by tomorrow she'll be laughing at how worried we were—I say, she's going to be fine, Frank! Tomorrow I'll be kidding her about breaking the fall with her head," Dandy said, but even he couldn't force a smile onto his white face.

Tacey Thompson suddenly whispered to Frank, "Are you going to call Christine?"

"Not unless I have to." He made another path across the room and back. "Call her where?"

"The Broomes must have a number."

He shook his head and again set off pacing.

Softly she called, "She's Mary's mother."

"What?" Miss Peters dropped into a chair. "But Mary told me her mother was dead!"

The others stared.

"She said so just this morning."

"Well, she's not, but she and that horse could both be dead and it would suit me fine!" Dandy moved out of his wife's reach. "Mary Grace was ten years old when Christine Broome went off one night, went off with a scoundrel, never left a note or a kind word. Never been back since."

"We're divorced."

"I'm sorry," said Miss Peters, "it's none of my business."

While she walked around nervously, Dandy wiped and replaced his glasses to see her better. He cocked his head to examine the back of her tight jodhpurs. "You're mighty young to own a riding stable. And what kind of riding teacher lets a little girl gallop on her third lesson?"

When she snapped toward him the long plait flew. "I wouldn't call what old Ralph did a gallop. Mary's class is still developing balance, so of course I didn't *let* her, as you put it. They're only allowed to trot a few steps at a time. I'm not much older than Ralph, in fact—he's twenty. And I lease the stable." She eyed Frank. "And I carry insurance, of course, but in this case there was no negligence."

Frank didn't hear, but Dandy said, "You know what has four legs, eats oats, and sees just as well from either end? A blind horse, that's what, and maybe that's old Ralph's trouble—he's blind, and when some noise scared him, he ran her into that fence!"

Jill planted herself in the path Frank was pacing. "If I know Mary—" she began.

"And do you know her? After three lessons?"

"Three Saturday lessons, yes, but Mary's been coming to Centaur Riding Stable every Saturday morning since New Year's, just to watch and do chores."

Frank stared. He'd thought on Saturdays she and her best friend, Kay Linda, shampooed each other's hair and set it with the hot rollers he'd pretended were a gift from Christine.

"I was saying that if I know Mary, she was trying to become

an instant advanced rider by following directions in some book."

"Or five books. With contradictions." He frowned. "Mary met you through some of her girlfriends?"

"She said she looked up riding stables in the yellow pages."

Frank leaped forward when Dr. Seagroves appeared through the swinging doors. "How's Mary?"

The other three ran with him. Dr. Seagroves felt his slick bald head for reading glasses and set them on his nose. "She's got a concussion," he said, making notes in a file, "and I took eleven stitches where her scalp split open on that rock." He wrote something else, then smiled at them all. "We'll watch her for twenty-four hours, of course, but I think she'll be all right."

Sudden relief almost made Frank's chest cave inward.

Miss Peters sounded defensive. "All my students wear helmets. Every student in that class had on a riding helmet."

"Mary left her chin strap off. Now, Frank." Dr. Seagroves drew him away and down the hall. "Mary's generally feeling all right? I haven't seen her since September."

"I was sending her in next week. She's been fine except for a sore throat and cough that hung on half the winter. Mama thinks she's thin, but she's growing so fast, and Mama always—something wrong?"

The doctor looked at a page Frank couldn't see. "Her blood count's all right, but as long as she's here I'll just update her medical history." He kept reading silently. Frank couldn't make sense of the figures upside down. "Maybe repeat the urine tests," he said half to himself.

"What's the matter with Mary?"

Dr. Seagroves snapped shut the file. "Don't start worrying, Frank. I'll take a bet nothing at all is wrong with Mary."

From a distance, Jill Peters was trying to read the doctor's lips. She frowned like someone about to be sued who can't afford a lawyer. Frank deliberately blocked her view.

"Can I see her now?"

His parents crowded forward, also wanting to go in, but the doctor said just Frank at first. The others could visit once they moved her to a room upstairs. He held back the Thompsons with one pink, soft hand—Frank hated the texture of doctors' overwashed hands. With the chart he tapped Frank's arm. "Don't be alarmed," he said, "if Mary doesn't remember eating breakfast. In an hour she probably won't even remember arriving at the riding school, and in another hour she may forget the fall. Sequentially she may lose memory of the whole day, but that's not significant."

"But she *is* conscious? She's coherent?" Frank suddenly wanted to examine Mary's eyes and make certain their pupils were the same size.

"Conscious and talking; takes after her talkative grand-father—how are you, Andrew? Tacey? And of course when she does sleep, we'll wake her up regularly." He broke off his handshake with Jillian Peters to hurry after Frank and stop him at the door. "Just a minute! Don't you go in there looking scared to death. You hear me?"

Nodding, Frank—like his mother—remade his face. He pushed forward both doors and immediately saw Mary, eyes closed, lying on a hospital cart beside the black X-ray machine.

A nurse looked up from tucking the sheet.

"I'm her father." It was hard not to run to her. "Mary?" Above her white face, a bandage was tilted like a beanie cap down on her brow. "Look at me, Mary Grace Thompson!"

With false starts her eyelids struggled to open and stay open. At first he could not tell if the pupils were even. Now both blank eyes and, yes, they matched, each iris greenish blue with darker edging. As he watched, the blankness melted while he came into focus for her.

"Wow," Mary said, and blinked. "What a dumb thing!"

"That's all right. Are you hurting?"

Tentatively she fingered the gauze. "They shaved some? I'm numb. How many stitches?"

"Eleven." To Frank's terror she was closing her eyes to drift into a final coma! "Mary?" He grabbed the nurse, who, shaking her head, spoke Mary's name softly several times.

"What?" Again her blue-green eyes came into existence and in them so did Frank's wide and frightened face. She said, "I was cantering."

He made himself pull back a little, watching his image shrink in her wide, clear gaze. "Miss Peters should never have let you canter. It's a wonder you didn't break bones." His voice sounded weak.

"Miss Peters didn't." Mary lifted a hand—coordination seemed OK—and waved it in one direction, then the opposite. "Correction. The *horse* was cantering. I was not."

"You'll be fine, honey. Dr. Seagroves is keeping you overnight to be safe, and Dandy and Grandma are waiting outside. What should I bring you? What pajamas do you want?"

"A milk shake and French fries."

Smiling, the nurse rolled the cart toward an inner door. Frank started to follow, but she said they had to transfer Mary to a third-floor room now.

Mary called, "Is Ralph all right?"

"Ralph? Who's Ralph? Oh. He's fine. Went straight to the gate to be let out, I'm told. I'll come up to her room in about ten minutes, then?"

The nurse said firmly, "Thirty," and rolled her out of sight.

Absently, Frank reached to spread his palm and lean his full weight on the cold X-ray table. She'd be fine. Of course. This dangling camera had looked inside her body and made certain that underneath her red hair there was no crack in the skull, no snap between the vertebrae of her neck, though he had heard everything break in the instant she flew over the fence railing. He could still hear those bones breaking. Dozens. Like a string of firecrackers.

He spread precisely the fingers of his other hand by the first. Neither one was steady.

But Mary could remember the horse's name. Ralph. And she was hungry. Good signs.

He kept bracing his sweaty palms, releasing, watching the uneven tremor in both hands. This kind of love—it was all hazard. Never with any woman had he been so vulnerable. Not Christine when they were first married, certainly not Cindy Scofield on an occasional Saturday night now. Never with his parents. Not with one single friend.

Caring so much can't be good for people. Men especially. It leaves us too exposed.

Dr. Seagroves came in from the hall. "They've already moved her?"

Before turning, Frank interlaced his fingers and tugged hard to be sure they would not shake in public.

"I sent your parents to eat lunch in the cafeteria while Mary's admitted. You do the same." He held back one of the doors for Frank. "You worry too much about that girl, you know that. Ought to get married again."

"She looked so pale."

"That's to be expected. I was just telling Miss Peters she'll probably be back in the saddle next Saturday."

"Oh, I doubt that." But in the hall when he spotted Jill Peters at the far end, he called and caught up with her. "Mary says she was trying to canter, but not with your permission."

"So long as Mary's all right, that's the important thing." Down the hall she moved, her long blond plait in rhythm. Its sway made him look at her ass.

"I'll be back in thirty minutes," Frank called to the doctor, hurrying after. "Miss Peters? I promised to bring her a milk shake and French fries. Come with me and have lunch."

From her handbag she showed him a small carton of yogurt, low fat. In her tight jodhpurs he couldn't locate a pound she needed to lose.

"Come have a napkin and water at least. I'm sorry I blamed you."

"You were worried," she said.

"NO WONDER SHE LIED about her mother." Jill Peters bit deep into the cheeseburger she had claimed not to want. "Couldn't you have kept the details secret? At least until Mary was older."

"She brought the whole story home from school."

"And what did you say?"

"That it wasn't so, that Christine had a good sales job, with traveling, so we both just decided not to stay married, since we couldn't get along." Jill's black-rimmed eyes belonged in a harem, he thought. Her tears would flow like ink. And she stared straight into his eyes with the gaze of a dominant animal. Frank was determined not to look away if he had to salt and pepper his food by guesswork.

From somewhere behind her serene contemplation, Miss Peters said sarcastically, "So if she'd come home, you'd have taken your wife back."

"No. Not this time."

"Mary must have thought so. Does she think so now?"

Frank shook his head, snatching a quick estimate of the seasoning that speckled his food. "She chose to believe her school friends. They answered all her questions. Some told her stories I thought nobody knew except me. Older stories." Men's names came into his mind and went. "Worse stories."

Embarrassment finally made Jill look away. With care she dipped into ketchup and ate potato strips.

He decided her hair must be yellow naturally, its roots pale all the way down to a paler scalp. "You're not from Chapel Hill."

"Is anybody? Are you?"

"From the countryside in Orange County, or it used to be

countryside. Now we're in an apartment building like everyone else, on the edge of Carrboro."

"I know." She set a container of apricot yogurt out of her purse, fished among keys and coins even deeper, then spread a crude map on the table. "Mary's asked me to dinner several times."

He saw the red crayon circles—the wide one marking their building in a crowd of buildings, the smaller showing their door in a long line of identical doors. The sameness of layout rose before him—all those bathrooms piped vertically together, those TV antennae, everything squared off as if made for angular, metallic people.

"She never mentioned—wait a minute? Saturday evenings?" Jill nodded. "A woman cleans for us on Fridays and does some cooking for the weekend. Fried chicken or homemade soup." Maybe Mary was matchmaking? "I work late shift Fridays." He touched with one finger the red mark along which he drove very late, out Highway 54 to the rows of blocky buildings, and turned by the sign RAMSHEAD CHATEAUX into the perfectly drawn parking spaces. "There are too many things Mary isn't telling me."

"Naturally. She's what, thirteen?"

"This August."

"I stopped confiding even younger, to protect my parents from finding out how disgusting my mind really was compared with theirs. Not only the thoughts of boys but the emphasis on me, me, me, while Mother was out doing good works in the parish and while she thought my only flaw was this over-bite."

Jillian showed her extended upper teeth. Something instant, like a chill, flashed across his groin. "And your father?"

"He kept his charity at home. Once a year he went to confession, always in April, when he also had his chest X ray and paid his taxes. The rest of the year he was a farmer and a part-time electrician on hourly wage who worked overtime so I could ride in horse shows with the daughters of doctors and lawyers. You see where it led."

"They're still alive?"

"Mother is, in St. Paul. Does Mary have grandparents here?"

"You met my parents at the hospital."

"Not exactly," she said, but interrupted his apology to repeat, "You were too worried."

"My wife's family grew up around here, too, but those grandparents live in Durham now. What brought you to North Carolina?"

"The new vet school at N.C. State. As soon as I accumulate some more undergraduate hours and tuition money, I hope to enroll, and it's cheaper for an in-state resident."

Frank had a brief pastel vision of Jill cuddling puppies in both hands before she added, "Equine specialty, of course. Maybe cows." She glanced at a wide man's watch on one arm. "Your thirty minutes have passed."

"In this hospital—I know too well—everything takes longer than announced."

"You work there?"

Though out of uniform, he was surprised. Maybe law enforcement embarrassed Mary, whose seventh grade was full of professors' children, world travelers all. "I'm a patrol sergeant." Jill looked puzzled. "A trooper. The North Carolina Highway Patrol? Come on, you know me. I wave cars by so taxpayers can see football games and the state fairs. Sneak up on safe drivers with my evil radar. Falsely call you a drunk when you only drank just one beer with a big dinner."

Once more came her long, appraising stare. "Except for your defensiveness, I'd never have thought you the type."

At fifteen, he had considered the ministry. The thought of Christine, a sensation in any choir loft, made him grin. "Broderick Crawford being the right type?" Jill was too young even to remember the TV reruns. "You're twenty-one? Twenty-two?"

"Twenty-four."

The waitress brought his prepaid sack of food for Mary. As they slid from the booth, Frank decided to ask Jill Peters, decided not to; yes and then no; then elected to ask Mary instead. But when they reached the hot parking lot, where sunstroke might excuse it, he stared overhead and said in a rush, "I guess you've got a special boyfriend or an engagement here or something still going on in Minnesota, pretty as you are?"

"Not any longer."

He went on sounding a fool. "I'm thirty-four."

"That's all right." She pointed to a side street. "My car's there; you'd better hurry unless you want to take her cold French fries."

She was turning, that long plait swinging round like the tail of a painter, a mountain cat in the rocks. Her hair was not long enough to sit on like his grandmother's had been, he saw, but it could be loosed and hang wavy in front across her breasts like a curtain, or knotted below them. Down the sidewalk she moved. Her jodhpurs fit as well as a panther's skin.

Hair like that: in bed it makes trouble, he thought. She rolls on it and it yanks and it gets into everybody's mouth.

Halfway down the block Jill Peters swung to face him and the plait slapped over one shoulder and quivered.

He shouted, "I'll call you!"

Almost without pause she spun back as smooth as a ball-and-socket joint, so quickly and without answer that he was disappointed and took a step forward to call after her, "Say 'Good!' "

Effortlessly she made the same dance whirl, and the hair went around the maypole—"Good!"—and she turned the corner out of sight.

ALTHOUGH FASTER HELICOPTERS have largely replaced the patrol's medical relay, North Carolina still has more square miles than England, with its wide 500 running east to west still mostly in woods and fields. Sometimes the hospital where a cornea transplant can be scooped out before the bone socket is allowed to cool may be in an isolated town; or the National Guard is away on maneuvers; the TV station's chopper usually borrowed may be temporarily poised like a hummingbird over the red blooms of a burning forest. Then they go back to using the automobile marathon again.

Frank Thompson, headed home late Saturday after watching Mary slide safely into a natural sleep, got the radio call. A cooler containing some dead woman's eye was being rushed from Wadesboro to U.N.C. Memorial Hospital, but the Chatham County intercept had blown a tire. Could he head south toward the unit northbound on U.S. 1, now a dozen miles below Sanford, and make the pickup wherever they met?

Frank acknowledged, checked the gasoline gauge, put on his blue light without flasher, and made a swift road turn.

Months had passed since he last carried body parts, antivenom, or rare blood type in his cruiser, speeding between county lines to beat some thunderous death knell set to go off God knew when. In all these races, he would assign himself cumulative wins against losses. To take this curve smoothly, to beat a traffic light, to make some farmer swerve his pickup truck aside without danger—each of these moments tallied and turned back time by force until, in Frank's mind, carpenters unbuilt the bier, wreaths were dismantled in reverse, and unction was reduced from extreme to casual.

Tonight Frank's blue light met blue counterpart in the valley between Deep and Rocky rivers. They spun the cars in a dusty stop by the highway, the moves as reflexive as when one shoulder lifts without thinking the weight upon it. As easily as that, Frank, one eye on rear mirrors, gunned his engine and moved alongside, leaned out, and from the window took without words from Patrolman Flynt the white icy belted box, set it beside him, and already was moving onto the pavement, driving, third gear, fourth; then smoothly at speed.

He thought of Mary as if he were carrying the magic of sight to her alone.

In Pittsboro, too many late drivers were still out—teens, early vacationers headed east; Frank had to flash and siren around the old courthouse and then north between old houses dark at the back of wet green lawns. Although the trip was routine, it seemed secretly heroic. The dragon, he thought. The Black Prince.

At the hospital, after giving up the treasure, he hurried to the third floor and tiptoed inside Mary's dark room. She was sleeping. He stood by her bed as he had stood by bassinet, by crib; she looked one year old, then four. Under her pillow he had just replaced a yellowing incisor with two half-dollars. She was eight with the Halloween false face lying nearby. She had chickenpox. Nightmares.

Once Mary had sleepwalked. A few months, maybe, after Christine went away. He could still remember hearing a swishing noise on the hall carpet, coming forth to see her flowered nightgown going out the far window and onto the small, projecting roof that overhung their front door. So thickly had his heart stuck in his throat that he had to croak her name soundlessly, over and over, a running unreal dreamer himself, before she dimly heard the hoarse anguish and turned. Only that one window was raised on winter nights; after that night, all were kept locked. He reached it at last. Under her bare feet, snow powdered the asphalt shingles. Mary's blank face was turned to the window he was struggling through, his arms out, gasping a dried husk of her name. Her eyes were so wide and joyous that who would have thought her sleeping? At sight of him she cried, "Mama!" Awkwardly he kept coming. His voice returned, saying "Yes, Mary. Yes." They sat enwrapped on the roof, Frank wearing only his undershorts but not cold, numb and unreal, no longer himself but a creature who from now on could live iced over on roofs and in treetops.

He grew numb again watching her sleep. Tonight in the

hospital bed she slept well below dreams, far from the risk of sleepwalking. Almost as deep as death, he feared.

Frank worked the old trick: laid his forefinger over her upper lip to let her warm damp breath blow evenly, miraculously, over that knuckle. Against hers, his skin was ugly and corrupt.

He tiptoed away. Outside her door he stopped to read rapidly her posted chart. A blood count without comment. No surprises. Normal temperature. Low blood pressure. The volume of nourishment matched to the volume of waste. X-ray report. Reflexes. Sleep.

There it was.

Below the other listed numbers and cc. dosages signed by Seagroves came tomorrow's orders. Frank began moving his lips. Repeat hemocrit. Repeat urinalysis, all. GFR. Check with Fishl: IVU. Frank squinted, not certain of the handwriting, much less meaning. He reread and changed the scrawled numbers and letters without making the content any clearer.

Maybe he would telephone the doctor, late as it was.

Or maybe it was best if Seagroves got a good night's sleep before doing a single test on Mary.

At the nursing station, Frank asked what tests Mary Grace Thompson would undergo tomorrow and exactly when. Nobody seemed to know.

He promised himself not to worry. In the elevator he reminded himself she was strong and healthy, a girl with a body built of alternate layers of vitamins and milk. He was always nagging about milk.

And in the parking lot he remembered that, besides, tonight he had brought some stranger a human eye; that was on record; by any system at all he was owed one. He was due.

IN SPITE OF Dr. Seagroves's written schedule, the few hospital technicians at work Sunday were concentrating on emergencies.

At Mary's bedside he had to tell Frank and his mother that the tests would take one more day.

"But tomorrow's my last day of school—we don't even pick up final report cards until tomorrow!"

"For you, summer vacation starts a day early, that's all. And how are you this morning, Mrs. Thompson?"

"Fine." Tacey Thompson, who did not like this particular doctor, inhaled deeply in hope of giving her face a healthy glow.

"I'll pick up your report card, Mary." A natural list maker, Frank jotted that on an envelope. "Or do you want me to call Kay Linda to do it?"

"Never. She's the biggest snoop in the seventh grade."

"And I'll have a television set moved in," he murmured, continuing to write. "I thought Kay Linda was your best friend?" He walked Dr. Seagroves to the door without learning anything new.

"Kay Linda only likes boys now." With both feet, Mary pedaled her coverlet into a wad at one end. "Any other time my English class would write me letters. And there's no telephone in this room."

"You'll survive. I want to talk to you about Kay Linda and hair shampoos and Saturday mornings—Mother? What is it? I've never seen you so restless!" Tacey was winding her watch. "If you're worried about making Sunday school on time, go on; I'll be here."

She looked surprisingly guilty. "I'll be back about twelve-thirty so you can take a break." She took her hat off Mary's steel chest of drawers and pinned it to her bluish curls.

Frank made the mistake of getting in the mirror image with her and saying, "I bet you're the only woman in the congregation who still wears a hat."

"If you came more often," she snapped, "you could see for yourself."

Mary sat up in bed. "Grandma? You won't send your preacher, will you?"

"A father's influence." Any other time Tacey would have expended more rolled eyes and spread hands, but it was already nine-thirty. She kissed Mary's chin and hurried out, her patent-leather pumps making too much noise down the tiled corridor.

But there were advantages in having a set routine of church attendance when your husband and son did not. Why, she thought, I could have committed adultery fifty-two times a year with no suspicion at home, just a polite question about the sermon text!

Today she was not going to church.

Halfway to Durham she bought an area map but had trouble reading the tiny names of streets. When she stopped for gasoline, the attendant marked the route to Cromwell Street.

"But, ma'am, I don't know which way the house numbers run." She thanked him warmly, knowing her hat and Sunday clothes had triggered his good manners. Doubtless he knew he should not have been at work on the Sabbath Day. Anyway, she would have no trouble locating number 906 as it said in the Durham telephone book. Today she moved under the power of a vision.

Yes: a vision. Nowadays people reduced the sources of dreams to bad conscience or salami or—even more indigestible—something insensitive Daddy had done forty years before; but Tacey Grover Thompson, reared on the Old Testament, believed in Jehovah over Freud, the same Jehovah who came in the night to wrestle Jacob or warn Samuel.

Last night in dreams Jehovah had showed her a woman in a long green dress sweeping a city street, sweeping it endlessly despite passing trucks and cars and buses, even a horse-drawn wagon now and then. It was a wonder so much traffic did not run the woman down as she darted among wheels, sweeping, and behind bumpers, sweeping. Then came a large flatbed truck, which she, Tacey, could see turning into the street. It was loaded with children who were standing in a thick pack—perhaps kindergarten age. They must have been riding to a country picnic. As the truck turned the corner the mass of their bodies swayed and staggered. She saw that those at the back were being pushed to the edge. Though she began screaming, no matter how loud she screamed nor how fast she ran, she could move very little, and her voice strangled. Her whole body agonized with effort. One step. A croak. Slowly and silently the first children fell and rolled; the woman in green swept them easily toward the curb. They rolled so lightly, like tumbleweeds, that the struggling Tacey wanted to believe them false children, air filled for this effect, especially since there was no blood. But they kept flying from the truck as it moved down the street, bouncing off pavement and being steadily swept aside like huge but weightless dust motes, and Tacey recognized the faces of some.

Although there was more to the dream, Tacey remembered only this scene. She had been still running and screaming through it when she woke this morning and managed to get some sound out of her mouth at last. "Broom!"

"What?"

"Nothing, Andrew, go back to sleep." Broome. Did "green" rhyme on purpose with "Christine"? Or stand for leaves, springtime? She could not for certain remember whether one of those children had been Mary Grace; they seemed much younger, five or six, blowing out of that truck like fat, white thistles.

But definitely it was a vision meaning she must find the Broomes, maybe even Christine.

Her neck and jaw felt sore from the effort those muscles had made in her sleep. She had gotten up and dressed, waking Andrew only to say she would go first by the hospital, then to church.

"I meant to go with you to visit Mary."

"Better this afternoon." Against the pillow his pink unfolded face was itself childlike. Had it been worn by one of those boys tossed from the truck? Suffer the little children. She bent closer. Andrew, now sixty-eight, would die ahead of her—she had always known that. By now she had expected him also to know and at last become concerned for his soul.

He was not. By habit she said to his closed eyes, "Coming to church?" and he without movement, "Not today."

She could imagine how many middle-aged and older women were at this very moment saying and hearing the same. Very early the first Easter morning, only women had climbed out of bed to go together to the empty tomb. Now mostly women sat in the pews of Damascus Baptist Church, and sometimes they —like Tacey—must wonder if Christ had risen and, like the other men, departed from this place, also.

Now as Tacey entered Durham through wooded neighbor-hoods near Duke University and then drove between smaller, crowded houses with less shade, she kept watch for any street matching the one in her dream. It was too much to expect that Virgil and Georgia Broome would live in the exact neighborhood as the sweeping woman and the falling children with marsh-mallow bodies, so she was not surprised when Cromwell proved to be a poor man's street with no shade at all and mixed black and white residents in peeling old houses. Their sheds and front rooms sold the services of home hairdressers, photographers, and knife sharpeners. Too many cats and dogs could be seen.

At 906, a crudely lettered sign nailed to a porch post offered HOUSEHOLD REPAIRS. KEYS DUPLICATED CHEAP. And—good Lord! MADAME GEORGETTE, PALMIST.

With tongue against teeth, she tocked several sharp disap-provals. After parking at the curb, she walked to the Broomes' front screen door. Through the mesh she could see a short hall with stacked cardboard boxes.

Tacey knocked. A human voice far away said a word or two—probably profane—but nobody came, nor to her second knock. She caught hold of the handle and banged the screen door against latch and frame.

The noise brought a frizzy head poking out one doorway into the hall. Tacey recognized the hair color—that of an overripe peach. "Georgia Broome, you get out of bed and let me in!"

The fat woman stepped squinting into the hallway. "Who's that?" Her nightgown with crooked hem was a shade lighter than her hair.

"It's Tacey Thompson, Frank's mother, and I need to talk to you."

"Is it morning?"

"What does your palm say?"

Georgia Broome snapped upright and evened the straps of her gown. "It's you, all right. Anytime you did talk it was sharp like that. My palm don't tell time. You wait on the porch."

With Kleenex Tacey wiped out a rocker and sat, eyes on the blue sky. Lord, you might as well forgive me for being a snob—it's what they call a besetting sin.

Not that her own Grovers hadn't been poor themselves, uneducated, rural, the older ones as far below her present level of taste as she was below that of people who liked opera and poetry.

But the Broomes fell below them all—below Average, below Common, below Tacky. The Broomes were *trashy*. Wasn't it just like Virgil Broome to hire out to fix houses while living in this unpainted wreck, and to cut door keys even if his own door was tied shut with a string! It was no wonder that for Christine, who had been so unexpectedly neat about her own person and surroundings, the trashiness had to seek some other outlet.

Again Tacey flung an ashamed look skyward. *As we forgive the trespasses of others.*

Georgia Broome's idea of dressing for company was to put on a cotton robe stamped with improbable violet blossoms two feet wide. She squawked the screen door shut behind her and, without a word, pulled up a second rocker and set it in motion with Tacey's, who immediately broke rhythm.

"It's been a while," said Georgia, placidly rocking. "What's the emergency?"

Who discusses dreams with a paid palm reader? "Mostly I want Christine's telephone number."

"And why is that?"

"Mary Grace is in Memorial Hospital—nothing serious. But I thought Christine might like to call her."

"So you drove all the way to Durham instead of calling *me*. In the hospital with *what* that's not serious?"

"She fell off a horse. They're just doing a general physical and some tests while she's in there."

"Tests for what?" Georgia Broome put her bare feet on the flaking yellow banister. She must have been almost Tacey's age but looked older and fatter, like someone who had one dark night agreed to let time and mortality have their way. The only resistance was her defiant pink hair, but even that looked accidental, something she had put on as carelessly as the outlandish robe, something made of tangled yarn and tossed overnight on a closet shelf. Georgia said, "Is she really sick?"

Pity and grief, which swam up, filled Tacey to the edges. "I don't know."

Georgia rocked, relentless.

"Maybe," Tacey said. "I'm afraid of the possibility."

They moved nervously in the two chairs while traffic went by. Perhaps every tenth car, Tacey thought, contained a church-goer, lost in the stream of travelers, water-skiers, picnickers. Aloud she said, "Mary hasn't looked well all spring."

"At the school play she looked all right."

So, Tacey thought. You did come after all. The balcony, maybe, which was half-dark. "That was April."

"I know when it was." She leaned forward to finger a hard callus along her big toe. "But the doctor hasn't said much yet? Tina's living in Jacksonville."

"I believe Frank said that, but he only had a general delivery address."

Georgia stood up and checked that her front zipper was pulled to her throat. "I'll get her number."

"You've spoken with her recently?"

"Last month. It was Virgil's birthday."

Some joke, thought Tacey, watching Georgia in her broad iris blossoms fade into the dark house. Virgil was her second husband—a toucher, a feeler—the kind of stepfather girls wished had never been born at all.

She caught herself. Missing church one time, she decided, has robbed me of all charity.

Then Georgia carried back to her the phone number scrawled on a torn newspaper margin, obviously from a household where there was never a sheet of blank paper anywhere. "And I added my number, too. If anything's really wrong, you call me. Collect."

Collect. Noblesse oblige. Accepting the paper, Tacey was glad for her Sunday hat and the way its ornamental fruit would bob and click as she nodded and got to her feet.

Thinking: You raddled old bitch.

On the steps, though, she turned slowly back. "Georgia Broome, what in the world do you know about reading palms?"

"What do you care?"

She swayed against the untrustworthy rail. "I have these dreams."

Georgia shrugged and went back to rocking.

"Mary Grace used to sleepwalk. Once," she whispered as Georgia began to nod, "once Frank was hurt at school and I knew it, this baseball hit him? Here? And at home my rib snapped in like a stave in a basket." Tacey moved up a step and extended her left hand. "Read mine."

Georgia stretched it as if flesh were rubber. "Um."

"Dr. Seagroves can say 'Um.' What else?"

"Long life—too long. You'll outlive some."

"Outlive who besides Andrew?" Tacey gasped when again her hand was wrenched out and pressed thin as pie dough between the plump fingers. She saw that Georgia was wearing dime-store glass finger rings, one size fits all, set in gold-colored aluminum.

"No money problems. This is a hard year for you. And the next. After that: nothing."

"Nothing?"

"Nothing important. You'll likely die easy yourself. Hardly knowing it."

"I want to know it." Tacey snatched back her hot hand.

"Well, now that you've been warned you'll get false alarms."

She'd done harm. Her kind always did harm. "Thank you, Georgia. What's the charge?" Tacey snapped open her pocket-book.

"Watching you—that was my price."

In a flood Tacey saw how her snobbery had always offended, had hurt, how by discomfort Georgia had earned fair spectator rights the next decade or so, could see why any pain of Tacey Thompson's would feed a Broome appetite. Too late she blurted, "I'm sorry," then hurried to her car and raked its gears badly getting away.

She stopped to enter the first phone booth she saw, stacked her quarters, did breathing exercises, and dialed Christine in Jacksonville, North Carolina. A man answered. What had she expected? In another moment she heard the familiar high voice and fast breathing: *Hello?*

"It's Tacey Thompson. How are you, Christine?" Into the silence she added, "Frank's mother."

"Is he hurt again?"

"No," she said, surprised, though suddenly remembering the night Frank had been shot, and she and Christine had something briefly in common. "No, it's nothing serious, but you should know that Mary fell from a horse yesterday and got a concussion. She ought to be out of Memorial Hospital late Monday."

"That's good," Christine said, "that she didn't break any-thing. Or scar her face?"

"No, but they're doing more general health tests—she's been run-down all spring?"

"At her age they grow too fast." Beyond the telephone Christine was answering somebody unseen. She came back on the line saying brightly, "You'll give her my love, OK?"

Tacey said firmly, "Room three-two-nine."

"I appreciate it. Now you let me know if everything doesn't turn out one hundred percent, OK? I'll call soon as she's home. Tomorrow night, OK? How have you and Mr. Thompson been feeling?"

"We've been feeling our age."

"I hope you're just teasing. Do you happen to know if Frank got my letter?"

"He mentioned it."

"About her birthday?"

"Her what?" It wasn't like Christine to plan two months ahead. "You may remember Dr. Seagroves. He's still Mary's doctor."

"Oh good, he's wonderful."

He's not, Tacey thought. "I got your number from Georgia. Frank really ought to know how to reach you all the time, you know, if you want to be reached." Nodding so vigorously, Tacey had struck her hat against the booth's glass wall, and it slid sideways down her face.

"I'm on the road so much," said Christine vaguely. "Is Frank answering my letter—do you know?"

Her voice got suddenly too loud. "There's been no time to think about anything but Mary."

"Thank you so much for calling, Mrs. Thompson."

"If you should get worried," Tacey managed to say at a lower volume, "you can always call me if you don't reach Frank." She listened to murmurs and breathing. "Yes, certainly." She gave her telephone number, twice, and pictured Christine tearing off the corner of a magazine page, finding no pen, making a wide pantomime shrug to the unknown man across the room. "She'll hear from you, then," Tacey said.

In the hot booth, blank-minded, she hung up the phone and stood as still as a caged monkey that has completed one more pointless task. Her head ached. Slowly she took off her crooked hat with its heavy grapes and flowers.

There's something really wrong with Mary. She closed her eyes and felt blindly for her pocketbook.

LATER THAT WEEK, Tacey was to meditate on how many entries her Bible concordance had for blood and heart, but none for kidney, though Jehovah above all had to know how Adam had really been made: of one-quarter dust, no argument; but three-quarters water.

On Wednesday morning, while Dandy was staying with Mary in her hospital room, she had listened like a recording machine while Dr. Seagroves explained that humans could only survive on land because their cells were laved in a kind of soup that the kidney kept constant. The doctor preferred, she saw, to go on talking of systems, to sketch the little suspended organs in their matching cushions of fat, to brag about two million nephrons—anything but to speak to Frank and her directly about Mary Grace Thompson.

Acute problems were, in some ways, to be preferred, Seagroves said. But chronic symptoms were often low-key by their very nature—feeling tired, getting pale or silently anemic, passing more water at night, the growing pains of early adolescence? Such vague complaints rarely brought a patient in—

"Chronic what exactly?" Frank broke in.

He said it as fast as possible. "Chronic renal failure."

That last word, "failure," batted against the office walls like a bird trapped indoors.

From that point in the explanation, Tacey's understanding

failed. Filtration rates. Something about a Dr. Bright. The accumulation of creatinine. Often from a known, identifiable cause. Not in this case.

While Frank paced, she heard him barking a long list of Mary's doctor's appointments and regular checkups, but Seagroves said protein in children's urine was very common, had not showed up consistently. He ostentatiously held out the open file folder to share. Maybe her childhood scarlet fever had triggered a mild, progressive problem? Or sometimes these things were the result of an inherited immune system.

Maybe this, maybe that. I'm glad I called Christine—not that anything came of it. Tacey forced concentration.

Frank said, "Just tell me how you cure it." His mouth had flattened around his teeth on all sides; he used to look that way as a small boy, just before rage would make him cry—she had forgotten.

"First, some more tests will help measure the degree of Mary's problem, and of course we'll keep trying to pin down a cause. We've done an IVU, X ray of the kidneys; maybe we'll look at the renal blood vessels." He kept turning old sheets in Mary's folder, records of smallpox shots and a broken wrist, age five. "Whatever the cause—and in some cases we never know— there'll be at least diuretic drugs and a special diet."

"Fine." Relieved to have something he could write in the small notebook he was taking out, Frank sat again near the doctor's desk. "We can do that. You mentioned salt—what else?"

"We'll get you a food list, high calorie and low nitrogen," he said, while Frank carefully wrote the categories down. "As to dialysis, we'll cross that bridge when we come to it. *If* we come to it."

"What?" Tacey cried. "A machine?"

"Even a transplant. I'm only trying to reassure you, Mrs. Thompson, that times have changed; there are many options of treatment all the way from mild to severe disease, and research under way all the time. Mary's young and strong. We may have only a mild situation here."

But Tacey, not reassured, had gone to stand behind Frank's chair. She watched Dr. Seagroves rereading his own handwriting all the way back to Mary Grace's birth, seven pounds, thirteen ounces, twenty-two inches long. High forceps, she remembered, though she herself had stopped going to Dr. Seagroves years before her granddaughter was born. She changed doctors over the question of regular douching. He would have had her pump sterile solutions into herself night and morning, even when in perfect health, and when she had only raised the possibility that what was inside might clean itself, he had betrayed such facial distaste that she sensed vaginas were nasty to him. She never went back nor told her husband why nor interfered when Frank and Christine kept him for their family physician. But she had hoped soon to transfer Mary's medical care to her own gynecologist.

She realized from the motionless body in the chair before her that Frank, too, had stopped hearing a word of Dr. Seagroves's muttering about sodium and edema and blood pressure. Frank just kept moving his pen in squiggly borders around the very short list of things he could do.

Stepping closer, Tacey dropped both hands on his shoulders. While Dr. Seagroves droned on about CAT scans, she pressed, then squeezed, then slowly began to massage with her thumbs behind his neck. At last Frank reached to pat her fingers while the doctor finished listing the urologists who would consult on the case. He suggested all three of them go now to Mary's room; she would need medical facts from him, but love from her family. Tacey thought of her husband waiting by Mary's bed. He would be silenced for once.

But Frank shook his head. "I don't think I can watch while you tell her."

"You'll not watch," said the doctor. "You'll hold her hand or whatever else does her some good."

Frank continued to shake his head. To stop him, Tacey bent and laid her cheek by his. She said, "That's always the way— you don't even get to the middle of your own fear before you have to set it aside and deal with hers. It's just as well, Frank." His face felt cold against hers. She longed to make promises: *Everything's all right. Tomorrow it'll go away.* She said a silent prayer that these be true.

IT WAS 10:00 P.M. the following Saturday when Frank parked in the Ramshead Chateaux apartment lot and spotted someone wearing a pale skirt seated on his front stoop. Because the shadowy sight was as unexpected as that of Mary leaning off a snowy roof, he leaped from his patrol car thinking irrationally that she had sleepwalked across town all the way from her hospital room.

In midleap the long blond braid gleamed to him through the dark. He felt foolish.

She watched him regain balance.

He said, deliberately flat, "I never called."

"No wonder."

"What are you doing here? It's late."

"I was surprised to hear Mary was still in the hospital, so I dropped by to visit her this evening. She told me."

"Was she upset? She hasn't *been* upset." He slumped beside her on the concrete step. Every bone was tired.

"Not upset enough. You wait till she gets to a library and checks the prognosis herself," said Jill Peters. "That's what I did."

Not talking, they sat side by side until at last Frank took her hand and worked the fingers, one by one. It was not how he had meant the first touch to be. Hers was a lean hand meant for work, meant to go on working long after . . . after Mary's? He dropped it. "Let's go inside." He unlocked the door and turned on lights.

Behind him she said, "This is the first time I've seen you in your uniform. It looks good, I guess, though I've never been drawn to uniforms."

Frank's slow turn was deliberate and, he knew, theatrical. She gasped when in the glare she saw the stiff and bloody stains.

"A bad wreck." He moved to the serving bar Christine had ordered from Sears, silly looking with its black bar stools facing flowered chintz. "Fix yourself a drink while I change."

In a stiff, formal tone she asked, "Somebody died in the wreck?"

"Three."

Upstairs, ashamed, he washed quickly and changed into jeans and a worn shirt. Death by vehicle had begun to seem less real in life than in movies, even to Frank. In real cars by actual highways, the scene looked crudely staged, the patchy grass low budget, every actor a has-been forgetting his lines. Tonight: a dead man with his oral cavity still crammed with unchewed Big Mac hamburger. The two younger passengers had been thrown some distance; God knew where their food and drink had gone.

At Christine's mirror, Frank absently pressed his hair with one hand. As a rookie he had seen a human head sliced off its normal neck and glued in red jelly to an automobile hood like some garish enameled ornament. Since then he'd read that the decapitated Jayne Mansfield had in some similar wreck rolled out her wide mascaraed eyes and sexy starlet's pout—disconnected—to confront some other stunned lawman. Body and mind. *I'm losing the latter.*

When Frank let go his hair the fool-boy cowlick stood up. He thought: *I could have been selling liability insurance. To horse stables. Been betting* against *accident.*

He ·came downstairs to find Jill, in the kitchen, pouring

herself a glass of milk instead of bourbon. She licked white smile marks from the corners of her mouth. He decided she was much too young for him.

"What did Mary have to say?" He put one ice cube in his drink.

"She said kidney failure."

"Kidney disease. Disease. Disease," Frank repeated. "Kidney problems."

"Failure," she said, and she looked like someone had just given her an F on her whole life."

He didn't want to hear this. "Come in, let's sit down." He led Jill past the photograph of Christine, taking a good look at how the two women contrasted. Ten years' difference, though. Chronologically Jill fell halfway between him and Mary.

"She talked mostly about you, and how lonesome you are with no woman in your life."

He couldn't stop himself from saying, "I'm not without women in my life."

"Cindy Scofield—Mary mentioned her."

He grinned, sat on the chintz couch. "She's not all that depressed, then, if she's minding my business."

"Oh yes she is," Jill said. "I think she's trying to make provision for you. Mary plays the piano?" She set her milk glass on Tacey's crocheted scarf.

"Yes." Years of the John Thompson music books plinked through his head: melodies meant to glide like swans, crackle like fires, flit like glowworms.

Die away like piano students.

"I can't stay long, I've got a late date." She did not look at him, moving the framed photographs here and there on the piano. "How old was Mary here?"

Posed that last day of kindergarten wearing a silly graduation robe sewed by Tacey from a bedsheet. "Not quite six." He took a good swallow of the bourbon. "Later that day she broke her wrist. Christine was hurrying her off the platform—it was just a jerry-rigged plywood platform—and she fell, and that wouldn't have been so bad, but one of the fathers stepped on her, on her hand or her arm."

"You were there?"

"No, I was on duty. My mother was there." And has blamed Christine ever since for jerking Mary off balance.

He watched her drink milk. Cindy Scofield drank nothing but wine, Fetzer's white; her refrigerator was always full of the big green bottles lying down. On most of their dates he went with her to public events she was covering for the local newspaper. He had sat with Cindy through the whole Cane Creek watershed controversy, had waited on a retaining wall while she interviewed university students who were living in temporary campus shacks to show sympathy for South Africa. Often he and Cindy were present at the same traffic accidents.

Cindy was by no means as pretty as Jill Peters.

"And this is Mary's mother?" As if catching his own word out of the air by psychic contagion, Jill added, "She's pretty."

"Pretty enough." He watched Jill drift from desk to table, aimlessly touching a book, a cigarette box, a brass turtle; he hoped she was feeling objects for his pulse. "I'm glad you came, but surprised," he said, remembering that one reason Cindy seldom came here was the lack of privacy, Mary upstairs, Mary being influenced by parental behavior.

"I don't know if she'll be well enough to keep on with the riding lessons," Jill said awkwardly, as if this explained her presence. She was reading titles in his collection of musical tapes. Nothing she wanted to hear, evidently, the hits from a decade too soon. "Nice lamp," she murmured, though it was ordinary. Rather primly she sat on a chair across from him and finished the milk.

Suddenly Frank wanted to put a hand, both hands, inside her clothes, and roughly. Maybe she even wanted that. He thought of old photographs of girls at Kent State, teasing the uniformed men with their gifts of a single daisy, half knowing that something violent hibernated under all that discipline. Sometimes he thought women were never young in the same way that all men had been boys, that even in Mary there had always been in childhood a capacity to manipulate and disguise.

"The reason I came," Jill blurted suddenly, "was that when I was going out the door Mary asked me how long it took for chronic renal failure to turn into final renal failure, and I just said I didn't know, and ran."

"You should have said that wouldn't happen." His voice had grown angry, loud. He stood up to telephone Mary and say the words himself. "What was so hard about that?"

"She's been talking to nurses and doctors, she said so. She was just testing me. It'll be your turn tomorrow."

He turned from the telephone to watch Jill pacing between the false fireplace and the fake-walnut arch, feeling something between pain and desire, anger and passion. Altogether, a mess. *If I touch her, I'll hurt her. I'd be glad to hurt somebody.*

He said, "Sit down." She joined him on the couch. "I'm glad you told me. It gives me time to think up an answer."

After a silence Jill clicked open her brown shoulder bag, took out a wallet, and flipped through the plastic photo holders. He was thinking about Mary and hardly noticed.

"You're not the only one with pictures," she said, and passed one to him. "My parents."

A plain stocky couple, once blond and ruddy, now bleached by the same work and weather and habits, they might have been siblings in matching eyeglasses and colorless hair, Frank thought, or resemblance might deepen over the years from steady absorption of each other's bodily fluids, decades of excess sperm and lubricant. *Ye shall be one flesh.* His own parents also looked like fraternal twins.

Christine had always looked like her unaffected self.

He looked closer; that was snow underfoot, although Mr. and Mrs. Peters were standing there in short sleeves, thin garments.

"Here's me as a child."

The younger Jill Peters was not much different except that the hair was in double plaits, the eyes untouched by makeup. "You must have been about . . . about Mary's age," he said uneasily.

"And my sister. Her two children here." Then Jill turned to her own driver's license and slid it back to reveal a photograph underneath: a dark young man with an untrimmed mustache. Curly hair—his shirt was carefully unbuttoned far enough to show he was curly all over. "He's my Christine," she said before snapping shut the wallet. Out of those black-rimmed eyes she shot her gaze, double-barreled, into his face and through.

Frank let her click shut her pocketbook before lightly touching her neck. Under his fingertips the carotid artery, the one you could feel even if a victim was in shock, throbbed steadily. He bent and pursed his lips into a whistle shape above that rhythm. Under his mouth, her life in years pulsed by—too few, enough, too few, enough.

The telephone rang. He whispered into her neck, "I'm off duty."

But already he knew no dispatcher would call him after a shift with three fatalities unless it was necessary. The ringing kept up until he was suddenly certain that Mary was worse and snatched up the phone.

"Who? Oh. Miss Torrido." On his tongue was the taste of Jill's skin. He smiled at her across the room. "Really? How long since you called 911?" Absently he began fastening his top shirt buttons and standing straighter. "Sure. I'm leaving this line open, and a friend will keep talking to you." He handed Jill the phone, saying softly, "Next-door neighbor thinks somebody's cutting her back screen. Just keep talking to her. Lila Torrido."

"Hello? Lila?"

He heard Jill's soothing answers as he got his gun and holster off the closet shelf.

Not that any burglar would be there. Frank eased out front while settling the belt in place. Lila Torrido, sixty-five, had criminals on the brain. She claimed to be the only surviving (illegitimate), daughter of Frank—not Al—Capone, still sought by Chicago hoodlums who believed she had received secret underworld funds.

Frank Thompson had heard Lila's stories before, had checked out strange noises and footprints and menacing parked cars. Now he slipped along the dark wall of his building, feeling ahead with one hand around the scratchy brick corner toward the back of Miss Torrido's adjoining apartment. It pleased him how Jill had so easily begun to speak into the mouthpiece toward the woman's fear: young, but mature. By friction his hands led him around the next corner. Then he dropped behind shrubbery. He could hear a ragged sawing noise at the kitchen door. For once the old lady was right! The form hunkered there was not likely to be the ghost of Frank Capone, slipped shining from his silver-plated coffin, not even one of Frank's kin or henchmen, but some local two-bit doper planning to feed his veins from the price of stolen necklaces and stereos.

Since Lila had already phoned the local police, Frank wanted a challenge no sooner than necessary. He squatted to wait, prickling numb toward each foot.

The burglar broke through the outer screen and entered at a crouch. He began working the back-porch door lock with his plastic card. Frank edged closer, hoping the Carrboro police had not this time discounted still another of Lila Torrido's frightened calls.

Then car doors slammed in the front parking lot and glimmers began enlarging toward the building. Frank and the burglar both held still to evaluate. Uncertainly, the burglar slowly turned away, back to, then from the door again. Frank could dimly hear Miss Lila's faraway voice.

The man sprang for the screen door. "Freeze!" Frank shouted as more voices grew clearer inside. The man jumped the steps to land on all fours on the asphalt. Frank stood up in the bushes, gun level, and held himself as still as a great insect.

There were running steps, noisy, then noisier, steps inside and closer.

"That's right, hold it!" Frank called. "Police officer!" He didn't want to get shot by mistake. The figure stayed knuckles down on the pavement while rooms kept lighting up, doors banging loud and louder, light pouring from doorway to doorway toward them until the back door burst open and it swept across them both, making the bent one cry, "Don't shoot!"

Damn right, Frank thought, and called, "Police officer here!"

A city policeman barely old enough to flunk algebra, perhaps one of Jill's contemporaries, came squinting into view. Again the immediacy of the scene shifted, and Frank stepped into the spilled light as if on camera, into a moment that had more filmed reality and class than plain reality ever would. He holstered the gun that shone in the light like a melodramatic prop. "Turner, is that you?"

Most of them knew one another—state patrolmen, sheriff's deputies, city policemen.

"I thought this was your neighborhood," Turner said after he got the burglar handcuffed. "You could have saved me some gas."

And pissed you off. "Your turf, not mine," Frank said. He caught himself looking over one shoulder at other lighted apartment windows from which residents were hanging now, calling out questions. The studio audience. It all felt like a movie, a TV show, with the director temporarily off the set for coffee break. Not until recently had Frank felt this artificial overlay, and he thought it must be coming from the contrast with Mary's life or Mary's death, that everything but Mary's fate was on the level of a matinee.

He stepped back toward his own door and halfway listened to Turner read the burglar his rights. At first he thought Mary had materialized there on his porch alongside the tools and garbage cans, but it was Jill's shadowed face, and on the other porch, Lila Torrido's old one. They waited until police had taken the burglar away and Miss Torrido was safely barricaded indoors for the night.

Then Jill said, "I need to go home, Frank. I feed horses early."

"I thought you had a late date."

"I lied about that."

He nodded. In the living room she picked up her pocketbook full of pictures, and he followed to her car, where she found keys, dropped them once, at last unlocked the door, and stopped with one foot inside.

"This wasn't a good time for us," he said, tentatively.

"I don't think there's going to be a good time, with Mary sick and everything."

But in the dark he could feel she was looking straight at him. The plait had worked its way forward over one shoulder; he wondered if she practiced ways to move it—the way a lecturer might direct a pointer at titles on a blackboard. He took and wound it lightly over her throat, across that durable pulse. "I'm too old for you," he said.

She shrugged, dropped into the driver's seat.

He kept hold of the door. "I'm off Monday night."

Something inside the windshield drew her attention; she scratched at a flaw or dried speck that Frank could not make out. "I doubt," she said slowly, "that you're going to have enough energy for anyone or anything but your daughter. For a very long time. But even if you did?" Her head tipped toward him. "Even so, I plan to go to vet school in the fall, so I wouldn't want to get really involved in a relationship."

"Shit," said Frank. "That's such a stupid word. *Relationship.*"

She turned on the engine, but he would not let go the door.

"One thing at a time," he said. "And Mary's going to be fine."

"I hope so." She got the door loose and slammed, but he had already reached around to spread one hand on the windshield. Then he lowered his face onto the thick glass and mouthed "Monday night." Jill finally nodded. He held up eight fingers and tried to decide whether she had smiled or sneered. Then he stepped back so she could drive away.

BUT MARY WAS ALLOWED to come home Monday, so Frank couldn't go out on her first night home. When he called Jill from the patrol station, she didn't seem surprised. In fact, she said she needed to stay at the stable anyway, to keep checking on a colicky horse. They had tubed him and poured down mineral oil, but she had to be sure he was up. "Up?" asked Frank.

"You don't want a horse to go down and stay or start rolling—they can kink an intestine."

He had already noticed that horse people gave most of their conversation to horse care, horse shows, horse prices, and other (dishonest, incompetent) horse trainers. "If you get free, come on over here," he said. "My parents are coming home from the hospital with us."

But Jill said she'd probably walk the horse awhile, and at the end of it all she'd smell like a barn.

So Frank met the others in the hospital lobby, where Mary was making her wheelchair fly up and down the broad room and threatening to try to balance it on the up escalator. She looked rosy, energetic, with no marks of illness except the head bandage over the shaved patch of scalp.

She rode home in Tacey's car while Frank followed, watching Mary's restlessness through the back window, guessing at his father's constant complaints and road directions in the front seat. From time to time Frank glared at other motorists who might sideswipe the car with Mary in it, pass on the right, lose control on a curve. Jerking his head toward every vehicle made his neck hurt.

In the apartment, Tacey started upstairs to transfer Mary's pajamas from suitcase to washing machine but stopped midway to call, "I've left you a macaroni casserole to heat up. And Miss Torrido from next door sent over a pan of candy if it ever gets hard. I need to give that woman my recipe."

"Fine. Sit down, Mary. You want this hassock?"

Not moving, Tacey said slyly, "I thought maybe some of your friends would have brought food in. Maybe this newspaper reporter? What's her name?"

She knew Cindy Scofield's name as well as her own. Frank almost enjoyed saying, "She hates to cook." Probably Jill also hated to cook; he'd had no luck with any of these thin and busy women.

He got Mary to sit down but from the kitchen could see that she kept popping up, pacing. He hurried to get the casserole into the oven and checked Miss Torrido's fudge. They'd have to eat it by the spoonful.

"Looks like mud," Dandy said.

"Go back in there with Mary. Make her sit still. What?" he called in answer to Tacey. Then, "No, I can set the table myself." Overhead the washing machine began to rumble.

"Francis, if I don't make your mama go home and leave you two alone," Dandy promised, "she'll be scrubbing the wood-work, that's how she does her worrying."

Frank nodded as he finished with plates and silverware. He could hear the three of them murmuring in the living room, then Tacey's call: "I feel like I ought to stay and help you."

He decided to skip over that and call back, "Thank you again, Mama, see you tomorrow or the next day!" The grumbles got softer and then the door closed.

Frank eased to the doorway, watched the way Mary moved to turn on the TV and then turn it off, watched her visits to one corner of the room and then the next. "Hope you're hungry!" She still looked healthy, but her mouth had somehow solidified. He came in and sat on the edge of the sofa cushion to show her his food list, in triplicate, taped here and there in the kitchen so it would always be handy, he explained.

She answered in monosyllables, walking through the room, into the hall, over to a window to look at the empty space where her grandparents had been parked. He found himself following her, talking about anything that came to mind and mouth.

When they ended up in the kitchen again and Mary slowed down enough to pause at the open refrigerator door and stare inside it while absently relocating bottles and jars, Frank finally asked how she was feeling.

"With my fingers—that's what Dandy would say." Her voice sounded gloomy.

She closed the door and gave him an opportunity to tap the food list hung there by a magnet. "It won't be as hard as you think to keep that chart of your diet and food intake and to bring the doctor regular urine samples. It'll soon be a routine. You're going to be fine."

Her eyes rolled to him and away. She was holding her mouth the way Miss Torrido sometimes did, clamping her dentures against gravity.

Frank didn't like it. "Want to go to the movies?"

"Naw, I'm tired." She put up a hand against the worry that must have leaped into his face. "Just plain tired, nothing worse. Don't we have anything good to eat?"

"Staying in bed will make even a prizefighter feel weak. If you don't want your grandma's macaroni, we could order pizza. You want me to call now, or do you need to get on the telephone to all your girlfriends?"

"Not tonight."

"Not even Kay Linda? She came to the hospital to see you. She brought all those photographs."

"Of her and Jimmy Rosemary, sure. I wasn't in a one of them. Sometimes Kay Linda is just disgusting."

Frank checked to see if the oven was up to 350 yet. He didn't trust Christine's aging microwave. For all he knew it had leaked rays straight onto Mary's kidney. None of the doctors' explanations made any better sense. Some people got scarlet fever and strep throat and got over it easily. "With some," Tacey had tried to explain, "it just *settles* somewhere." Nothing Dr. Seagroves had said made any better sense than that. Frank looked at Mary, imagining old germs in her body turning into the sediment of illness and gradually drifting down into the kidney.

He forced himself to say cheerfully, "Well, I'm glad the worst is over and you're home. Anything special you'd like to do tonight?"

"I don't want to *do* anything. And Miss Torrido's fudge is always grainy, even when it does get hard." But she slid the pan across the table and raked up a corner piece that sagged between thumb and forefinger, then absently sucked on it. "All this eating is disgusting, too."

Frank was getting out a spoon to sample the candy, but now he left it in the drawer. "I don't know what you mean."

"I mean it just is. Don't you ever look around Kenan Stadium and think about that ton of food going down everybody's throat and then how everybody runs to the toilet at halftime to drop it out? It's disgusting."

"No," Frank said, reaching for her. "The human body is all right."

"It's not, it's ugly." She twisted aside and popped the rest of Miss Lila's fudge into her mouth and blew her cheeks into distorted shape. On purpose she showed him her brown front teeth.

Then she darted out of the kitchen to the piano, where she thumped the very lowest key a few times. "What else did old Seaweed tell you that he didn't tell me?"

"You heard it all, Mary. The medicine and checkups." He stood behind her, helpless, while the bass note struck over and over. "If things don't improve fast enough we can consider dialysis or surgery, but that would be a long time off. You'll probably be long since grown-up by then. Maybe a doctor yourself." Her red hair gave a negative shake so he said hastily, "Or whatever you want to be. An airplane pilot, I don't care. Married," he said nervously. "Married with children."

"You'll get married before I do," she said, almost accusingly. "You'll marry Miss Scofield so you can go to wrecks together."

"I hope I never see another wreck."

Smudges of chocolate were showing on the lowest ivory key. *Bum bum bum bum bum bum.* "Do I eventually just fill up with pee like a toilet?"

He caught hold of both her shoulders, saying, "Of course not." *Bumbumbumbum.* Faster. He had to speak louder because the piano sound got louder. "This is a major teaching hospital with researchers and the latest equipment and treatments and specialists that . . ."

Her hand slid up the keyboard, and at first he was relieved to hear middle C over and over. "I think that's what people do," Mary said softly. "They drown from the inside."

"No." He reached over her shoulder to keep that restless hand from carrying fudge smears to the very highest note. His fingers got sticky from hers. "I don't want you to worry." When she tried to pull loose he found himself shaking that hand almost angrily. "And quit feeling so sorry for yourself, Mary Grace Thompson! You could have broken your spine when you fell off the horse—ever think of that?"

She was not, he saw, thinking of it now, either. He dropped her candied hand and sat beside her on the piano stool, giving her body a push that would move her from bass toward treble.

"It's important to expect the best because mental attitude's a medicine, too. Dr. Seagroves was very strong on that. Good thoughts have good physical effects." He got his awkward right arm around her.

"Whether the good thoughts are true or not?"

"When have I ever lied to you?"

"Plenty of times," she said calmly, "but only one other time was it important." She sucked fudge off a fingertip before beginning to play her spring recital piece, Chopin's Minute Waltz, at a tempo so slow it might last all evening.

"If I've ever lied to you, then I'm sorry, Mary Grace. I'm not lying now."

"You lied about Mama."

"I didn't want you to stop loving her then." The labored notes kept thumping wearily on. His arm might have been laid on a machine. He squeezed. "Or me now."

But she could not attend to his feelings yet, playing in slow motion. "Have you stopped loving her?"

Well, he had asked for it. He said, "I think so. But you don't have to."

She played on. After a while she said, "Did I inherit this kidney thing from the Broomes or the Thompsons? Your side or Mama's?"

"You didn't inherit it from anybody. It's a fluke that you got this thing; it's like being struck by lightning."

"It sure is." She hit a wrong note and then stopped. "I'm not some terrible person, am I?"

"You're a wonderful girl, so don't start blaming God for this, either. He's not getting even with you or me for anything. God doesn't do that."

"Hah!" Mary said, and spun out from under his arm. "You haven't been to Sunday school in twenty years. Ananias. Uzziah. Jephthah. King David. The whole Bible is lousy with people that made God mad and paid for it."

Tacey's territory; she should have stayed after all. Frank said

uncertainly, "That must be in the Old Testament before—"
"Ananias is in Acts. And his wife got it, too, for practically
nothing. Talk about getting hit"—she made a discordant crash
with both palms flat on the keys—"by lightning!" Then she
slid quickly off the piano bench to drop onto the couch, lying
down so her red hair hung off its edge, the bandage stuck there
like a mailing label. "I'd a lot rather have got TB like Elizabeth
Barrett Browning and laid on my couch with my dog and the
poets."

"That must have been crowded."

But she would not smile. Frank was afraid the blood that
probably needed to go calmly in and out her kidneys was rushing
to her head and clotting there. Soon those eleven stitches would
bulge and snap out.

"I don't want to die, Heaven or no Heaven."

"You won't, Mary, I promise that. You can have my kidney
anytime." Both of them. Liver, heart.

"You can't promise about dying." Her face was getting red
and puffy. "And I could die even with somebody else's kidney
stuck in me. I've asked around; I know."

"I could get run over by a bus tomorrow, too. Same risk."

"It's not," she said. "Is that cheese I smell burning?"

She followed to watch him take out the glass dish, now dark
on the bottom. Through a tear in the quilted oven mitt, he
felt his finger burn and was almost glad to have pain pinpointed
like that. He wondered if Mary had done any crying, if she
ought to do some, and how he would stand it if she did.

"Here, put this on." Mary broke off a piece of the potted
plant that was growing in the kitchen window. "Grandma
Thompson calls it heal-all." The aloe juice felt cool, soothing.
As if it were step two in first-aid treatment, Mary added, "She's
praying for my kidneys to be well. Her whole Sunday-school
class is praying."

"That will make her feel better and you feel loved, but I've
got more confidence in doctors than—"

"Listen to you!" she exploded. "Talk about making God mad! I sure don't need you making trouble in Heaven right now!" Closing her flushed eyelids she added, "And it wouldn't hurt if you came out to Grandma's church from now on, either."

"OK, fine," said Frank. "Fine, we'll all pray."

She looked at his reddened finger and then dropped it. "See how you're giving in to me because I'm sick? It's disgusting."

The deep breath he took filled his lungs with the smell of charred food. Slowly he said, "I'm trying to be patient with the way you're taking out your feelings on me because I know you'll get over this mood when you're feeling better. We can make sandwiches, I guess."

"I hate it when you act like you know me better than I do." Abruptly she reached into a cabinet and announced as if it were maximum threat, "I'm making popcorn now, a lot of popcorn."

While she was locating the packet exactly in the middle of the microwave, Frank said, "Don't stand too close to that thing."

She turned it on, arm's length. "I don't care if popcorn is on that list or not!" He could hear kernels begin to ping and snap. "Is there any mail? I thought my riding class might send me a card."

He went to their front door and the basket that caught mail put through a slot. A horse-show announcement for Centaur Stable—he'd take Mary; afterward the three of them . . . Then he lifted out the square envelope with its fat, ornamented handwriting. He could smell the popping corn. "Mary? You've got a letter." The postal cancellation showed Jacksonville, North Carolina.

"Who from?" she called.

"Looks like your mother's writing." Sure enough, on the flap was one of those return-address stickers sent out by charities. This one had the Lung Association symbol on one side, then MRS. CHRISTINE B. THOMPSON, River Haven Mobile Park, Rte. 1, Jacksonville, NC 28540.

The noises were slowing and stopping. In another few minutes she came with her bowl of popcorn to the television set, turned it on, and sat watching a game show. He held out the envelope.

"I'm in no hurry. She wasn't in any hurry. Want some?"

"No." He opened other envelopes, discarded unread every sweepstakes offer that promised him good luck and a bright future. He wondered how much time he would need to improve his own attitude, this unfamiliar sense that even the air had changed so there was nothing to inhale but irony.

"Just mail it back."

"It's your letter—you can mail it back."

Without turning her head, Mary reached out, took the envelope, and slid it into the hip pocket of her jeans. She switched by remote control to another channel and, like an automaton, began feeding herself popcorn with alternating hands.

"Don't get butter in that thing," he said, watching her. "If you continue to get along all right, the doctor says you can go back to horseback riding."

That stopped her. She must have been afraid to ask him.

"With all that bouncing around?"

"It's the inside problems, like infection, that we have to worry about."

"And diet."

"Yes."

She set the popcorn bowl on the coffee table and slid it away. "Why don't we ever keep any orange juice in this house?"

Frank said there was a carton in the back of the refrigerator. He reminded her there was also a list stuck on its door about vitamins, calories, high-carbohydrate foods, low-protein ones.

"OK, General Franco," she said with a long look at the popcorn. "I didn't salt it."

"Good."

She was in the kitchen a long time. He turned off the television to listen for those earlier restless movements. Finally he found her sitting at the table, chin on hand, with her empty juice glass next to Christine's opened envelope. In a tired voice she said, "Mama sent a get-well card."

Over her shoulder he saw a picture of fluffy white kittens rolling a ball of yarn toward a bluebird singing amid flowering twigs. Mary flipped to display the inside verse:

> You are a sweet young thing like these
> So may your illness be a breeze
> Then sunshine warm from head to toes
> Till good health blossoms like the rose.

Nobody said anything. Finally Frank prodded the address sticker. "Probably your grandmother has reached her by telephone and given her more details by now."

"I wrote her myself." Mary slid the pastel animals into the envelope and propped up her chin again.

He stayed behind her so she could not see his face. "Listen," he said urgently. "She had you. Even I can't stay mad at Christine when I remember she could do that one wonderful thing, could have you, Mary. Mary Grace? Your mother could mess up everything else from then on. She doesn't have to do one single other miracle all her life. Or me, either, for that matter. Because? Because we—"

But Mary was crying by then, and she *did* need to.

By holding on to her, Frank was able to stand it.

ONLY TWO FACTS—that Tacey was freezing strawberries and he had a secret appointment—forced Dandy to drive the car himself all the way out to the patrol station. He wanted to look at Frank's face and deduce how Mary was. Frank's face said: so far so good. Relieved, Dandy stood in the doorway watching a classroom of people including Mrs. Wilmot (size eight, sandals) taking written tests to renew their driver's licenses. Mrs. Wilmot was whizzing through the questions, although she had nearly driven up Tacey's exhaust pipe the week before. "That woman," he said over his shoulder to two troopers, "studies up before she even goes in for a blood test." Since neither laughed, he pretended seriousness as he joined Frank and Elmo Wicker, acting this morning as dispatcher. Elmo said, "I was just telling Frank how sorry I am about Mary, but at least you've got the best doctors."

"Doctors? They every one think they're God. That's what 'M.D.' stands for, 'Major Deity,' except when I'm a patient, then I'm pretty sure it turns into 'Mentally Deficient.' "

"You'd better be polite," Elmo said, "to any man that's going to decide someday whether to call you brain-dead or not."

"That Major Deity Seagroves wants more than polite—he wants people to put on their sunglasses just to look at him. Last week I was in Mary's room when he made rounds—the way he put out his hand you could see he'd like me to kiss it or something." He gave Frank a pat. "Mary's going to be just fine. You bear in mind that a Major Deity would rather have a serious case than a plain case, isn't that so? Isn't every doctor a born alarmist? Who can make a reputation curing dandruff?"

"OK, OK," said Frank.

Elmo had a story about doctors he wanted to tell, but he was too slow getting his mouth open.

"You notice your mother quit going to that particular Major Deity. I've always thought he did something, something no gentleman would do—Nosir, I couldn't warm up to Dr. Seagroves if we was being cremated together." Dandy snapped his head forward so sharply that his jaw teeth clicked. "And he always expects the worst over every little symptom, a pessimist, Frank, the kind of man that fills his tank every time he sees a gas station."

"The other doctors, specialists, they agree with Seagroves about Mary's kidney problem, Dad."

"Damn shame," Elmo murmured.

"Every doctor I ever met would magnify everything. Too many years with a microscope must cause it. Besides, wouldn't all those Major Deities stick together in front of us lesser mortals even if behind their face masks they disagreed? You ever tried to sue one of those doctors?" He stopped while Elmo took and dispatched a call because, just once, Dandy would have liked to be needed in an emergency, to make a citizen's arrest.

Elmo said, "By the way, Frank, this punk you caught next door couldn't make bail, so you can tell the old lady he's off the streets." Elmo kept making notes in his log as he talked. "Just for the hell of it, I put your questions about Frank Capone on the wire. Al never had a brother named Frank."

"I'm not surprised. Making things up must be a hobby with her."

Elmo Wicker shook his head. "It's more interesting than that. Their first report said no; but the next day somebody remembered his brother Salvatore. It turns out he was always known in the family as Frank."

"In the family!"

"That's right, a.k.a. Frank. But not in his obituary. He's been dead since 1924, shotgunned down in Cicero where he was fixing an election. So if she's old enough?"

Dandy said, "Does he mean old Lila Torrido? She really could be a bastard Capone?"

"It's barely possible timewise, that's all I'm saying. Didn't you say she was born in Chicago?"

Frank nodded. "Claims she lived with her mother somewhere in Cook County till the early thirties. She's got a big box full of Capone clippings, but that doesn't prove anything. Why would she end up living here?"

"Everybody has to end up someplace," Dandy said with growing excitement. "Why not here?"

Elmo consulted a printout. "Al Capone had brothers, and one was still in the Chicago gambling business until recently. He had only one son—well, one known son—and that boy finally changed his name."

"Run Lila Torrido's name through, by itself," Frank said,

settling his hat. "Time to go ride the roads, Dandy. You driving on in to see Mary?"

"Not this time."

"She's been home a week, and everything's going fine, so lay off criticizing Dr. Seagroves, will you?"

Dandy bounced behind Frank to the door. "She's fine no thanks to him." Even the thought of Mary Grace strung every tendon and ligament so tight that Dandy twanged when he moved. The prospect of actually being in her presence alarmed him worse. She might look tired, or puffy, or terrify him by emitting some ammoniac smell he could neither mention nor terminate. "Just driving this far has doubled my pulse, the fools that are behind the wheel these days, and I sure don't want to be on the road if Mrs. Wilmot is driving herself back to town."

He waited while Frank's black-and-silver car with its STATE TROOPER markings drove off toward Hillsborough. Then by nervous fits and starts he backed up his own car, raking its doors twice against the same shrubbery, and drove on to the main post office where a certified letter was waiting. Such a letter, Dandy knew, meant he had won another contest, maybe even the Cadillac offered in the subscription sweepstakes (Tacey wouldn't complain about driving him around in a Cadillac!), or maybe he'd won the soap company's vacation to Miami, where sun and air so expensive would surely heal Mary Grace before she even left its airport.

On the other hand, he might have won another gadget.

Tacey was dog-tired of gadgets. She already had apple peelers you cranked, hamburger grills, yogurt makers, baked-bean bakers, and a kitchen tapestry with a gold-thread perpetual calendar from which only Einstein could figure out today's date. She owned serrated knives and spatulas in graduated sizes, sausage grinders, toaster ovens, and portavacs. Rusting on their back porch stood a Marvo-Mop that would scrub floors with electrical brushes and then slurp up the dirty water. He had won for Tacey a kitchen radio shaped like a fat green pepper, shoe trees, and padded dress hangers, and six tapes for which they owned no tape player.

Today's letter came glued onto a box too small to contain a car. Too large for airline tickets, even the wrong size for the ranch mink or golf clubs. He dumped excelsior into the nearest trash bin and felt around inside.

This smaller box contained a digital watch. Half its face flashed time, date, stopwatch seconds. Another window blinked out the parallel times in London, Rome, Moscow, and whatever that newfangled Chinese name was for Peking. The third display (so the instructions said) could be set to read out the wearer's pulse rate, handy for jogging and other aerobic exercise.

He tossed the watch into the glove compartment. With anxious glances into his side mirror and an uncertain foot on the accelerator, Dandy drove into the edge of Durham to keep his private, even secret, appointment with a urologist and have his questions answered.

"I SEE." Though his thick glasses were ground for an old man's eyes, the doctor's face was pale, smooth, almost adolescent. He couldn't have learned many fine points in so few years.

"Of course only those doctors handling your granddaughter's case can give reliable answers. Did you want me to consult? Examine the child and give a separate opinion?"

Dandy said no, then flooded him with talk. He pressed and insisted and demanded while this preadult Major Deity checked his wristwatch. It glinted; it had not been won from any soap company.

Finally the doctor broke in, "Naturally your entire family is probably overreacting, trying to work out a worst-possible scenario. There are many different forms of nephritis and renal disease, different treatments, different expectations." Seeing that Dandy was in danger of speaking again, he made himself patient by biofeedback, deep breaths, slow exhalations, a slight tug of one hand by the other, then overrode him smoothly. "Your granddaughter has had no sudden attack? No emergency? Not the horse accident, I mean a kidney emergency? Good. I would guess that your granddaughter contracted some time back an infection and then a quick secondary infection that did its damage without leaving anything to identify itself in the blood culture. What damage is there is just there—you can't rebuild organ parts by taking medicine." With one hand he stopped questions from getting through. "But her kidneys must be functioning now, or there would be other signs such as high blood pressure, swelling, high rates of potassium and electrolytes. Probably you should call it chronic renal disease rather than *failure* to stop scaring yourselves to—" he decided not to say the word "death." "Even if her condition worsens, she'll be a prime candidate for dialysis."

"Don't beat around the bush—can I donate to Mary my kidney or not?"

This time the doctor's exhalation turned into a sigh. "The ideal situation would be a kidney donated by a twin. From that ideal on down, they tissue-type from zero to four. A four is the next-best thing, and a sibling is usually the best choice. Then comes a parent. When you move out to the kidney of some stranger who's an organ donor, well. I'd go ahead with surgery given any two-point match. A two would allow about a forty percent chance of success."

The low figure shocked him. Dandy tried not to look at his own hands, where he felt four of his digits quiver.

"I'm too old?"

"Your *kidney* is old. Tell me, do you take medication for high blood pressure? I thought so. High pressure damages organs, you know." He studied Dandy as if debating how much mortal time he would want measured. "If a transplant patient keeps a kidney six months, she'll keep it a year. Keep it a year—three to five years."

"Mary's only twelve."

"Then there are years of scientific progress ahead of her."

Finally he had to ask. "A girl—what does this do to a girl? Who is just growing up? In this bodily area, you know?"

"At twelve, at puberty, with associations to the genitalia, what will it do psychologically to a girl *or* a boy? Nothing good. Get her some therapy, Mr. Thompson."

Afterward Dandy sat in the car with his two moldy atrophied kidneys ticking inside their fragile container and made stubborn plans to think of other things. Quit dwelling on this; all doctors exaggerated! Expect the best, chin up, cheer up, and so on, he recited to himself. He'd need to take with a bag of salt all he had heard from a doctor too young to be more than a Minor Deity at best. Still too young to know the dotted *i*'s and crossed *t*'s and exceptions to rules that experience would teach him.

Dandy sat for ten minutes, at least, cheering himself up.

Then, heavy from effort, he drove badly toward Chapel Hill. He debated a side trip to Cromwell Street just in case it would cheer him even more to see how poor a provider Virgil Broome still was, but saw there were too many parked cars with bumpers and fenders stuck out in the way, while on the four-lane he could drive at a sane speed on the right side and let lunatics whiz by on his left.

At thirty-five miles per hour he entered green Chapel Hill, a university town he loved but could not understand. Most of the time its neighborhoods were chock-full of friendly, likable people whose ideas he disapproved of: liberals favoring abortion, welfare, eminent domain, peace at any cost, fornication, homosexual weddings, and the secularizing of American public life.

Not that Dandy went to church much himself, but he *approved* of church.

Every summer, though, when the liberal professors and their ultraliberal students went away on tax-supported travel, the main Franklin Street recovered from them all. In every lane relatively calm drivers would pass; there were empty parking spaces; prices dropped. Not a single summer sport produced bonfires or riots by Tar Heel fans. For summer school, the student body was split between anxious kids who might flunk out and fattening schoolteachers, all wearing eyeglasses, the latter clearly homeowners and taxpayers.

In the summer even an old man with old kidneys could buy a cold beer without anybody's smart-ass remark.

Dandy was walking toward a bar to overload those kidneys on just such a beer when he spotted Mary Grace Thompson ahead of him, talking to a black-haired man who moved beside her while rolling every bodily joint, especially the hip joints, like a pervert.

"Stop!" he called. "Mary Grace!" She turned. So did the Dirty Old Man, her other grandfather, Virgil Broome.

Right the first time.

Dandy hurried forward, suspicious in every prickle of his skin. "What's going on?" Mary's hug made it hard for him to keep his stance ominous.

"Oh, good!" she said. "We can all have a Coke together."

The two men eyed each other with a dislike that went back to fights on school playgrounds in the Lowes Grove community outside Chapel Hill. While Virgil had been in Korea, Andrew Thompson had even dated Georgia a time or two, but had too much sense to marry her. Too bad Frank ever married Christine.

"I thought you lived in Durham," Dandy said.

"That's right. You've gained some weight."

"Not an ounce." Since he was a few years older than Virgil, though, he was allowed to weigh a little more.

The grandfathers seemed nailed into the sidewalk, swaying, pretending to look in a shopwindow at Indian earrings. Mary managed to squeeze between them.

Dandy washed venom in the space between his teeth before asking, "How's your Christine?"

With slow, well-spaced words, Virgil Broome said she was "putting her life back together after a mizzable marriage." He was the taller, with an outsize face, long as a mule's, big teeth.

Her miserable marriage! Dandy decided then and there that having a reliable enemy must guarantee vitality. By his own rush of sensations he understood how, by instinct, a threatened tomcat or rooster cock would swell its hair and feathers into aureoles. Adrenaline crackled now through his vestigial mane and comb. He could feel his eyes bulge and shine. "Well, they married for better or worse," he said briskly. "Christine couldn't have done better and Frank couldn't have done worse."

"That's enough," said Mary, and with fingers as sharp as Tacey's took hold of the skin on both men's arms. "Let's go downstairs here. Watch your step."

She led them into a basement bar; it must have been a gay bar; it looked gay. Dandy became instantly certain its location was metaphorical—but the air between him and Virgil was so electric with Y chromosomes that they'd be as safe as in church.

Even so, he sent out a threatening glare like a searchlight after they had lurched downstairs into cool dimness, where dark-green plants were sucking light below the sidewalk grating.

Nobody bothered them. Two suspiciously dainty men at a far table went on discussing something unspeakable. Soon two beers and a milk shake were placed before them while Virgil set down a box of rolling metal. Dandy felt out his iron soda-fountain chair, which was insecure and too small. "What's that?" he asked with a tap of his shoe on Virgil's box.

"Keys and tools."

Skeleton and burglar, Dandy almost said. From her back bench, Mary smiled around a creamy straw at them both. She might be enjoying this tension, Dandy thought suddenly. She's Christine's, too; she might not be innocent at all.

"I've been hoping we could get together like this," Mary said.

He tested the air for sarcasm.

"Dream on," said Virgil. "This old fart used to turn me in to the principal for smoking. Grade six!"

"Didn't." Falsely accused! he thought. It was grade seven.

There swam in memory the playground lowlands, a valley below mountains of furnace coke, where a young pine forest was smothered under kudzu. Here the girls had built playhouses during recess or performed in leafy theaters. Here the boys had spied on them, not even certain yet what they hoped to see up their skirts. Here Virgil Broome had once leaped off a pine onto Andrew Thompson's back and knocked the breath out of him. Here they had found used condoms and filled them with rainwater.

"You're both my grandfathers," Mary cautioned, though Virgil was only a grandfather by marriage.

Dandy couldn't resist it. "But he's Georgia's second husband, and now she's got a new louse on life." He went off into giggles and got beer foam up his nose.

Virgil concentrated on Mary, asked about her diet and how she was feeling. Too fresh from his own doctor's visit, Dandy tried to change the subject. "And how's Georgia, the misfortune-teller?" He was noticing that Virgil had grown thin and stringy this past year, looked faintly yellow, might have blown out his liver at last. Smiling, Dandy leaned forward to check his complexion.

"You're altogether gray now," Virgil said with spite. "She's fine." He saw Mary's expectant look. "And Tacey?"

"Just fine, thank you, fine. Did she tell me you make keys these days?"

"I spend a lot of time changing locks," Virgil said. "There's a lot of crime in Durham."

"I see it on TV," Dandy said, as if well satisfied that this should be so.

"I've been thinking," Mary Grace put in, "there's not a thing wrong with everybody in our families getting together this year for a Fourth of July picnic. We used to do that. We could get all the Broomes and Thompsons together."

Dandy wondered if she still hoped her parents might reconcile.

"Anything you can imagine wrong with it is about half of
what's wrong with it." But Virgil smiled at her. "You was
good in that school play."

Noel Coward, Dandy remembered. *Blithe Spirit*. Every bit of
cleverness wasted on the Broomes. The Broomes thought Bee-
thoven's Fifth was a bourbon. "Y'all didn't come to her piano
recital, though, and she was good there, too."

She said, "Why am I supposed to love all the family on both
sides when they can't stand each other?"

They had no answer. "I don't think Georgia got told about
the recital," Virgil almost whined.

"It's a wonder," Dandy said pleasantly, "those green plants
live down here with no light. Just that little bit and the beer
signs." The beer signs, in moving multicolors, washed Mary
from brow to chin in a recurring rainbow. "We're not all that
bad," he told her.

"I'm not, I know that," Virgil complained.

It was true that after Frank's marriage the Broomes and
Thompsons had held joint family reunions in the summer, since
the families were obscurely related, generations back. One year
they had met in the fellowship hall of Tacey's church, and she
had stood in the vestibule checking off strangers as they came
in, sheep from goats, Thompsons from Broomes. "Blood will
tell," she'd said, and it was true that on looks alone not a single
Broome was as refined as a cabbage. They gargled up tea and
siphoned up soup. They talked louder than TV commercials.
Even the Broome kids looked as if they'd been born dumb and
then had a relapse.

Though Dandy enjoyed feeling superior to every single visitor, the gatherings had stopped after Christine ran away. "It's
not as easy to book space at Damascus Church as it used to be,"
he began now.

"Even the apartment complex would be big enough for a
reunion if we catered the hors d'oeuvres, ham, potato salad,
you know. We could eat in that little park. In summer, people

want to be outside." She touched Virgil's sleeve. "I know you could get Mama to come."

"Never been able to make Christine do anything."

"How about just the Thompsons this time? It's easier to get in touch with the Thompsons." He gave Virgil a look meant to convey that none of the Thompsons were in jail or skipping out on child support or unable to drive because their licenses had been revoked.

"I want everybody." Something new came over Mary's face. "I'm sick; I want everybody."

The two men eyed each other.

She asked Virgil, "Mama wouldn't have to bring along a boyfriend, would she?"

"Lord, child. I guess not." Virgil's answer almost made Dandy feel sorry for him, that and the way he gulped the beer.

"Well, if she does, she does," Mary said.

"No, of course not, she wouldn't do that even if . . . would she, Andrew?"

"No, even Christine wouldn't do that, there's a limit. Think about your daddy."

"But he could bring Miss Jillian Peters," Mary said and sat dreamily tearing strips of napkin and rolling them into tubes between her fingers.

"Or Cindy Scofield, for that matter. Is that all over with? Tacey says the Peters girl is way too young for him."

"She's not," Mary said and gave Virgil a challenging stare. "Wouldn't you think Mama would at least like to meet Miss Peters?"

"Well, if she's got to come stag I don't see why Frank Thompson gets to—" He noticed Dandy's rapidly shaking head.

"I could be sicker by September," Mary threatened.

The grandfathers tried to find help in each other's face. Dandy decided Virgil had become very seedy, an imitation urban gypsy, learned it by mail order from California. And to him I must look pink, tightass, trivial. All they had in common, he thought, were their monthly Social Security checks. And Mary.

Virgil said slowly, "Georgia could maybe get Christine to come."

Georgia. Dandy took a long air-conditioned breath without stirring up her old scent (Evening in Paris) or memory, though once Georgia had been able to give him a hard-on merely by stirring his armpit with her fingers. Even then, such power had scared him—and he was by no means the only farm boy she tested it on. Instead of Georgia—a Saturday-night girl—he chose and married Tacey, the Sunday-morning type, a good, even a loving, woman. Tacey's armpits had proved free of the very nerve endings he had himself intended to master and arouse. He had planned on their honeymoon in Asheville to amaze her by releasing her own unsuspected passion. For forty years she had remained amazed at his.

Then Georgia had married Willard Beak, wore him out, had Christine, left her alone a lot. For years if they met downtown Dandy would say the same chiding thing to her, "I hear you been on more laps than a napkin," and she'd say, "Well, every once and a while I feel like a new man—and don't you wish you could say the same!"

He wondered now what married life had been like for Virgil Broome, who had come late into Georgia's life—four? five? number fifteen or twenty of Georgia's men? Whether he tickled and shot up still, whether Georgia as an aging slattern could still ply her will through her fingertips, whether every man's powers wore out over time more rapidly than borrowed kidneys were scientifically predicted to do. Well, Willard Beak had burned up his kidney. Georgia could probably pee straight scotch. Maybe there were reasons to get on Christine's good side, just in case. Organ donor reasons.

"Wake up!" Mary ordered Dandy's face behind the mug.

"I'm just thinking about July fourth." Splendidly, Tacey's kitchen perpetual calendar rose in his mind and functioned for once. "It's a Wednesday. We could do it the Sunday before if any of Virgil's kin have to hitchhike in." But Virgil shrugged. "And you're not going to be sicker by September," he told Mary.

The line of her jaw went flaccid, as if her face had begun to wilt. He remembered her broken wrist—age five—how she had tried to keep the cast on extralong so Christine would dress her, comb her hair, pay close attention. Changing the subject, he said, "You remember in 1776 what Martha Washington said to George when the redcoats appeared outside Mount Vernon; she said, 'Don't just stand there, slay something.' " A pause. "Never mind. I thought you might smile over it. Well, just for you, Mary, the Thompsons and Broomes will bury the hatchet, won't we, Virgil?"

She broke in, "Don't overdo it. It's just one simple picnic —skip the hatchet; I wasn't even there for the hatchet."

"I hope you're not there for the blow," Dandy said.

Virgil set down his almost empty beer and said to her firmly, "You just let us Broomes know where to come and we'll come, but tell your grandma Georgia exactly how you want things done. Invite the first cousins? Second? Kissing? The Beaks, too? Covered dish or what? And you want to entertain this crowd of people? Georgia can put on her moon-and-stars dress and read palms."

The Broomes had begun to seem more generous than the Thompsons. "I can juggle! I whittle whistles and toys! Tacey makes the best chess pie anywhere around." Inspired, Dandy leaned forward. "We'll have it out at the Thompson homeplace." He knew the Broomes had never had a homeplace; one time when Virgil's daddy had been in prison, the family had lived a whole summer in a parked truck. Most of Georgia's kin were dead, now.

"I don't know. With that field all grown up and so much stuff to carry up that hill," Mary murmured.

"How heavy is a folding table? The road to the house is grown up, but you can still get a car through there. I can call the man I sold it to. There's the shopping center right close for last-minute things. And that highway's easy for everybody to find, even the Broomes that can't tell fortunes like Georgia. There's plenty of places in Happy Creek where the children can wade."

"Snaky, I bet," said Virgil.

"I know a man will run over that hillside with a bushhog a few days before, clear it out for us."

"The way that leaves stobs sticking up and poison oak scattered—I don't know." Virgil shook his head, matched the movement by shaking his empty glass, as if the last malt drops could be consolidated.

Laughing, Mary waved her hands. She said maybe the reunion picnic would be a big celebration. They could send postcards to invite people from out-of-town. Draw maps. They could invite good friends from Chapel Hill; now that school was out, she hadn't seen many of her friends.

"All right, fine!" said Virgil, grinning at her, and Dandy said, "Sure. Great, that Sunday! Don't just stand there—slay something; didn't you get it?"

"We didn't want it," Virgil muttered.

After Mary excused herself to go to the ladies' room, they were left staring at its closed door. Virgil tried to order another beer, but Dandy advised against it. "You're driving, right? So how's the key business?"

He rattled the box onto the table. "Half of this stuff is knives to sharpen." But they both kept their eyes on the bathroom door. Virgil said softly, "She don't seem so sick."

"Right now she's not. And I want Mary Grace to have anything she wants, to have it any way she wants it." They watched the door, wondering if she was taking too long inside.

"We'd hate to bring Christine all the way from Jacksonville if she was going to be insulted, you can understand that."

"Nobody's going to insult her."

"When Georgia called her up with the news about Mary, it made her cry."

"That's such a big help," Dandy said.

"There you go. Insults."

"No more. I promise." Both were leaning forward now, waiting for that door to swing open. "I can handle Frank if you can handle Christine, and we'll make this reunion just the way Mary Grace wants it. We got through other reunions. We got through the wedding ceremony all right."

"Fourteen years ago. I'm out of practice."

They had gotten through visiting the same hospital ward thirteen years ago, had stood at the nursery window, and picked out the wrong red lump of infant as their granddaughter.

"I forgot you and Georgia have been married that long. You think this time is permanent?"

The door opened and both men relaxed.

As Mary joined them Virgil said, "I'll outlast you."

She said, "I don't think we need to plan any formal entertainment at this picnic, but you tell Grandmother Broome I want her to read the future in my palm."

Uneasily Virgil answered, "Never thought of that." He stood up.

Dandy slid the heavy box toward him. "You're sharpening knives for customers over here in Chapel Hill?"

"There's a man here does sharpening real cheap—I carry them back to my Durham customers and then charge my profit. People that moved down here from the North expect to pay high."

"You could just sharpen the knives yourself!" But you're too lazy to scratch when you itch, Dandy thought.

"Sometimes I have to." Virgil touched his none-too-clean

fingers to Mary's red hair. The stitches were out, but she kept Band-Aids over the wound to cover the fuzzy new hair. "You do what them doctors tell you."

Naturally he left Dandy Thompson to pay for his beer.

AS DAYS PASSED and Mary took up her normal summer routines—on bicycle to the swimming pool, then home with her basket full of library books, afternoon TV, a slumber party at Kay Linda's—Frank could feel his fear loosen. He invited Jill Peters to a movie, behaved politely as a boy, kissed her goodnight far too lightly for them both, and hurried off—knowing she frowned after him. Pleased by his strategy of restraint.

For Saturday's horse show, he and Mary sat in folding aluminum chairs by the ring at Centaur Stable to watch Jill lead a demonstration clinic over jumps. The way her ass rose and floated in midair when the horse extended himself gracefully over each barrier made Frank ache.

There came into his mind a scrap of graffiti—scrawled in the men's toilet at the patrol station:

I'd love to be the ruby ring
Upon my true love's hand
Then every time she wiped her ass
I'd see the Promised Land.

He shifted in the lawn chair. Thinking such a thing about his daughter's teacher while by his daughter's side! But on her next jump he responded even more strongly to the smooth line of Jill's curved body, high and inclined forward over the powerful neck of the thoroughbred. On each approach, just before the barricade, the horse seemed to pause, to gather himself, then fly. The pause made Frank tense up, since each time it appeared the horse might crash into the heavy poles.

"I hope you don't want to jump like that," he murmured to Mary.

"It's not hard. First they teach you to rest your hands in the mane and rise up in the stirrups to ride over cavalletti—I've read the book." She concentrated on a line of intermediate students who followed Jill, practicing their form over the lowest jumps.

Jill stood holding her horse's reins while encouraging each young rider who passed. "Head up!" she'd call as the girl cantered by. "Look ahead to where you're going. Let your knees absorb it!" and so on. Sometimes she would turn her body's silhouette to demonstrate how the spine should arch.

Frank kept watching her and not the jumpers.

Not that he lived a celibate life. Celibates got ulcers or nervous disorders. No wonder priests needed to pray a lot just to sustain their bodily health without permanent harm. Frank had an ongoing arrangement, after all, with Cindy Scofield. They had met after a false bomb threat and evacuation of a U.N.C. basketball game. Cindy was almost thirty and had dark wiry corkscrew hair; on sight he had known how her pubis would feel. In a few years Cindy would move on: from the *Chapel Hill Newspaper* to the *Charlotte Observer*, *Atlanta Journal-Constitution*, *Boston Globe*. Her set career plans did not seem to include Frank Thompson. As she had saved him from ulcers, he saved her from jitters and severe female chauvinism, she sometimes said, since in the journalistic world it could be easy to hate men, the bastards, if you didn't immunize yourself by always maintaining a tie to one good, sweet backup man; "And you are a good sweet man, Frank," she'd say in bed, drowsing afterward, absently sucking his chin or earlobe or shoulder, wherever her mouth had ended up.

By now they knew each other too well, too long. Like an old married couple, they had to plan sex within their work schedules, build up to it, shift out of the good-buddy stage in which they had just compared their wreck reports.

Frank watched Jill Peters bend again to curve her beautiful back.

Cindy was scarred on the right buttock. She had only one younger brother, a child always bruised and scratched, since he was able to feel only very high levels of pain, who could work higher math in his head but could barely speak. Most of the time he scrubbed his small world with saliva—table, wall, chair—and gave small moans. Spittle on people, too. One winter night when Cindy was baby-sitting—most sitters would not keep so severe an autistic child—twice Bobby spat in his hand, dipped his fingertips, reached to smear her face. This once she forgot how little he could comprehend and, by reflex, shoved him away. Laughing, he snatched the kindling hatchet off the hearth and hacked her quickly, as if she, like he, could feel no more pain than the trunk of a tree.

Cindy's brother lived in an institution now. None of the patterning exercises that had exhausted their mother altered his mind enough. He could still chalk on a blackboard algebraic formulas that might reflect either genius or nonsense—how could the average licensed practical nurse determine the difference? Maybe the circumference of Jupiter was always running through his head, maybe relativity, maybe in sequence every license plate he had ever seen.

Frank had early kissed Cindy on her scar, knowing how much emotion its swerve must represent. Instantly she had shivered and cried out. Until then he had not been able to bring her to orgasm.

Jill was probably too young to have any hurt worse than some boyfriend in a wallet photo who had ditched her at the prom. Whereas Tacey had buried two miscarriages; Frank had been shot; Dandy had had one silent and one all-too-loud heart attack. Christine, he guessed, had had a hangnail or two.

Helpers ran forward to dismantle the jumps for Jill's final demonstration, the one Mary said was guaranteed to attract new students. First she took the horse through small circles at different collected gaits, then executed smoothly the moves of third-level dressage.

Mary clapped so loud that Frank blurted, "You want a horse of your own?"

"Are you kidding?"

Now Jill was side-passing her mount precisely along the fence so everyone in the stands could see how easy it looked.

"Yes or no—you want us to buy a horse?"

"We can't afford a horse."

"I'll manage." He could increase his loan at the bank when it opened Monday. "Miss Peters have any for sale in the barn?"

"No, but this doctor never rides his—Chancy, an Arabian; we could make an offer? His daughter grew up, and his wife doesn't come to ride very often. I bet they're tired of him." She was getting excited. "Gambler's Chance is his registered name. He's a purebred gelding with four stockings, and he knows me already."

"That's too high-strung a breed and too expensive."

"Shows how little you know. A horse acts gentle if it's treated gentle. Come see him, Daddy. I already can pick out his feet and groom him and pet him; he likes me." She was tugging Frank out of the aluminum chair through the applauding crowd while Jill demonstrated how to back and roll back her horse. Mary kept talking as if greater volume would persuade. "I'll feed him myself. I can get a newspaper route to help out. And baby-sit. And mow grass. I'll give up going to movies and buy hay instead. I don't even like the swimming pool much."

As she hurried him by, Frank tried to read rapidly the monthly boarding fee plus lessons on the Centaur sign. She pulled on his arm all the way down the barn aisle.

"He's got Raffles blood and a little Egyptian and he used to show English when the daughter lived at home and he's smart; he understands half of what I say." She suddenly cooed "Don't you, Chancy?" into a dim stall, shot back the bolt, and disappeared before he could stop her.

Frank leaped forward.

She was standing with both arms wrapped around the powerful neck of the bay. Gambler's Chance hung his head down her back to nibble the hem of her T-shirt.

"Ah, what doctor owns him?" Frank took a tentative step into the stall and across manure. He knew little about horses. This one looked glossy and well fed; it was not flattening ears or twisting tail or showing the white in either eye. On the Thompson farm as a boy he had dropped off tree limbs to ride surprised mules or cows. He knew a lot about falling.

He patted the withers. After a pause he slowly ran the other hand over the horse's loin.

"Dr. Weaver is some kind of cancer expert so he travels a lot to give speeches, and the poor horse just stands here except when Miss Peters turns him out for exercise. See how level his topline is? Arabians have one less rib than other breeds of horses, and look at his skin." Mary parted hairs. "It's black, that's another trait of Arabians. Look how well his shoulder is laid back."

"I'd think black skin would have been hot in the desert sun. How old is he?"

"I'm not sure, maybe ten."

"Too old." Frank thought of a ten-year-old dog he knew, gray at the muzzle.

"No, it's not—we don't want a young, unseasoned horse. Ask Miss Peters."

"Maybe we could take Miss Peters to dinner to talk about it?"

"Terrific. I'll go invite her!"

Mary ran off without questioning his motives, leaving Frank half-glad and half-sorry. One time—just one—he had taken Cindy Scofield as his guest, to Mary's music recital, without telling Mary first. From the piano bench she had looked once into the audience at him—stricken, betrayed—before playing badly the Chopin waltz he had already heard perfectly a hundred times. Later, introductions had been polite and frigid.

"I know who you are. I see your name in the newspaper."

"I enjoyed hearing you play, Mary."

"I don't see how, I was awful. Are you covering the recital for the paper?"

"Well, no."

Mary's look blazed through her to hit Frank beyond. "You're dating? Like teenagers? Dating?"

He said, "That will do."

Mary began moving off. "I've already got a ride home with friends"—she said "friends" very loud—"so you two can go to the soda shop or park or make out, or whatever old people do when you're *dating*."

"Mary!"

But Cindy had held him back while Mary slipped easily into a crowd of giggling girls and hid herself there like a herd animal. Had he and Cindy been seriously considering marriage, he would certainly have pressed the issue, would have made Mary apologize, then brought Cindy to dinner at home and made Mary be gracious there. Maybe he should have disciplined her anyway. But Cindy only said, "Forget it. If anybody deserves to indulge her Electra complex, Mary does. Give her some time." Later when he lectured Mary, she said in disgust, "If you could have seen yourself! Teenagers, and you with a potbelly!" Frank said, "I do not have—"

Suddenly Chancy kicked back, threw his great head around, and with his teeth snapped some yellow fly off his flank. Frank was already half out the stable door. Feeling embarrassed, he slid the bolt home and stood studying the pedigree of Gambler's Chance, done in calligraphy in a small picture frame hung on the outside wall. It made no sense to him, and he couldn't pronounce most of the horses' names.

Jill's hand went suddenly past to lift the frame off its nail. "We'll carry it along so I can tell you what his forebears were known for. How are you, Frank?" Her handshake gave the same tingle as touching an electrical switch with damp fingers.

"You looked wonderful on that horse," he said awkwardly; he knew liberated women hated to have emphasis put on their looks.

Without answering, she handed the pedigree chart to Mary. "I need to shower and change so everybody else in the restaurant won't have to sit upwind. Can you two pick me up at my apartment? I'll hurry. Mary can have a Coke and maybe Frank would like a drink before dinner."

Mary, he saw, was gazing at Jillian Peters with an awe as great, though different in kind, as his when he looked at her ass. Mary said, "We can follow your car. We're parked close by."

"Even if you should lose me," said Jill with a smile, "your father knows where I live."

"Oh?" Frank got ready for Mary's wisecrack to whiz over the plate dead center. This time he'd clamp down; he'd insist she apologize, sick or not.

Mary said, "Can't I just ride on with you, then?"

"If *you* sit upwind!" Jill said with a laugh.

"You bring this with you, General Franco." Mary thrust the pedigree into his hand and set off with Jill Peters, calling back, "Any horse you see on there with an asterisk is imported."

Buying a horse now might bring his own ass to risk. Financially.

He loaded the aluminum chairs, then drove slowly behind Jill's car but lost them at an intersection while he followed heavy traffic out of Carrboro, a mill town that over the years had merged imperceptibly with the college town of Chapel Hill. Jill lived on Airport Road in a high-rise whose halls were depressing concrete-block tunnels between blank doors, their peepholes placed as if someone had systematically shot through each one, head-high. Real crimes took place in her building, too, mostly drug busts or an occasional domestic fight between a graduate student and his worn-out waitress-wife. One rape that he knew of. One fatal leap from the roof.

He already knew which monotonous balcony on the fifth floor was Jill's. After their first date he had ridden by several nights, watching her light, wondering who else was inside. He had very carefully kissed her good-bye in the hall and not gone inside himself.

"Oh, you look so funny!" Mary crowed behind the apartment door when he knocked, her eye obviously stuck to the peephole. He knocked again. "Stick out your tongue," Mary called through the flimsy door.

Somebody got rich on this construction.

She finally opened it, moved to the outside to peek through the hole in reverse, then stepped aside. "Miss Peters is in the shower. Why didn't you tell me you took her out? She says it's just once to the movies."

"I didn't think you'd like it."

"Who cares what a kid likes? Do I ever mind your business?"

"All the time." Though small, the living room was more pleasant than he had expected, airy with painted wicker and translucent curtains at the sliding glass doors. There were many books on shelves made of white boards and white brick, under bright impressionist prints and travel posters.

"She set out scotch on the kitchen table."

"Scotch?"

"She didn't have any Jack Daniel's."

At least it was a good malt scotch. The kitchen area was clean but cluttered, canisters everywhere, a sweet potato vine clogging the window, carrot tops growing in jar lids on the sill; and before he tasted his drink Frank sniffed the air. "She got a cat?"

"I haven't seen one."

Definitely the smell of a cat's litter box. Must keep it in the bathroom, from which he could hear running water. Cindy owned a yapping Pomeranian that would swoop, bite his ankle, flee, then do it again.

Suddenly Jill appeared from the bathroom wrapped in a beach towel. "Oh!" she exclaimed at the unexpected sight of him staring. Frank lifted his glass in a silent toast as she stood, pink and evaporating, even her long hair in wet dark strands. "You're supposed to be in the living room with Mary." She wheeled through an adjoining doorway.

He called, "Where's the cat?"

"Top of refrigerator." The door closed.

The yellow tabby, huge, probably a neutered tom, had all this time been fixing on Frank a gaze so green and judgmental that his neck should have prickled. He called to Mary, "Cat's on the refrigerator," and reached to scratch its chin. Without effort the cat placed one paw on Frank's knuckle to prevent the caress—he could barely feel the dots of claw points on his skin.

Mary, of course, came right in, climbed up the kitchen ladder, and hauled him purring into her arms.

Frank hated cats. Probably he and Jillian Peters would never find a thing to talk about either. To check it out, he went to read titles in her bookcase. Dog books and cat books and horse books. Farley Mowat on wolves and whales. Roger Tory Petersen. Falconry. Encyclopedias of animal tracks and scats; he had to check what a scat was—yes. Shit. Audubon. Raising baby birds by hand. Thor Heyerdahl. The desert, the seashore, the mountains, the rain forest. In any books about man, man was a predator or polluter, unless born Indian or Cro-Magnon.

Mary rearranged the limp cat hanging off her lap. "Look up Arabians in that big horse book."

He turned to the pictured gray stallion under sheik's saddle with pom-poms and tassels. He skimmed silently, "oldest pure breed in the world . . . Lady Wentworth . . . Army Remount . . . Polish stud . . ."

"Hold the cat—I'm going to the bathroom."

"Take him with you. There's nothing wrong?"

"Nothing except you're turning into a pest about my health." The cat did follow and washed a foot while waiting outside the door. Frank sat with the book, trying to understand the Darley Arabian, the Byerly Turk, and the Godolphin Barb. He read the paragraph twice.

Dimly he heard Mary call out, "Miss Peters?"

"Be out in a jiffy."

"That's fine, no problem." In another minute Mary came back into the room and moved rather stiffly to the glass door, slid it back. Noise and exhaust came into the cool room. She carried the cat onto the balcony to watch cars passing. Then she carried him back, closed the door, and stepped carefully to look at one framed poster, then the next. In detail.

"Sit down," Frank said. "You're making me nervous."

"No, thank you."

Something in her voice? No matter where Mary moved in the room or what she did, she remained no more than half-turned toward him. He put down the book to watch. Still, her face looked secretive and tickled.

"Something on your mind?"

She edged along a bookcase at the same odd angle, checking this houseplant and then another.

"Mary, what *is* it?"

"It's just so funny, I mean it's so perfect, to happen here and everything!" She giggled.

Jill stuck her head into view. "I'm dressed, but I still need to braid my hair. Mary, you want another Coke?"

"No, but can I come in?" At the same skewed body angle Mary slid to Jill's bedroom door and disappeared inside.

For what seemed a long time Frank read about the escaped horses of the Spanish conquistadores, probably Arabian, and the Cavaliers bringing Arabians to Virginia and the ancestry of Justin Morgan.

He looked up once when Jill went alone into the bathroom,

then back again. They were talking beyond the thin wall. Not laughing. Once, he decided, they were arguing.

When Jill hurried out, her wet hair was only caught back with a rubber band in a long ponytail. "Frank? I don't want to worry you."

Frank dropped the book, leaping from his chair.

"Mary thought, well, she thought she was starting her first period, and so did I at first, but now I don't think so, Frank. I think she's passing a lot of blood in her urine and turning that red, and where she hurts on one side doesn't sound like a menstrual cramp at all. She feels a little sick to her stomach, too."

"Call Seagroves. At home, Dr. Donald Seagroves. And tell him we're on the way to the hospital."

Jill began thumbing through the telephone directory. "She doesn't want to go."

"She'll go."

He found Mary sitting on the edge of the bed, determined by fury not to cry. He heard his own light, false voice. "Come on, Mary Gracious. You know we've got to see the doctors." Silence. "You know this is just what they warned us to look for."

"There goes the horse, the horse, there goes the damn damn horse."

"Of course not. Come on, now. Feel like walking?"

"So now it's OK to say damn? That's how sick I am?"

"It's not OK." Awkwardly he stood alongside her, intending by leaning down to pull her to her feet; even more awkwardly, she turned her face suddenly into his hip and hugged both his legs hard. He was off balance, afraid of falling on top of her. He said, "Maybe we'll even see the doctor who owns him at the hospital, who knows? In fact, I can make a point to look for him. Dr. Weaver, you said. Mary? The sooner we go the sooner?" He glanced at the nodding movement Jill was making in the doorway. "The sooner you'll get out of there."

She swung away, got up slowly. "My head hurts."

They walked her carefully between them to the elevator, on to Frank's car in the parking lot.

"I'll lock up and"—Jill had to raise her voice as the car pulled off—"be about five minutes behind you!" Then she sprinted inside the building, pressed the elevator button, watched the light linger on the third floor, jabbed it again. While she waited she fingered in one pocket the tampon Mary had thought she needed.

LATE DURING THAT long night in the waiting room, Tacey Thompson remembered she had earlier passed the open door to a chapel somewhere in this vast hospital. She pulled her husband's arm.

"Come on, Andrew, we're going to pray now."

Tired and numb, he could barely hear her; he managed to ask, "What?"

She grew louder. "You heard me. I'd hate to poke you right here in public. Get up this very minute and come with me."

He looked anxiously across the couch to Frank. "Has she snapped or what?"

"Pray," Frank said. "She just wants you to go pray."

In a corner sat Jillian Peters, with her eyes closed and an open magazine forgotten in her lap.

Dandy got up uncertainly from his hard plastic chair. "That's no way to ask a fellow—I'm sure Jesus never—look here, Tacey! We're all under strain!"

She said angrily, "Never mind strain! This time you will, I mean it, Andrew. This time you wouldn't dare not to." She was dragging him toward the hall. "We'll ask the nurse where." He was pulled behind her, rolling both eyes, spreading a palm toward Frank when he could get one free.

Frank didn't care. "We'll be here," he mumbled.

A nurse directed them downstairs to the All-Faith Chapel.

"I can," Dandy grumbled at its door, "pray just as well"—
Tacey shoved him onto the back bench in the dim room—
"upstairs!" he finished.

She sat close to him on the dark-red cushion. Like a drill
sergeant, she ordered, "Twenty-third Psalm, then the Lord's
Prayer." She began mouthing words in a stage whisper.

The Twenty-third Psalm? It had always made him nervous.
It gave in. It acquiesced. Soon as it got down to brass tacks
and left the still waters to walk down the Valley of Death,
God-as-*He* was begged to turn right away into God-as-*Thou*.
Serious business. So wouldn't a need that extreme bring
Thou, Him, It, Whoever, into the valley right away to fix
things up?

Not a bit. That psalm acquiesced to dying!

For the rest of the verses no mention was made about escaping
Death thanks to Him (thanks to Thou). The most that could
be escaped was the fear of Death. Just the Fear. Second best.
You got goodness and mercy the rest of your life but no insurance
beyond, except someone to walk the last mile with you. Even
convicts got that.

Dandy mumbled so Tacey would think he was keeping up
with her recitation. Besides, this room with its stained-glass
windows picturing nobody special and its pulpit on which any
stranger's Scripture could be laid and then read out in a crazy
language made Dandy shift and stare into each corner.

In a dead-serious whisper he told Tacey, "I don't think Jesus
is *in* here."

"He's everywhere, hush up and pray like I said."

He guessed she was doing by rote the psalm and straight
into Our Father, but his mind could not grab hold of either.
Imitating Tacey, though, he bent forward to press his forehead
onto the cold edge of the bench in front of them. Touch is
important, he thought. Those old Jews wearing their phylac-
teries—good stuff. The polished wood pressed his skull like . . .
like a halo? Like a crown of thorns? Like Cain's mark.

Tacey was nudging. Evidently they were supposed to recite the prayer together.

When it was over (he could never predict the choice between "debts" and "trespasses") she did not rise, so he could not. He squinted between folded hands at the rug. Oriental. Somebody rich had once been scared to death in this hospital, then lived long enough to make an offering of this Persian rug in deep blues and scarlets. The intricate design reminded him of veins and arteries.

"Bless Mary," he whispered, reminded suddenly of nothing but failures. The year they gave her the wrong thing for Christmas and suffered through her polite thanks. The time he had fallen asleep when she was staying overnight, and she ate baby aspirin and slept too deep and long before they knew. The earache into which he had blown tobacco smoke when she needed penicillin. He had quit smoking then.

From the corner of his mouth he whispered to Tacey, "They've built this chapel all wrong."

He heard her breath escape as if from a punctured tire but kept talking anyway. "Less is not more." He peered through his fingers to examine the churchy but anonymous room where "All Faith" meant first no faith in particular and then no faith at all. Alongside, Tacey was clearing the lowest level of her throat. "You need to put everything into a room like this. The Virgin Mary. And the Star of David and a crucifix or two and an Indian thunderbird and—who's the ugly female? Kali? The place ought to be jam-packed with statues and candles." She was squirming. He lifted his head. "Ain't it silly to keep this room so bare when even the doctors wear that snake and staff? Isn't that from Moses?"

"I'm warning you, Andrew!"

So he was forced by her stiff body and silence to leave these general complaints, to go specifically back to Mary Grace Thompson, all hundred pounds of her, all he would be leaving behind when he died, now lying upstairs in a state some baby intern had called preconvulsive, and—

And listen.

Here.

Jesus? he finally prayed.

Listen, it was bad enough when I saw she'd grow up and marry some asshole and have babies who never knew about me and they'd all forget all of it, and the ants would dig anthills on my grave that nobody visited—that was a Valley of Death, all right; but listen?

Not to have anybody left able to do the forgetting? Even to send her into the ground before me?

Oh, that's a torture! That's cruel and inhuman punishment, he accused.

That's mean as hell!

Near him Tacey whispered, "I'm so glad you were able to pray. Don't you feel better now?"

He could not get up, not then, not with his eyes so hot and his silent throat so red with rage.

IN HIS BED, Jill Peters had tucked Frank's head between her face and shoulder and rocked him there as if he were no lover but a large hurt child.

Her left arm was numb from his weight. He had forgotten to turn on the apartment air-conditioning, so she felt clammy where her sweat was stuck to his. Over his damp hair she could dimly see a clock—5:00 a.m.—and the bedside telephone. She willed it not to ring; if it did, she demanded that the call not be from Mary's doctor; if it were he, she ordered the news to be good.

When they had been sent home at 2:00 a.m., Mary was responding to medicines they hoped would reduce the toxins in her bloodstream. They saw Frank's parents drive away, then without a word Jill got into his car, leaving hers somewhere forgotten in the six-story parking deck. Though both remained silent in the car, he never thought to take her anyplace but here.

They had passed through his apartment without touching a light switch, she hanging on to his shirt or belt while he led them down a dark upper hall and at last into this room. When the light came on, Frank seemed to notice the room and her for the first time.

He said softly "The sheets!" in a tone that implied sheets were a wonderment.

"It doesn't matter." She saw Christine's ruffled curtains and spread; otherwise the room was so austere it almost appeared unused, except that the bed had not been made. The framed mirror had a second frame of curling snapshots of Mary. Below them a hairbrush and comb were exactly parallel to the edge of a white dresser scarf. His slippers barely showed under the bed. There were two stiff upholstered chairs nobody ever sat on or dropped the day's soiled clothing across.

Jill began taking off her clothes. Without glancing up, Frank called the hospital and again sent his phone number to the nurse's station near Mary's room. "For insurance," he said vaguely. "Things get lost." Jill could hear the empty humming on the wire, though he kept sitting there holding the receiver.

"Let's go to bed, Frank."

He hung up the phone. He untied a shoe.

"It's late." She was down to her slip, wondering whether to go on or not. "She's improving now."

He came and held her. With her face tight against his, Jill could feel that terrible pressure clamped on him from ear to chest; she'd never understood why people belittled it as a "lump in the throat." More like a rigid ache, it bore down heavily on chest and neck and over the jawline into the temple. As a weepy teenager, she'd thought such solidifying came from swallowed tears that were running down unseen paths inside the head and hardening; she could picture salty stalactites growing down from the cheekbone, getting sharp in the tube of her throat.

She suggested to Frank in a whisper, "If it were me, I'd cry."

"I never could."

That's why she had come. Still in his taut embrace she felt blindly to undo his shirt buttons.

He let her, though his arms tightened. She got the front shirttail pulled awkwardly above his belt. His tense jaw barely moved when he said into her ear, "Tonight I'm not sure? It might not work tonight."

"Nothing has to work. Maybe you can sleep."

He backed away to finish taking off the shirt. His eyes were still too full of Mary having a slight convulsion to take in Jill at all.

She watched him hang up clothes, drop underwear into a closet hamper—the whole comfort of ritual. As his clothes came off, she saw that he weighed less than she had expected, though his muscles were full and tight. Hair fanned on his chest, then grew down in a dark narrow line. Beyond it was a round scar on one side.

When he climbed into bed, she turned off the light before stripping.

"Why did you do that?"

"I'm shy. Where did you get the scar?"

"It's a bullethole. I stopped two guys for a traffic violation but they were in a stolen car. It's old—I guess Mary was five or six."

She supposed all parents told time by their children, but she rubbed her own forehead to avoid thinking of that. Naked in the dark, listening to his monotone, she decided it was a bad idea to sleep with Frank, done for all the wrong reasons. Her armpits were smelly, breath sour; she was tired. Besides, there were pimples on her rear, with streaks of calamine lotion on top. She did not even know Frank Thompson very well nor, at the moment, desire him very much. She felt uneasy, even irritable. At least she was on the Pill.

She got into bed feeling like some ultramodern nurse engaged in mercyfucking on schedule.

She almost smacked her head deep into the pillow. It and the mattress were too soft, she saw right away. That he did not immediately touch her was a relief. She listened to him breathe. Then to herself. She was gradually relaxing when his light fingers, like a blind man's, examined her face. Then her throat, softly under one breast where the heartbeat was, plucking this nipple, then the other. As his easy touch played on her body, her increasing symptoms were familiar enough, though she had not felt them for some time, not since Sonny Howard had touched her there and, yes, there. Less patiently, though. Sonny had been more like a foreplay expert giving samples.

She stretched out longer, as if because of his moving hand her expanding body required more room. This was no time to remember Sonny Howard.

In her flesh a sweet yearning made her roll against Frank and trap his hand where she needed it, eager to touch him, too. He was not ready. She kissed away some kind of apology he tried to whisper, then sent her own hands to coax him. Every skill, even this one, comes right back, she thought. Finally he fell upon her with a groan and amazed her by lasting so long that a second time she forgot how to think, but lost herself in their faster and harder moving.

When it ended she was altogether red and swollen and out of breath. So limp did Frank's body feel that she knew even those hard, unwept deposits clogging his throat and chest had been shaken loose so he could sleep a little. He did; they both slept. She had meant to get up and wash, but the next thing she knew he was making an incoherent growl of speech and it was nearly 5:00 a.m. Frank lay on his back, dreaming, his neck strung with cords and blood vessels, saying some angry thing.

Jill rolled him into her arms for comfort. He still mumbled now and then as she rocked him.

At six, she eased her stinging arm free and got out of bed to rub back its circulation. Instantly Frank fell onto his back, muttering to or about Christ, probably swearing; then he snored lightly.

For a robe she put on the shirt he had hung up so carefully and tiptoed to the kitchen phone. The hospital said Mary Grace Thompson was still asleep and stabilized. After some switchboard work she learned that the doctors would see Mary at nine, that Dr. Weaver—the Arab's owner—usually made his rounds at the same time.

She stepped onto the screened back porch, curious to see the next one where Frank had caught the burglar. Lila Torrido, sitting on her back steps drinking coffee, called, "Is Mary sick again?"

"Took her to the hospital last night." Miss Torrido made noises of distress. In Frank's shirt, Jill was glad the screens did not show her below the waist.

"I'm so sorry, and poor Frank, poor Frank. It's Jillian Peters, isn't it? The one who doesn't spell it with a *G*? I've left my glasses inside."

"That's right." Jill wanted to stretch but thought such a move would make her appear brazen. "It's already a hot day."

"You can't really tell with the sun hitting all these buildings and parking lots and those air conditioners blowing out so much humidity. Maybe it's very pleasant five miles away."

"Maybe."

"How much worse is Mary?"

"She had a restful night, that's all I know."

"Is the next thing to put her on one of those machines?"

"I don't know. That's an option, certainly."

"What will he do then? It's not as if that hateful wife of his is ever going to tend the sick. That woman *is* the sick."

Jill glanced toward the closed upper windows, wondering if Frank could hear.

"I didn't know her."

"They were living here when I moved in." Miss Torrido tipped her cup toward the round webbed clotheslines on their metal stands. "I'd come out here to hang clothes on my rack —she'd have aluminum foil pinned to hers and a lounge chair drawn up so she could quick-tan while she played the radio."

Jill stepped closer to the screen. "Lots of women aren't good at housework; I'm not myself." She waited. "I'm a bad cook besides."

"No," said Miss Torrido, "you just spend your cleaning time and cooking time on other kinds of work. Christine spent all hers on herself. You run a horse business?"

Feeling generous now that her whole body smelled of Christine's husband, Jillian said, "She can't have been too bad? Mary's turning out very well."

"Thanks to her father. Are you Catholic?"

"Yes," Jill said, surprised. "Why?"

"So am I, but I haven't gone to mass in a long time. They've got a church here, St. Thomas More, and a school and a Newman Center, so we don't have that excuse."

"I meant what made you think I was Catholic?"

"I meant it takes one to know one. I worry about Frank Thompson with no religion to hold him up."

Jill thought she must be growing warmer and more awkward. "I'm not a practicing Catholic. And it didn't hold me up when I needed it."

"Of course it did—you're still here, aren't you?" (Jill hated that—giving God credit for everything you'd done yourself the hard way.) "And probably you were just trading off the baptism alone, not even praying for special help when you needed it." Miss Torrido wavered to her feet. "I can get you a cup of coffee if we're going to talk religion."

"We're not, but thank you," murmured Jillian. "I have to

fix Frank's breakfast anyway." She decided to stretch and give a postcoital yawn after all, defying Miss Torrido to fling up the Sixth or Ninth Commandment so early in the morning.

"I've got extra coffee cake—you can warm it in the oven." Before she could be stopped, Lila Torrido had hurried indoors. She carried back a foil-wrapped package. "Need anything else, let me know. I don't know what the grocery situation is like over there."

"Thank you." Blushing, Jill had to come down the back stairs wearing nothing but Frank's flapping shirt. She took very tiny steps, but Miss Torrido didn't even blink. She said as she handed over the coffee cake, "I do like Frank."

In the kitchen, Jill opened too many cabinets and drawers trying to find what she needed, stopped to frown over Mary's food list stuck to the refrigerator. She gagged when the third egg she cracked contained a hardened embryo chick in a pink mucus, and lost her appetite for an omelette.

She had not cooked breakfast for a man since Sonny Howard. He had liked fried potatoes. Jill never cooked those anymore.

When noises began upstairs, she set the table, trying to overhear a whistle, a hummed melody. The sound of an electric razor made her feel forgotten. Scullery maid. She slammed a cabinet door, then two. He did not call out to her.

She had gathered ingredients to be folded inside and was ready to put on the omelette. "Frank!"

"On my way!"

She tipped up the pan to spread the sizzling butter and poured in four beaten eggs. Four was the magic number according to her mother; if you needed more, you made more four-egg ome-lettes. She could hear Frank on the stairs at last, at the door, but she was lifting with the spatula to rearrange the uncooked part until it grew creamy.

He said softly, "Good morning."

Her angry voice surprised them both. "You just took it for granted I'd still be here!"

"I didn't think you'd slip off in the night, no, did you want to?"

"Just took it for granted, took me for granted."

"Besides, your clothes were in a chair, and my shirt was gone."

After what seemed an hour he was behind her, arms around her waist, face in her long, loose hair. She looked down at his hands. She was certain she could see the pale flesh where his wedding ring had been.

"Careful! I'll burn it! I've got to add the cheese and chopped bacon now—move back!" A nervous cook, she shook loose. In her hands whatever could stick or boil over or catch fire would do so, but this egg mixture was easing up nicely on her spatula, was folding over, sliding neatly onto the plate she had preheated for Frank. She breathed, "By God, look at that!" She set it before him on the blue place mat. "Eat it this instant."

He kissed her, but Jill was serious about the omelette and pushed him into a chair. These were omens: having the food do well while the coffee stopped perking at just the right time.

"Is it good? Is it still runny in the middle?"

Frank said her omelette was wonderful. She poured two cups of coffee, the right color, neither weak nor strong. He asked, "Aren't you eating half of this?"

"I hate breakfast." She sat in another chair near him, then —very slowly—put her hand through the air to touch his intricate ear, his face cool from shaving.

He cocked his head to trap her fingers in place, saying, "I'm full of things to tell you, Jill, I just don't know which one to choose. I'm trying to imagine how I'd ever have faced this day if you weren't here. Pretty selfish. Then I start to tell you how good you look and how good you feel, and they say that all the time on TV far better than I can. And there's last night to talk about. Tomorrow night."

"Eat." She took back her hand and looked at it as if the molecules had been rearranged. The happiness rose in her and vanished just as quickly. "And there's everything we don't know about each other to talk about. There's the picture in my wallet to talk about. How about Christine?"

"Not now." He was eating—she saw with surprise—the whole damn omelette.

"I can't even cook, Frank, this is dumb luck." She suddenly cried out, "Oh!" at a faint, sweet smell and flung open the oven door to rescue Miss Torrido's cinnamon coffee cake just before the raisins dried out.

Then she sat watching Frank eat, trying to decide what she saw in him. He finished the omelette and toast. Sonny had been younger, bigger, handsomer. A dancing fool—she thought Frank was probably too self-conscious to dance well. He cut a slice of the sweet cake. Sonny had been the hit of every party, could remember jokes, movies, could imitate their friends, made other women envious. He would have been doing a Jimmy Cagney–with–the–grapefruit routine at this point in the breakfast, not chewing solemnly like Frank. He cut another slice, and she refilled his coffee. Sonny read the newspapers looking for unusual places to go; other than that he read nothing. Sonny had even been charming when drunk. He could drive a car with one finger. Sonny had played the harmonica, during his spring break had persuaded her to get a butterfly tattooed on one shoulder. Sonny had made her mother giggle.

Had left Jill to go through pregnancy by herself.

She leaped up to empty her coffee down the sink. "I called the hospital—Mary's stable this morning."

"I didn't know that." He gave her a grateful smile. "So I called from upstairs too."

In spite of herself she felt slightly jealous that he had thought of Mary before her. She ran water to wash down the last grounds. "I need a shower."

"Wait awhile—it's a small water heater, and I probably used it all. And look straight at me, not out of the corners of your eyes. What's wrong?"

"I told you; I'm shy. It's daylight, so now I'm shy again."

He tried to touch her, but she kept busy scraping the skillet. "Jill, you're not going to be sorry, I promise. Unless—unless you only stayed because you felt sorry for me?"

"Partly," she said.

His face changed and changed back. "Well, partly I let you do that. I wish this had happened some other time, some better time. Hell, I even wish it was the first time for us both—you know? In a way? But in another way, I was stupider then."

More bitterly than she had intended, Jill said, "Makes two of us." He sounded too serious. He sounded as if she might skip vet school and sew curtains instead.

"I promise not to hurt you."

"People can't keep that promise. Finish eating so you can see Mary. The doctors come by at nine, including the owner of that horse—Dr. Weaver? If that's still a possibility."

"God, yes—if Mary wants a horse, she'll have a horse." She saw by his blank eyes that he was seeing Mary's face and not her own, the way sometimes she held on to a foal's front hooves and eased it free of the mare's birth canal, but somehow looked at a baby boy instead. For all Jill knew, her baby son was dead by now—in a wreck in Noplace City, from meningitis, beaten by some child abuser posing as his adoptive father, fallen from a high window. Dead of Nothing. Anywhere. They ought to have, in Arlington, beside the soldiers, the Tomb of the Unknown Baby.

When Frank rose quickly to put his arms around her she knew he had seen the glaze of tears, had mistaken Mary's illness for their cause. She made them go away, inside, down the throat, hard, chalky, while he said, "You're wonderful, Jillian."

"I'm not," she whispered, holding on to him. "I'm not, Frank, I'm not."

The phone rang. As she washed dishes, sniffling, Jill gathered from Frank's answers that it was Cindy Scofield, that she had gotten the news from somebody named Elmo, that she wanted to help.

So where were you last night? Jill wondered, and moved a glass too strongly from the soapy water so its rim grazed the edge of the faucet and a long silver crack ran all the way to the base.

IN A FEW DAYS, Mary came home. Dialysis had almost proved necessary, but then an enema, which first attracted and retained, then expelled potassium, also lowered the levels of all the electrolytes in her blood samples. The renogram scanning was better than expected. It was a respite.

In the car Mary said, "I look like an addict!" She said it with some satisfaction, rotating both arms outward to show off rows of blue punctures. "Next time they're going to leave a spigot stuck in and just taped to my arm."

"There won't be a—" Frank began, but let Tacey's face in the mirror silence him. She didn't believe in lying to children—so how had he grown up believing so much foolishness? He drove while watching Mary beside him, trying to gauge her strength, wondering if tomorrow would be better to reward her with the horse.

As if reading his mind she asked, "What did Dr. Weaver say?"

Immediately he gave a turn signal and swung the car toward Centaur Stable. "Said yes."

"You mean it? You're going to buy Chancy?"

"I've already bought Chancy."

She squealed. In the rearview mirror Frank saw his mother's troubled face change. She had held out for a dog, a cat, goldfish, or gerbils, even a ferret or mynah bird, instead of pairing a dangerous horse with a sick girl. But now that she saw and heard Mary's joy, she became its reflection, almost bouncing herself in the backseat.

"You and Dandy can ride him some," Mary offered. She got on her knees to face her grandmother in the backseat.

"Thank you, but no thank you."

On her knees, Mary kept leaning toward her grandmother, suddenly still. "That's right," she said, going solemn all over. "You've got arthritis. Dandy's blood pressure is high. I'm going to pay attention to those things from now on. In the hospital for the first time I realized?"

Tacey bent forward, kissed her chin. Frank was glad to be driving.

Although there had been telephone conversations, he had not seen Jillian Peters since their one night together. One day she had a horse to trailer to Alabama. Others, he was with Mary, or he had night duty to make up.

So he let his mother and Mary walk ahead through the barn toward Chancy's stall while he tried to find Jill. In the tack shop at closing time—no. In the riding ring too late in the day—no.

But in the second barn he found Jill mucking out the stall of a horse turned out for exercise in the cool of dusk, halfway between fly time and mosquito time. She did not at first notice him, busy lifting manure off wood shavings into a wheelbarrow with her wide, thin-tined rake. By their shape, he understood why people said "horse apples." At the sight of her, various alterations in his chest and stomach made him uneasy. There was Mary to love, with nothing left over. His breathing got shallow nonetheless. "Jill?"

The rake stopped moving, but she continued to look down its long handle. "I knew the horse would bring you."

"Not just the horse." When he put his hand on her back it was like touching a wall. He said uneasily, "How was Alabama?"

"Hot. How's Mary?"

"To look at her, you'd never guess. She's playing the proud horse owner for her grandmother."

Jill straightened, wiped sweat off her forehead. "I hung a plastic bag outside his stall—apple, carrot, sugar cubes? I guess she'll find it."

"Sure she will. When can I see you, Jill?"

"Not often, I expect." At last she faced him. Her eyes looked hollow. "Mary has first claim on your time, Frank, I understand that." With both eyes outlined in black pencil and puffy pale bruises underneath, she burned him with the gaze of some righteous angel.

Under its power he even took a step back before saying, "I need to see you."

"You don't need to build any more guilt than is normally there, Frank." She propped her rake against the wall, swiped both hands down dirty breeches. For an instant she looked old, disillusioned; then something flickered either inside her face or his optic nerve, and she was a beautiful girl again.

He said, "Please come here."

The feel of her plus her sweaty smell hardened his entire body. He could not stop his hands from roaming over her, dipping into the curves of waist and hip, at last finding the crotch that fitted so well to the palm of his hand. He pressed hard, then soft, then began slowly to stroke her there. He closed his eyes.

But she pulled back. "I don't know," she said vaguely.

"What's to know?"

She resisted his arms, finally unwound them and pressed them to his sides. "You know I'm taking some science courses at Carolina. This fall I go back to school full-time."

"Fine," he said. "Fine." She was wearing what Christine had always called a halter, a brassiere in flowered cloth, but he thought a horse trainer must call it something else.

"So I'll be gone a lot, and I still hope to run this place. I'm hiring some girls. I can still give lessons at night in the arena."

"You plan to be too busy—is that it?" He watched her wrap one end of her plait around her wrist like a blond chain.

"If I had a sick child," she said almost fiercely, "there wouldn't be much time or love or anything left over for anybody else."

"That remains to be seen."

"Though men are different about children than women are —I do know that much!"

"Now wait a minute, Jill." As she tugged up a shoulder strap he suddenly spotted the color printed in her skin. "What's that?"

She let the strap sag down her arm. "It's a butterfly."

"I didn't know you had a tattoo." He stopped short of touching the small black-and-yellow wing.

"Oh, yes, I'm marked all right. And it was dark; you didn't notice."

He said to himself, "Elmo's got a cross," then louder, "I don't know that I've ever seen a white woman with a tattoo."

"If you're thinking a man had something to do with it, then you're right."

"The man in your wallet."

"Sonny Howard."

She was waiting for him to ask something more. Frank took a step back.

After a silence Jill carried the rake out of the stall and hung it on a peg. "I wasn't saying that I wouldn't see you, just that this is no time for serious commitment on either side, yours or mine." He said nothing. Abruptly she shouted, "Mary Grace Thompson!" Someone answered from a distance. Down the barn aisle Jill's voice seemed a bellow. "You think you can post on the right diagonal on your own horse?"

He watched her move off while they kept calling back and forth—Mary with faint giggles, Jillian's answers going farther and farther away. He rolled the loaded wheelbarrow out of the stall.

She moved into sunlight at the sliding door and crossed its brightness to the entry to the other barn. The shine of her hair sent a dull throb through his groin, inside each thigh, low in his tailbone. After the ache surged and subsided, he felt almost weak and moved slowly past the Appaloosa in the next stall, then a grade horse, next a mare with a baby colt. Here he stopped to hang over the half door, watching the chestnut give suck with a hind leg cocked while the flimsy foal—one bony body misaligned on four long stilts—tottered to her udder, lost it, crashed into her belly again. The mare watched Frank with the wet flat eyes of a stoic who hoped to leave it at stoicism, who didn't much feel like kicking a human intruder if that should be required. Something about the way she waited, available but not generous, while her foal lurched in and out of feeding range, made Frank want to watch as long as necessary until the new life would triumph and feed with complete self-ishness from a nipple that even at this distance looked cracked and sore. He started to summon Mary to watch this colt stum-ble, recover, step on its own foot before skittering backward on tangled legs, already sucking the mare's hock and smelly flank. Frank wanted Mary to see Nature's Way and realize through indirection that even the old marrow of every Thompson bone would be hers on demand: she could have kidneys, hearts, anything.

And Jill might be right. Whatever he felt for Jill was nothing that strong or passionate.

He heard Tacey calling, "Where are you, Frank?"

In cadence he marched toward the musical voices inside the other barn.

The three women—no, two women and a girl—were clus-tered ahead of him down the aisle with Chancy out of his stall on halter. They were petting him, feeding him sugar, lifting his feet, combing his mane with spread fingers. Frank had not expected to find all three united in such a female tableau: his mother who had groaned him forth no easier than a mare on bloody straw; the young woman in whom his semen had so recently burst like fireworks and died; and the girl with half her chromosomes matching his, though Mary was like nobody at all but herself.

Facing him, she looked a little pale, or perhaps her freckles were darker on both cheeks. "Jill will not let me stay in his stall tonight, not even in a sleeping bag in the loft with the hay bales."

He said with a grin, "She's cruel," and wanted to catch Jill's eye, but she disappeared behind the Arab.

"I must say you've made a good buy," Tacey remarked, coming around the tail end with her hand trailing over the horse's muscled rump. "I used to go sidesaddle, you know, as a girl. Not that the Grovers owned horses, but our neighbors did. I even jumped sidesaddle." Her fingers ran up the ridge of Chancy's spine. "He has good conformation, Frank."

He couldn't find Jill but in the pause said, "What?" In all the years, he'd never known his mother rode. "You women are full of secrets," he said, stepping nearer to the horse.

"It's really safer than jumping astride, since there's a special grip you lock your legs into and—well, it's complicated to explain, but my knees remember perfectly." Despite her weight, Tacey made some kind of half squat and bounced lightly on air. Then she moved briskly to measure her height against Chancy's withers.

"Watch this," Mary said, and showed him how to pick out packed dirt from a front hoof. He could see Jill's boots by looking under the horse's belly.

When he reached for an ear, Chancy shook free. Frank was thinking how if women-strangers had five minutes together they would become either enemies or bosom friends. They would come out of an impromptu bridge game knowing how much the car had cost, who slept with whom, and whose uterus was ailing.

The boots moved, and then beyond Chancy he saw Jillian seat herself on a hay bale. He smiled at her. Was that a nod or a headshake? He remembered barely introducing his mother to Christine Broome before Tacey had somehow learned that the girl had monthly cramps for which she wrapped up her electric iron, set on low, in a towel on her belly. "She'll have hard labors," Tacey warned him later, "and they'll all be in her head."

And while showing Christine where the bathroom was, she had learned that Georgia Broome occasionally stayed out overnight without explanation, but that the one night Virgil had tried it, Georgia had lain in wait in their automobile and tried to run him in the yard.

Leaving Christine in the bathroom, she had brought this last news forth to tell Dandy Thompson, adding with a thump to his skull, "You'd have liked a wife like that, I suppose." Then she gave Frank a hard look, conveying her certainty that he should never marry Christine. But he did anyway.

He wondered what Tacey had learned today about Jill. Circling the horse, he came to stand over her, to pluck out a stalk of hay and run it between his front teeth.

Jill asked him when the doctors said Mary could ride again.

"She can begin now if she goes slow. Carefully."

Jill knew he was making a suggestion about the two of them, also. "Mary?" she called. "I'm through class tomorrow at twelve if you want to come out in the afternoon." She was flung half off the hay bale by Mary's excited hug, the extended hoof pick in danger of putting out an eye. "Good then. All right, all right."

"And we want you to come to a big picnic Sunday, July first, so don't make any other plans, OK, Miss Peters? We all want you to come!"

"Yes, we do," Frank said, though he was thinking that he might call Cindy tonight. It had been a while.

"Sure, I'll come." Her level look came from made-up eyes as ringed as a raccoon's, the lids painted the color of U.N.C.'s Carolina-blue uniforms. There was something childlike about so much makeup, as if she were primed for Halloween or pretending onstage to be older than she was. She said directly to him, "It's long-term commitments that are hard to make right now."

"Short-term is fine," he answered, but he still thought he'd give Cindy a call.

NOW MARY WAS UP early every morning to be driven to the stables. She was faithful to her diet only so she would stay well enough to ride Chancy. Some days she insisted on staying in the saddle so long that her aches might have originated either in muscles or organs; no way to tell; she had become one long fiber of aching. After supper and a hot bath she was ready to sleep without dreams. In the fall, she planned to ride him in the Raleigh horse show.

She knew that at home her endless horse talk was boring, yet wouldn't stop long enough for her father to ask about symptoms. Sometimes for him she summarized the day's workout with Chancy twice. Her riding class had trailered their horses to Duke Forest for a long slow ride along woodland paths; she told Frank in tedious detail how she had learned to lean going uphill and down, to cross water, how to pull him in if a lizard should suddenly rattle dry leaves nearby.

Her closed piano was gathering dust while she memorized saddle parts and bits (out loud). At the walk she did mounted exercises, then brought them home for demonstration during meals while straddling a kitchen stool. She learned how to lunge Chancy when he needed to settle down, and how to explain the process to Frank, standing and turning slowly in the center of the living room carpet. Daily she groomed and bathed him; nightly she discussed it; she babied his slightest nick or sore. Late every afternoon she brought home the blended smell of his sweat and hers in her clothes.

Mary almost hated to wash away these odors for fear something medicinal might leak out of her instead.

Often Frank stopped by the stables to watch her ride. Mary admired him for being so pleasant to Miss Jillian Peters on her behalf. He even went riding through the pastures with Miss Peters once, on an aged quarterhorse almost as placid as Ralph. Another time he took them both to dinner at Hotel Europa, at prices he couldn't possibly afford, and treated Miss Peters almost as politely as that Cindy Scofield from the *Chapel Hill Newspaper*.

For days after her spring piano recital, Mary and her girl-friends in bike relays had pedaled here and there to spy on Miss Sinful Scofield, had watched her buy produce at Kroger's, gather the news at city hall, even stop in the late afternoon at Crook's Barbecue to order a beer by herself.

"Hoping to be picked up," said Kay Linda darkly.

Mary wasn't so sure—she planned to drink beer (and worse) alone in Las Vegas, then she'd lure the cowboys out of the bar beyond beaded curtains and into her gambling den (and worse).

But after her most recent stay in the hospital, Mary thought less about fancy houses in towns where tumbleweeds came rolling down the street; she had decided to become an Olympic equestrienne, amazing the television announcers by her courage despite a chronic illness; after winning the gold medal, she would then do cancer research—cancer because she didn't have it. Already she knew it was impossible to be cool and scientific about pains that were your own.

Not only had her fantasies changed, but she spent less time with Kay Linda also, now that Kay Linda had already bled for three days in early May and not a drop since; now that she claimed to have breasts, though they were really only enlarging nipples. From Mary's body the news was less exciting. She now carried in her purse a notebook and small measuring cup so there could be a daily record of how much she drank and how much she peed, and there were regular pills to take and times she had to poke her ankles to check for swelling, and once a week she went to Dr. Seagroves's office for a blood test.

Mary treated these medical activities as if they were some

complex form of toileting—regular, necessary, but unnatural to contemplate. She thus assigned to Dr. Seagroves and the urologists the same managerial role she took herself with her horse—watchful in case Chancy's manure contained undigested grain, grew hard, grew soft, turned black. Chancy himself produced it carelessly and walked away.

Besides long hours at Centaur Stable, Mary and Tacey were planning the picnic the weekend before Independence Day. They studied road maps and drew their own after using the odometer to plot exact mileage to the Thompson homeplace. Addressing the invitations with maps enclosed proved to be an education in family history.

"Dorman Gilley?"

Almost defensively Tacey said, "Well? His parents were named Dorothy and Norman—they thought Dorman was cute. They were very young then. Dead now. Dorothy drove them broadside into a fast train. I think Dorman runs a Dairy Queen and never did marry." She saw a question on Mary's face. "Dorothy was deaf, you see, and it must have been a very quiet train."

This came early in the invitations when Dandy was still allowed to help and to comment. "Dairy Queen, my foot. Dorman never held any one job longer than sixty days. By the time any woman decided to accept his proposal, he'd be working in another state. Dorman's idea of home is a suit of clothes with a roof on it."

"We may be doing my family now," said Tacey in a threatening voice as she slapped down envelopes in front of him, "but soon we'll get to do yours." She whispered to Mary, "Wait till we hit Hurley Thompson. His blood nephew."

"At least Hurley won't come to the picnic, but if his mail's being forwarded, Dorman will." Dandy made his fist a hammer to bang down every stamp.

The blows made Mary's handwriting waver. "Stop shaking the table, Dandy!"

"Hurley lived up in Cherokee County. Tell her what Hurley does."

"He's a gardener."

"The very western tip of the state. Tell Mary what kind of a gardener he is."

"Works for this mountain park some church has started."

"They have built," announced Tacey, "a copy of Joseph's tomb and planted trees from the Old Testament, and last I heard they were carving the Ten Commandments on a mountain in letters as tall as Mary is—did they finish all ten?"

Dandy muttered something.

"Hurley will show up now and then in the *Charlotte Observer* claiming that Abraham Lincoln's real father is buried in Murphy. There's always a picture of him pointing his hedge shears at the grave."

Dandy began waving an envelope. "You're asking fat old Maude? Now there's one for you, Mary—fat old Maude would have been counting calories at the Last Supper, and she'll still be eating at the Last Trump. She's what, Tacey, a dietitian?"

"You know perfectly well she works in a lawyer's office in Winston-Salem. And it's not her fault she's fat. It's her glands."

"Yeah, her glands weigh two hundred pounds." He sealed and stamped the envelope. "Seriously, now, your cousin Maude suffers from Dunlap's disease."

"What's that?"

He gave Mary's shoulder a shove. "Her stomach done laps over her belt!" He went off in a frenzy of snickers and giggles while Tacey said she would just as soon lick the stamps herself.

Eventually the notices were mailed on time, despite his comments: on old Whit Wakely (whose face looked as if it had worn out three or four bodies) and Uncle Elbert (rare intelligence—very rare) and Mary's favorite—that Ruth Carrington's mouth was so big she could eat a banana sideways or sing duets by herself.

For revenge Tacey made him drive by himself to the post office and back during the busiest time of day.

When he was gone, she said to Mary, apologizing, "You have to understand why your grandfather will make a joke about anything—back in grade school, he was *short*."

Soon they were getting return calls and letters from distant kin who would be making motel reservations or staying with friends; a few asked about pitching tents Saturday night in the old meadow if it would be freshly mowed.

Mary kept the master list and checked off those who were coming, those who could not. She refused to ask anyone whether or not her mother planned to come. Asking would bring bad luck. So might lying or overspending her allowance.

On June 28, while she was cleaning Chancy's stall for the second time, a student rider called Mary to the phone that hung between racks of saddles in the tack room. She climbed on the crate to talk.

"Mary? It's your grandmother—I'm sorry to interrupt your ride."

Why was she saying "grandmother" in such a loud emphatic voice? "It's OK, I'm through."

"Georgia and Virgil Broome are here."

"Here? At your house?"

"They've brought a list of who's coming from their side, and would like to see you before going back to Durham."

"One minute." She called to the people in whose car pool she rode. Yes, they'd drop her off at the Thompsons. "Grandma? I'll be about thirty minutes."

"The sooner the better, dear."

The Thompsons owned a small bungalow in Chapel Hill with a rented garage apartment in the back, and a carpet of zoysia grass that was so heavily fertilized it thrived even under thick maple shade. As Mary closed the car door, she saw Tacey and the Broomes in three metal chairs, widely separated, on the front lawn—drinking iced tea, not even pretending to talk. Of all things, Grandmother Georgia Broome was wearing green shorts.

"Why there you are!" Tacey rushed forward to embrace her more tenderly than felt normal. The other two set their tea on a glass-topped table.

Despite his long face, Virgil Broome had dark, rather sinister good looks suitable to an assistant villain in the movies. He dyed his black hair; in fact, on scheduled Saturday nights he and Grandma Broome dyed each other's. Once when Mary was small they had dyed hers halfway black for a lark. For weeks she seemed to have a splotchy polecat wrapped round her head.

She hugged each of them. "Thank you for sending the perfume and the manicure set."

Virgil said, "Now when you going to ride that horse over to Durham and show him off?"

"We'd never live through the traffic, Virgil." She always called him Virgil, her mother's stepfather, nobody's blood kin. "But here—I've got pictures." Her purse was cluttered with Kleenex, pencils, her medicines, the measuring cup; but at last she found the envelope with the color photographs.

"This is your hotshot riding teacher?" Georgia studied the snapshot at arm's length. "I thought she'd look butch."

Grandmother Thompson became slightly strangled on her tea.

"She's coming to the picnic."

"Oh, is she?" Very delicately Georgia passed the picture to Virgil, who whistled. "That's really why we waited, Mary, to tell you your *mother's* coming. Some friend is flying her up in his Cessna."

"That's wonderful," Mary said. Of course. Wonderful. Why was she getting a stomachache?

"She's coming June thirtieth, this Saturday, so we'll pick her up at Raleigh-Durham airport. Wouldn't you like to meet her with us? Maybe stay in Durham overnight?"

Rapidly Grandmother Thompson said, "Of course there's so much to do getting ready for this many people."

"Been a long time since you've seen Christine," Virgil offered as he handed Mary the picture. "She'll be surprised how you've growed up."

It turned out not to be an ache in Mary's stomach after all, but something hard and cold, like a great ball of snow that had been rolled and rolled, packed hard and harder for a long time. "Why couldn't Mother fly up in this airplane when I was in the hospital?"

"It ain't *her* airplane," Virgil explained.

But Grandma Broome reached for Mary's hand. "She didn't think it was serious, honey. Even Tacey here didn't think so at first."

"OK." Mary put the pictures of her horse and of Jillian Peters inside her pocketbook. "I'll just see her at the picnic, since I'll be helping get things ready."

Georgia had risen even as Mary spoke. "Thank you for the tea."

"You're going to read my palm at the picnic, aren't you, Grandma Broome?"

She seemed flustered. "I don't, it seems—I might be losing my power; well, it comes and goes." Her face grew redder, and something was twisting her mouth. "You can't tell anything from young hands that aren't finished, anyway. When you're twenty, twenty-one, I'll read you everything, Mary, and it'll all be good." She snatched Mary's head suddenly against her large breasts, which were crammed inside some heavy undergarment in a size large enough to boggle Kay Linda's mind. "I'll be a better palm reader by then, too; I'll have more practice. See?"

It was hard to breathe anything but loose talcum. "All right," said Mary. "I just wondered." Though she took one step backward, she could not free her head.

"I know Christine just can't wait to see you."

The noises in Grandma Broome's chest, a cycle of swallows and gulps, became magnified in Mary's ear. When released at last, off balance, she lurched into the edge of the table. Tea and ice cubes went everywhere.

Delighted that some physical action was at last required, Tacey mopped the glass top with her apron while the others retrieved tumblers from the grass and shook liquid off the list of Broome relatives coming to the picnic. The moment rescued them from any more farewells; almost before they knew it, Virgil and Georgia Broome were in their old finned Buick, a long white gas guzzler with three strange airholes above spreading scabs of rust. Mary stood by the driveway calling, "Tell Mother I'll see her at the picnic!"

Georgia put her pinkish hairdo out the window and remarked as the car began to back, "You ought to write Christine letters."

In sudden fury Mary screeched, *"I always have!"*

The Buick backed into the street; hands fluttered above its roof; it drove away with extra clanking. Mary, ready to cry, waved with large furious slaps against air.

Behind her, Tacey Thompson murmured, "I never should have called you at all."

"Oh, phooey," Mary said, not willing to turn until her face and eyes were under control. Oh, shit, she thought.

"At least we can now estimate paper plates and cups. And Georgia did write down what food everybody plans to bring." Tacey made a gargling sound. "Can you imagine the nerve of Milton Broome to be bringing meat loaf? A taxidermist? This is Georgia's idea of a joke, I suppose."

Able to face her now, Mary was surprised by her own sullen tone. "I don't see why you wouldn't let me spend the night over there."

"What? Oh, Mary. That's not fair."

"I don't ever want anybody to say 'fair' to me ever again." She threw herself into a lawn chair and grabbed a damp page covered with large and awkward handwriting. "Where's Dandy?"

"You know perfectly well the minute that car drove up he marched straight out the back door. He's probably in the garage."

"I never heard of most of these people," said Mary, reading. "Here's somebody coming from Washington."

"Must be Little Washington. D.C. or N.C.?"

"Oh. But here's another one coming all the way from Pittsburgh."

"That has to be Clinton Broome, the one your grandfather calls the big iron-and-steel man—his wife irons and he steals."

Mary couldn't help laughing.

FRANK HAD NOT SEEN Christine since the day she left home.

Early that morning, actually. Even now he was outraged to remember that normal, ordinary weekday morning—Mary's cornflakes left floating in the milk, the newspaper, their talk of a movie they might see that weekend, her smile—when all the time Christine had known these were the final cornflakes, and they had seen the week before the last film they would ever see together.

During several weeks of anger at that memory, Frank came to appreciate the phrase: insult added to injury.

As well as several others. Beauty is only skin deep. Pretty is as pretty does.

If he lived long enough, Frank thought, he might find that everything his English teacher had labeled a cliché proved out to be a nasty, universal truth.

The good die young.

He came downstairs Sunday morning, July 1, thinking that the empty kitchen still looked much the way Christine had left it three years ago, the dishes she had chosen still stacked in the cabinets in the places she had assigned. Whatever happened, he dreaded to see her today at the picnic, in the crowd. Looking beautiful, she would be alone or with the latest man, might smile or freeze him with a glare; he would have his anger made fresh again or, worse, his desire.

"Mary?"

He found her note addressed to General Franco under a magnet stuck to the refrigerator door. Gone on her bike to Grandma Thompson's early, and from there to the country. He was to bring ice—a big block plus bags of cubes—and also charcoal and be out there no later than 10:00 a.m.

Frank carried his coffee to the phone and dialed his mother's number. Before he had more than said hello, Tacey cried, "How can you bother us now, Frank, when there's so much to do! We're loading the car!"

"I want to be sure Mary's all right! She seemed very tired and irritable at bedtime. I didn't mean for her to go off on that bicycle this hot morning."

"Lately, Frank, you're always expecting the worst."

"Damn right."

"And don't swear. She seems fine—except you know she must be nervous about seeing her mother today."

"We're all nervous."

"Not Christine, I expect. Christine is sleeping late, I expect."

Let sleeping bitches lie, he thought.

First he picked up Jillian Peters, standing in front of her apartment house with a bag of chicken she had fried herself, though he'd explained how easy it would be to buy a Family Tub from a Chic Chick restaurant.

Jill was wearing black jeans and a black top. He wondered about the color symbolism.

"Is she here?" asked Jill as she settled her greasy paper package on the seat between them.

"Christine? I guess so. We're to bring ice."

"And Mary?"

"Mama says she's all right. She was barely ten years old when her mother just disappeared from her life like that. Last night she was so mean . . ." He drove a block without finishing. "I think her face looks puffy, too."

Jill rubbed one hand on the back of his neck. "Try to remember that any normal adolescent is an abnormal human being."

"I wonder. In Africa? In this country in 1700?"

"You sound depressed."

"I'm not. Oh, hell," he said.

Not only depressed, but confused. During the past two weeks he had been seeing Jill more than he'd expected; what he could never predict were her hot/cold moods. Some evenings, if he was off work and she was on campus for her chemistry lab, he had lately been going to Cindy's. If he got out of bed in the dark to go piss, he sometimes was uncertain which animal not to step on—tabby cat or Pomeranian.

Frank shot a glance across the car seat at Jill—happy today —and argued with himself that he needn't feel guilty. Both women had told him: no commitments. It was like alternating chiropractors whose offices were on different sides of town; both made him feel better in slightly different ways.

If some man ever thinks that way about Mary, I'll kill him, he thought.

"I hope you're not going to scowl like that all day," Jill said.

Not even when you and Cindy and Christine all get together, he decided, and shook his head as they parked under the signs ICE, COAL, BOTTLED GAS, ORGANIC MULCH, SAND, and GRAVEL. He was relieved that the place was open, probably because it was a holiday week full of July fourth celebrations.

He had to drive through alleys to a low, nondescript building cramped beside abandoned railroad tracks, selling also bag coal to the poor, plus septic tanks and cement steps, run by one old man with bulky shoulders and two black helpers soon to have hernias.

The man said knowingly, "Not many private sales ask for a

block this big. They get 'em to carve out at the big hotel. You got tow sacks?"

"Just a plastic garbage can and plastic bags."

The man hollered, "Tow sacks!" and one black man appeared rolling a dolly with the block of ice already wrapped in burlap, held with twine.

"Fifty cents extra. Hot day like this, it'll go fast," said the foreman wistfully while directing how the ice should be loaded into Frank's too-small trunk and the lid tied down. "I'd get it into a tub quick. In the shade. Tea?"

"Whatever," Frank said, counting out money.

"You got a ice pick, a course."

He paused. "At home I've got a pick."

"One dollar."

He bought the ice pick, which Jill put into her pocketbook. "Why did all that cheer you up?" she asked as they drove away.

"Just did. You look pretty."

"That's all you notice when I had my hair done and the braid"—she turned and displayed—"divided and wound up over both ears? The women in Flash Gordon had braids circled like this, my beautician said, but that was before my time and probably yours, too." She looked back when they crossed the railroad and the trunk lid banged against the ice. "It's not that I'm competing with Christine."

Or Chiropractor Number Three. "You don't need to. It doesn't apply."

"I wonder what she's like, though. You never say much about her." Jill waited, but he did not say anything then, either. "Maybe a white dress and a wide straw hat would have been better. Did she call you or anything?"

"Of course not."

"I'm sure Mary hoped she would."

They came to the shopping center where they filled insulated coolers with ice cubes. From its parking lot they could look across the busy highway up the mowed green hill where long white tables were stuck on the meadow like Band-Aids. Jill shaded her eyes. "Somebody's already up there."

"Mama and Mary, I guess. I wanted to rent a porta-toilet but Dandy planned to dig a trench himself."

"He could get sick in all this heat," she said, squinting under her hand.

"I see they cleaned out the old farmhouse."

"They must have sprayed it with weed killer. I see lots of brown vines and dead stuff."

Poison. The thought of it made him slam the second cooler in the backseat.

Getting into the car Jill noticed the box of bottles on the floor behind. "Is that liquor?"

"Bourbon. Wild Turkey."

"Exactly how much liquor is it?"

"More than my mother would allow if she knew about it."

As they drove fast down the highway, Jill giggled. "I can't get over how you Southern men fake things for your mothers."

Frank drove them down the highway until the Thompson homeplace was out of sight before turning back onto a gravel road that soon became ruts through hard clay. They passed one low field where someone had stuck up a cardboard sign that said PARKING, and crossed a log bridge over a rocky creek, turned uphill by a ruined molasses-cane mill, and began climbing through dense shade on a rutted wagon track. Its surface was so eroded that roots of giant white oaks had chopped the old road into a set of irregular stairsteps.

Flung about, Jill said, "Will we make it?"

The engine kept whining while the car's rear end slewed to one side on wet leaves. It had rained the night before, and sometimes a pack of brown vegetation hid patches of mud and water. She could tell by Frank's tense hands that they were being lifted up that hill as much by willpower as internal combustion.

Farther and farther they rose above the whoosh of traffic on the interstate, surely much higher than the Thompson house had stood on the hill. She wondered if Frank had taken a wrong turn, if this was only a logging road that ended with a small sawdust mountain atop the larger one. She rolled down the window; Frank told her which singing came from mockingbirds, katydids. Between sycamores and ragged pines that shaded out honeysuckle they slipped and slid. On her side, slabs of rock showed through the slope like broken bone.

Into sunlight they burst suddenly atop the hill. The rough road turned into two dim parallel lines through weeds. Frank turned off the engine, then stepped outside the car.

More slowly Jill got out on her side to face falling black barns, a slouched outbuilding, one weathered shed that had folded on itself into an obscure origami shape. For this part of piedmont North Carolina, the prospect was high. She looked down into treetops first, then saw that they had come out of the forest above the old Thompson farmhouse, whose roof she recognized by the dead vines that lay on its rusted tin like a rusted crown. Even farther downhill lay the weedy plains with their old neat furrows drawn in straight lines through the green mat, the even greener bottomland sloping into the curves of Happy Creek, with thick water the color of a sorrel horse.

There stood the picnic tables with tiny ant figures in motion nearby, and, in the valley beyond, the toy highway seemed glued in place with flat plastic vehicles sliding along it in slow motion.

Frank had walked to the small collapsing shed and rocked it with one hand. With a groan the nails slid back and forth in the wood.

"I wanted to live up here," he said, but he took his hand off the old shed and waved it behind him. "Before that shopping center."

"I wanted to live in the limestone part of Kentucky," she said, "and get racehorses ready for the Derby."

He shook the building once more, as if to chide it. Then he

moved onto a path past a flattened brood house for chickens and told her to walk behind him, out of the poison ivy whose three leaves he indicated. She tried to get in step with him but his stride was too long.

"Why did your parents sell it, then, and not save it for you?"

"They needed the money when Dandy retired."

His foot rose in an unexpected high step, so sudden that she stumbled into his back and onto the low stone wall he had crossed. Rocks like those in the outcroppings they had passed had been awkwardly piled knee-high in a square that enclosed rows of small headstones. She dropped back without stepping inside. She did not like coming upon the dead like this, abruptly, in the open air, with her fingers still smelling of fried chicken. Instead she longed for the scale of St. Paul's Cathedral at home, not these shrunken, sunken, country graves with unlikely markers and dragonflies drinking some invisible vapor off their names.

"I see Old Man Chaney kept his promise about the family graveyard," Frank said, "even if he does plan to park trailers in the bottomland."

"Is that more poison ivy?"

"Virginia creeper. Five leaves."

It was clinging to faded words: CARRIE BRADFORD THOMPSON, twenty-one. MARY ELLEN HUGHES THOMPSON, thirty-two. Both of them wives of JOHN GUY THOMPSON, 73, whose third wife, tenacious JUNE SALLY, lay by his side, sixty-eight herself, and entitled.

And the babies!

She watched Frank step with ease over the little space each infant had required. Nor had their small decay caused earth to cave in where they lay. She edged around the stone wall, watching for snakes, reading the names blurred by gray lichen. LUCINDA, 1894. CHARLES MARION, 1895. Both stillborn. No Unknown Babies here. Nearby lay their sister, ALMA QUEEN, who at seven had been old enough to read the inscriptions on others, before her own tombstone was cut. She turned away from the other small graves.

Jill almost said: *I had a baby who's now dead to me.*

No. She had worked too hard at forgetting. She had wrapped that memory in exuded crust the way an oyster wraps sand, but she was not getting any pearls for all her effort.

"We ought to go," she said tensely.

"These are my grandparents—William Rufus and Rebecca Eleanor Thompson. Grandma lived thirty years beyond him in that same house downhill with my parents looking after her. People don't do that anymore."

"By people you mean women, and women have jobs outside the home now."

"I guess that ice is melting. You want to ride on with me or walk straight downhill through the pasture? There's a path."

She did not want Frank to drive off and leave her almost adrift on this small island of the dead. "Through those thickets?"

"It's mostly sumac and saplings. But I'm going around the wagon road if it's not too overgrown."

"It can't be any worse down than up. I'm with you." She wondered if Frank, who had wanted to live here, wanted also to be buried here, decided to ask if his parents planned to be put in this cemetery.

"I guess they'll go out at Damascus Church when the time comes."

They drove onto a track that once had carried hay to livestock or wagonloads of corn to be thrown in the crib whose foundations the seasons had finally eaten away. Skidding down was easier than their bumpy climb.

Jill said once, offhand, "That was a little creepy."

"Creepy?" It was a mistake to turn his surprised face to her—Frank nearly skidded them into a cedar.

"Graves on the way to a picnic. You know."

Perhaps he did not hear as he swung them on downhill and aside into the wide meadow stretching on all sides of the house.

From that farmhouse, so festooned now with dead vines that it looked scorched, Tacey flew toward them, both arms out, as soon as they bounced to a stop in the shady oak grove.

"I thought that was your car on the high hill, Frank. I suppose you forgot the ice?"

Still silent, he untied the trunk and tipped the wet block into a washtub, then dragged it past her into the shade.

"How you, Miss Peters?"

"Please call me Jill."

"Don't they plait their hair like that in the operas, those German operas Hitler liked? Oh, good. You stopped at the chicken place."

"No, ma'am. I fried it myself."

Frank finished wiping his hands and frowned at them. "I don't see Mary."

"She's snooping around inside that old house. Let's put the food on this first table."

He yelled, "Mary!" then scolded his mother. "She could fall through those old floors or something!" Despite Mary's answering call he leaped over the millstone onto the porch and skipped the holes where boards had dropped out and stood calling inside the crooked doorway, "Mary? Come out of there."

"I can't stand to go inside an abandoned house myself," Tacey was saying as she covered Jill's chicken with a cloth. "Especially one I lived in. Empty houses are pitiful."

"We stopped at the family graveyard."

"Here, catch your end of this bedsheet," Tacey said, flipping it up like a tent. "We can cover these tables and weight it down. I hate that greasy wall where somebody did all that cooking for years and years. Oh good," she added after they had stretched the white cloth in place. "Set a rock on your corners. The graveyard, you say. I've got two started babies buried up there, not far enough along to name, everybody said. But they're named to me." She caught herself, embarrassed. "Frank, how about all that other ice?"

Jill set and reset the stones, unable to find exactly the right spot on the table's corners, thinking: Sonny Howard, Jr. Never. She had resisted the thought of any name. Baby Boy Peters, the small blue beaded bracelet had said. B. B. Peters. She had left it at that.

Frank went into the house after Mary.

"Where's Mr. Thompson?" Jill said when the stones were finally in their proper places.

"Working on the, ah, latrine. He's nailed up plywood to trees around this hole with a shelf over it. You're supposed to sit on the shelf like a bird on a wire. If you ask him, you'll have to go praise every detail." Tacey was setting out napkins, paper plates, plastic cutlery. "As for me, I am going to drink by the teaspoonfuls."

Above them, Mary's head and Frank's appeared in a house window. "I used to sleep in this room," Frank called to Jill. "I was probably up here the night you were born. When's your birthday?"

"September fifth."

"Mary's is in August. The rest of the ice is in those two coolers, Mama. You need any right now?"

Tacey said she needed it not to melt. "Here comes somebody. After that climb they everyone will want a drink. You bring an ice pick?" Jill found it in her purse.

People on foot were trailing uphill from where they had parked, hiking an easier route than Frank's car had barreled through, on a path marked by the pink plastic streamers that surveyors use. These stairsteps between tree roots had originally been worn by hungry cattle making a path to the barn. As Tacey went to meet them, Dandy Thompson appeared at the edge of the woods and waved Jill toward him. She shot one glance at the shape of the new arrivals—all too bulky to be Christine—before crossing the meadow, her ankles nicked by low briars, to where Dandy was nailing a board on which he had lettered TOILET to a tree trunk. "You've got to see this," he said as he led her down a path neatly clipped back. A second sign had been posted by an upright broom handle with a roll of toilet paper stuck on its top. This sign explained that users should carry the paper with them, then replace it as they left to signify the latrine was no longer in use. Dandy even carried the roll along when he took Jill behind the underbrush to admire everything—the leafy barrier, plywood wall and shelf, the ditch, an open bag of lime with a flowered teacup inside.

While she was smiling he took her off guard. "What about Christine?"

"What about her?"

"Meeting her. I don't know if you and Frank—"

"Neither do I."

"Oh." Jill watched him test the plank for splinters with one hand—this small man whose knit shirt made his shifting flesh look even more plump and loose. It bounced below his chin when he cocked his head to align his bifocals, so intent on the board that she was able to say softly, "Naturally I'm curious about her."

His voice sounded mild, even flat. "You'll be able to know which one she is, even from a distance. Give Christine an inch, and she'll make a dress out of it."

Jill giggled.

He started to say more but changed his mind and by her elbow steered her back along the path, where he replaced the roll of paper. "Mary thinks the world of you, so I will, too," he promised in an offhand way, "and here we are! Oh look, there's going to be a crowd, and it's a good thing after all Tacey's hard work. I won't remember half these people." As they broke into sunlight he was already counting and comparing the number who represented Tacey's family and his with those more kin to the Broomes, the Beaks, and Georgia's scattered cousins. Some, it turned out, were confusingly related to each other besides. "Christine ain't here yet," he muttered, "'cause I don't see a thing worse than short sleeves."

In what had once been the Thompson yard grove, people were setting up aluminum chairs and playpens and spreading quilts in the oak shade, maybe twenty-five adults so far, and others in sight climbing the slope. A few children were already running in the meadow the way colts will leap and frisk when released at last from the barn. She could not see Frank. Downhill an odd hopping motion caught her eye—a large man was helping an old woman climb despite her metal walker. At each tree root and large rock he would bear-hug her waist from behind and toss her upward. Then she would manage a few more steps inside her aluminum cage before his next heave.

Mary ran to Jill for a quick hug. "I'm so glad you're here!" she cried, but her glance was already sliding away toward the climbers, looking for her mother.

"Who's the woman with the walker?"

"Grandma Georgia Broome's oldest sister. Wait'll you see her husband. They had to bring him the way you came, in the car. He's in a wheelchair and Grandma says the doctors gave him some kind of L. dopa-dope and now he reaches up your skirt. He must be eighty-five."

"Are they here yet? The Broomes?"

With elaborate unconcern Mary said she wasn't sure. "I've been busy."

They met two men who introduced themselves and went down the path to try Dandy's toilet.

At the tables, Tacey began introducing Jill to the women who were unloading bowls and boxes of food.

"Frank's friend," Tacey said over and over with no emphasis. "Frank's good friend. She fried this chicken herself."

With one glance, each woman measured Jill's every part.

One of those women, Layla Thompson, got Jill to help set up and brace a card table on which she then stacked Thompson family histories, photocopied books at twelve dollars per copy. Jill opened one to the first page, where a family tree traced ancestors back to Norfolk, England, and showed a tentative branch toward poet Francis Thompson, who was said, in a footnote, to have written a famous Christian poem in which Jesus, like a hunting dog, ran eternally after the scent of human souls.

Jill folded out the family tree and ran one finger down to find the box for Francis and Christine Broome Thompson, now divorced, with their daughter, Mary Grace, suspended neatly below. Below Frank's name she located the bare space in which her name (or some other woman's) could be inserted, the way second wives sometimes get buried on the very edge of crowded cemetery plots unless they have the last word, like June Sally, uphill now and underground. She felt depressed.

"People chipped in to fly me to England to do research," Layla Thompson explained. She rearranged the booklets and a cigar box already primed with some dollar bills, then opened a large album to show Jill plastic pages holding postcards and photographs of English graveyards, with additional snapshots of creeks and homesites here in Orange and Chatham counties. "That's Terrell's Mill; the Yankee professors have restored it now. And here's an old picture of Alexander Thomson—sometimes it's spelled without a *p*—who died at Fredericksburg. And here"—she pointed to a circled gray face smaller than a grape seed among hundreds of other flung seeds—"here is Billy Jewell Thompson in the infantry in 1917. This was taken at Camp Sevier?"

The way she looked away from the photograph, suddenly doubtful, at first made Jill think the name of the army camp was dubious, but she followed the woman's stare and ended up staring herself as a wave of silence rolled across the enlarging crowd toward them.

No question. Christine.

Like Mary's her hair was red, but it bobbed uphill into the sunshine showing highlights only bottled chemicals could supply. She was shorter than Jill. There was nothing else to criticize. Even if her breasts and hips had not been round and full, her narrow waist would have drawn attention to all that swelling above it and below. In high-heeled sandals, she seemed ready to pirouette in a beauty pageant. And, as Dandy Thompson had predicted, her black shorts and top were a small, close fit.

Jill smoothed her own black outfit, which now seemed wintry and mournful as she turned back to Layla's photo album. "Is this downtown Chapel Hill?" Though she shot forth a scatter of glances, she still could not find Frank anywhere.

"In 1925. Franklin Street wasn't paved then."

She finally spotted him near the ice tub with Wild Turkey dark in his glass, she thought—not tea. "Excuse me."

Maybe she was halfway to where he stood when Frank saw her and almost instantly also saw some explosion of red hair in the background. If her hearing had been better, Jill could have heard him switch focus the way big trucks bang hard into a different gear. Looking past her, he lifted his glass and drank slowly to build up his strength.

Jill put out one hand to touch him. His concentration was passing through her just as a microscope on higher power will leave the gross behind. Jill shook his arm. In a loud, surprisingly angry voice she said, "You'd better tell Mary her mother's here."

Frank put one arm around her like someone feeling through the dark.

"Her pictures don't do her justice," Jill murmured.

"Mama always said Christine's looks were her affliction. If you're big as Goliath, she'd say, somebody's going to be picking fights all your life. And Christine was doomed from birth to get more offers than fifty average girls."

Jill said, "I'm grieved for her."

"That's Virgil and Georgia coming behind her. They always let Christine go ahead. You know what slipstreaming is?"

"Like a motorcycle close behind a truck? Not that Christine's built like a truck."

Frank gave Jill a squeeze that felt absent, minor. "What can I say? A book and its cover. Already you know it all."

Say something good about *me*, she thought.

The crowd reaction was jerky, as if in a silent film—people speaking to Christine and then snapping heads toward Frank and away to Christine and back to him. A cluster of people formed around the card table with its family histories and rolled their attention back and forth.

Jill asked, "You going to introduce me?"

"Let her come to us. And I wonder where Mary is." He held on to Jill and made them pivot as a pair. "There. Upstairs window, see?"

"I can't make out her facial expression from here."

"She's probably not wearing one. She's got that wait-and-see look; I used to call it her Gray Fish Look. Big eyes. Pop eyes, almost, but blank, no reaction showing. As if she was drifting through water and even her skin had cooled down."

"But she remembers Christine was always beautiful."

"A lot has happened since a little girl thought her mama was always beautiful."

Now it was Jill's turn to circle his waist and pull. "Mary's going to be all right, Frank. She's going to grow up like every other girl."

He said nothing, but his body felt so stiff she wondered if he might not be wearing a Gray Fish Look of his own. They watched in silence as Tacey left off swatting flies, entered the cluster of people, and soon came out again, shading her eyes. Frank waved toward her. She made a shrug and went to sit alone on the grass and lean back against an oak trunk.

"Has Mary moved?"

"Not yet."

"Get ready, then. It's our turn."

Christine came laughing out of the group, touching a shoulder here and an elbow there—all male, Jill noticed—and made a show of spotting them for the first time. With some care she stepped into the meadow and walked toward them, balancing uphill on wedged heels that were wooden—"Good; her feet'll get sore," Jill whispered.

"What?" Frank said.

Christine was walking as if she took secret satisfaction in how smoothly both hipbones rolled in their pretty sockets. Halfway she called, "How are you, Frank? And where's Mary?"

"She's around." He stepped forward, leaving Jill without the comfort of his arm. "Hello, Christine." They extended stiff arms and shook hands across distance. "Come and meet Jillian Peters. She gives Mary riding lessons."

"Oh yes. Where she got hurt."

"How do you do?" The women tapped each other's fingers and pulled back.

"I'm anxious to see Mary."

Jill tried to prevent it, but her eyes rolled overhead to check that the window was empty.

"Call inside the old house," Frank said.

"Thank you."

When Christine had smoothly moved her polished hip joints and carried her auburn highlights into the shade, Jill whispered, "Why not let Mary pick her own time?"

"Because they need to see each other alone and there's no privacy out here in the open. Come on. I'll pour you some of this bourbon." He led Jill to the ice tub and began chipping some into a glass. "It's the right place, anyway, that broken-down house. Everything's over inside that place. Ivy's faded and left behind. I almost feel guilty sending Christine inside, since I couldn't have staged things better on purpose."

"I hope Christine picks up on all your symbolism."

"Never mind Christine. I'm thinking of Mary."

FROM CHRISTINE'S point of view, she had produced her particular beauty the way Henry Ford produced the Model-A car.

Souls Raised from the Dead

Every person born, she believed, came into the world with at least one potential for success—call it X—perhaps mechanical ability or good temper, musical talent, even pretty features, but most people squandered their energies everywhere from A to Z instead of concentrating on the X. Even those lucky enough to be born with two gifts or three needed to recognize young the major one compared with those so clearly minor and added on. Ford, had he made the mistake of diversifying, could have invented household doodads by the dozens.

She'd had no trouble spotting her inborn X. A single distraction, her mistaken marriage to Frank Thompson, had only delayed focus on it. Since leaving him, Christine had made beauty her central choice, her profession. She was now district manager for door-to-door cosmetic sales. Regularly she posed with exactly eight teeth showing for travel posters in Wilmington and Kitty Hawk. She even had a weekly phone-in radio show in Jacksonville, advising callers on makeup and diets and facial hair. "Tina's Arena," the show was called. A training ground for women pursuing, while gladly pursued by, men.

Christine herself had the same level of interest in men that Ford must have had in auto buyers. Would this man contribute to beauty or not? Recognize it, compliment it, prefer it, pay enough to maintain beauty in the style it deserved?

Just last week on "Tina's Arena," an angry feminist (ugly or—worse—probably lez, in Christine's opinion) had called to attack her basic attitudes, had offered as a parallel how in the last century women would sometimes have their lower ribs surgically removed so they could be corseted more tightly. As if Christine would recommend such an operation; she hated pain, herself! A nose job, OK for the unfortunate, an eye tuck, maybe even breast enlargement for those poor women whose X had been badly proportioned by nature, but Christine was not even in favor of corsets or their greedy salesmen. She was in favor of health and exercise salons—OK? Like the one she hoped to open in January if the lease went through? OK?

She stopped now at the edge of the unsafe porch and tested a board with one toe. The very place to twist an ankle, get a splinter. Frank would have liked living in this lonesome wilderness where any woman was bound to be disfigured by hornets and lye soap. She called, "Mary Grace?" It was important to modulate the voice so it would carry without strain, and to project without wrinkling the face. "Oh, Mary!"

Inside the house came an answer. Though she waited, Mary did not come out to cross this rickety porch. They got so moody at this age! Christine moved cautiously from one sound floorboard to the next until she could catch hold of the door. "Are you upstairs?" The things a mother goes through! "Mary?"

At least the hall floor seemed solid enough. By noon in these shoes her arches would be aching, but Christine was carrying fold-up slippers in her large purse, which about now ought to have its strap shifted from left to right shoulder to keep those muscles evenly developed. She wrestled the handbag across, calling, "Mary? It's your mother!"

At the top of the stairs, Mary appeared. Bad angle. At my age she'll have jowls. She has my hair, but Frank must trim it with hedge clippers. Taller. "Oh, Mary!" Christine clattered recklessly up the narrow stairs. Midway they ran hard into each other, clutching. The wobbly banister barely held them. Already Mary had lost her baby fat, so Christine could feel through her T-shirt the soft early nipples. How terrible to be this age! For an eternity, Christine remembered, back when she was endlessly turning thirteen, a fat boil had appeared and reappeared above one eyebrow with its white top growing over and over like a snow-swollen mountain peak in spite of every cream the local drugstore sold. A miracle that it left no scar!

But Mary's skin seemed clear unless you counted freckles. Christine drew back to examine Mary's face more closely. How amazing that this separate body and person had come out of herself—though *that* experience she'd just as soon forget, OK?

Ruined her vagina. Why don't the plastic surgeons put their talent to work where it's needed?

"How pretty you are!"

Tears sprang into Mary's green eyes. Their sudden appearance sent body heat surging through Christine, who cried "I love you, baby!" the minute a hot flash rose in her throat. Crying, Mary hung on so tightly she was apt to make them both fall. "Up here," Christine murmured, turning her slightly aside so they could slowly climb the stairs. "Let's find a place to talk, OK? Is there anything to sit on? No?" She checked one empty room with stained walls while Mary snuffled against her shoulder. "Honey, let's sit on this top step then before these shoes throw me down, OK? Right here. Don't cry anymore—it makes your eyes swell. I'm here." Inside her shoulder bag she found the makeup kit with premoistened tissues. "You're growing up!" Mary swabbed out her eye sockets. "And you don't look a bit sick. How's that going, Mary? What does the doctor say?"

"He talks about options."

"Should you be sweating like this? We're both damp! What options—tell your mother, OK?"

"Medicines first. Then dialysis. Then a transplant. If I should need all that, of course." Mary blew her nose. "He says science is working on my problem every minute."

Christine felt very much relieved. "Oh, they'll solve it. They'll fix cancer next. Even in my business, Mary, everything depends on science. I'm thinking of putting out a face cream myself once I get the formula just right."

"I thought you just sold Avon."

"No, I'm handling a whole new line with women working under me. Hypoallergenic. That means you won't break out. And I've brought enough cosmetic samples to last you five years if Virgil's carried up my cases by now." She touched the widest freckle on Mary's cheek. "You don't need much makeup yet, but some sunscreen?"

"Chapel Hill would be a great place to sell cosmetics, Mama. New college girls move in every year."

"Not for me, baby."

"You could get your own separate apartment and everything."

"Listen, I'm all set up on the coast, OK? I travel up to Norfolk and down to Charleston. Never mind college territory—anywhere the navy goes, there'll always be a market for lipstick and perfume. I'm expanding to Mayport next. That's in Florida."

Mary pulled away. Christine frowned; she didn't even pluck her eyebrows yet!

"I wrote you letters," Mary said.

"Honey, they were just fine letters, just fine." Christine leaned down—well at least she was shaving her legs! "I keep every one in my sachet box, but, Lord, I'm no letter writer myself. You'll just have to accept that. People are good at one or two things and bad at all the rest—you learn that now, and no man will ever be able to disappoint you, I guarantee. Look at me now, Mary. Was that the only time you ever thought about your mama? The times when you wrote those letters?"

"I kept thinking about you plenty."

"See there? Me, too. We're just alike. Let's go get those cosmetics, OK? In a case all your own, a Samsonite; now you can start yourself a luggage set to match. I hope you like blue." Christine patted Mary, then used her shoulder for support as she stood teetering on the step. She lifted one wedge sandal, inspected her polished toenails, and then stepped down, talking. "Too much horseback riding and you'll bow your legs, Mary. You need to swim this summer to keep your body structure in balance." At the foot of the stairs she shifted the strap of her bag to the opposite shoulder before smiling upward. "Is that riding teacher your daddy's girlfriend?"

"I guess so."

"But Virgil said he had some newspaperwoman?"

"I guess it's Jill Peters now. She's nice." Mary had to hurry downstairs to catch up in the dirty hall. "Did you fly here in your own airplane?"

"It's my friend's airplane. He had to come to Duke anyway to find out about the rice diet program for his wife, so he arranged his trip to suit mine. He might invest in this exercise spa I want to start. He's a good friend." Christine walked ahead but thrust back an arm with a gold watch on the wrist, bright stones set around its face where numerals belonged. "He's a jeweler."

"What happened to the one you were staying with?" Mary broke off to cough. "The one from here?"

"Mr. Lassiter was a free taxi ride from the courthouse to the beach. OK? Once. I don't know where he lives now, and I never miss him." You never knew anything about men except in close quarters, and it turned out that no matter what Jip Lassiter ate, he got gas. Every morning Christine would rush to the shower, his fart smell sunk into every pore. No gasman for her, OK?—not even a millionaire, which he wasn't!

They came onto the dangerous porch, where, with an overhead flash of gold and gems, Christine made a flourish toward the high oaks. "These old trees—don't they make you feel like a little bug down in the grass sometimes? I love the beach, Mary, where it all opens out, and the air and sun are just everywhere with nothing in their way. California, now. That's my natural habitat, I'll bet."

"You're not tan."

"No, and with our kind of skin, baby, we'd better just *moon*bathe and let it go—oh!" She teetered alongside a hole in the floor but caught herself by the ornate porch post and swung around it with a wave toward the gathering picnickers. "Have you ever seen so many ugly people in your life at one place? And fat? I treat fat as if it was an overall cancer of the system; that's how seriously I treat fat, OK?" Christine frowned across the crowd. "Even my mama is letting herself go now. But your grandmother Tacey Thompson has looked exactly like that since she was forty-five, when she went into a size fourteen and just stayed there. There must be a whole factory turning out her little flowered size-fourteen dresses. I think she had on that very one the day I first met her. Other people her age wear pantsuits now." Christine pivoted on the post for a different view of the picnickers. "Even the strangers have all got those round North Carolina faces that make you just die to see one Jew or a Mexican. Mary, I don't see how you can stand it! You ought to go to the Bahamas once." Suddenly she yelled, "Virgil?" Then she called a second time, more musically.

He waved to her from a group of men watching someone drive in an iron stob for horseshoes. While motioning to him, Christine asked Mary softly, "Has Frank already told you not to spend any time with Granddaddy Virgil by yourself?"

Mary shook her head.

"I'm telling you now, then, OK? You're not his blood kin, which might make you fair game as I damn well ought to know." Christine decided privately that today she would warn Frank one more time and maybe mention eyebrow tweezers, too. Virgil never went further with young girls than feeling their bodies, but Mary might not know how to handle his sudden, rapid touches. When Virgil had been Christine's step-daddy for about six months, he'd begun walking up behind her and sliding one hand so quickly across her budding breasts that he might have grazed her by accident while his arm was extended for something else. But the third time she was ready, grabbed hold of him quickly, and sank her teeth into the back of his hand. When he howled and yanked it loose with a perfect semicircle of purpling dents in the skin, he drew back to strike. She yelled, "Mama!" They both froze, listening to Georgia's heavy footsteps coming. "If you ever touch me again, I'll tell *her* and she'll kill *you*." Virgil had stuck the bitten hand deep in his pocket, for it was just possible that Georgia might have actually killed him. She was known to have one of those cold tempers that almost on the instant of recording an injury begin to calculate a vengeance; and they both knew any of her long-lasting grudges could be temporarily quieted without being entirely satisfied. Waiting for Georgia with her whole mouth salty from the taste of Virgil's hand, Christine had watched all the long possibilities cross his mind and face—from slow poisoning on up and down: and when Georgia finally came into the room they both made up some story. After that Virgil never bothered her, though she'd heard he began riding Chapel Hill buses and pressing himself against nurses and college girls. He even adopted her. She never trusted him.

"See where Virgil's pointing? That's where he's put all my stuff—come on."

"But walk slow, Mama, so people can meet you." Mary lifted her head in a way that lengthened her neck, threw back her shoulders, and began to speak like a queen as they crossed the meadow. "Miss Walker, my mother." Murmurs. "And Mama, this is Mr. Elmo Wicker from the patrol station."

"We've met," said Elmo with no smile. "We was in school together."

"Can you add and subtract now?"

"Enough to get by, Christine. Where's your daddy, Mary? I want to tell him about that Torrido woman?"

"What about her?"

"She really is a Capone after all. Some people," he confided to Christine with a wry smile, "ain't what they seem to be, I guess."

"Elmo always was deep." Christine swept by, dragging Mary's arm, then whispered, "I like to remember things like that Capone woman, the criminal friends your daddy has, just in case I'm ever in a position for custody." Suddenly a pimply girl who must have painted ink or laundry bluing on each eyelid blocked their way. Her red mouth, slightly open, was wiping lipstick across her front teeth.

"Why Kay Linda," Mary cooed, "I'm so glad you could come to our picnic. You remember my mother?"

"Hey there, Kay Linda." Christine kept pulling. "We've got to get out of these flies or we'd stop and talk."

When they reached the oak shade, Mary gloated. "She is eating her heart out with ketchup and mustard, she is so jealous of how pretty you are!"

Grimly Christine said, "I hope you don't get much older before you figure out it don't make no never mind what the Elmos and Kay Lindas of this world think." They sat on the grass by luggage and tote bags that Virgil had dropped in a pile. "Now take a look, OK? Isn't this fine?" She snapped open the large blue leatherette case, whose inside lid had a recessed magnifying mirror. In interlocking plastic trays were stacked layers and layers of tube creams and gels, with sable brushes for blushers and powders in neat compartments alongside skin toners and cleansers and facial masks. "What's wrong? You don't like it?"

Mary fingered items in the top arrangement. "I tried to put on false eyelashes once and they got glued all over me."

"We all improve with practice, OK? Mama said she'd bought you a manicure set—not that you've been using it." She snatched Mary's hand and tossed it back. "Don't tell me you still bite your fingernails!"

"Not all the time."

"There's a quinine polish you wear to discourage that—I'll tell Frank before I go." She relocated the case on her lap until Mary's face was centered and widened in the mirror; then she floundered for a comment. "There, now. Ah. See yourself? You've got, you've got good bones."

Mary's mouth jerked out of shape twice—on her face, in its reflection. "Bones are just what I'll need if I don't get a kidney transplant!"

Christine slammed shut the lid. "Don't talk morbid, Mary

Grace Thompson! I did not come to this awful picnic to find out they'd turned you morbid. You wipe those eyes, and I'll put a little liner on; with our pale lashes we need it, OK? Now you just perk up." Christine made herself busy choosing the right color and instrument. "You see mine?" Suddenly she leaned forward and with one finger pulled down distorted skin below one greenish eye. "It's tattooed on. Permanent. I never have to do a thing. Now you hold still." While she pulled Mary's eyelid and held it half-shut by its outer corner, she began painting the base of her upper lashes dark brown. "For about a week after it was done I looked like I'd been punched in both eyes, but now it's worth the price. Just local novocaine. I was scared he would slip and the electric needle would go right through my eye, and he couldn't get anything done with me crying and not holding still. I couldn't stand to go through all that medical stuff like you do. OK, baby, now for the other one. You be pretty instead of dwelling on all that medical stuff, OK?"

Christine allowed herself a small, nearly wrinkle-free frown while she worked. Poor Mary Grace Thompson was never going to be truly beautiful, though she'd be attractive enough to manage, she'd be weekday pretty. C average. Seventy-five percent. But never beautiful. She decided whatever was Mary's special X must be located inside her head, since it didn't show on her face. "Now with the dry brush, hold still. You still practice the piano?"

"She doesn't teach in the summers."

"There. Oh, good, try the mirror. Isn't that an improvement? Now what about this horse your daddy bought? Does he race?" Mary shook her head—so there went National Velvet at the Kentucky Derby. "Do they give an Olympics for horseback riders?"

"Sure," said Mary, blinking hard at her image. "Miss Peters knows somebody on the team."

"Don't rub! When you get to be fourteen, you can put liner

on the lower lashes." Abruptly Christine leaped up to call Layla Thompson, "Where did you get that card table, honey? Is there another one?" In no time some soldier on furlough had found and carried her a small table, set it in place under a tree, and evened the legs with chips of bark. He waited awkwardly to one side in case she should also need chairs. "I might as well take some mail orders," Christine explained softly to Mary while she unzipped and unbuckled her other bags and began to set cosmetics across her unfolded red velvet cloth. "It keeps the other girls on their toes when the manager outsells them. On a weekend, too. Just setting an example." She unpacked printed signs of her brand names also, which the soldier was happy to thumbtack to surrounding tree trunks. Christine stacked her order blanks by a box of ballpoint pens and stood back, nodding. "You want to be some help, Mary? OK, how about if you circulate and show that darling little case and just tell people where you got it. You mind, baby? Go show that Kay Linda —she'll make her mama outbuy you."

Mary started away carrying the case.

"Show her the eye shadow especially!"

"I will."

Christine called, "They can't see inside if you leave the lid on!"

To display its contents, Mary had to bear-hug the leatherette box with its mirrored top folded open and hooked underneath her chin, so when she glanced down she could see up the double-barreled hairy holes of her own nostrils. Finally she got it all balanced on her chest and moved with her stiff back arched past the table of family histories and downhill where young women were sunning in the meadow on spread coverlets. Already she was rehearsing in her mind what she would say and the careful breath she would take while she smiled between each sentence: "Look what my mother brought me! Yes, she's got lots more. That's her at the red table. Isn't she pretty?"

Souls Raised from the Dead

* * *

LYING WITH HIS HEAD in Jillian's lap, all Frank could see with his eyes open was the cover of the Thompson family history she was reading, so he relaxed and decided to nap on the sunny grass.

Behind the book she said, "I get tickled every time I read how Layla Thompson is bragging about being kin to this poet who saw Jesus as a hunting dog. It makes that Elvis Presley song run through my head, remember? You ain't nothin' but a hound dog?"

Frank made an agreeable, drowsy noise.

"You don't fool me by peeping, Frank, I know who you're looking for."

"No, I'm not, but I'm probably the only male who's not. Christine is something." In the dappled sunlight he felt pleasantly dotted with warm and cool. "In fact, she's even more than she used to be. Must be taking lessons. Mary says she's even on the radio now."

"Some TV station is bound to decide that's a waste."

"Guess so." Under him Jill suddenly shifted in a way that banged her knee against his ear. He added, "She's already developed that artificial look," and felt Jill's muscles slacken.

After some pages had been turned, Jill said, "You must have loved her when you married her."

"She claimed to be pregnant."

"Oh."

"In spite of what she said, Mary wasn't born for over a year."

"Proving she wanted you enough to lie."

"Not a whole lot of motivation is required for Christine to lie. No, I think she just wanted once in her life to be married. Come six months, seven, and she thought, 'Well, I've tried that out.' And started looking around."

Jill sounded far away. "It's ironic that you married Christine thinking she was pregnant."

"How so?"

"Because some men. Well." Her drooping book shadowed his face so that inside his eyelids it grew abruptly dark. "I had a friend and when she got pregnant the man lit out for California. So she had the baby and gave it up for adoption."

"Not many do that now that abortions are easy."

"We farm girls grew up with animals, so we're used to helping things live and not die."

Now the book was actually touching Frank's forehead.

"Everybody told her she was crazy."

"Even you?"

"No. Not me."

"Hers probably got a good home, the way they're so careful placing babies. More careful than Mother Nature is—would you give a baby to Christine Broome?" With one hand he pushed the booklet aside. "Elmo Wicker, down at the patrol station? They adopted this baby a couple of years ago, and he was so happy he got right silly for a while."

"Boy or girl?"

"Little boy."

"This was a boy, too. Isn't that Dr. Seagroves? I didn't know he was a member of your family?"

Frank sat up. "I think Mary invited him. The whole family reunion gets complicated because Christine and I are second cousins or something, so we're kin to a lot of the same people. They started these combination reunions soon after we got married and quit them the year she left. But some of the guests are just friends—Elmo Wicker's here with his family and Lila Torrido and some of Mama's canasta players, and I think Mary asked half the nurses from Memorial Hospital. If they'd all come, there wouldn't be enough chicken to go around." He waved at Dr. Seagroves, who came to sit by them, carrying a soda and a pimento-cheese sandwich.

"Lunch already?"

He shook his head at Jill. "Only for those of us who have to leave early. It's good to see Mary enjoying herself."

"Where is she?"

"Up on the porch getting her fingernails painted. Silver, I think."

Frank reminded him of Jill's name and said while they shook hands one more time, "Mary's feeling fine today, but every time she frowns I expect the worst."

"Remember dialysis works wonders, Frank, and rests the kidneys so they can work again on their own. Even if her condition worsens, we can use it a long time while we're finding a suitable transplant for her."

Frank drew closer. "I've been wanting to talk to you like this, when Mary wouldn't know. Why wait, Dr. Seagroves? You know I'm probably the best match." Dr. Seagroves put his sandwich onto the paper plate and stopped chewing. "Why don't we go ahead and schedule transplant surgery this summer while Mary's still strong?" Frank said.

"You?" The doctor looked surprised. "You give Mary one of your kidneys?"

"Well, certainly. Who else!"

"But of course you know, Frank, why that won't work."

"I don't see any reason why not. I'm in excellent health, you know that."

"But have you forgotten? The time you got shot?"

"What's that got to do with it?"

"Everything, Frank. You know perfectly well the bullet damaged one kidney—the left, I believe."

"I don't know any such goddamned thing."

"We told you at the time. How could you forget it?"

"Nobody told me a fucking word!"

Jill whispered, "Frank?"

"It's hard for me to believe the matter wasn't thoroughly

discussed with you before you left the hospital." The doctor lifted his chin. "Why, I myself talked it over with Christine when she was signing the release forms. I distinctly remember that conversation!"

"She never mentioned it. Are you saying, Seagroves, that I can't give Mary my other kidney?"

"No physician would approve a donor who'd be left at risk."

"Fuck the risk. It's been years, and I've never had any trouble at all. And it's my life. At this point all I care about is Mary."

"That's understandable. But a doctor has to care about you both. Besides, it's not as if this is Mary's life-or-death choice, between you and nobody."

Frank stared at him.

Dr. Seagroves said firmly, "Apart from other possible donors, Mary has a mother, and her mother, so far as I know, has two healthy kidneys."

"Christine? Are you crazy?"

"Am I crazy, Miss Peters?"

Jill said no, but Frank jumped to his feet and began to circle them, grumbling. "She'd never do it, not old Christine. She can't stand to be hurt physically. She used to have to check into a hospital just to have a tooth pulled. And don't you remember when Mary was born? She was hysterical most of the nine months and for a week after the birth and then depressed for God knows how long." He wheeled around them, waving one hand. "Hell, she can't give Mary a routine letter or a phone call—she'll never give her an organ somebody's got to go in and cut out!"

To follow Frank's frenzied march through the drying clumps of Queen Anne's lace, Dr. Seagroves spun his head this way and that. "Just because you and Christine have had your differences, Frank."

"Do you really know her, Seagroves? Do you really know Christine a damn bit?"

"She's a mother."

"You go ask her, then." Frank could feel his teeth snap shut biting off each word. "Ask her now. While she's right here, while Mary's in view. You tell her why it's vital. I want things settled before this day is over."

"All right." The doctor got up, looking at his watch. "But I need to find her in the next fifteen minutes."

"You make her look straight at Mary the whole time she is giving you her answer."

Jill pointed. "Christine's selling cosmetics at that table. The second one, see?"

"Any potential donor would need time to think it over and make her plans, Frank. Naturally she'll want to talk to her own physician."

"Don't say that to her, Seagroves. Bear down on the urgency. With Christine you've got to talk about *now*. She's got no talent for promises." Nodding, Seagroves moved away. As he watched him go, Frank kept muttering to Jill. "See, what happened is that Christine just forgot all about my kidney damage because that emergency passed, and other things took her time right then. She never thought it might be important to tell me or that we'd ever want to allow for it in the future. She was always getting Mary's ears pierced young or giving her a home permanent with the alarm clock set, but she couldn't remember how many sugar cubes she'd had for polio. Jesus!"

Jill stood to touch him, but he kept marching out of reach, shaking loose when her hand came near. "I don't know why I'm even surprised! And I can't tell Christine what a goddamn stupid thing she's done now on top of all the other goddamn stupid things because right now she's got the one thing Mary needs!"

"He's talking to her, Frank. Calm down."

He stopped abruptly to watch Seagroves bending behind Christine's shoulder. "When I look up that hill all I see is kidneys walking by, everybody but Mary with two healthy kidneys. Old kidneys, young kidneys. For a change, Christine's don't look any better than average—I bet she's got two goddamn ugly kidneys—but right now they're the best kidneys in the crowd, the first-prize solid-gold kidneys."

"They're moving over to one side to talk, Frank. That's a good sign."

"Beauty ain't skin deep at all, it's bone deep, organ deep, and Christine right now owns the prettiest goddamn kidneys in America."

"She'll do it when the time comes, Frank, anybody would."

"Just a little below that small waistline, Jill, she's got one on each side. A regular and a spare."

Unconsciously Jill slid one hand into the small of her own back and rubbed herself there.

"There goes the doctor to his car. How do you interpret that wave of his—good? Dismissed?" Frank waved; he lifted Jill's hand until both were waving. "And we've just got to wait and not say a word that might spook Christine. We've got to hope she'll come of her own accord and tell us that she's agreed."

"She's back at her table again. Surely she couldn't just keep selling cosmetics if she'd told Dr. Seagroves no?"

"Could you keep selling them if you'd said yes?"

"Oh, Frank, who knows! We can't walk around all day trying to read Christine's face. But we do need to walk by her ever so often in case she wants to discuss it with you."

"I'm sure she told him no. If Mary was at death's door, maybe then, but not while Mary's just had her fingernails painted silver."

Jill took a few steps as if she were leaving. "I hope you're not just a pessimist by nature. That's hard to live with."

"Are you going to live with it?"

"I don't know. I haven't been asked." She became flustered. "Too soon to think about that."

SOMEBODY RANG A COWBELL when the food was spread on the long table, and Gordon Thompson from Pennsylvania

—because he had come the greatest distance—was chosen to pronounce the invocation. He prayed so long that Dandy soon had his eyes open, mapping the quickest route to his favorite foods.

The prayer swept backward to the earliest Thompsons who had bought, in the 1700s, a farm for fifty shillings, lingered there to praise early thrift and piety; then the petitions inched forward one gratitude at a time down the generations. Dandy slid nearer the corn pudding and a selected platter of ham biscuits that had fatty edges showing all the way around. In order, the prayer was allotting regret to each war in which any Thompsons had perished—though it passed rather quickly over the 1860s when some had fought on opposite sides.

Dandy could not help it; during one petition he snatched a deviled egg and popped it into his mouth, where it fit snugly inside his upper plate. The slow melting of its spicy yolk made him close his eyes in sweet earnest.

"Shame!" Mary whispered behind him with a giggle attached. "Pig!"

Somewhere near her Tacey's soft but pungent voice added, "Infidel."

He pressed upward with his tongue to further the dissolving of the yolk while loud blessings reached the Depression and world wars and at last rained in small thumps upon the crowd gathered in the meadow this very day. Amen. Dandy snaked his hand between others to grab a paper plate and filled it quickly with chicken, fried okra, potato salad, baked beans, banana pudding, and blackberry pie. He turned from the loaded table with his loaded plate held high to find Christine staring at him.

"That ham will be in your big artery by sundown, right next to the heart," she said with a pleasant smile.

"Tasting good all the way," he snapped. He stood next to her table of creams and sweet waters, with his fingers wiping a little chicken fat onto this jar and that. When finally able to think of something unpleasant, he said, "I'd a lot rather harden my arteries than my heart like some people I know."

"Don't start with me," she said. "I used to have to control myself when you treated me like dirt, but now I don't have to."

But she had given him time to sharpen his tongue. "Go right on and lose your head, Christine; you'll never miss it." He rushed away before she could come up with an answer and collected a large cup of cola from Tacey. As soon as possible he poured out half and filled it with Frank's Wild Turkey. He carried everything behind the house, where he could sit in the cool shade by the well, whose flaking bricks he had whitewashed many times. He wanted the back of his shirt made dusty from whatever coating remained.

Eating here, away from the noise, Dandy tried to summon up the faces and forms of his parents by reciting their full names like an incantation through his full mouth—William Rufus Thompson, Rebecca Eleanor Thompson—then to locate their images behind him on this back porch. His father would be washing his hands as usual in the basin that used to hang there, then flinging water through the air over Dandy's head and downhill in a silver sheet. And his mother? Winding the bucket down into the well again, letting it settle there and fill. From memory he called up their voices, made them talk softly between themselves about chicken hawks and neighbors. About their son Andrew. Favorably. But just as he had the scene fixed now as it used to be then, the shape of them wavered behind him like steam, and their voices turned into birdsong and leaf rustle and at last into his own heartbeat, a little fast now as it fought the forbidden ham biscuit.

Perhaps he was unable to keep them pictured in his mind because he was older now than his father had been when his own heart failed. Papa died at sixty; Mama not until ninety. When such a married couple came through his gate, would St.

Peter split the age difference? And how could Papa ever recognize his son Andrew grown old? If Heaven proved to be
inhabited (as Tacey claimed) by more elegant versions of everyone's last earthly body? How could mothers identify one stillborn infant from another? And only God knew what became of
the borderline abortions or patients kept in a coma for years on
machines. And what about his own slow-witted brother Bobby,
who had died of quinsy sore throat when he was only ten? If
God had now promoted Bobby and made his brain smart for
eternity, how would he seem, to his family, the real boy they
had been so patient with? But what kind of cruel Heaven could
keep unaltered the same handicaps and ugly faces and flawed
IQs forever?

Nothing suited Dandy Thompson better than to be chewing
good food slowly while his mind turned and tasted and retasted
these indigestible questions that Tacey always dismissed with
a wave of one hand and her standard murmur about God's grace.
She had chosen Mary's signifying middle name. But Dandy had
always dared ask such questions. In his youth he had collected
those blue E. Haldeman Julius five-cent booklets that were most
radical: Darwin, Marx, Freud, Thomas Paine. It had surprised
him to discover these condensed versions were still hard to read,
but just their ownership had set him apart from those other
Lowe's Grove boys who only owned their sixth-grade Bibles
with Sunday-school catechisms stuck in the center between Ma-
lachi and Matthew, turning yellow there.

Elmo Wicker from Frank's patrol station bent over him.
"You OK?"

"Just eating with my eyes closed. Makes the flavor better."

"Never heard of that." With a grunt, Elmo lowered himself
alongside and set his plate and cup on level ground. "Your
people didn't dig this well with shovels, did they?"

"No, it was drilled. They used a spring for a long time. Did
you try the sweet potato pudding?"

"I couldn't tell that's what it was. Had pecans on top?"

His glass, Dandy noted, had also been sweetened with bourbon and, from the pauses in Elmo's speech, must be his second or third drink.

"Makes me wonder," said Elmo, pointing overhead with a drumstick.

"What? What makes you wonder?"

"Days like this make me wonder about my boy. He's adopted, you know, he won't ever meet all his blood kin like this. He can read names in the Wicker family Bible till he's blue without looking or acting like any of those dead people, you know what I mean?"

"Oh, that might not matter," Dandy lied politely, since the older he got the more blood kin mattered. Every family needed some old maid every fifth generation or so with nothing better to do than rediscover ancestors and make the others pay them homage. He closed his eyes again. But if he could not sustain William Rufus Thompson's face motionless in his mind, would Frank ever remember his? A name on a tombstone—that's all that was left of the unknown grandfather of Elmo's adopted boy. Maybe no more would be left of Andrew Thompson. Plus he would be wearing this old man's body in Heaven trying to introduce himself to a father whose hair had already turned divine without ever turning gray.

He said angrily to Elmo, "If we lived in a different country, we'd think people got born and reborn over and over anyway. Why, Elmo, maybe I was your son over in England sometime and maybe you was a French hoor some other time."

"Speaking of hoors," Elmo said—which made Dandy open his eyes in a hurry. "It looks like Miss Lila Torrido really is the daughter of one, and you'd never guess it, would you? So you must be right. Blood don't tell after all. She sure learned how to be a lady somewhere."

"You know what a hoor is, don't you? A busy body." But

after a halfhearted snicker Dandy looked around uneasily. "I don't think you ought to be telling it that Miss Torrido is a real Capone."

"She's the one telling. I'm just confirming it."

Behind them, hollow footsteps sounded inside the abandoned house, so they ate in silence in case something might occur worth overhearing. Then Dandy said, "You think Miss Lila got any of the Capone money? She sure lives a better life than Social Security can buy."

"Maybe she's like you and won some big contest."

"The biggest thing I ever won was that FM radio. You tried my latrine yet? You ever seen such a good job in your life?"

"Not since the army," Elmo said. "Can you pick up this beauty program of Christine's on your radio?"

"You couldn't pay me."

"There's some complaining about her selling stuff at the reunion. People are saying they could have done the same, written up insurance policies, for instance, or handed out advertising. The woman that teaches dancing lessons is sorry she didn't do a demonstration, she says."

"Trust Christine." He decided to change the subject and share with Elmo his speculations about Heaven and its confusions, but Elmo was a regular Sunday-school teacher for the Methodists, so he was barely getting started when Elmo said, "You're doing just like the Pharisees when they kept asking Jesus about the woman with several husbands and whose wife she would be in Heaven."

Dandy, who didn't appreciate being classified with the Pharisees, stood up. "If you want any cake you'd better get there before Virgil Broome eats it all." He carried his plate around the house to the end of the table, where flies and yellow jackets were finding the desserts.

"How you, Andrew Thompson?"

He shook hands with the woman whose name he could never remember—one of Tacey's relatives. She collected salt and pepper shakers. Had 'em made like Philip Morris bellhops and Kool-cigarette penguins and God knew what all. Couldn't stand it that restaurants gave you little paper folders nowadays, just wouldn't modernize her thinking. He edged away past pound cake and meringue pies, picking up brownies and nougats as he went.

Somebody rang the cowbell again. He tasted a date bar, then dropped the rest on the ground as people began gathering near the millstones his daddy . . . with that, a full unsolicited picture of his father sprang suddenly into clear focus: William Rufus Thompson the day he had rolled the first millstone off the wagon bed. Dandy could see every detail about him now, as plain as if he were the boy still standing too close to the wheel and getting axle grease on his overalls. His father's eyes? A blue whose vividness he had forgotten until this very moment! And the shorter left leg that made his gait uneven. The way both ears stuck out. Some people's earlobes are joined to the face, but his had been loose and wide enough to waggle, and hair grew visibly inside both ears and in his nose. Together they had dug these old millstones out of a creek bed and hauled them home. And now, yes, now his mother was coming out of the house to see them set in place, her features clear and youthful. She was not only pretty; Dandy realized from all these years beyond that she must have been desirable then, with her pert smile and slender waist and—

"There you are," Tacey said and by speaking sent Mama back into oblivion. "I'm not going over there and give Georgia Broome the satisfaction of watching her read palms. Are you planning to fill up on all that sugar?"

"Every grain," he said, smothering a sigh.

She stuck her mouth against his ear so hard he could feel her teeth. "Listen, Dr. Seagroves has told Frank he can't ever give Mary a kidney because of the time he got shot, did you know that? I didn't know that, but Christine did and kept it to herself. Don't look at him, he's upset. We're both upset." She held on to his shoulder and kept him from pulling free. "Christine is the one who'll have to give a kidney when the time comes. Doesn't that beat all?"

At first he was too shocked even to speak. Then he blurted, "How you can believe in God is beyond me!"

She let go of him in a hurry. "Andrew!"

He lurched away through the crowd, not sure whether bourbon or bad news was making his legs so unsteady. At Christine's table, he stopped to fix her with a stare meant to convey long, enraged demands.

"Hey Dandy," she muttered, then she turned to smile at the woman getting cologne sprayed on her wrist pulse. "It's a floral bouquet. Not too heavy, OK?"

He continued pouring his gaze into her, flattening his mouth, hauling his eyebrows down hard.

"But what I really like is the perfume that pairs with it. Just a hint of musk underneath. Smell."

The woman smelled the glass stopper so long that Dandy's face muscles began to ache. He decided to join the others seated nearby on the grass around Georgia Broome. Georgia had laid out playing cards on a towel and from time to time also held up a poster and pointed out certain standard wrinkles in an average human palm. At her elbow sat Mary, who was either getting a fever or had both cheeks painted. He went closer, squinting. Rouge. And her mouth an unnatural red besides!

Georgia said to the woman whose palm she was reading, "You are going to have some health problems."

"Honey, there's no going-to-have *to* it. I've been sick all my life."

"They'll come to a head," said Georgia. "But you've got up to twenty more years of life ahead of you."

"Is that all? My mama lived to her nineties."

"She had a different palm. Now something intersects right here. Something good. Maybe you'll remarry?"

"I might be sick, but I ain't crazy," said the woman, rolling her eyes.

"Somebody's coming into your life, that's for sure. Any family that could be moving into your house?"

The woman's smile disappeared. She gave a hard look to somebody in the crowd. "Not a soul."

Dandy moved forward with hand extended, and as soon as possible Georgia made a smooth transition out of that boring life and into his. "You need to sit all the way down so I can see better." Squatting had made him dizzy. He half fell into place. Georgia said for him she would deal out cards also, since trying on shoes was easy labor and didn't mark a man's hand enough.

Insulted, he said, "I'm no sizzy."

"Sissy." Georgia waved a hand to disperse his whiskey breath, then snapped cards facedown on the grass, talking patter that didn't interest him. Something large was swelling in his chest. He bent forward and past her. "Hello, Mary."

"Are you all right, Dandy?"

"The question is you, you." A long paragraph went on in his mind, but did not need to be spoken. In silence he finished it to the final word and period before Georgia began turning over cards and talking:

". . . travel across the ocean . . . careful of banks and investments for the next six months . . . control your temper . . ."

When the time came, Dandy decided, he wanted to be buried in the old family graveyard up the hill. Probably he had never explained this to Tacey, who might plant him in the municipal cemetery with professors and Rotarians. Might even cremate him! He'd end up smaller than a shoebox and prayed over by that deaf preacher who wouldn't wear two hearing aids because he said his affliction forced him to listen to people's souls! He only wore one. He heard them half-assed.

". . . and sometimes cards also read the past, though that's rare," Georgia was droning on. "Why, yes, this queen of hearts is a love of your youth!" With a smirk she pressed the card to her forehead, then briefly blocked each eye. "I see a green and shady place. The university. The arboretum! You and this young woman are there on a moonlit night, but I can't see exactly what you are doing."

The bystanders sniggered, and Dandy, who remembered exactly what he and Georgia Lambert had been doing, gave her a wink. "Never mind the past. Tell me the part I don't know."

Georgia smiled, but then her eyes rolled toward Mary once. She turned away from Mary but raised her voice so even Christine's sales pitch could not override, and began telling him loudly that he would have a long and happy old age, one in which *all* his family would be a pleasure to him, with no particular illnesses or sadnesses for him *or his loved ones*—she said that twice, *or your loved ones*—to mar the years ahead.

Motionless, Dandy let her lies pass through him to reach Mary. He half believed Georgia Broome really could read the future, so he knew she must have seen something very bad to prettify like this.

The Wild Turkey bourbon seemed to be coming back, solid, into his throat. He touched Georgia's hand, managing even to forgive the old bitch for giving birth to Christine. He swallowed the lump and decided that everybody expected him to joke, so he said, "It'll be terrible to grow old alone." He rotated toward the surrounding audience to deliver the punch line: "Everybody knows Tacey hasn't had a birthday for years and years."

Over at the food table Tacey made a noise that could have been a hacking cough or a controlled growl. I'll explain it to her later, Dandy thought.

Georgia flipped over another card and pointed it toward Tacey first, and then to him. She predicted they'd both live a long life, then die within days of one another.

"That's sweet," somebody (but certainly not Tacey) whispered.

Mary had left Christine's cosmetic table and drawn nearer. That artificial mouth looked as if it had been made in her face with a dull knife.

"One reason my wife lives in the past is it's cheaper," he announced to onlookers. Laughter.

Georgia whispered, "Are you drunk?"

He picked up and studied a card himself, glancing aside to his audience. It was either a spade or a club printed badly. He winked at Mary. "Just tell me, Georgia," he said, "if my ship is going to come in before I'm too old to navigate."

Was Mary smiling? Yes. That was good. Red mouth and all. So good.

Water rose up suddenly and drowned his view of Mary's painted, smiling face.

CINDY SCOFIELD did not arrive until some of the perishable food had been packed away. "I can't eat much anyway, I'm working," she said to Tacey, whose picture she took.

"Don't you keep that picture! I'm not getting my hair done till Thursday!" Tacey cried with both hands pressing down on her skull.

Cindy snapped that one, too. "We're doing a feature on how people celebrated July fourth. I've been to a ball game and a parade and I've got fireworks Wednesday night." She accepted a chunk of coconut cake that had to be eaten right away before the sour-cream icing got way beyond sour.

Georgia posed with her playing cards. Then Cindy called over Rosa Venters, the black woman who cleaned Frank's apartment on Fridays, and wanted Georgia to read that palm on camera. Neither woman wanted to—Georgia because she did not like to hold a colored woman's palm, and Rosa because she thought all that stuff was the work of the Devil. So Cindy got one shot of the two women gaping away from each other, as if mutually recoiling from bad supernatural news.

She wouldn't photograph Dandy at the latrine, but she did get one of him, arm extended, sending a lucky horseshoe through the air. A nice contrast, perhaps, to the dire predictions of the cards. Mary wanted her photo made holding a blue weekend bag—who knew why!—but Cindy could send her some prints to keep.

And the old lady in the walker with, of course, a baby crawling underneath. She might send that one to the *Durham Herald*.

By stages she worked herself through the crowd, photographing Elmo Wicker out of uniform, and some old woman who was telling a group of boys that Al Capone had chewed Sen-Sen, that she'd gone with him in the summers to Beaver Lodge in Wisconsin, that he played bad pinochle. How warm it had been when he died in Florida, how cold when they buried him in Chicago. The boys were disappointed that he had died old and sick and not in a machine-gun massacre.

It made a good shot, Cindy thought, and would look as if a refined old lady were telling young boys about patriotism on Independence Day, and from this angle no one could tell that their faces were bored.

"And it's eight feet high, his tombstone, black granite," the old lady said, standing tall to measure. "My father's in the same plot. QUI RIPOSA, it said!"

Cindy got another quick picture; the old woman looked like the Statue of Liberty with that arm upraised. One boy made an ugly farting noise with his mouth.

"But of course they had to move Al to Mount Carmel, there were so many vandals," said Miss Lila Torrido as she sat down again. The boys were peeling away from the edge of her audience and moving toward the old orchard to climb trees. "Now he just has a flat stone marker like all the others, and it just has his dates and a cross. And MY JESUS MERCY. He had the last rites, you know."

The boys were gone now, and Cindy considered but did not take a shot of them swarming up the limbs. From the hairy, snakelike trunk that grew attached to the old apple trees, she thought they would break out with poison ivy by morning, and she didn't mind. She wrote down the woman's name and address for a cutline.

At last she came to Frank Thompson and Jillian Peters, seated on the steps of the old house. She stood without moving, like some sluggish boulder that had just rolled downhill and stopped, until Frank had no choice but to introduce her.

They shook hands. She knows who I am, Cindy thought. And I know who she is.

"I see your byline a lot in the paper," said Jill politely.

"I read about you in the horse-show results." Two noncommital exchanges. She's pretty. Wearing her hair like Freya and the Valkyries. Or is it Frigga? Or do I have a dirty mind? To Frank she said, "I took Mary's picture. She's looking well."

"So far."

Something in his face made her ask, "Is something wrong?"

"We just found out I can't be a kidney donor if it comes to that. So it's up to Christine, of all people."

Cindy frowned toward the table where Christine was showing some kind of bottles to a crowd. "She's her mother, after all," she said, remembering her own mother and the endless hours she had spent bending the knees and elbows that were supposed to set nerves to firing in her sick boy's brain.

"She's Christine," he said.

As if she had read Cindy's mind, Jill quickly said, "Don't say anything about this or to her. She'll have to work up to it. She's got to agree."

"But she's Mary's mother!" Cindy kept staring across the green yard toward the cluster of people who seemed to be spraying and smelling and wiping their skins; she hardly noticed the murmuring behind her until Frank said, "Jill has to feed horses early so we need to go."

"Yes." She turned back and lifted the camera. "Let me get a picture of you together."

"Oh," said Jill, "not now." She turned to pick up her purse, and the movement showed something colorful on one shoulder, a flying bird or something.

Frank shrugged and followed her.

Through the lens Cindy continued to watch them move through the meadow together, stop at the horseshoe game to speak to Dandy Thompson, nod to Christine. Frank had to bend down to hug his mother, who was seated on the grass. She did not click the shutter.

They talked to Mary; maybe they argued about who she'd ride home with; then they both got into Frank's car, the one with the bad shocks that Cindy knew so well.

She made herself photograph a fat man sleeping, the kind of cliché her editor would like. Then she strolled toward the table with a red velvet cloth on top, where the woman with hair almost as red was selling tanning cream and roll-on deodorant and hairspray.

"Just let me get the cutline down," Cindy said as she made notes on her pad. "Christine Broome Thompson, I believe?"

Quickly the bottles and jars were being turned, label out, with one of Christine's manicured hands, while the other smoothed down the hair and moved it subtly over the shoulders so it would hang like twin pointers toward the breasts. "That's right, from Jacksonville, where I have my own radio show, 'Tina's Arena,' on lasting beauty for women. That's 'Tina' with an *i*, OK?"

"I've got it. And I want to get a picture of you hustling your product."

Christine did not think that statement through but was just getting her chin the right height and turn and her model's smile spread to the ideal width when Cindy snapped all that muscular effort in progress, and turned away.

"Is that all? Just one?" Christine took a step after her. "Did you get my good side?"

"I don't know," Cindy said. "Which one was it?"

LATER, Frank was to remember that Sunday, July 1, 1990, as the last good day.

They drove Lila Torrido home from the picnic, and, before Frank could even get his own door unlocked, she came screaming out of hers. Her apartment had been ransacked. Sofa cushions cut open. Drawers dragged out of bureaus, then upturned so their bottoms could be stomped.

After the Carrboro policemen had come and gone, Frank remarked that obviously Lila had "succeeded in convincing somebody" that she had Capone money.

"Somebody stupid," Miss Torrido answered. "Would I keep a lot of money here?"

"Where would you keep it, then?"

"Safety-deposit boxes."

Her choice of the plural left him wondering.

But that next week Mary became suddenly, acutely ill—her blood pressure rising so fast that she became, not simply asleep, but deeply unconscious in front of the television before Frank realized—and for the first time she was placed on a hemodialysis machine. The sight of her still body hooked to snakelike plastic tubes in which pulsing dark blood surged past sent Frank on a run for the hall, gagging.

"As many wrecks as you've seen, Frank?" Dr. Seagroves shook his bald head. "Remember when that gasoline truck exploded out on the interstate? Nothing could be worse than that pileup."

"They were strangers," Frank muttered.

"They were burned-up pieces of strangers, but I never saw

you turn a hair. Naturally it's worse when it's your own child
—but, Frank, stop being a candyass. You've got to call on your
professional discipline now for Mary's sake. She mustn't feel
like some kind of freak lying in there. Some families even learn
how to do peritoneal dialysis at home."

"I never could."

Dr. Seagroves drew down his glasses from his forehead as if
with magnification he could see to Frank's core. "Then show a
little understanding for things that come hard to Christine."

Like motherhood. Fidelity. Frank turned away, saying, "One
of those other kids on a machine has already had one kidney
transplant. His mother says he rejected it. So he's right back
where he started."

"It happens."

Frank waited until a teenage girl had buzzed past in an electric
wheelchair. "And this hospital is full of other kids with all
kinds of infections, but none of those germs destroys their
kidneys."

"There were plenty of cars on the highway when that gas
truck turned over and blew. Do you think I know why one
particular station wagon ran right into the tank?"

A particular wagon loaded with Cub Scouts.

But Frank glanced at the door marked HEMODIALYSIS.
"No, a better parallel would be if two station wagons had hit
the truck and one exploded while the other one didn't even
burn."

"My answer's the same, Frank. I don't know why. I just
know that Mary's biopsy showed scarred nephrons and I know
they don't regenerate. I know a name: nephritis. I know some
diets and treatments."

"It's not enough—what you doctors know."

"Maybe not, but it's better than nothing, a lot better than
what doctors knew a hundred years ago. And in the future—"

Frank interrupted bitterly, "In the future you'll be able to
save all the children Mary will never have."

A nurse passed, eyes fixed way down the corridor, and after she had entered the room whose overhead light was blinking, Seagroves said in a cold, superior voice, "No wonder Mary shows so little self-pity. You've got it all."

"Son of a bitch!"

"Well, use it up now, Frank, get it all over with, then leave it out here in the hall when you go in to Mary."

Frank might have hit the pious bastard if Tacey had not just then come out of the dialysis center, her face limp and old.

"Mother?"

"Hospitals," she said with an aimless wave, "and the children? I always forget so many children?"

The nurse reappeared at the unknown patient's door and motioned for Dr. Seagroves. Children burned and injured, thought Frank to the doctor's back. Children in comas, with cancer, deformed, on respirators. He nodded.

Tacey dropped onto a narrow bench. "When I go to the airport I'm always surprised to remember that all over the country thousands of people are heading off into the sky constantly, over and over, and when I come to the hospital?"

"Yeah. Over and over."

She brought herself visibly under control. "Did Dr. Seagroves have anything new to say?"

"I don't like that man. He's callous."

"He's not callous to Mary, and I'd call up the Witch of Endor if she could help Mary. Did you meet Mrs. Alpern?"

"Whose son rejected the transplant, sure. That's what we were talking about."

"I've been sitting with her. It's all the steroids Charles has to take that make his face puff out like that."

"And he's no taller than a ten-year-old," Frank reached down to touch his mother's shoulder, as if measuring.

Tacey said carefully, "He hasn't matured in other ways, either."

Gelded by chemistry. "How much longer do they keep Mary on that damned thing?"

"Another hour, Frank. They fill her and then leave it awhile and then drain—you know the cycle. It hurts when they're filling."

He knew that after the biopsy they had for this very purpose left a length of tubing that stuck out through Mary's stomach—he knew that but had not seen it, did not want to see it.

"I know I've got to get used to this. Seagroves was raising hell about that."

"Yes," Tacey said. "It won't be the last time."

"Some of them vomit."

"You still have to get used to it. By the way, I notified Georgia and asked her to tell Christine."

"That's all we need."

"It might speed up Christine's decision, you know?"

"Don't hold your breath." Frank snapped to attention. "At the elevator—is that your preacher?"

"*Our* preacher, yes, Mr. Ware. Don't stare around so wildly. There's no place to take cover."

"I need some cigarettes."

"You stopped smoking in March."

"And started again this morning. Hello, Mr. Ware. It's good of you to come."

One reason Billy Ware looked so serene was that he was deaf. It wasn't much of an occupational hazard, Frank supposed, for a man who could respond to anything by quoting Scripture.

Cocking his head so the hearing aid on his left could be trained to receive what they were saying, the Reverend Billy Ware shook Frank's hand, then held on to both of Tacey's and murmured. In the pulpit, Tacey said, he wore hearing aids in both ears. He was chubby with very dark hair and eyes and a swarthy complexion from his Lumbee Indian forebears. Frank could hear him whisper something about the afflictions of the righteous and how God delivered. As for Frank, he had never felt less righteous, and he wanted God to impose no conditions of righteousness or anything else, just the compelling, sufficient one—that Mary Grace Thompson was Mary Grace Thompson.

"Now that Mr. Ware can be with you, I'll get us some coffee," he said. "Can I bring you some?"

The preacher shook his head as he sat with Tacey on the bench, still pressing her hands. On a velvet string he wore a carved-wood cross that rose and fell on his fat breath. A bit High Church for the Damascus Baptists, Frank thought as he walked down the hall.

"They don't allow you to smoke up here!" Tacey called after him. A lie.

A good lie, she thought, holding herself very still while she watched Frank hurry away, her hands growing warm and damp between the preacher's while he talked on. Since she had already cast her burden upon the Lord as Ware was advising now, she felt free to concentrate on organizing her day. Her lunch appointment, for instance. You had to keep moving. If you once stood still, fear could find you and drop down like an avalanche.

She broke into some long and comforting train of thought Mr. Ware was expounding. "You want to sit with Mary awhile? We try to keep her distracted." He smiled so sweetly that Tacey repeated herself, louder.

"That's why I came."

"It's very boring for her, this process. Now, Mr. Ware, I don't want to tell you how to visit the sick or anything, but if I were you I wouldn't insist on praying with her today. Mary's not in her best mood. And as for Frank's mood! Whew!"

He nodded, smiling.

Tacey said, "So much anger."

"At her illness? That's understandable."

"When I was a girl," said Tacey, forgetting to speak loudly enough, "my mother assigned me scrapbooks so I could fill them with ideas for amusing myself on some later rainy day. I used up a lot of perfectly good sunny days expecting the worst with Mother's help, but today I've wished I'd been making a long list saving up against this day. For Mary. Saving jokes and things?" Surreptitiously she stole a look at Billy Ware's facial lines, too many of which were level calm, too many of which suggested that if she were not there to stop him he might talk in the dialysis room about what he'd saved up to share— the blessed endurance that suffering provides.

He murmured, "Beg your pardon?"

"Never mind." They can hear me in the street, she thought. "I'll keep an appointment while you're with Mary if you'll be very, uh, diplomatic."

"Glad to." He tiptoed into the room where the noise of machines, overhead television sets, and nauseated children might deafen him even further. So what if he says the wrong thing? she thought; he can't hear her complaints. Mary might not hear him either over all the racket.

Still, Dandy and Frank were wrong—it didn't matter that Billy Ware was deaf nor that half his church pews were empty while those seated in the other half heard only half of what he said and less than he meant; it didn't matter that the Women's Bible Study that Tacey regularly attended sometimes became either obvious or silly. Tacey herself could be the silliest member, but God was willing to use whatever flimsy thing might come to hand: she was certain of that. Once, leading a W.B.S. devotional, Tacey had drawn parallels comparing the early job training of a Nazareth carpenter to the later mission of a Savior—how from the beginning Jesus had to allow for knot-holes, use primitive tools, work with the grain. She had been very pleased at thinking up this illustration all by herself and had expected to hear herself respectfully quoted churchwide thereafter—but never did.

Pride, she thought now. How it leaks in!

Outdoors she decided it would be easier to walk to the Carolina Inn than move her car off the high hospital parking deck.

Across lawns and parking lots she walked briskly between shrubbery to the slope of Columbia Street, past redbrick university buildings whose windows were still open to the warming day, through which came a flow of scientific talk beyond her comprehension. She was puffing before she passed the naval R.O.T.C. building, with its gray gun mounts guarding the flagpole, then more slowly uphill to the handsome old stone Carolina Inn that always seemed crowded with alumni and conventions.

In its lobby, Cindy Scofield rose from a deep upholstered couch. "Thank you so much for coming, Mrs. Thompson, especially while Mary's in the hospital. Things must be difficult."

Tacey nodded, extending her hand. The girl's touch was warm. She wouldn't have minded Frank marrying this reporter, even though she had known for a long time what everyone else knew—that they'd been sleeping together regularly, and what man buys a cow if he's getting milk free? She could not help a slow, thoughtful survey of Cindy's body now. Sex was more important to men than it had ever been to Tacey. Maybe those old Jewish male prophets valued sex so highly it had attained to them the level of sin; she did not, so it had not. Briefly she wondered now if Frank, unlike his father, might know how to do those secret things that could make Miss Scofield shiver and squeal the way all the women did in beauty-shop magazines nowadays. With rumors so widespread, there must be something to this orgasm business, but the most Tacey had ever felt was some brief internal reflex, as if her womb had sneezed.

"I made reservations in the Hill Room."

Good, Tacey thought, as the dark young woman led her down a broad carpeted hall. She seldom came on campus and never to the Carolina Inn; perhaps Dean Smith would be eating in its dining room. She thought it was sweet the way his wife worked against pornography, even criticized the swimsuit issue of *Sports Illustrated*. At the entrance she swept her eye over the tables, but the coach was not there.

As they sat at a small table, Cindy said, "I appreciate you keeping this confidential."

Tacey was thinking that Cindy Scofield might still hope to marry Frank, though she had certainly seen him with Jill Peters at the picnic. She decided to head off one possible conversation by saying suddenly, "I try not to meddle in people's private lives." (That's one reason I don't know if other women have multiple orgasms or are just bragging, if they only happen in New York City or just what.)

If Cindy was surprised, she hid it by handing a brown envelope across the table. "You might like these."

The first eight-by-ten print showed Tacey herself six days late for a good shampoo and set. She was mashing her own pompadour as if to hold the dandruff down. With a sniff she snapped past Georgia trying to look mysterious. "Oh, that's good of Rosa!" she said, lingering. After Christine had run off like a harlot, she'd asked the janitor at Damascus Church who still did maid work. And he'd sent Frank his sister. At least Tacey hoped Rosa was his sister; they lived in the same house. "May I keep this one of my husband?"

"You're to keep them all."

In his photograph Dandy had thrown the horseshoe high so it flew prongs upward, the way it needed to be to capture and hold good luck in its curve. She had known city people to nail one on a car shed for cute good luck—but place it upside down.

"I tried to get Frank and Jill, but they were leaving early. You saw the feature, I hope? They only used group shots after all."

Tacey nodded. In the last picture Christine's face must have oddly twitched to one side. It reminded her of something, maybe those pictures she had seen that illustrated the right and left sides of the brain; Christine was a Total Right, all instinct and self, and part of her expression had always seemed dimmer, like the moon in half phase. No, there was one specific face in an old magazine, some killer she remembered who had the two sides of his face misaligned, as if his head had been halved like an apple and then set back a quarter inch off. The Clutter murders, she remembered suddenly. An innocent, normal American family and this man with his face jarred off center had shot them in their own home. Had watched them die with one big eye and one little.

"Christine won't like hers" was all she said as she slid the brown envelope into the big purse under her chair.

Cindy didn't bother to open her menu. "I eat here a lot, and it's always the same," she said, tapping the cover with its faded Old Well landmark. She got a club sandwich with coleslaw and coffee.

Tacey could fix sandwiches at home. "Shrimp cocktail," she decided, wondering why they made shrimp sound alcoholic.

Clearing her throat, Cindy said, "I know what you mean about meddling in people's lives, and I hope you won't think Frank's friends are doing that. People have heard about Mary. They'd like to help."

"Help how?"

"Money for one thing. Lots of people know Frank, and they're also the very ones who know the kind of insurance state employees have. Especially if there's to be a transplant."

Tacey said quickly, "I doubt it comes to that."

"And blood transfusions. I'm told kidney patients require a lot of plasma."

"Dr. Seagroves mentioned that." Her food had come, and she did not like the looks of the thickened red goo in the middle.

They took their first bites, politely not watching each other.

"State troopers," said Cindy, "well, they investigate so many car crashes that sometimes they know about a possible, uh, kidney donor before anybody else might even think of that possibility. The patrol wants to make it known to the family now that they'll be watching out for Mary's interests, but they don't want to say the wrong thing. They don't want to sound like vultures or something."

This time Tacey stared as Cindy bit into the too-tall sandwich and chewed.

"I was asked," she said, chewing fast, "to pass. That along." She put the toasted segment back on her plate. "Woman to woman, I think, is the way Elmo put it."

"I see." Tacey leaned back, sorry now that she had ordered shrimp, disliking their tiny kidney shape. "This needs to be talked over directly with Frank."

"In Elmo's opinion, Frank just isn't psychologically ready yet to look that far ahead."

"Neither am I." Tacey took a hot roll from the basket.

"And Frank and I don't talk as much as we used to."

It's not you! Tacey thought. "He never did talk things out very much, even as a boy. And Mary, Mary's just—"

"His whole life, yes."

After eating in more silence, Cindy said while she forked into the slaw, "Frank has a lot of friends. You'd be proud to know how many people have been calling Elmo wanting to help from as far east as Wilson and back west to Winston-Salem. Everyplace he's ever been stationed."

Everyplace Christine hated. "I never expected this. I just thought about how we'd get through this experience, ah, privately."

"There's bound to be a Mary Grace Thompson Fund one way or the other. And the time may come when it will be useful to publicize the existence of such a fund. What about the Kidney Foundation people—is Frank in touch with them?"

Less and less did Tacey find appetizing the curled shrimp that bled seafood sauce down her too-sharp fork. "We're just trying to get through today, Miss Scofield, and hoping for the best."

"Cindy."

She pushed the dish away. "We don't let ourselves believe that any days to come will get worse, so it would seem like bad luck to provide against it, Cindy. Well, weak faith, bad luck —you know." She thought about Dandy's horseshoe.

Cindy was nodding. She was not as pretty as Jill, not as pretty as Christine; in fact, Tacey thought as a young woman she had been a bit prettier herself. A good straight gaze when she chose, however. A nice voice; maybe an alto. Maybe a church choir?

"I've lived day by day myself. But it does get worse faster than you can believe, and a tired family gets up one morning and finds itself an exhausted family. People fuss at each other, people drink, people quit speaking and move out. The strain gets to be, well . . ." Cindy frowned, said rapidly, "That happens even when the patient recovers as we all trust Mary will. In my brother's case—"

Tacey waited while the young woman's mouth and eyelids clamped down hard; her features compacted briefly in a way to convince anyone—even sunny Mr. Ware—that a flood of suffering did not always leave behind an unexpected high-water mark of good. She touched Cindy's arm.

"He's in an institution now." After a deep breath came the short, flat sentences. "And so is my mother from time to time. She and my father finally divorced. Now his blood pressure and his guilt are both way up there."

Tacey took her hand away so Cindy could busy herself with napkin, iced tea.

"Thank you, Mrs. Thompson. I'm only telling you this history, this—ha!—private business so you'll understand that I really do know what chronic illness can do to a whole family. Frank ought to take any help he's offered, from anywhere, anytime. He's going to need it." She swallowed. "Being his mother, maybe you can tell him so."

She loves him, Tacey thought.

When Cindy lowered the napkin, her mouth had smoothed itself. "People think they're going to bear up like saints, but if there's any of that, it comes a long time afterward. Not during."

She means me, Tacey thought. "I hope you'll keep on being Frank's friend," she decided to say. Because I don't think Jill's old enough. Inside.

"Meantime," said Cindy, nodding, "Elmo and I will just put any contributions into a bank account and wait to see what happens. We're not soliciting donations."

"Thank you." Tacey nodded when the waiter came to remove her dish. "Leave the bread," she said, nibbling. "I hope the only money Mary will need is for college."

Across the room she spotted Lila Torrido near a window, eating lunch with a young man whose slick black hair and black mustache looked oiled. Tacey had never seen him before. She smiled, then nodded, at last lifted and waved her own napkin but could not catch Miss Torrido's eye. "Sorry, one of Frank's neighbors," she explained.

"I should have brought you her picture. My editor says she's supposed to have ties to the Mob."

"Oh, I doubt that. Sometimes lonely people will say anything to be noticed."

"We reporters find people don't even have to be lonely. Would you like something else? Dessert?" Tacey said no while she continued to eat the yeast roll. "You, though, Mrs. Thompson, you're the quiet type; I guess Frank gets his reserve through the genes. I have too many conversations that are really interviews in disguise, with everybody trying hard to seem quotable."

Talk's cheap, thought Tacey. By now Dandy would have been entertaining this entire dining room. She nodded, her mouth full of expanding bread.

"But it's hard to tell what quiet people are thinking."

Tacey supposed this comment obligated her to speak her thoughts aloud. "I see people on television all the time telling the world what they ought to tell God alone."

Cindy blinked. She lifted the glasses hanging down her chest by a chain and set them over her deep-set dark eyes so they sprang slightly forward, larger. "Don't you think it's mentally healthy to be open about your feelings?"

"No."

From her impatience, Cindy must have argued this with Frank before.

"It causes new trouble," Tacey said, "when there's enough old trouble already."

"We ought to be willing to run the risk of being psychologically vulnerable."

"Who's willing physically?"

"But we no longer go about armed. We don't keep up our guards physically or keep looking over our shoulders." She gave up on the sandwich in favor of slaw. "Do you think being emotionally reserved keeps people from being hurt?"

"No, you get hurt either way. It's easier to handle hurt in private."

"Well, that's what Frank's doing, all right."

But Tacey didn't want her to confide too much about Frank in the name of all this vulnerability. She let her gaze wander to other diners at other tables, stopped where Miss Torrido seemed to be having a strong disagreement with her luncheon guest, a nephew perhaps? No. He looked the way Tacey thought burial-lot salesmen must look in New Jersey, more sinister than here. Miss Torrido was shaking her head so fast that the gray hair slapped back and forth.

But she could not hear their private quarrel and didn't want to; let them go home and fuss with the door closed.

"Where are you from, Cindy?"

"I started out in Pineville—where President Polk was born. But we moved a lot. My mother's in Louisville, now. Dad's up in Norfolk. He was a navy veteran, and he wanted to retire where he could still see the ships."

"When Andrew retired, he took up contests." Tacey stuck

out her wrist with its new watch showing international time zones. Then she showed the one on the other wrist, which had Elvis Presley on the face.

Cindy laughed. "I wish I'd gotten that shot of him having his fortune told. He looked as if he believed every word."

He was drunk, Tacey thought.

"It was a wonderful picnic. I got so interested in the people that I even bought a copy of your family history."

Because it was Frank's. "The book disappointed some. They had hoped after they paid her airplane ticket that Layla would trace them back to lords and ladies."

"I'd be proud enough to be traced back to Francis Thompson. Especially to carry his name, like Frank does."

Tacey let her face show that she didn't remember that particular namesake. She didn't. She had named Frank for the saint who loved animals and whose prayer was carved in the vestibule floor of her church, *Lord, make me an instrument of Thy peace.* It was a jolt when Cindy lifted one hand over the table's small vase of flowers and announced dramatically, "I fled Him, down the nights and down the days!"

"You fled who?"

"He fled Jesus, of course. Or Christ, he'd probably have said. Being Catholic."

The waiter refilled their coffee cups and asked if there had been something wrong with the shrimp.

Tacey shook her head. "Jesus?" She sat straighter. "I never realized." Quickly she shook her head to his offer of dessert, leaned forward to exclaim again, "Jesus! Imagine that!" The frowning waiter stepped quickly back.

He thinks I'm swearing.

Cindy Scofield ordered lemon pie. "It's a long poem."

"Was all that in the family history? Can you say more?"

"Just a mention. I was an English major, so I know the first lines of a hundred poems. I wandered lonely as a cloud. Comrades, leave me here a little. Little Lamb, who made thee?"

"Oh, that's sweet!"

"No, no, they're different poems!"

"I'm not much of a poem reader. What's the name of Mr. Thompson's poem?"

" 'The Hound of Heaven.' "

Having grown up on a farm with beagles and blueticks and redbones, Tacey suspected it might be sacrilegious. She watched Cindy skim off and taste the meringue. "This poem takes place in Heaven?"

"It's about how God pursued Francis Thompson's soul here on earth until he finally hunted it down. Saved it, I suppose the church would say."

Tacey wondered if the poem was like Jonah's story, except that there God *used* a whale, he didn't go turning into one. But the hound might be symbolic. When anything got hard to understand in the Bible, Mr. Ware always said it was symbolic. "You don't remember more of the lines?"

"Not really. It's quite long and in a repeating rhythm"— Cindy tapped the white tablecloth evenly with her knife handle—"all about those feet that followed, followed after."

"Then I suppose," said Tacey with some regret, "a lamb wouldn't have done as well." Really, though, Cindy's thumping made her think, not of dogs, but of horses' gallops. The sound-effects man did it with coconut shells, as she recalled, for the Lone Ranger and his great horse, Silver.

Still, it was always a comfort to uncover some clue that God was still imposing His patterns on current ordinary affairs the way He used to in Canaan and Galilee, where you might meet an angel while you were threshing wheat. Frank's name might be as divinely chosen as John's or Abraham's. Tacey said, "I'll try to find a copy of the whole thing."

"You could make a photocopy over at Davis Library."

They sipped coffee before Cindy said, "I know all this is hard on Frank. He dotes on his daughter."

"Well. Being both parents. You know."

"It's more than that."

Tacey hoped she didn't mean something unhealthy. "Children grow up so fast that every change is wonderful to them and seems slow, but it's fast to parents. When you add sickness to that?"

The lemon pie must have been very sour. Cindy stared at it and laid down her fork. "If Mary dies it'll kill him."

"Goodness!" Tacey leaned back, napkin pressed to her lips. Why tempt the death angel by saying such things aloud? "It would grieve him deeply, of course."

"Take it from me, he'll quit. He'll lay down and die himself."

Tacey said stiffly, "That would do Mary no honor."

"I wish I were in a position to help him."

Tacey thought that a sign of maturity; Jill Peters, she believed, wanted Frank to help himself while she went off to vet school. She said, "Mary needs the most help right now."

"Of course." Cindy couldn't eat any more pie. "But will you call me if I can ever do anything? For either of them."

"Yes."

Cindy insisted on paying the check with her credit card. Tacey insisted on leaving the tip. They gathered purses, Cindy's clipboard, Tacey's envelope of pictures.

As they rose, Cindy said, "My mother used to say that when her clock ran down and her engine quit, she could refuel with vodka and orange juice. So of course in the end she turned into a heavy drinker. What do you do, Mrs. Thompson? Or does that time ever come?"

Tacey winced, because her reflex, truthful answer was "Say prayers." She never knew whether at such moments God required her to testify to her faith like St. Paul or whether He had taken into consideration how pious and awful it would sound. She stepped out in front of Cindy and wordlessly lifted one feeble hand shoulder-high with a weak finger that jabbed once toward the ceiling and then fell.

They said no more but parted in the lobby, from which Cindy hurried off to a called meeting of the Chapel Hill Board of Aldermen.

Tacey came out of the Carolina Inn onto Columbia Street and hurried through the humid afternoon across the U.N.C. campus, along brick walks that the roots of old trees were undermining, past the YMCA, which still had pointed windows lighting its former chapel, now a snack bar. The asphalt parking lots were hot enough to melt her shoe soles.

At the new modern library, the automatic door flew open ahead of her. It was her first visit. The banisters, she saw, were made from painted plumbing pipe. Davis Library had replaced an older building that had marble stairs and brass handrails and a domed reference room in which even scoundrels would find themselves tiptoeing.

The truth was, any kind of library made Tacey feel illiterate. She wandered uneasily among dozens of busy people who already knew where to find everything. At last she threw herself on the mercy of a graduate student who understood the massive card catalog and its on-line computer, and she waited patiently by the elevator while he went into the stacks to locate Francis Thompson's collected poems. The young man was so solicitous she decided he must be researching Alzheimer's disease, and it seemed a useful strategy to collaborate with his concern for her advanced age that had killed off so many brain cells already.

She carried the book to a long library table and sat between two young women with skirts nearly up to their navels. It had already been explained to her that all the Thompson collections were on reserve, but she would find the poem in this, an anthology of Christian verse—raising for Tacey the possibility that there might be Buddhist verse, even atheist verse.

"The Hound of Heaven" went on for five pages, in small print. She moved her lips around its unfamiliar words. From time to time, a verse—like a dark room lit up by passing headlights—would be briefly clarified; for instance, she lingered over the verse about "little children's eyes" and was almost smiling when the stanza closed:

> But just as their young eyes grew sudden fair
> With dawning answers there,
> Their angel plucked them from me by the hair.

Some light that had been sweeping through the poem departed and went on.

What she did understand of it hinted at an unexpectedly mean Jesus, as if the Good Shepherd were suddenly to materialize in the fold with rod and staff and begin beating some sense into members of his unwilling flock.

Finally, sensing that weight at her nape that meant a headache was in ambush, Tacey wasted a quarter before getting the book lined up correctly in a coin-operated photocopier. She folded her copy of the pages small enough to fit in her wallet.

When she had walked all the way back to the hospital in the afternoon heat, the tips of her fingers were throbbing to Thompson's rhythm, though she could not have recited a word. And what little shrimp she ate had disagreed with her.

WHEN MARY GRACE THOMPSON was about ten, a television series on murderers and the insanity defense had left her uncertain about how the human mind—that is, her *own*—really worked. If you were inside your mind, how could you ever go out of it, and where would you go? Going crazy seemed to her as complicated as a soul going to Heaven, but was not even mentioned in Sunday-school lessons.

Neither Tacey's nor Frank's answers about mental illness helped her much. If the body got sick, the mind knew every symptom; but should the mind become sick, since nobody was minding the store, even madness must feel perfectly normal? Frank told her soothingly that people who fear they might go crazy probably won't; really crazy people insist they're fine. Immediately Mary knew her own mind was fooling her with false reports of happiness.

For long hours of her tenth summer Mary went to stare at enigmatic photos of Ted Bundy, the Hillside Stranglers, Son of Sam, Charles Manson, Richard Speck, the Atlanta children's murderer, Sirhan Sirhan, Lee Harvey Oswald, Charles Whitman, John Gacy, Albert DeSalvo, Bruno Hauptmann—page after page of faces not different enough from those she passed every day between home and school. During prayers at Tacey's church she studied in every pew expressions that could have belonged to missionaries or cannibals.

One of the infamous Hillside Stranglers, Kenneth Bianchi, had under hypnosis convinced one doctor he had several other personalities crowded inside his mind, and the doctor had testified that one of these had actually choked the California girls while Kenneth himself was not at home.

At such knowledge Mary pressed both hands around her head. Why had his mind and not hers turned into a swarming Pandora's box? Could anybody tell which teenager was predestined for acne and which for murder?

When she did not "go" (nor even "get driven") out of her mind that tenth summer in spite of avid reading of police/detective magazines that she stole from Snipes's barbershop, Mary began slowly to regain trust in her mind again, though never in the easy old way. For instance, she was no longer sure how much she slept during the nights. Maybe, like Snow White, she was actually asleep for weeks at a time while those who loved her kept concealing her affliction in silence. It would account for many lost books and forgotten instructions if others had been living through ordinary days while she was absent in a stupor she could not recall.

In fact, perhaps she had already suffered a nervous breakdown. (Just the term made Mary shiver so violently that her vibrating brain could easily break itself down against bone.) And the same amnesia that plagued so many in films had ever since kept her from remembering life in the recent asylum. Maybe she even had multiple personalities, like Dr. Jekyll, like Eve, like Sybil, and had once turned into somebody else, perhaps one of those characters who seemed so real in her dreams. Wouldn't Frank and Dandy and Tacey conspire to conceal these horrors, hoping to prevent her insanity from happening again? Especially if it had been her sick but unremembered mind that had driven her mother, Christine, not crazy, but away?

Age ten was Mary's worst year to date. Into that fall and winter, she listened alertly for clues to some large-scale conspiracy about her mental health. She took note of every time she was being humored. Probably even her daily vitamin pills were actually tranquilizing medicine to cure her mind. She tongued and spat them out for a week, checking symptoms. Or maybe Rosa, the housekeeper who came at Thanksgiving, was a nurse, disguised in her apron. Did all Mary's so-called friends at school know the secret? Or were they, like she, being fooled by a communitywide conspiracy? Remember Kay Linda's wild temper and her mysterious allergies? Perhaps more than one child had lost her mind sometime in the past, but knew no more about that experience than she knew exactly what took place and how in her parents' bed.

One December night, Mary woke to find herself outdoors, standing on the small roof above their front door, barefoot on a crust of snow, numb in her flannel gown. General Franco appeared behind her, murmuring, and gradually coaxed her back through the window and to bed. In daylight, the experience became a half-forgotten dream, until Frank had a long, confusing talk with her about sleepwalking.

As he kept being kind, Mary thought her heart would stop. Murderers and rapists had already explained her experience better. Had said: I don't know how I got there . . . like a dream . . . movie unfocused . . . blur . . . not real; I can't remember.

Sleepwalking. On long January days in school, drowsy in a

humid and stuffy classroom, Mary would wonder if this was actually the sleepwalk, her real body left behind, still spending the previous night in bed. She resigned herself to a lifetime of secrets and puzzles.

But gradually during that next spring, perhaps for no better reason than time and buttercups, her uncertainty about the separation between what was and wasn't real diminished, and at last disappeared. Until her present illness, she had never again thought of all those anxious months.

Now, perhaps because the long dialysis treatments produced a familiar dissociation of mind from body, the old feelings crept up on her before she could even identify why they felt old. The first effect of division was that she began to feel like a good letter in a bad envelope. Then: maybe two letters, one good and one not.

But this time Mary became the secret-keeper. It was her duty to protect adults. She let the self that was attached to a rotten kidney sleepwalk through the dreamed U.N.C. Memorial Hospital, certain that somewhere else her real and healthy self was taking ballet lessons or riding Chancy or acquiring over a single weekend her first menstrual period plus a pair of boobs with nearly magenta nipples. She would lie very still while machinery filled her and flushed her, trying to be Ms. Hyde changing through chemistry into her better, higher self.

Naturally none of the doctors or nurses or family members knew that she had only dreamed them into this convincing but temporary existence, any more than the real Christine at the picnic could have guessed how often in Mary's dreams she lived out a perfect mother's role. Why, even if on this dream plane Mary were to someday, well, die, she would only be falling into one of the old sleeps of uncertain duration that were necessary to let her wake from this one into her real life; she would certainly wake, maybe at age nine, before Christine went away, perhaps on that remembered Saturday morning the three of them got up early and drove to Kitty Hawk for the weekend and her parents were laughing, and on the long sleepy trip home that strong natural body that her mind deserved had been so sunburned that Mary drowsed in the back seat, pulsating from radiant heat like a giant firefly.

Yes, from that trip and on that good day, she would wake up and be nine again to find that Christine had become her Girl Scout–troop leader and her fourth-grade helper mother, and her Damascus Sunday-school teacher and a P.T.A. refreshment mother as well as the pretty front-seat mother who periodically would lean back to touch the slumberer and whisper, "Isn't Mary wonderful? Frank? Isn't she?"

MARY WAS FROWNING as she pushed her bicycle behind Kay Linda's. "Let's ride," she said. "We can ride *slow*, but let's ride." Kay Linda did not answer, although one shoulder twitched as if to dislodge a bug. "This sun is hot," Mary said louder.

Kay Linda's face snapped into view. Her teeth were showing. "Hush up."

"He's not at home anyway."

"This is when he mows grass, between Donahue and the game shows."

"I don't like his attitude," Mary said.

"Nobody asked you." With her back again turned, Kay Linda began to march forward in an unnatural and stately way, as if the bicycle were lightly clinging to her fingertips by magnetism, as if she were surrounded by a force field that made her body flow forward without effort. Not only did her shoulders grow straighter and smoother under the T-shirt, but Mary would almost have sworn that her pale-brown hair was combing itself with air alone. "I don't know what you see in Jimmy Rosemary," Mary muttered, though she did know—it was the hope of stationery imprinted KAY LINDA ROSEMARY. Perhaps even posters, a theater marquee. Kay Linda Eubanks planned to become a starlet. A starlet developed younger and earlier than a star. A starlet first acquired a name better than Eubanks; then she began her career by being long-legged and pink on calendars, moved on from the *Playboy* centerfold to television soap operas, became the gasping victim in science fiction and horror movies, and at the height of her popularity would be filmed kissing men of all ages with her mouth open.

Well, Kay Linda had the mouth for it. Frankly, Mary couldn't see the point. Last year when she was spending the night at Kay Linda's, they had kissed their own upper arms and produced no passion whatsoever; at last, in desperation, they had tried kissing each other.

"Ugh," said Kay Linda. "This is kind of pukey, you know that?"

Mary made spitting noises in the air. "I bet boys taste worse." But this year Kay Linda was only interested in the imagined taste of Jimmy Rosemary, whose house they were walking by for the third time this morning. Usually this was Jimmy's day to mow the Rosemary front yard. Usually the girls would stop to talk with him, Kay Linda speaking sentences quite unlike her own, in a recently acquired laryngitis. Afterward she and Mary would mount their bikes, would pedal gracefully around the privet hedge on the next corner, and collapse giggling at its base while Kay Linda reveled in her normal high-pitched shrieking about how sexy Jimmy Rosemary looked with his shirt off and his armpits visibly wet.

"This is my last trip," said Mary, bored. "Let's go to the Record Bar."

"They know we don't have any money. You know how they'll act. Isn't that him out back? I can't look—you look! Is that Jimmy?"

"It's his mother. Carrying trash."

"I wonder if he's sick."

She was already, Mary knew, picturing herself at Jimmy's deathbed promising never to forget him. "I can't stand it."

Mary stepped onto her pedals. "I'm going to get a Coke or something."

"That's his room upstairs, the one with the curtains blowing?"

But Mary was already riding away, down the sidewalk and out the next slanted driveway into the shady street.

"Bitchy thing!"

She knew from the repetitious squeak that Kay Linda was coming behind her. "Don't you ever oil your wheels?" she called back. Last summer she and Kay Linda had spent Saturdays taking apart their bikes, understanding the chain and crank axle and how the caliper brakes worked. This year Kay Linda deliberately cultivated squeaks and rattles so she could ask Jimmy Rosemary to diagnose their cause.

Mary pedaled at top speed under the green arch of tree branches that overhung one of Chapel Hill's old and narrow streets. The Rosemarys lived within walking distance of the university, where Billy's father worked in Student Affairs. These were not love affairs, Kay Linda had explained in a superior voice, but cases involving fraternities or the honor court. Over the years, Mr. Rosemary had known, had often protected, the sons of judges and governors. Somehow Jimmy had thus acquired gilt by association; his family's statewide contacts would someday advance his starlet wife's career. Although as recently as last year Mary and Kay Linda had been planning to drop out of high school when they were sixteen and bicycle across the country, this year Kay Linda was afraid of windburning her complexion.

Pulling alongside her now, Kay Linda reached out and shoved Mary's handlebars. She fought for a wobbly balance.

"That was so bitchy! See if I ever do anything for you!"

"See if you ever *have*," snapped Mary.

Again Kay Linda aimed a push at her, causing Mary to turn into the rough gutter. "See if I give you a blood transfusion or anything."

"I wouldn't have your old cold blood."

"I'm going back," said Kay Linda, making a wide road turn.

"Go, go," said Mary, though she was disappointed when the squeaking of Kay Linda's bike faded in the opposite direction. Mary was then left to ride straight ahead very fast, pretending not to care and muttering, "Keep your nasty old poison blood."

From time to time, because she could no longer produce new blood, Mary's regular blood tests showed anemia, and she would be given a transfusion of packed cells. She had finally been able to ask one of the woman doctors, "Is that why I don't get my period? I'm all dried up inside?"

"No, dear. Your hormones aren't developing the way they normally would. So there's not enough to trigger your flow."

Kay Linda had enough hormones for every girl in the eighth grade. One transfusion from Kay Linda and blood would pour right through you; they'd have to send fast for a truckload of Tampax.

For some reason Mary felt like crying. Christine would have been the perfect mother for the starlet Kay Linda Eubanks. The perfect backstage mother. Christine: the only one who could ever get Kay Linda's makeup and hair exactly right just before the curtain went up.

And Kay Linda would have been her perfect daughter. Curly and creamy. No sunburn, even. With eyes so blue they looked artificial. Last year Kay Linda had stuffed her bra cups with toilet paper. This year she didn't need to.

Mary rode to Franklin Street, walked her bike across, and then pedaled slowly along the brick walkways of the U.N.C. campus. During the summer, the university became boring. Schoolteachers were everywhere, overweight, overdressed, giving her schoolteacher looks as they stepped aside into the grass while finishing sentences about their difficult courses in education and sociology.

Mary was never going to be a schoolteacher.

Some days, like this one, she thought she was never going

to be. Period. On days like this she could see and hear too much, literally—she could hear her heartbeat pulsing in each fingertip; the wrinkling of her own clothes crackled at great volume; the sight of her own nose could not be overlooked but loomed just ahead of her like a mountain. I won't look at my nose, she thought fiercely, pedaling faster past two more frowning schoolteachers, but immediately she crossed both eyes and —Yes! There it was! Huge!

She had to jerk her vision overhead by will, where in a slight breeze the leaves of ancient campus trees were banging together like cymbals.

Sometimes such moods were a sign that Mary's blood pressure was going up, though it had been fine this morning. Of course—according to General Franco—she was not supposed to be out on her bicycle, using up her strength and risking falls. She stopped pedaling and coasted along the main road of the campus. No headache. Some fly was stomping across her sweaty forehead. No dizziness. General Franco was right, though, in saying it was bad to sweat, since she could only drink 1,000 cc. of fluid in a day, and that included any food that would *turn* into a fluid, like ice cream or Jell-O.

It was an easy ride downhill on West Cameron, past the university laundry plant with its smokestack, and on into Carrboro. Its boundary reminded her of melting Jell-O, as there was no way now to tell where Chapel Hill left off and Carrboro began. Once the railroad tracks had marked the line, but when the trains stopped coming, all the book lovers had poured across from Chapel Hill and turned Carrboro into its imitation. On the whole she preferred the faded mill town that used to be, Carrboro before cosmetics (population 7,500). General Franco said once that if you woke up an Englishman in the middle of the night he would talk like anybody else; Mary thought when the train tracks were crossed eastward at midnight the snob town of Chapel Hill (population 45,000, not counting students) might turn into the ordinary town it really was. In a repainted

Carrboro, where former mill houses were now considered "historically restored," still lived the orderlies and clerks and cooks and repairmen and highway patrolmen; and their physical work propped up the mental work of doctors and lawyers and professors who lived over the line in Chapel Hill.

Mary had not noticed this division so much until this past school year when the children of both groups of parents began to make it visible, as if all of them knew by instinct how in every classroom the same old railroad tracks snaked invisibly up and down the rows of desks, taking in some and closing out others. Some of the university's children, of course, went away to northeastern private schools or at least as far as Durham Academy. Other academics on principle kept their richer, more culturally advantaged children in the public schools, where they could learn about "all kinds of people." And they did learn: they learned it was easy to sort their own kind from other kinds—sometimes by race or grammar, by clothes, by bus riders versus car-pool riders; they got the athletes separated from the bookworms, and the criminals-in-training set aside from the boys who were wild now but would later polish their wildness to a social grace in some good fraternity; by grade eight everybody knew which pretty girls would get away with being pretty and which would be betrayed by teenage pregnancy.

For most of last year's sorting Mary had teetered between categories. She could have gone either way—she had enough brains to notch her way upward, and knew it; she shared with surgeons' daughters the lingo of horses and showrings; she was going to be just pretty enough that the popular girls could have taken her into their group and felt democratic about it.

But now, even though the eighth grade had not yet started, she knew the invisible railroad tracks had thrust themselves like a sudden eroding flood surge of the Mississippi. She, like a sandbar, had been cut off, left after all on the Carrboro side to be sorted neatly with her own kind of people—the kind who had hay fever or fits or rode in wheelchairs.

No one had said this to her. At first her girlfriends had telephoned often. A few even came to the Ramshead Chateaux apartments to visit, but not twice. This summer when she and Kay Linda met to go bike riding, their meeting place kept moving, like a war pin on a map, closer to Kay Linda's shaded Chapel Hill house, farther from Mary's sun-baked Carrboro apartment. A few times the other girls had slept overnight with one another and not invited her: "Well, we didn't know what your schedule was with the machine and all." She couldn't eat many potato chips or fast-food hamburgers and fries, laden with salt.

As she pedaled slowly down Carrboro's Main Street, Mary thought: I'm stuck over here with the dumb and the poor and the crips.

She stopped at a convenience store to choose a soda—and choose it carefully, as its twelve ounces were a large proportion of her daily liquid intake. Sometimes she thought of only rinsing her mouth with ginger ale or Coca-Cola, like someone dying of thirst in the desert. When she got rich and had a new kidney of her own, she would do exactly that—buy champagne by the case and merely rinse her mouth periodically, then throw away each whole bottle before its bubbles grew flat.

She rode home one-handed, sipping from the warming can from time to time.

Their cement steps, the flimsy black railing to their front door, made Mary think of how Jimmy Rosemary's bay windows looked out on old brick patios with roses blooming on white fan trellises. She chained her bike to the rail that Frank said had been welded out of recycled beer cans and then spray-painted, wouldn't hold a June bug; when she shook her bike the whole row vibrated. Jimmy's house had stained glass in its double front doors. Kay Linda lived in a low, shaded house that was very modern and uncluttered, with wall niches by the entryway holding plumes of beach grass in pottery jars. Maybe living in such an Oriental house had given Kay Linda the mind of a geisha.

Sighing, Mary had to fish deep inside her T-shirt for the string that kept her door key dangling round her neck. Next year, or at least the year after, she had planned to become better organized, start using key cases and scrapbooks and bulletin boards. Now? Maybe not.

When she opened the door, a blast of air-conditioning made her skin clammy. She carried her soda inside carefully, having counted the very last ounce into the day's allowance.

From next door thumping noises could be heard through the thin walls. Absently Mary reached into the hall closet and rapped her drink can three times so Miss Lila Torrido would know she was home. She waited, but there was no answering knock.

Mary shrugged and went to check Frank's schedule, held by magnets to the refrigerator door. He was patrolling near Hillsborough today and had left underlined the phone number that in any emergency could be patched into his car radio.

Again there were bangs and thuds next door. She wondered if Miss Lila was turning her mattresses. Loud music and artificial announcers' voices through the walls made Mary frown. Ordinarily Miss Torrido did not turn on her television set until the six o'clock news, WRAL, Raleigh. She had a crush on newsman Charlie Gaddy, with his silvery hair. Daytimes she did her housework with a radio in one pocket and earphones on both ears. She preferred country music. Willie Nelson daytimes, Charlie Gaddy from cocktails on. Playing on the other side of the wall now were unexpected violins.

They modulated into a brassy commercial, but Mary could still hear furniture being moved. She threw her empty drink can into the trash on the back porch. On the next porch, as usual, Miss Torrido's pale-blue underwear from yesterday was drying on a line—she would never dream of hanging lingerie outdoors on one of the community racks for the public to see.

"Miss Torrido?" No, TV and air-conditioning would keep her from hearing. Mary hopped quickly off her own back stoop and onto the next, but Miss Torrido's screen door was latched. She knocked. Nothing. The underwear, always pale blue with one pink set for Sunday, looked dry, even a little dusty. Miss Torrido seemed too skinny to need such floppy underpants.

Mary decided to go home and write Kay Linda the letter she deserved. "I will always think of you as a friend," she would begin, her virtue in every way superior. "Whatever seems to have come between us cannot . . ." No, "can in *no way* . . . wipe out . . ." No, "can in no way *erase* . . ."

At Frank's desk she sat writing, curling every capital letter so it became neat and well bred. "I have nothing against Jimmy Rosemary but has he ever lent you his math homework?" she was writing when Miss Torrido's front door slammed. The bang of it made her sit back, and at arm's length she suddenly saw her handwriting as a copy of Christine's—embroidered, self-conscious. Almost immediately the Thompson front door quivered in its frame, and Frank's leaning umbrella slid down the wall and fell. Miss Lila never closed her own door so hard. Mary turned her letter over and rose slowly to her feet.

She stood by the desk, motionless. Listening. Miss Torrido always closed her door gently, and usually stood aside keeping hold of the knob so no visitor could bang it shut, either. In fact, when Mary was eleven Miss Torrido had paid a call to ask Mary not to slam *theirs* because the vibrations sometimes caused her wildflower prints to leap off their nails. And after that I never did, Mary thought. I pressed wildflowers. I put some in Saran Wrap for her to use as a bookmark in her Catholic Bible. Miss Torrido had shown her the New Testament Confraternity with the Protestant version printed in a separate column for easy dismissal. The division made Mary nervous.

Though Mary sat down to her letter again, she did not write. No furniture was being moved next door, but the TV was still loud.

Soap operas? Never. She tore up the letter. In the kitchen Mary dialed Miss Torrido's number. No answer. Through the wall she could hear the phone ringing on the table in the room just beyond Christine's china cabinet. Mary set her own phone on the counter and went to press an ear against that wall and thus locate Miss Torrido's footsteps moving through the apartment, but she heard only murmuring reconstituted lovers' voices and ringing. Plus, of course, Mary's own body noises to whose volume she was miserably sensitive today. The cola seemed to be boiling in her stomach.

Leaving the next-door telephone to ring (nine . . . ten) Mary opened her front door to make sure Lila Torrido's car was still in its usual parking space (twelve . . . thirteen). Slowly, then, she walked down the front steps past her bike and turned up Miss Torrido's stairs, where the black railing had been made to support a clematis vine with blooms like purple saucers. Surely if her door had been slammed its lock had caught, but, no, when Mary touched the knob, it lightly turned. Miss Torrido's door eased slowly back of its own weight—nothing was plumb in these buildings, Frank always said; nothing was level. Mary waited immobile while the door drifted very lazily downhill.

The first thing that came gradually in view was broken glass on the floor—a small piece, then the shattered frame of one wildflower print (columbine, said Miss Torrido), and at last she was staring at the print itself, the flower stepped on and dirtied.

Mary would have run, but hadn't this front door been slammed behind whatever thief had dumped out those chiffonier drawers? Besides, the telephone was ringing (sixteen) from her own call (seventeen), and it seemed important to disconnect from this end that disturbing noise she had set jangling.

Mary kept her mind locked on that ringing telephone as she stepped over glass into the living room and tried not to focus on opened chests or overturned chairs. She picked her way around cushions and over lamps to where the phone (eighteen . . . nineteen) kept ringing even louder; then, with a snatch, lifted and set the receiver down again as if the plastic might burn her hand. In the new silence her eardrums continued to vibrate, and she glimpsed, not even cross-eyed, the pale quivering bulb of her own enormous nose, like Everest. Mary closed her eyes. Over distant television noise she called, "Miss Lila?" There was rust in her throat. She looked past the shambles someone had made of the living room toward the small hallway and swung her full attention there like a searchlight, moved toward that space unerringly, calling louder, "Oh, Miss Lila?"

In the narrow hall even the flowered carpet runner had been wadded against the baseboard. The bedroom door stood open. Mary absently tried to kick the rug back into place as she walked toward that open door and the sound of television. "Miss Lila?"

And Miss Lila almost seemed to be waiting for Mary and watching from where she sat on the floor, wide-eyed and wide-legged against the bureau, had it not been for the bloody hair strung down her face and even trailing into her half-open mouth.

Mary cried out, but the name twisted itself into a moan.

She wanted to run, but it seemed impossible to stop hanging on to the doorway and to move back from the sight of Miss Lila Torrido with her nightgown crumpled around her waist and her false teeth lying on the floor near one stained hand.

That's what *dead* is, Mary thought. And still her hand would not let go; she could not move.

Another gasping noise came out of her throat by itself.

That sound, so obviously unheard by the bloodied Lila Torrido, helped drive Mary one stumble backward, then two, then she was falling over the lumpy hall carpet and scrambling over things that lay broken on the floor to fly out the front door— not slamming it—and in great jumps over stairs into her own house to the kitchen phone.

She tore off Frank's number for the Hillsborough sheriff, then forced her jerky hand to dial twice. As it rang she lifted her right hand in midair; the fingers would not tremble to her direct gaze but became shaky just out of sight; the backs of her legs felt limp as ribbons. She slid down the kitchen wall and sat on the floor (too much like Miss Lila, she thought wildly, and clamped together both legs) as she told the dispatcher that yes, she was the sergeant's daughter, and yes, a real emergency. Help.

In fact, she did not sound like Frank Thompson's daughter, even to herself. She sounded old.

Her ear filled up with the static of false tries and then, at last, with her father's voice. In the middle of trying to tell him, she started to cry.

OTHER LAWMEN whom Frank radioed reached the Ramshead Chateaux ahead of him. By the time he came screeching down the road in his black-and-silver patrol car, police had sealed both gates to the parking lots and were systematically searching the grounds and buildings. Though other drivers had been stopped for questioning, they waved Frank through. Already an ambulance had backed up the short walk to Lila Torrido's door, and someone crowding inside had leaned too hard on her stair rail of imitation wrought iron and snapped off the flowering vine of which she had been so proud. Neighbors, in fact, had vowed that Miss Lila diluted her own piss in a jar to fertilize organically those purple blooms—all wilted now.

Frank asked the man at the door, "Where's Mary?"

"She's safe in your place."

"How long had the woman been dead?"

"Two or three hours at least. We didn't make Mary look at her the second time."

"Thanks, Harold."

He found Mary telling her story to a tape recorder and to Marlene Fowler, a city hall secretary the police had borrowed. They must have thought Mary needed a woman's touch.

She came into Frank's arms, but not headlong. One thing illness had already taught her: how to endure. He put his face into her red hair, wondering how much taller her kidneys would allow her to grow.

"They hurt her," Mary was whispering over and over into his chest.

"It happened early this morning; we were both already gone," he said, not wanting Mary to think some rescue should have been attempted.

"I heard them hitting her."

"No, you didn't," said Marlene Fowler quickly. "That was all over before you got home. What you heard was them wrecking the apartment."

"Them?"

Marlene shrugged at Frank.

Pulling loose from him, Mary said she should never have gone riding with Kay Linda in the first place. "I should have been visiting . . . her."

The proper name had become unnatural now that "Lila Torrido" no longer described what Mary had found next door.

"Honey, you'd only have been hurt yourself."

"Killed," said Marlene flatly. So much for a woman's touch. "Probably raped."

"Oh, surely not," said Frank. "Raped?"

"At least molested, that's for sure."

He saw Mary's throat and chest lock and spasm once, but she was able to swallow her need to cry. The tape recorder was still operating. "Have you gotten all you need from Mary?"

"A few last details?"

He patted her awkwardly. "Then I'll go see what I can find out. You'll be OK here, Mary? You need anything?" She shook her head. What if the murderers had come into the wrong apartment? As he left, he could hear Marlene pressing for which TV program had been playing, trying to pin down the hour and minute the murderers had left. Or trying to pin down when they had finished with the old woman and decided to mask the noises of their search.

From the door he asked Harold softly, "They beat her to death?"

"Looks that way. Somebody hit her with his fist and then it got out of hand with shampoo bottles or something. She had on one of those little headset radios? They drove one earphone all the way into the brain."

Frank hoped Mary had not seen that. Miss Lila had maybe been raped while Willie Nelson was still singing deep in her ear. "Is it the same old thing? They thought she had Capone money?"

"I guess. How's your girl?"

"OK. Considering."

"Be glad she didn't come in sooner and catch them."

"I am."

The ambulance pulled away, its light no longer blinking. There was no rush to an autopsy. Frank started aimlessly up Miss Torrido's stairs, stepping carefully over the torn vine.

"Not yet," said Harold with a nod at her open door. "They're still working in there."

"I wonder who ought to be notified? The Capones she claimed are all dead."

"I bet there's nobody at all."

"Mary said she had a nephew to come this summer."

"If he was really a nephew."

"Yeah."

"Probably drugs involved; nine times out of ten it's drugs. And the way they did her—somebody was crazy on drugs and planned to buy more." Harold leaned over the railing to spit, but the sight of wilted clematis stopped him. "Used to, people shot boyfriends for jealousy or maybe they poisoned kinfolks so they could inherit the farm, you know? Today that would be almost a clean murder. The kind they talk about in the Ten Commandments. But these dopers that will put a knife in you fifty times and write words in your blood? I don't think they used to have dirty murders like that."

Preacher Ware could probably recite him a verse about one, thought Frank. I better call Mama.

"I'll be glad to retire," Harold said.

"If I send for my mother, can she get by the barricade?"

Harold lifted his walkie-talkie. "I'll tell them. Miz Thompson?"

"Mr. and Mrs. Andrew Thompson," said Frank, for she'd never get Dandy to stay away.

Marlene joined them on the stoop. "I'll get this typed up," she said, "so they can decide if there's more they need to ask. Listen, Frank, the coroner offered to give Mary a little tranquilizer, but she wouldn't mix it with the other medicine she takes. But she may not sleep tonight, right next door."

"I'll send her home with her grandparents."

"Even now she keeps staring at the walls on your side as if she could see right through."

Harold finished talking into his radio. "I was just telling him, Marlene, how drugs have ruined this country. Not only murders like this, but every sport is rotten with them."

"The niggers lowered the standards," said Marlene briskly. She snapped her recorder in its case while Harold was glancing nervously on all sides for black policemen.

He said, "I think it's TV, myself. Those boys dropping big rocks off the overpass in Harnett—they was all white. Kids learn on TV you can ride by and just shoot at somebody for pure-T entertainment." He shook his head. "The way we used to shoot at road signs."

Marlene said firmly, "Mostly niggers."

Since the murder was outside his jurisdiction, Frank watched for ten minutes while local officers nodded and passed by. Then he went to his own apartment and paused halfway up the stairs to see into Mary's room without being seen. She was lying in bed, back turned, one palm laid flat to the wall as if picking up vibrations.

Frank moved toward the voices coming nearer his front door,

then met his parents just inside, a finger to his lips. Tacey nodded, but nothing could stop Dandy's stage whispers. "She didn't see them, did she? She's not an eyewitness? I already told the cop outside that Mary's not up to a court trial or anything." Frank kept shaking his head. "Or a lineup, for that matter. I wonder if Tacey and me didn't pass them on the way? Old blue truck, driving too fast. Two white boys in the front."

"Shhh," Tacey said. She raised her eyebrows at Mary's open door. Frank spread his hands in the air.

They did not realize it, but Mary found the drone of Dandy's voice comforting. When its volume dropped she knew they had moved to the kitchen, so no murderers would be coming in that back door. She lay there wondering if there was any age too old or too young for rape. The thought made her clap both hands to her crotch. She thought Miss Torrido hadn't been growing much more hair down there than Mary herself, so hair was not the appeal—no matter what that boy had whispered to her in the school hall about "hair pie."

Beyond the wall policemen were lifting fingerprints and trying to decide what was missing from the apartment. Sometimes she caught their raised voices, but mostly the sounds of movement were muffled. They were there, though; no murderers would be creeping back down Miss Torrido's hall and leaning tonight against this wall to guess where a girl the right age for rape might be sleeping.

Not that Mary would ever sleep again.

She must have, though, because Tacey was whispering overhead when Mary smelled food and opened her eyes. "A little soup," Tacey said as she set down the tray. "You haven't had any other liquid today besides what's posted on the refrigerator door?"

"No," Mary lied. The back window was dark. Was it locked?

Her grandmother clicked on the bedside lamp, though Mary said she wanted to get up and eat at the table.

"Be lazy this once."

From a distance, as dependable as a furnace noise or air-conditioning, they could hear Dandy talking. Not only was that familiarity comforting, but so was Tacey's well-known face, the ugly tray with the picture of George Washington that she had put under varnish with decoupage while in Girl Scouts— even her regular water-soluble vitamin pill seemed trustworthy and customary.

She sat up and accepted the soup bowl. Tacey said, "It was a terrible thing, honey, and I'm so sorry you saw her. But it's over now. They'll put him in jail."

Mary said nothing. She was glad to see this particular soup-spoon, which Christine had once ordered with Betty Crocker coupons.

"I'll leave your door open?" Yes. No murderer would be able to come down the hall without being heard. "If you're not sleepy afterward, you can come watch television."

Eating, Mary decided against it. There would be surprises on television programs. Unexpected entries and departures. She wanted to finish her soup and then linger over the gumdrops and hard candy she was allowed while controlling sodium, potassium, water. She wanted to sleep tonight without the muscle cramps that sometimes snatched at her calves, thighs, toes. Tonight they would feel like tightening fingers; she knew that.

"Call if you want anything?" said Tacey from the door.

She wanted Miss Lila Torrido to come down the hall, healthy and fully dressed, carrying a plate of grainy fudge.

The food almost made Mary's own body familiar again. Refreshed, she got out of bed and pressed her head to the wall, but the policemen had gone, and the room on the other side was empty, silent. She toed off her tennis shoes. Miss Torrido had been barefoot herself. It did not seem right for death to come between breakfast and lunch, before you had even got dressed.

She carried the tray out of her room. Just at the living room arch from which she was admiring the constancy of Dandy's steady monotone, she heard Frank's sharper voice. He was on the kitchen telephone. Mary waited.

". . . that's what they said at the scene. Yes. Terrible. No, but I can check through her apartment if the police haven't already done so? I see."

While Mary listened she looked at the picture of George Washington she had glued to the tray. He was at Mount Vernon, painted by Peale, with his right hand stuck inside his coat, like Napoleon. His face looked sinister.

"No, I didn't know that. Thank you for calling. She's been asleep, yes. Thank you." General Franco hung up. He said vaguely, "That was the hospital. Miss Torrido had had a mastectomy—I never knew that."

The dishes shivered over Washington's military coat while Mary tried to remember her last sight of Miss Torrido. Half of the nightgown bodice had been flat; of course it had—flat but lumpy with scars. Mary could feel soup boiling up in her stomach, wanting out. She backed away, timing a hard swallow to match each step. At her room she set the tray on the hall carpet, then crept inside and closed the door. Now she could barely hear the murmur of Dandy's voice, no longer comforting. She got into bed, touched her own barely budded breast and jerked her hand away. Which cancerous one of Miss Torrido's had been sliced away?

The left, she decided. Over the heart.

IT HAD BEEN PLANNED that Mary would soon bring home a portable dialysis kit packed in a fake suitcase with tooled imitation surface, as if made to hold salesmen's samples. Earlier, nurses had taken her to visit Rodney, a twenty-five-year-old beginning lawyer, who was experienced in its use, telling her he simply took all his legal trips carrying his briefcase and pee-case. Rodney was jovial, with freckles; she imagined him in medical journals featured in before/after ads for the dialysis machine. At Mary's age, Rodney said, he'd often gone to the hospital for the procedure, and sometimes—bored—he would suddenly pound on his chest to set the electronic equipment skittering, with nurses flying down the hall to the rescue. "Not that you should try that," he said, though of course Mary did. He was a handsome boy, almost pretty. She wondered if he plucked his eyebrows.

But the week after Miss Torrido died Mary felt much worse; her urine increased; both eyes looked puffy under a sudden deep tan and dry skin. She felt itchy and sleepless.

Deep in her restless nights, certain she was wide-awake, Mary would hear the slipping sounds of Miss Lila Torrido's bare feet coming down the hall, would turn to see her standing in the door—one arm upraised like Lady Liberty. It was her left arm held overhead and, just as Mary had suspected, underneath was the rough scarred crater where her breast had been hacked away. The warrior's metal hat Miss Torrido wore was not starred like the one on the Statue of Liberty, however, but cupped her head like an Amazon's helmet. Amazons had been single-breasted, too—Mary remembered—but by choice so they could draw a bow more easily.

Miss Torrido kept her arm uplifted so the ragged hole in her chest could be clearly seen, but her right hand rhythmically motioned Mary forward. Out of her bed. Toward the door. Away.

Mary sat up in bed and caught hold of the rope ladder hanging there. Although the hall light only outlined the shape of Miss Torrido, she thought she could barely see the tiny white worms of cancer working away among flesh and ribs. Mary pulled hard on the ladder, but it collapsed heavily onto her from a great height, and she woke tangled in the sheets, frightened.

AS SOON AS they had come down the steps from his apartment, Frank said, "Well?"

"It's hard to tell." Jill let him open the car door for her.

"It's not a bit hard. She's gone downhill, anybody can see it."

Waiting in the front seat, Jill thought through an answer. "Naturally this murder has affected Mary," she said as Frank slid in beside her and turned the key. "You'd worry about her if she showed no effects at all. So she isn't sleeping well—no wonder."

Frank was only driving her home. They had planned to go to a movie, but some anxiety in Mary's face at the thought of their two-hour absence had canceled plans. "Last night I found her standing beside her bed making these noises, these grunting noises. She doesn't even remember it."

"She had a nightmare and stood up in her sleep. Nothing worse than that. With time, her fears will pass. You know that, Frank."

"Time is exactly what I know the least about. Mary doesn't have any to waste, I'm sure of that."

"Nobody does, I guess." The angry flattening of his features made Jill regret her tendency to generalize, even to put Mary into context with *any* girl who'd found a murder victim, *any* person with a chronic illness.

"I'm sorry we'll miss your movie," said Frank—meaning he wasn't.

She waited for several blocks. "She could spend some nights with her grandmother?"

"We tried that. She hollered in her sleep."

"Or with me."

Like a sharp outline suddenly smudged, his profile changed, and Frank reached across to take her hand. "Thanks. Maybe I'll ask you."

"Could you move out?"

"It's a lease. And you know how crowded this town is on rentals."

"When somebody new moves into Miss Torrido's apartment, won't that help?"

"I hope it's a family with two fat parents and five fat children, everybody laughing every minute, everybody singing in the shower, you know."

"I know."

"But it's physical with Mary, too. They talk more about a kidney transplant now."

"What does Christine say?"

"When I couldn't get her on the telephone, I wrote her a letter. No answer yet."

"Does Mary know her mother's been asked?"

"Not from me. But she can figure it out—it's bound to be Christine or me. I haven't said anything. Maybe she wonders if I'm not willing."

"You should explain."

"And give her more to lose sleep over?"

At her apartment building, Jill waved him back into the driver's seat. "Just watch my light come on and then go. She shouldn't be left alone for long."

When Frank slid toward the car window, she was afraid he might say "I love you," mistaking gratitude for more, so she turned quickly away. "Tell her to come spend tomorrow night if she wants. Or pick another night."

He was saying something as she hurried up the walk, so she covered the words by hand waving and shouted good-byes— much like Dandy, she supposed, outtalking reality. She shoved the door, waved again, stepped inside, and slammed. It was no good being angry—who would quarrel back? Miss Lila's killer? A kidney?

Even before Jill's light went on, Frank had thrown the car in first gear, so when her window lit up he could be on his way across town to Mary and her nightmares. He found his own apartment streaming light from every opening, from blazing floor lamps and ceiling globes and both porch fixtures, leaking through every drawn drapery or closed blind, and showing Miss Lila's entryway still sealed with crisscross police tape—a yellow X to mark the spot. With exaggerated noises he rattled keys, banged the car door, loudly whistled his way up the front walk until at last Mary's bedroom curtain twitched overhead while he was posing face forward in the spill of light. Without alarming her, then, he could work the new double locks on their front door and step inside, calling. Her answer from upstairs sounded listless.

"Mary? Want something to eat?"

She was reading, she said. "Maybe later."

Standing by the banister, Frank blew out, inhaled a sniff. He could smell illness in these rooms. His skin could almost feel its dank mist. Someday it might become a visible fog floating above the floor. He called, "Sorry I took so long."

"No problem."

Frank went around clicking off lamps and wall switches but leaving the light on the desk where he spread his folder of clippings about the Torrido murder, plus photocopies of police reports a friend in the department had made for him. Neighbors interviewed. Miss Torrido's acquaintances from St. Thomas More Church—Jill had said she, too, was Catholic. So were the Capones, he supposed. Alibis checked. Lists of similar crimes here, in Durham, Cary, Raleigh, other nearby cities. The methodical search for pattern that had led, in the end, to nothing so far but the isolated event.

Rereading the file, as Frank had been doing for many nights, left him in chilly helplessness. This night as for so many others he finally went to bed too depressed to sleep, too lethargic even to toss and turn with worry. He lay rigid under his sheet as if it were a snowslide.

So he heard Mary from the first: the barefoot steps on her bedroom carpet followed by her opening the door, then down the hall her voice, slightly numbed by sleep. "Wait," said Mary's voice to Nothing in the dark. "Wait, I'm coming."

Frank rolled out of bed too fast and fell over a chair that was always there. Then he was in the hall facing Mary, though she looked through his face at something else.

"Where?" she asked it.

Slowly Frank raised one hand into the path her eyes were making through the air. He had heard that to scare a sleepwalker awake might shock the heart. He whispered, "Mary?"

Almost within reach she came toward him, perhaps toward the window he now kept locked and would tomorrow nail shut. Her eyes were open.

With his hand he blocked her lightly, but she stopped and felt space as if for a high wall that had materialized. Gently with both hands he turned her round. "This way, Mary. It's all right." She led easily to her room door. He murmured, "Time to sleep, now, back to bed." Unerringly she moved to the mattress, sat on its edge as if in thought. "Go back to sleep, Mary." She lay down and drew her knees high, the way a baby sleeps, while he covered her. He waited in case she might rise again.

He did not trust the deep sleep Mary seemed to be in. It took a while to drag the recliner into the hall and block the stairs. Frank wound a sheet around himself before getting into that tilted chair from which he would be able to see her door between dozes. Though his naps were brief and every passing car roared him awake, her door never opened the rest of the night. At daybreak he carried the chair out of the hall, trying with strain to tiptoe. His stiff back and shoulders ached.

At breakfast Mary said, "You catching cold?" when he rubbed his eyes.

He said nothing about her sleepwalking but left early so he could call Mary's urologist from the patrol station. Many calls were necessary, as usual—first he was on rounds, then with a patient or in consultation—but at last Dr. Gorbin listened to his concern and promised to examine Mary carefully when she came for dialysis. He asked about Mary's mother and a possible kidney transplant.

"I'm calling her next. Does it sound to you more, well, urgent? Can I tell Christine that?"

Dr. Gorbin said, "It would be best if surgery could always be done well in advance of urgency."

When Frank got through to Christine's number, a man said she was at a lotion convention in New Orleans.

"A what? Lotion?"

"Lotion, powder, all that stuff." No, he had no telephone number, did not remember the hotel. "She'll be back next week. Thursday or Friday."

Frank left his name and number. "And tell her Mary's sick."

Slowly the man repeated the words to Frank. He sounded like the type who would spit on his pencil point between drawing large, laborious letters. Why, at 9:00 a.m., wasn't the man at work, some work, any work?

"If I don't hear, I'll keep calling."

The next day he went with Mary for the dialysis and met with Dr. Gorbin after his examination.

"There does seem to be a progressive reduction of renal blood flow," the doctor said, "and Mary's blood pressure is up. We're increasing her iron because the hemoglobin has dropped and adding more calcium and vitamin D." He sat there tapping his pen on the desk, like a Dutch boy who might have to use it to plug up the dike and hold back the entire Atlantic.

"I don't want to wait too long," Frank said.

"Of course she's already on the waiting list for a kidney from a cadaver just in case."

Ugly word, "cadaver." He wondered if doctors used it because it didn't sound human, didn't sound like a dead human being. "But that's not the best choice."

"Even if it were, we've got patients who have been on dialysis for several years. Who've been coming three times a week for years to be plugged in for four hours each time. People begging for transplants who have no living relatives to donate." He sighed. "I had one man take his vacation last week, went to Brazil. He never told me, but I know he's gone to buy a kidney from an unrelated donor there. It probably won't work."

Talking with Dr. Gorbin always reminded Frank of the one trip he had taken to Grand Canyon, his walk to the edge, the terrible expectation of the abyss that might any moment open up before him. He made some vague murmuring noise to let the doctor know that he was listening but would just as soon hear no more, a noise that reminded him of the grunts Mary was giving in her sleep.

"Then there's a teenage girl," said the doctor doggedly, "who got her sister's kidney and six weeks later began to reject. We increased the cyclosporine, tried prednisone, tried O.K.T. Three, but she's back on dialysis, back on the list. She's very depressed."

Probably suicidal, thought Frank as he dizzied by the abyss. "You'll have to forgive me, Dr. Gorbin, but I can't weigh which case is more or less deserving—all I think about is Mary."

"Of course." His face in which every cell seemed heavy showed how well the doctor knew each father and his priority, each mother and hers.

But Frank could not think of the others. Instead, he wondered if his friends on the highway patrol could find him a severely injured motorcyclist and get him sent to Memorial earmarked, kidney-marked, for Mary's aid. "You do these transplants all the time, the ones from"—he hardened himself—"cadavers."

"We don't *get* kidney donors all the time," said Dr. Gorbin with a headshake.

The doctor widened his lips almost imperceptibly—a mini-smile. "But I've got one patient—seventy-two—who just left for a Caribbean cruise! It's a dialysis cruise. They have a special room and the passengers rotate in and out." He saw that Frank was unable to smile at this prospect. "But of course more and more people sign the organ-donor cards these days."

Frank wondered who on the list ahead of Mary deserved a kidney more. What about age, reputation, character? Shouldn't there be such a thing as Time *On* for good behavior? He wondered if the doctor's depressed teenage girl was white or black?

He was ashamed.

"YOU'VE GOT TO STOP avoiding all direct contact with Mary's illness," Dr. Gorbin had told him. "Stop sending her grandmother, stop turning your head aside when Mary talks about dialysis—yes, she does mention that you do. As soon as she improves I want to try the home unit, and you'll have to know how to help in case she needs help. Don't treat dialysis like something people do in the toilet."

So Frank had made an appointment to tour the hospital's outpatient dialysis unit in Carrboro—recently moved from a shopping center into a renovated furniture store. From its hot parking lot he noticed how former display windows had been subdivided, curtained. Before opening the broad glass door he tried to close off his own nostrils against the expected smells of piss and blood.

But he stepped into an ordinary office hall, cleaner than most. Two black men were waiting on straight chairs. He could not tell what kind of kidneys were inside either one; perhaps both men were uncles or taxi drivers.

The woman at the desk wore not a white nurse's uniform but something nylon and bright blue.

"Yes, Dr. Gorbin called. Maybe the first thing to do is sit and watch. Later I'll show you around and answer questions."

With dread he dropped into another straight chair and forced himself to face into the large open room where couches and end tables had once been lined up for sale. Now there were rows of long blue recliners that matched the nurse's dress, and by each a stack of blue machines that looked like stereo equipment or VCRs with dials and knobs and fat white tubes.

No, there! In the third chair a young woman lounged with her eyes fixed on a high television screen: the tube *drooping* between her and the blue machine surged red with blood. Frank glanced at the pamphlet the nurse had put into his hand. "Your blood leaves your body a cupful at a time," it said—though that was the biggest cupful Frank had ever seen, and because he kept picturing Mary in that chair, Mary's arm invaded by something alien, artificial, Mary's tube torn loose so that her life would run out by accident, red on that vinyl floor—he felt as faint and sick as at his first car wreck years before. He closed his eyes.

But then the girl patient laughed at some joke on her television program and—when he unwillingly made himself watch—she lifted the arm that seemed so securely harnessed and flapped one hand in midair, giggling.

He saw, then, that in the other chairs men and women were calmly working crossword puzzles or filling out forms, that some were sewing or knitting or reading, and that many kept talking back and forth as if all were traveling on the same bus this summer afternoon—from different homes, to different destinations—but now drawn into companionship by a mildly boring trip they shared.

The impression was so vivid that Frank almost felt himself flow down the road with them, and he caught hold of his own hard chair, unwilling to go. He became rapidly angry at finding them all so calm. One woman was dozing. When one man shifted in his chair and let out a fart that caused the first girl to whoop a laugh even harder it seemed like a sacrilege. To be dying? In such unconcern! Why weren't they making every moment count?

He leaped up, intending to go home and perhaps hug Mary

till she gasped, but the nurse gave a quick nod and came from her desk with a friendly smile. "Let me show you where we give home training, since Dr. Gorbin said you'd be coming in for that."

No, he could never do that. *Goddamn Christine!*

"You know what this one's for," said the nurse a bit wryly. She pointed to a separate room with its own chair and equipment. Frank wondered if the mayor, or perhaps doctors, warranted special treatment. "That's for AIDS," she said. He followed her into a small room where wall posters showed foods x'd out: eggs, cheese, meat, bananas, and salty foods, the watery ones; then the red check marks by favored items low in sodium and high in calories.

"Oh, Mr. Bolton. Do you mind?"

"Not a bit," said the skinny man lying down with a sheet folded only across his genitals. Frank snapped his eyes away from his flat furry chest and the plastic tube stuck straight into his abdomen as if it had been shot there. "You'll see it isn't so bad," said the man with a grin at Frank. "I play tennis and everything."

"I'm not the one—" Frank began, but the man was half flirting with the nurse and interrupted while winking at her. "I know this woman from Durham that rolls up her empty bag and sticks it right inside her brassiere—people think she's as big breasted as Dolly Parton."

Another nurse came in carrying a fat plastic bag full of clear liquid and larger than those Frank had seen hung over hospital stretchers for transfusions. "I think your tube's unplugged, now, Mr. Bolton, but let's test it."

Frank pulled back in case she might bend over to blow into the tube standing up from the man's belly like a drinking straw and distend him into a balloon. He hurried after the first nurse to study the poster that explained how Mary could carry her own bags of dialysis solution and do her exchanges by gravity four times a day and then a fifth time overnight. "So," finished the nurse, pointing, "she won't have to come in and have the process automated by machine."

"Wouldn't it be easier to use her arm?" Frank managed to ask. Behind him did he hear or imagine a liquid gurgle?

"Mary was hoping at first to avoid any scar that a fistula or graft might leave? Didn't she tell you?" The nurse smiled. "And how she asked the surgeon to locate her catheter low enough so she'd be able to wear a bikini?"

Maybe she had. Dr. Gorbin was right; Frank had closed his ears.

The nurse repeated all this to Mr. Bolton with his own inserted tube and even waggled her finger around the unbelievable place where it simply disappeared inside him as if into a milk shake of flesh. "This is Mr. Thompson's daughter we're talking about; she told Dr. G. that when she was rich and beautiful and transplanted she wanted to have a tattoo of a flower put where her catheter had been so she'd be a sensation on the beach. A yellow sunflower, she said."

Frank could not stop himself. "She's not that cheerful now. She's very depressed."

"Well, now, that comes and goes," offered the half-naked man. He tried to nod, hard to do lying down. "I spent a year thinking that since my kidneys had just shut off by themselves that they might turn back on again—remember that, Gloria?" The nurse nodded. "I'd sneak down to the laundromat and set my ass—sorry, Gloria—up against one machine after another while it was shaking? I leaned into clothes dryers and televisions and people's truck motors—you know? You ever had a clock stop ticking that you could shake and get started again?"

Frank nodded.

"A couple summers back I went outside every thunderstorm we had because it might help to get struck by lightning, just a little strike—and, hell, if it was a big strike who gave a damn!" He laughed. "But all that passes, Mr. Thompson."

After you got accustomed to being dialyzed instead of vibrated, struck by nephritis instead of a lightning bolt? Frank
couldn't see how any kidney patient kept on feeling *real*—why
blood would still feel like your own when it came back into
your arteries after being filtered through some sewage unit. Mr.
Bolton had not been far wrong setting his ass against household
appliances, getting ready for today when they unclogged his
tube so he could mechanically operate again. Frank thought
about inside and outside toilets. He wondered what nasti-
ness stayed behind inside machines and what the janitors did
with it.

Frank forced his attention back to Gloria, who was showing
him an empty plastic bag like the ones Mary would use for what
was called C.A.P.D., machine-free dialysis. Gloria lifted the
bag overhead, then held it below her knees—still talking—
finally rolled it into a long plump tube that could enhance at
least two flat-chested women. "Then after several hours, she
unfolds the bag and puts it lower than her abdomen so the
dialysis solution will drain back out. So do the toxic wastes.
You throw this away and you're ready to put more solution into
the peritoneal cavity." She lifted the bag overhead again. "It
takes about half an hour to put it in."

Frank cleared his throat. "I don't see exactly how I could
help with any of that or that Mary would even want me to."

"We'll teach her the procedure, of course, but you need to
see it done a few times in case you ever have to help. Part of
your job is supportive—to help her keep everything very clean
so she'll never get an infection, to double-check her schedule,
to keep a good supply of solution on hand. And you'll want to
help Mary think ahead. Where will she do this at school, for
instance? Or if you two take a trip?"

"Yes." He needed air. Frank really thought there were some
jobs women were biologically fitted to do while men were not.
He didn't see any male nurses putting needles in arms here or
unclogging people's tubes! "My mother has been the one in-

volved," he said. "Until now, she's gone with Mary most of the time."

"But she doesn't live with you, Dr. Gorbin said."

No, although maybe Dandy was right; maybe they needed one big house together.

Later, in Jill's bed, when the distinctions between men and women seemed especially clear and vivid to him, Frank tried to explain why he would have been a poor schoolteacher or nurse, why any man would. He was expressing himself very well, too, when she suddenly rolled over out of bed in one motion, hit the floor running, and slammed the bedroom door behind her.

"Shit." He got his voice in order and called very carefully, "Jill? Honey?"

Down her tiny hall he heard the roar of water entering her washing machine. He had noticed before that when she was angry she turned on electrical switches. It was morning; he doubted there was anything more to launder than her underwear from yesterday.

Naked, he went to the door and called her again.

She yelled back, "You're a very rigid man, you know that?"

Her last word was cut off by a ringing noise, so he wondered what appliance she had switched on next, only to realize it was the telephone.

She reached around the corner and thrust it at him. "And I don't like you leaving *my* telephone number!"

The phone chuckled in his ear before he heard, "That you, Frank?"

"What's wrong?" snapped Frank, for he did not have early shift and Tacey had stayed the night with Mary.

"They just found Wilson Clegg shot."

"Dead?"

"No, but he's critical. They got him at Duke."

And all the troopers were being called in—Frank knew that without asking. "I'll pick up a uniform and come."

Elmo hung up. In the kitchen Frank tried to get behind Jill, where she was grinding leftovers in her garbage disposal, to rest his face against her plaited hair. She wriggled loose.

"I've got to go into work," he said and took full advantage of the situation by adding, "A trooper's been shot."

She stiffened, then let his fingers creep around her until he tightened both arms.

"I didn't mean to piss you off. I'm old-fashioned."

"Sexist," she said. "If you weren't sexist, when I became a vet you'd come work for me in my clinic, and you'd be a lot safer."

"Work *with* you?" He put a wet kiss under the fold of her ear.

"With, with. Be careful, Frank."

"Always am." So was Wilson Clegg. Probably stopped somebody carrying heroin or coke.

The morning air was heavy with dew and the promise of heat when Frank let himself into his own Ramshead Chateaux apartment, quietly, but as soon as he closed the front door his mother came out of his bedroom carrying a rusty piece of plumbing pipe as long as her own leg.

"My God, where did you get that?"

"I found it in my backyard. You're lucky I wasn't waiting behind the door," Tacey said on the stairs. She gave him a look intended to measure the effects of a night of riotous living. "Came home to get a little rest, did you?"

"They've called everybody in," he said, already taking from the front closet his uniform in its dry-cleaner bag. He half hid the gun belt underneath. "Is Mary OK?"

"She seems much better. Why, I think they're finally getting this thing under control, Frank, don't you?"

He shrugged. Her optimism amazed him, but probably it was a help to Mary. If Jill were here, she'd see how the female instinct worked.

"Mary says you're to take her to the Carrboro unit yourself today."

On the stairs he looked back and saw from Tacey's bruised eyes that she had slept badly, that she was using the metal pipe like a cane. "That might depend on what else happens. Wilson Clegg's shot."

"He's not the Clegg that stood up for you at your wedding?"

"Yes."

Wilson Clegg. A bachelor himself, never planned to get married as long as his uniform was enough to get him one piece of ass per week. "Usually there's more," he'd say, "but when it drops to one every two weeks, I'll know I'm past my prime." The best year of Wilson's life he'd been stationed in the county he grew up in, where girls who wouldn't even date him in high school but who were now married and bored would wave their speeding tickets low above their laps and wink.

Frank was getting into his patrol car when a man walking by the apartment said to his little boy, "If you're not good, that policeman's gonna put you in jail."

It burned Frank up to hear parents say that. He slammed the car door and stepped onto the sidewalk, frowning. "That's not so," he said to the boy, "but I'll put your daddy in jail if he doesn't treat you right!" They hurried past. Frank got into the car and started it, but sat still until he had calmed down. Wilson Clegg. Goddamn.

He remembered seeing Clegg just after New Year's, when Clegg had made a resolution to give up drinking and women. Frank asked him January 2 how the resolution was working out. "Not so good," Wilson said, shaking the head that was beginning to go bald. "Most miserable afternoon I ever spent."

There was heavy traffic on Frank's radio as members of Troop C were called in or dispatched.

Headquarters was jammed, since everybody off duty had been summoned but not yet assigned. "What happened?" Frank asked in general. Like a jigsaw puzzle, pieces of news came back to him from the crowd—"Not far from Wake Tech . . . stopped a new Ford . . . van pulled up behind . . . called in one license but not . . . in the head and the neck . . . both of them gone by then . . . Jimmy Reece got there; the big one, naw. Not the white boy . . ."—and came back studded with "fuck" and "hell" and "bastard" peppering the words like buckshot. The roomful of troopers gave off a slight but sharp smell, something to make a bear throw up his head a mile away.

Frank pushed through to Elmo. "Who's been to see Wilson's mother?"

"Caldwell went."

"That's good. I guess it was dope?"

Elmo guessed so. "How's Mary?"

"With her it comes and goes," said Frank before he could stop the echo of Mr. Bolton from dialysis. "Comes and goes," he repeated. He knocked with one fist on his own chest. "You can see this thing did old Wilson a lot of good."

Elmo, too, knocked on his bulletproof vest, each proving its lucky presence to the other. Elmo said, "They got anything new on whoever killed your neighbor?"

"You don't think there's a connection?"

"Maybe a dope connection, but she probably got users; Wilson got dealers with a load."

There was a shifting in the room, announcements made. Some of the troopers left, and through the glass Frank could see them sprinting to their cars as if every second still counted. "There'll be a lot of Raleigh women crying tonight, and their husbands won't know why. Poor Wilson."

He saw Jimmy Reece come in, big as a wrestler, his skin so black that some troopers called him a blue gum, but not to his face. Frank reached through the others who were questioning him to touch Jimmy, who raised his voice, "Hey, Frank. He was still breathing when I got there but not talking, no. They got the plasma started before they even took him out of his car; that oughta help."

It seemed to Frank there was some kind of undertow that pulled across even the sky he had thought he knew—that under it at every moment troopers were carrying corneas in boxes, while machines were keeping livers alive long enough to be moved and reset, and blood was running out of Mr. Bolton's arm and in a long river overhead for miles and then into Wilson Clegg's; and that like an invisible cyclone these constant transfers of body parts and liquids were whirling in circulation at every moment but went unnoticed until something awful opened your eyes.

"You want some coffee, Frank? You don't look good."

He ended up spilling half the coffee on himself when he went with Elmo to set up a minor roadblock on one of the roads the killers were unlikely to take, or had taken already.

Touching the wet place that looked as if he had pissed on himself, Frank said to Elmo, "They're coasting me, aren't they? Giving me easy stuff, because Mary's sick."

"I doubt it," said Elmo, driving.

"They are. Hell, I want hard stuff. The harder the better."

"I hear Clegg was having a real light week, not but a few tickets here and there. You never know."

But why was it, Frank wondered, that you never got used to expecting the unexpected? That in your mind there was a normal night with no wrecks, and in your life there was a good marriage without arguments, with smart kids who would grow up into good citizens? Why didn't you come to know that burglary was normal, that shooting was normal, that everybody got sick and died no matter how sweet the delay?

When he threw his coffee out the window more of it flew back and stained his sleeve.

"It's not your day," Elmo said.

Let it be Mary's, then, thought Frank. He wondered whether or not, if Wilson died, his mother would donate his organs.

*   *   *

THE NAMES OF TROOPERS shot down while on routine patrol are fitted into the state patrol's long war story—James Brown, Giles Harmon, Ray Worley, Bobby Lee Coggins. But Wilson Clegg did not become a name on that roster, so Frank—who had visited the hospital room twice while Clegg was still unconscious and caught himself staring through flesh toward the place where his two healthy, functioning kidneys continued to operate unseen—was glad he had said nothing.

He went with Mary next morning to the Dialysis Center and steeled himself to sit in the same room while she practiced attaching the bag, walking around, taking it off again. He could not bring himself to touch anything.

"What if I spill this all over myself?"

"You won't," Gloria said.

"People bump into you at school and on the steps and everything."

"It won't come loose if you do exactly what we've practiced."

It was Frank more than Mary who cringed at the thought of a splash of this . . . this *chemical*, manufactured urine, sloshing onto her shoes and socks while her classmates snickered. When Nurse Gloria had him alone she startled him by laying her fingers on his face. "Right there," she said, pressing. "The frown lines in the forehead. The mouth turned down. You think Mary doesn't see?"

"I'll stop letting it show."

"No, what you need is to change your feelings, not struggle to control them."

"I will," said Frank.

She put the tip of one finger onto his chin. "Stop setting your jaw."

That afternoon they went to the stable to see Chancy for the first time in weeks. Mary seemed unusually well and happy. She turned sideways so Jill could see her new silhouette. "I'm at least thirty-four," she bragged, thrusting out her chest, "maybe thirty-five. And that's with no fluid in it!"

"Makes me jealous," said Jill. "Are you riding today?"

"Oh. Well maybe not yet. Till I'm used to it. And everything. Has Chancy missed me?"

"Every day."

She started to run down the barn aisle but checked herself, then moved sedately as if her shoes were touching not the pale wood shavings underfoot but the spaces between each one. Frank felt as if his Adam's apple had twisted in his throat.

"She's looking better," said Jill.

"Or trying to look better. I wish they'd find her a donor. I wish Christine would call."

Jill was frowning. "Your mother told me something different from what you said, Frank, about Dr. Gorbin having a kidney list. It's not some priority list the way you understood. Everything's on computer in the whole Southeast, and when a kidney becomes available the computer pulls out everybody who has that tissue match, and they go from there. Mrs. Thompson says she told you that."

"Maybe so. What a crapshoot, though."

Both of them watched Chancy nibble at Mary's shoulder. The sight made Frank think of the colored butterfly on Jill's shoulder, of the flower Mary had said she would someday tattoo around the hole where her tube had been inserted. He'd known a man once with a rabbit tattooed on his buttocks, escaping at speed into the anus.

Mary moved into Chancy's stall. Jill put down her rag so the sharp smell of silver polish drifted away. "What are you thinking? Something gloomy, from the looks of your face."

"No," he said.

He must have sounded short, even irritated, because she snapped back, "First you're upset because you're facing some unfair system doctors invented. But when it turns out to be no more than the odds about who will reject a particular kidney or not—is that just as bad?"

"You're not a parent. You just don't understand."

She looked as if she might cry. Frank knew they were quarreling too much, that in her presence he was either tense or focused somewhere else.

"I'm a woman," she said. "And I'm not stupid."

"You always drag men and women into it, don't you?"

"No," she said, in such a flat tone that he knew she was imitating him.

"I don't even know how stupidity got into this."

She gave him a look that pinned the label squarely on his forehead, and he turned away, muttering, "If you were more of a woman, you'd be more sympathetic."

"Oh, sure," she said, "because sympathy comes naturally to women, and all your goddamned silences come naturally to men."

He said wearily, "What is it you want me to say? There's always something you expect me to say, but I don't know what it is."

"Tell me what you're feeling."

Frank wondered what that was. Rage? Or just fatigue? Some time back Tacey had let slip her opinion that he was too old for Jillian Peters. She might be right. He was aging every day.

Into his silence she said, "Well, that's great, just great, knowing exactly how you're feeling in exactly those words."

He let out a sigh. "Jill?" But nothing else came.

She waited, then made the decision to quit waiting and dropped onto a stool near the western saddle whose silver fittings she had been polishing. With a dry corner of cloth she scrubbed a shine into what looked like a coin embedded in the tooled leather.

He tried what had always worked with Christine. "You look beautiful."

She made a sour face by folding out and down her lower lip. "Maybe you ought to get counseling," she finally said. "You need more than your mother and me to get you through all this."

"I don't need counseling."

"It's not manly, I suppose?"

"It's not necessary."

They were glaring at each other. Frank knew he should change the subject, but women always wanted more than that, wanted things withdrawn and apologized for, wanted every scab picked off. A man would just bring up the football score, and both men would seize on it with relief.

She snatched a handful of hay out of a nearby bale and pushed it prickly toward him. "Here, have a bite. Asses like it."

He hoped Mary would not come out of Chancy's far stall and see them frozen in this stiff tableau. The life of women seemed to him too intense, too tiring, always at flood. He doubted Mary would ever have the adult energy to live it, not now.

And in a flash came the sudden bright answer to practical problems. If he married Jill? If Jill lived with them, she and Mary could talk at the level females wanted. And Jill, who had gently tugged foals out of mares with an easy turn of the forefeet, Jill would know how to handle Mary's illness, what to say, how to touch her lightly even near the spot pierced by a plastic tube.

Without stopping to think, he suddenly bent and bit down on the stems of hay in her extended hand. "I'll eat it, crow too, if you want me to." There, he thought. Satisfied?

"Oh, Frank, for goodness' sakes, spit that out." She dropped the rest, frowned when he kept one stalk to chew. "I can't figure you out."

"It'll take years," he said with what he hoped was heavy meaning.

She rubbed absently at a bit of tarnish he could not see. "I've already committed some years," she said carefully, "to school." Then she changed the subject so smoothly it confused him. "It said on the radio that Wilson Clegg's out of danger."

"Better than that," he said slowly. "Doing well. And the Virginia patrol caught the men in the van. The Ford turned up empty last night in Elizabeth City, and they pulled the van this morning."

"Carrying dope?"

"Cocaine. From Florida."

When she tugged the stiff fescue stem from between his teeth and tossed it aside, he could smell the polish on her fingertips. What would it be like to live with a woman so centered on horses and other animals? Once he had gone with Jill to a horse show and on out to dinner with her and other trainers, and he had never heard so much horse talk in his life. It was a one-track life, like the showring. Round and round.

She was saying that maybe Frank ought to take up a different line of work. "Something safer. Mary needs you." She tipped her head to indicate Chancy's stall, from which Mary's distant cooing could be heard.

"If I started selling insurance, would you marry me?"

"That's the damnedest proposal I ever heard." She decided to smile, as if he were teasing.

"Or if I don't sell insurance. How about marrying me anyway?" He watched her smile twitch and shrink.

"Frank?"

"I not only turn into the most careful and safe trooper in North Carolina, but I come home every night and talk about my feelings. Will you marry me then?"

With a sigh, she said, "I can't tell if you're sarcastic or not."

"Not."

"You're forgetting my school plans."

"No, when they call the roll you can correct the name to Jillian Peters Thompson—how about it?"

"They know me on the circuit as Jill Peters. I've never once thought of changing my name!"

"Well, why not?" Privately, Frank expected that Jill would lose interest in vet school once married; tired of that long commute, she'd find herself pricing sewing machines and carpets. The change would surprise her.

"It's taken me some time to build up a reputation among horse people."

Some time—at twenty-four? He shook his head.

"I don't know why, Frank, but this . . . this proposal . . . but you don't sound sincere."

He spread his hands. "I am, though, I am. You want me to kneel and ask again?" With one shoe he scraped hay and clean shavings toward himself for a possible cushion. "Jill, will you marry me?"

She said nothing.

"Don't you want children? Will you marry me?"

"No," she said, catching him halfway down.

"No?" Almost on one knee, he stopped.

"Not now. Maybe sometime."

"Hell, maybe never." Frank jerked himself upright and headed for Chancy's stall at a near run. He called, "Ready to go, Mary?"

She called him back, hurried after. "Don't do this to us, Frank. Don't throw me a marriage proposal in some offhand way and then get pissed off if I don't swoon from pleasure."

He threw at her as he moved, "For somebody who talks about her feelings, I don't understand you a goddamn bit."

Mary's head appeared over the stall door. He hoped she had not heard.

But Jill called from behind him, "Are you just going to walk off without talking about it?"

He yelled back, "Talk about what? Talk about no? Come on, Mary." When he drew abreast of Chancy's stall he kept walking rapidly toward the bright opening at the far end of the barn. He thought it was as much light at the end of the tunnel as he had seen in a long time. "We'll go out this way," he snapped toward Mary's startled face.

"Oh. Well. I was thinking I might try to ride a little after all since—"

"Not today. When you've just started wearing that thing."

Behind him came Mary's uncertain, "Good-bye, then, Jill. I might try it Wednesday?"

Jill said something: "Fine" or "Yes" or something. He had thought she might keep running down the barn aisle after him, her face crumpled and her mind changed, that they might agree to marry while Mary herself completed the circle, but the only footsteps were his daughter's, and hers was the voice asking, "What's the big hurry, General Franco?"

A general in retreat. He kept marching. "You know you've got to change that fluid four times today."

"It's nowhere near time," Mary said with a pout when they reached the car.

After he got in, Frank gripped the steering wheel. What a relief it would have been to bend forward and tap his head against the horn. "I think about us having a flat miles from home."

Mary said she'd brought extra solution in the car. "I could hang it up on a tree limb if I had to."

Her cavalier attitude made him drive away from the barn far too fast, saying, "Listen, Mary Thompson, I want you to take this dialysis seriously. It's not some damn game, you know. This is a process that requires care and attention and absolute cleanliness, so—"

"OK," she said.

He shook his head. "With my schedule I'm not sure how much help I can be when—"

"I'll manage," she interrupted. "What's with you and Jill?"

"Not enough."

"You have a fuss?"

"Disagreement."

Though he was watching traffic, on Frank's right came a glimpse of Mary ducking her head. "Because of me? Because I'm sick?"

"Of course not. The world doesn't revolve around you, young lady." It did, though.

"I'm not afraid to stay in the apartment by myself now, so you and Jill should go out more."

"Aren't we getting new neighbors? I saw a moving van this morning."

"The Baileys. I've met Mrs. Bailey. She's got a little boy that's two, and her mother lives with her. Maybe I'll baby-sit."

And rock a child to sleep in the room where Miss Torrido died? Frank made a vague noise in his throat, then said, "What does Mr. Bailey do?"

"He's in jail."

After hitting the horn by mistake Frank waved meekly toward a jumpy pedestrian. "Jail for what?"

"He's in that prison camp up at Hillsborough, but I don't know for what. They've moved here to be closer for visits."

"What a great neighborhood we've got." Frank was wondering if they could afford better quarters on the other side of Chapel Hill; he decided to make some phone calls, test that lease.

"Daddy, did we send flowers to Miss Torrido's funeral?" He nodded. "I still don't see why I couldn't go."

"You weren't really over the experience yet." He had gone, with Jill. The first funeral mass he had ever attended. Had seen Cindy Scofield in the crowd. Well, journalism was a profession worse than Jill's. Feeding off other people's lives. He had watched to see if Cindy took notes, but she seemed to be staring at the priest.

He began asking Mary about Chancy's health, if the farrier had recently trimmed his hooves. "And are you sure the nurse said horseback riding was all right?"

At home, Frank wanted to pace off his tension downstairs while Mary emptied her plastic bag (early, in case inexperience might cause delays) and then refilled her belly with fresh solution. But she cried, "Go away! Go to work!" She rushed him outdoors and threatened to disrobe and spill everything right there in the yard if he kept making her nuts by hovering. He let her poke and push him into the car. She stood by the curb with arms folded (crushing that plastic bag, he thought) until he finally pulled away and drove around the maze of roads in the apartment complex to pass his own door four or five times, just in case.

Next door two women—one young, one white-haired—were unloading an old pickup in front of Miss Lila Torrido's. Already a blue plastic tricycle was parked on the narrow walk, though he saw no child. Another thing: he'd have to find out why Bailey was in prison.

At a Carrboro phone booth he called his mother. "Since I'm on late shift and Mary's still getting used to this home dialysis, would you call and check on her in about fifteen minutes?" Tacey said she'd do better than that; she'd wrap up half a fresh pound cake and carry it over, along with Better Boy tomatoes from her garden.

An hour later Frank and Elmo were stopping traffic on a back road in Chatham County, supposedly to check licenses and registration cards, but primarily to catch drunk drivers weaving home after a long afternoon with beer and chips under hot sun at Jordan Lake. Clegg had probably pulled over a too-slow vehicle with the same suspicion of drunkenness, not expecting the man's partner to park behind him in a van and leap out with a gun.

Not many of the trooper stories Frank knew would make good scenes on the television cop shows. His own shooting, for instance, seemed almost accidental, a link of ill luck at the end of its long but narrow chain. Two AWOL soldiers from Fort Jackson had held up a liquor store in Columbia, South Carolina, and at 2:00 a.m. were driving north too fast on the interstate. Frank clocked them at eighty and gunned his own car across the grassy median to pursue. When he got close enough to activate the blue flasher, the Chrysler—stolen, as it turned out—only drove faster, but after a few miles seemed to give up and ease into the right-hand stopping lane. Frank called in the plate number before he got out, leaving his own motor running. In his headlights he could see the short haircuts of driver and passenger, both of them unnaturally still and facing forward. The hairs vibrated at the base of his own skull as he called out, "Driver? Both hands on the steering wheel! Now!"

And every time since, whenever he stopped any other car at night, Frank still expected to see again that frozen moment in which the driver's head seemed so slowly to turn like a moon its dark side into the light, until the pale face appeared, revealing a bright row of teeth. Then one hand leaped over the seat back. Frank snapped to one side, but before he could get out his Magnum the driver fired through the half-open backseat window. The noise sounded very mild to Frank, a flat firecracker pop, not enough to cause the sensation of being slammed in his side by a two-by-four. He felt no pain at first, just one heavy blow and some nausea. He did not even fall to the pavement but continued making his pivot to kneel on top of his fallen hat, to aim, to see the glass shatter and, instantaneously, the driver's head as well. The other man then leaped from the car and instead of running down the steep embankment toward the woods ran straight into the busy highway. Frank had only time to call and shoot safely once, and miss; but the oil tanker did not.

Later he did not look back on the shooting itself but behind it down the further chain of fortuitous events preceding, any one of which might have happened differently or not at all. Only lately had he begun moving from the causes of that particular October night along the chain of events that fell forward to check on its effects, so that seven years later he had only one uninjured kidney he couldn't give a daughter who had no need for any of the blood or bone marrow he could offer in generous supply. He'd left off his bulletproof vest that critical night, but what if Frank had stood more erect, not turned? He might have taken the bullet in a shoulder, at worst a lung; Mary didn't need his lung. Or what if the Chrysler had been driving at the speed limit and passed that one spot on the interstate without Frank's notice? Or . . .

From across the road Elmo called, "You're not getting heat-stroke, are you, Frank?"

"No, but this asphalt sure holds the heat." It rose from black paving through his black shoes. "Crowd ought to pick up pretty soon." He had been checking his watch, thinking of Dr. Gorbin's statement that every twelve minutes a normal person got his blood filtered automatically, that he and Elmo had each gone through six cycles just standing on the hot road.

"Didn't that truck just pass through?"

"Yeah, going the other way." Elmo waved it by. Frank recognized the make and color, but the Bailey women weren't inside.

Something in the way Elmo stood, arm like a referee's, made Frank remember the adolescent mumps that had cost Elmo one basketball season and also rendered him sterile, how that bad luck had started another chain of events leading to some stranger's accidental baby he'd later adopted. Yet every Sunday Elmo could tell his adult Bible class that a good God ruled everything.

Next Frank checked the license and registration cards of a woman with a car full of children. Watching them drive away he said, "Were you and your wife both Methodists when you got married?"

"She was Primitive Baptist. Thought the Methodist was *High* Church. Hers didn't even use hymnbooks for fear of idolatry. And music? They wouldn't have a piano in the church. No, this preacher would just blow in a pitch pipe to start the tune, and you had to know the words yourself, since they never owned a hymnbook. We've had our problems."

"But you're still married."

"Still married," he repeated with a grin. "Like that optimist falling off the Empire State and yelling at every floor, 'OK so far!' "

"You serious?"

"No," Elmo admitted. "Things are fine." He began wrinkling his face as he always did preparing to force out some four-letter word whose use would enroll him as One of the Boys. "It beats fucking strangers," he announced after long facial struggle and new creases.

"Aw, Elmo, don't bother cussing with me. You never sound natural."

Elmo took off his hat and wiped the red ring around his hairline. "Mama didn't just wash my mouth out with soap—she used Octagon."

After stopping the next car Frank caught an expired driver's license as well as an outdated inspection sticker—little crimes; but they were on the radio awhile writing up the ticket, ignoring the driver's cussing, a natural talent polished to an art. Frank took the opportunity to ask the dispatcher for a background check on a man named Bailey, now serving time in the Hillsborough prison unit. To Elmo's raised eyebrows he said, "The Bailey family's moving into Miss Torrido's place."

"Mary doing OK?"

"Learning home dialysis."

"That's good; what about a—"

"Christine has took her kidneys out of state."

"Oh." Elmo said, "She was looking good at the picnic." He waited. "You ever think about getting married again?"

Frank grunted. "Funny you should ask. I thought about it once today and then quit."

"It would be good," said Elmo with growing enthusiasm. "She really cares about you."

He meant Cindy. Frank started waving at a car that was still very far down the road.

That night, taking off his uniform, he found in the hip pocket one of those postcards Elmo had printed at his own expense, with a color photo of his church on one side and on the back a map to get you there through a tangle of biblical place-names in central North Carolina, over winding roads among Antioch and Mount Carmel and Ephesus and Zion. There was also a schedule of weekly events arranged under the church slogan in capital letters: WE PREACH CHRIST AS HE IS TO PEOPLE AS THEY ARE. Elmo had told him once that this motto appeared twice in an ad the church had in the yellow pages of the telephone book, but Frank had never looked it up.

Frank had discovered Elmo's cards before: tacked to a bulletin board at headquarters for everybody, on the dashboards of patrol cars, taped at his own eye level inside his locker. Since Mary's illness they had been appearing more frequently. As before, he threw this latest card away.

THE MISSING HEAD of the Bailey family next door had been arrested several ascending times: for possession, then sale, of narcotics; for possession of stolen goods; he was now serving time for armed robbery of a twenty-four-hour convenience grocery. Bailey was only thirty, but his fuzzy photo showed he had grown a patchy blond beard to distract from his baldness.

On Sunday night Frank cautioned Mary not to get too thick with the Baileys and to watch for signs of too many strangers in and out next door, maybe buying dope.

"I'll never be any kind of policeman," she vowed with a stamp of one foot that made Frank afraid pungent fluids might spill everywhere. "The Baileys are very nice. You always look for the worst."

"So do lawyers and building inspectors." He stopped himself from adding: *doctors*.

"Schoolteachers grading papers?"

"Newspaper reporters. But in the Bailey case there's precedent. And how did they afford to just pick up and move here while he's in jail? They're from Conover. Nobody has any money in Conover."

"Mrs. Bailey works. She's a dental hygienist."

"Probably bootlegs novocaine."

With her tongue extended, Mary was rolling her eyes out of sight as the doorbell rang. A surprise: Virgil and Georgia Broome, and after dark. Frank was amazed that old car still had working headlights.

As they touched and then dropped hands, Frank wondered why Virgil had never tried the dope business, certainly not from law-abiding scruples. Virgil had convinced the V.A. that his permanent back disability had come from unloading artillery shells in Korea, so he drew that pension, some Social Security; he would take welfare food stamps as payment for key making or odd jobs. So far as Frank knew, Virgil had never paid a dime in income tax.

"Tacey's not here?" asked Georgia as she showed all her upper teeth in a smile. "Give me a hug, Mary." The bright colors in her dress reminded Frank of wallpaper.

"Not so hard, not so tight," Frank warned. "She's got on this dialysis bag that's—"

"Daddy!"

Nervously, Virgil encircled her in a fence of his arms without touching.

"Sunday won't end till midnight, so naturally Mama's at church," Frank said.

"I expect she needs a lot of church." Georgia's lip twitched into a sneer. "Mary, did your grandmaw ever tell you where she got her queer name?"

"It's old-fashioned, she said."

"No, it's not. I happen to know because *my* mama told me that Tacey's mama, your great-grandmother, named her in the outhouse. Well, she did, Frank! She was sitting out there, big with this baby, and they always kept old medicine bottles sitting around where the sunlight would shine through the cracks. Bottles had pretty colors back then, especially blue, and all that summer she was looking at an empty tonic for arthritis that everybody knew was half-alcohol—T.A.C. Eads' Elixir, it was called. 'T.A.C.' stood for the 'Tasty Arthritis Cure,' 'cause we had some, too, that a traveling show came through selling. I don't know how many trips she made out there setting in that outhouse and staring at that blue bottle before it turned into a name for a girl baby. Tacey never told you that? When she was a little girl she even had the very bottle or claimed she did, played tea set with it, I don't guess girls play tea set anymore."

Georgia's chatter grew softer and ran down while she dropped onto the couch, like an actress whose speech has finished.

Virgil had been waiting to get in a word. "We saw the place they choked that woman to death."

"New people have moved in, and we don't even talk about it," said Frank with a headshake.

"Talk about why we've come, Virgil. Sit with me, Mary. I know you're doing real well with this thing you've got to wear, smart as you are." Mary sat and, as if her arm had turned to a wooden handle, pushed her open palm into Georgia's lap. "I can't read 'em on a Sunday, honey, not sure why; it might be that there's too many prayers in the air—who knows? You tell him, Virgil, since we decided it was best not to telephone."

"We could drive Mary down to Jacksonville to see her mama," Virgil said rapidly.

"Start early tomorrow and spend a couple of days. Not right *with* Christine, no, we could park in a campground close by," Georgia said. She gave Mary a squeeze. "We've got the loan of a Ah-Vee."

Frank blinked before he heard it right: RV, recreational vehicle, camper. "No, she can't go, and Christine isn't even there."

"Georgia called her. She's there."

"No, she can't go; she's still learning how to work this home dialysis, and it's real involved. Who in the world would lend Virgil a camper?"

"It's a man owes him money," Georgia said patiently. "How involved can it be?"

"It's not a bit," said Mary, beginning to vibrate on the couch and to beg Frank with her eyes. "I just carry extra bags along and keep everything very clean, that's the main thing."

"In this Ah-Vee you turn a corner into a cutest little toilet you ever saw, and I can Clorox the whole thing tonight, it's that little."

"No," said Frank, "I don't know who's with Christine or what her, uh, situation is, and Mary can't go—"

"I won't even drive," Virgil said. "Georgia's been practicing."

"Because it turns wider than a car. It's even air-conditioned, Frank." He saw that Mary had slid her second hand into Georgia's lap as if grounding herself there.

"Please, Daddy."

Georgia sucked in a breath that seemed to make the reds and blues of her whole dress billow—it was loose and colorful, Hawaiian. "It's her own daughter that Christine will need to see, right in front of her, flesh and blood, before she can make any plans. You understand me, Frank?"

"That'll do it." Virgil nodded.

"We won't stay but a day or two." Georgia's eyes probed his. "However long it takes."

To talk Christine out of a kidney. He watched Mary's tentative smile get wider. It seemed to him one of her dimples had disappeared since spring, that it had been metabolized along with her baby fat and innocence.

"Not early *tomorrow*," he finally said, "because we'd have to clear it with her doctor and get extra supplies, and I want to see this camper for myself. If you went Tuesday morning and got home Thursday?" Mary jumped off the sofa to kiss him under one ear. He was certain he could feel the plastic bag beneath her clothes, that it was bigger than a real kidney, pliable as a giant cyst. He had recently read that poor Turkish peasants were now being paid to fly to London where a kidney transplant could be sold for 2,500 pounds. The chance of a kidney donor dying as a result of the loss was said to be 1 in 5,000. He dug his chin into Mary's red hair, wondering if he could send to Christine the second statistic but not the first.

"BLOOD WILL TELL," Tacey always said, so Mary expected blood to tell Christine and herself how to pick up as mother and daughter just where they'd left off three years before. She could hardly wait. As soon as they got east of Raleigh, she took out her blue makeup kit and put on lipstick. At first she read her library books to make the hours pass faster, but farther east she pressed her cheek flat to the window glass so her skin would buzz while Georgia drove fast down the long, flat highway and Virgil snored in the back. Mary kept her face there, even hours later, after they left pavement for a gray, sandy road. Off the driver's side, the land looked swampy here. Her teacher had said the Venus's-flytrap grew in these Onslow County swamps. On Mary's side were houses and patchy yards and finally a smaller road to the River Haven Mobile Park. She couldn't remember if this would be the Trent or the New River, though she had checked on the map at home.

Virgil woke up to read numbers on low creosote posts. Christine lived at 47. Hers was an older, narrow trailer with a fake bay window and two cars parked in the shade.

With one finger Mary poked her dialysis bag. She had been in a hurry at the last highway rest area, so it felt still half-full, sliding down and sticking out like a bay window itself. Georgia had to park the camper in the hot sun by a silver tank of bottled gas. The motor was still running when Mary jumped out and rushed to the back screen, through which somebody announced that WJNC-radio AM would continue the record show after a commercial break. "Mama? Mama! We're here!" The air had absorbed the smell of hot mud.

Maybe "Tina's Arena" was on the radio. Nothing happened inside until after a throng of females sang higher and higher and got rather screechy at the end; then Christine appeared, repeating, "You're here! You're here!" She wore a green sundress that intensified her eye color almost to artificial. "Honey, come in!"

This time as she swept Mary against a row of sequined buttons topped by a jeweled pin shaped like an elephant, one sharp rhinestone tusk was driven deep; Mary was trying to keep lipstick off Christine's shoulder when the scream burst in her ear, "My God, is that blood?" Christine leaped back, fingers spread on a wet blotch under her breasts.

"Oh damn," breathed Mary, "Hell, oh damn." Moisture was spreading down her new blouse, under the waistband of her shorts. "It's nothing, I'll fix it, Mama." It ran down her stomach and lukewarm between her legs.

"She's hemorrhaging!" yelled Christine. "Do something!"

Virgil shouted, "Where's your telephone?"

"Please," Mary said. "Just—damn." She was dripping onto the kitchen floor. "Just a leak?"

Christine fell back stiff against the refrigerator and held out a shaking hand as Georgia ran in from outside. "She's blown a kidney—what do we do?"

"No, she hasn't." Georgia touched Mary's shoulder. "Which bag has all the stuff you need?"

"It's a square bag, blue, with a red cross on it."

Christine was moaning. "Honey, does it hurt?"

"Where's your bathroom?" Mary asked. "I just need to change bags." She tried with both hands to hold up the collapsing balloon under her clothes, but fluid ran between her fingers. Georgia had jumped off the back stoop. Meantime Virgil had found a phone in the living room and dialed 911. Mary had to trail pale juice onto the edge of the carpet and grab his hand. "I'm all right. Hang that thing up." She whirled to snatch the case from Georgia, one hand still pressing what felt like a wet diaper wadded against her ribs. "Is it down this way?" She could hear Christine moaning. She stepped over Virgil's leg and left damp shoe prints across the tan carpet through the next door-

way, seeing a tiny bedroom first, then a tinier bath. She threw
herself inside and locked the door.

Virgil was bellowing, "See if she needs help, Georgia."

Mary screamed, *"No I don't need any help!"* Her hands began
shaking. When she had set the case on the commode her unsteady fingers could not undo the metal latches. She wanted to
cry, but she felt her whole body had cried already, had dropped
a great splash of tears down her front and inside her new sandals.
She found towels on a metal shelf, stripped, and then dried
herself, using an antiseptic wipe around the tube and its entry
into flesh. Georgia asked through the door if she was all right.

"Fine." Then she attached the new bag of fluid. There was
no place to hang it but atop Christine's douche equipment on
the back of the door.

Mary knew what women did with douche bags but was not
sure why.

Virgil was calling, "Now we can get her straight to a doctor
if we need to. You hear me, Georgia?"

A door slammed; the refrigerator opened. Mary heard radio
voices again, sounding serious—probably news or a thunderstorm watch. Then Christine's voice said at a distance, "What's
she doing now?"

Georgia murmured something.

"But what if now she puts in twice as much?"

Then I'll drain some down the toilet, Mary thought. She
knew what Christine was picturing, because originally she had
pictured it herself—that if you had filled yourself recently and
then did so again, you would run over—like a cup—or else
bloat into strange, sloshing abdominal shapes. She sank onto
the cold edge of the tub.

It felt strange to be naked in Christine's bathroom. Mary
tried hard to remember times her mother must have bathed
her, must have dressed her from underwear out, but it seemed
she alone had dressed herself forever, that no one now except
doctors had ever seen her entire body at once.

She calmed her voice before calling, "Grandma Georgia? I'll need some clothes?"

Just beyond the door Georgia said, "I've already got them —green shorts and a T-shirt."

"No," Mary said. "Not green."

"There's a denim pair?"

"Hang them on the doorknob, please."

But in a few minutes the door cracked open, and Christine's pale, white hand with its long, polished nails came barely into view, holding a pink silk robe. The hand shook it in midair.

"Thank you." Mary threw the robe onto the hamper as the door closed. She waited until the footsteps were gone, then reached around and took her own clothes off the outer knob.

From a distance Christine called, "I've got a big cake with your name on it, OK? They made it fresh this morning?" Virgil said something, and Georgia answered, "Well, it'll take her a little while."

Mary was tempted to send her grandmother back to the camper for one of the library books. This was the boring part —nothing to do but wait while the solution flowed down by gravity—through the catheter, inside. The radio had stopped. With a stretch, Mary opened the medicine cabinet and read softly names off the bottles there. The birth-control pills were the same as Jill kept in *her* bathroom. In the lower drawer was a jumble of specialized beauty needs—not just face cream but cream for certain sections of the face: cream to moisten around the eyes, cream to dry an oily nose, cream to tighten the neck and jaw. For a while Mary tried rolling her hair with an electric curler from Christine's cluttered drawer, then pinched her lashes upward using a tool wide enough for cow eyes. At the end of both failures the plastic container was still half-full.

From somewhere a man's voice said "—doing in there, I got to shave."

Must be the beneficiary of all these beauty creams and pills. It was easy to locate his drawer, containing its meager razor, blades, brush, tweezers. Mary lifted and sniffed his damp comb.

After a few minutes Christine called, "Are you going to want a Co-Cola with that cake?"

"No, thanks." Though thirsty, she was at her liquid limit for the day.

"Tea?"

She could hear Grandma Georgia making explanations. Suddenly a man's loud voice came right through the door. "You, Mary Thompson, how long's all this going to take?"

"Maybe ten more minutes."

"Goddamn. What if I come on in and shave?"

"No! No, don't you do that!" The door felt cool pressed against her bare back. "I can hand out your razor and stuff though."

Muttering about "the fucking kitchen sink" he went away, and Christine soon came to receive his shaving things. "That's Nolan Overcash," she said behind the cracked door. "We call him Nolo. It's just that he's got to be back on the base pretty soon. You're doing fine?"

"Yes, ma'am." Mary arranged razor and brush in Christine's spread palm. "I don't see any lather cream."

"Reach that white bar of soap."

Because the door stood between them Mary could ask, "Is Nolo your boyfriend?"

"Well, *he* thinks so." She withdrew her hand.

In about ten minutes when she had completed the exchange, Mary got dressed, then folded the empty bag under the waistband of her denim shorts, and rinsed and hung up her other clothes. She checked in the mirror that nothing showed under her loose T-shirt. Then she edged into the narrow hall.

The men sat in two facing love seats with a low glass table between. They appeared to be washing down small bites of cake with big drinks of whiskey. Virgil was claiming he had actually talked with General MacArthur once.

Mary stared at the very tall marine. His crow-black hair and sharpened face, deeply tanned, made Mary think he was maybe half-Sioux and half-Masai. When he stood and nodded to Virgil's long tale about the Eighth Army and the Yalu River, his haircut rose too near the ceiling.

Virgil interrupted himself to say, "That's Mary," behind his drink.

Nolo shook her hand in his long skinny one. He wore a gold chain on his right wrist. "You don't look so sick to me." His hand surprised her by suddenly running past hers and up her arm until it squeezed under the armpit. "You could use a little meat on your bones, though."

Mary jerked free.

He said to Virgil, "She must look like her daddy," and sat down, frowning.

"I saw Ridgway in Seoul, too, but he wasn't friendly," Virgil continued.

"Did it hurt, Mary Bones? What you just did?"

"No."

"But if somebody was to reach out"—he made grabs in midair—"and catch hold of that thing by mistake and pull it out of you—Jesus."

Mary stiffened her own hands against her sides so they would not fly forward protectively. "It's taped down," she said, and turned quickly past the bar and stools into the kitchen. Everything was built very close together here.

"Here you are at last!" cried Christine, but instead of trying another hug, she handed Mary a plateful of chocolate cake. Mary started to ask how many eggs in the recipe, but remembered that she was now allowed more protein. Besides, a bakery had made this cake; Christine wouldn't know. The word "Mary" and a scatter of rosebuds had been laid on its top in white icing.

Nolo called, "C'mere, Mary Bones, I want to show you something." He squatted to reach underneath the small couch, and she carried her cake (with no beverage its dry crumbs were packing down in her throat) to where he was arranging a long electronic keyboard across his lap. "Show you how to work this thing. Can you play?"

"Just the bottom part to 'Heart and Soul,' " she lied. She was not about to admit to years of piano lessons without knowing how good *he* was.

"Chords like that go on automatic." He flicked switches until the rhythmic bass accompaniment along with lazy drumbeats sounded through speakers high in the room's corners and seemed to make every object underneath vibrate. Then he showed Mary how to supply the treble melody in imitation piano, trumpet, or sax.

Over the noise Virgil shouted, "Loud! Deaf!" and pointed to one ear, but Nolo kept the volume turned high. An ashtray on the glass tabletop jangled softly. In Mary's head the orchestrated sounds thrummed. Making such massive music with only a forefinger made her laugh out loud.

Nolo, proud of himself, now showed her the button that would add a high-pitched violin to improvise around her tune. Mary's finger became symphonic. Just as abruptly he suddenly snapped off the rolling sounds. "I got to carry this with me, but you can play some more tomorrow."

Slowly, Mary withdrew her hand. Christine said Nolo played in a band downtown, and wasn't she going to finish her cake? Mary concentrated on serious chewing while Nolo unplugged and packed his instrument. "I'm picking up the roach"—Mary thought he said—"and we'll be at the bar till late. Bye, Mary Bones. Miz Broome."

"John Roche," Christine explained vaguely. She was putting a cover on the cake when Nolo turned her around. Maybe they always kissed good-bye, but he backed her against the refrigerator, straddling one of her legs, and tongue-kissed her deeply now for everybody's benefit. Then he reached overhead and got a packet of the green chewing gum that would take liquor off your breath and went out the door humming "Heart and Soul." Christine's face was blotched with pink.

Georgia had been watching it all from one of the high bar stools. In a neutral voice she asked, "Where'd you find him?"

"I was on another date in the club where his band was, and he found *me*, OK?" She finished covering the cake. "He used to play basketball for N.C. State."

"Till he flunked out?"

"I'm not sure what happened exactly. White boys lose out, you know? All I meant was that Nolo's like a big kid—he played ball, he plays in a band. He's playing soldier. When he's fifty, he'll be in the poolroom half his life."

Virgil came to add ice to his glass. "He ain't too white, looks Mexican, you don't plan to marry him?"

Pressing one painted fingernail to her throat she shaped her mouth ready to vomit. "Ack. I don't plan to marry a living soul, OK?"

"Not ever?"

She did not look at Mary when she answered. "Not anymore, not now that I understand the job description. If the man's hungry, you cook it; if he's horny, you fuck it; if a baby starts, you have it and look after it."

Still chewing cake, Mary edged away as Christine raised her voice. "That's right, honey, you look around; make yourself at home, OK?" She shook her head at Virgil. "Nolo's in *my* place at *my* invitation, and when his time runs out, I'm not the one that has to pack."

"He's younger than you," Georgia said, and Christine said, not much.

Mary moved farther away, picked up a figurine off a shelf, checked out both bedrooms, but there wasn't much to see. Everything looked neat and tidy because, except for cosmetics, Christine left no trail or clutter behind her actions—no cigarettes, books, magazines, hobbies, empty glasses, or food dishes. Mary pivoted as she pictured how Christine dressed from this

closet, weighed on these scales, watched TV. And slept with
Nolo, she thought, eyeing the pink bedspread. Her clean clothes
were hung in separate see-through garment bags with an index
tag about colors and belts. Every shoe was paired in place on a
metal rack. The second smaller bedroom, blue and white, looked
as if it had just arrived, prefabricated; even the blue guest towels
folded on the white chair seemed to have been manufactured in
place. While Virgil and Grandma Georgia were in the camper,
Mary would sleep here. From the doorway she swung her head
to check the other bedroom—yes, Christine's pink bed would
be flush against the wall, Mary's blue one just on the other side.
She almost thought of Miss Torrido then, but stopped herself.

Christine called, "Mary? We're going to this seafood place
for supper, so start now if you've got to do anything else to
yourself." Afterward they might stop and hear Nolo play; Christine said they'd probably dedicate a song to Mary. Them bones,
them dry bones, Mary thought.

Later in the restaurant Mary went off her diet, ate too much
of everything she wanted and drank two outlawed glasses of
tea. Guilty, feeling bloated, she lasted as long as she could at
the KitKat Club, where Nolo was too busy to notice them,
much less dedicate any songs, finally whispered to Grandma
Georgia that she ought to get home and make the day's last
exchange. Georgia frowned over the new word, filed it away
with a nod. And before they parted in the yard Georgia whispered across Christine's L.P. gas tank, "Let your mama see the
whole process, Mary, so she'll understand."

But Christine didn't ask to see, so Mary again sat alone in
the small bathroom, this time reading, though Judy Blume had
begun to bore her, since the life she presented and clarified to
other teens had so diverged from Mary's prospects that everybody
in those books seemed to be shrinking and moving away at
speed.

After completing her final exchange of the day, she got into
pajamas. The fluid would "dwell" overnight—such a biblical

word; probably she ought to be reading only *deep* things now, like the Bible. That would scare General Franco to death.

In the hall Christine was waiting with plastic wrapped around her wet hair. She, too, must have used the kitchen sink. "Come tell me all about yourself while this hair color develops."

Mary followed into her bedroom and sat lightly on the pink bedspread. Nolo's shoes were under its hem.

Christine (the word "mother" belonged back in Carrboro in her idealized thoughts, not attached to this woman at her dresser plucking eyebrows) said, "I could give you a permanent while you're here."

"OK," Mary said.

In the mirror Christine held both hands immobile near her face and met Mary's gaze. She said softly, "You don't want any old permanent, do you?" Mary shook her head. Each of them gazed at the other's reflection for what seemed a long time before Christine's tweezers went back to work. "So how's Frank? Is he going to marry that horse girl?"

"Wish he would."

"She's younger than Nolo. And what if the patrol transfers him? It's hard to move a whole stable." She winced, working. "Mama says you've been real brave and sensible, just like a nurse or something, to do all this medical business. I never could in a million years—you must get that from Frank's side. They'd just as well shovel me under the first day. With all you need to do to yourself, when Mama called about coming down I was surprised you even could."

Mary had hoped the invitation had been Christine's.

"She says you've even been riding that horse this week. What's his name? Gambler?"

"Chancy." Mary had sent the name and date written on the back of a snapshot that showed her in the saddle, but she had spotted no framed photographs of any kind in any of Christine's rooms. She said, "An apartment in our complex is lots bigger than this."

Tick-tick. Christine tapped her tweezers sharply against the mirror, right where Mary's talkative mouth appeared. "Get it straight, Mary Grace Thompson, that I'm never coming back."

Angrily Mary said, "I'm very sick."

"Here now." Christine turned halfway on her wicker chair, then lifted and rotated it under her. "I know that. What are you doing? Talking like that?"

"Whether you care or not I'm sick, that's all."

"Don't be mean."

As if tentatively approaching a wild animal, she gave Mary's knee some light pats before squinting at her own face. "Of course, I care. I'm your mother."

The word "mother" summoned from Mary's memory a dozen similar scenes. Those other light pats and touches of Christine's, which had never meant more than *Wait, hold still, be quiet.* Kroger's grocery store and Christine reading prices, never Mary's expression nor words. Mary, left behind wobbling on the curbing outside the school those mornings when Christine's car would roar away too fast. Long, bored waits on the benches at University Mall while Christine kept trying on dresses and dresses and dresses. There was the time Mary had asked to serve Kool-Aid when Kay Linda came over, so the envelope of lime powder was left for her in the middle of the table. All yesterday's grievances seemed tonight no more significant than that folder of sugary powder, but it took only a few seconds to tot them up like those water droplets of which the Atlantic is made. Mary wanted to count the secondhand Brownie uniform, add in every stray dog and cat she couldn't keep; now even those times Christine and General Franco had locked their bedroom door or gone Christmas shopping without her seemed affronts.

Motionless, she forced back this glut of recollections, swallowed it down, kept swallowing, and finally realized that not grievance alone but fish grease and vinegar were rising in her throat. With mouth covered, she scrambled off the pink bedspread and ran into Christine's toilet before supper erupted, brown and nasty, the iced tea burning now as it gushed through mouth and nostrils, each long spasm dragging out a groan and pulling her down until finally she sat on the floor with her head too close to some cake of raspberry sachet that hung in the bowl.

Behind her water was running. Then Christine pressed a wet cloth into Mary's hand. She wiped her face, retched up more scalding mouthfuls to drop into the stench.

"That tartar sauce did taste funny, you know? Poor baby. Unless it's the flu?"

Mary gagged, spit foam, and flushed the commode.

"If you don't quit you'll tear everything loose," Christine warned in an accusing whine.

"You go on, I'm OK," Mary managed to answer. Her throat, like a sock, had been turned inside out. She blew her hot nose. "Go rinse your hair."

Christine hesitated in the doorway. "I'd better get your grandmother. I could call Frank?"

"Don't you dare." The insides of her teeth were slimy.

"You don't even want your grandma?"

"Nobody." Mary waved the damp cloth overhead until Christine backed farther away, stood blankly in the hall, withdrew another step or two. Without rising Mary kicked the door shut and laid her chin on the cool white toilet seat. From the smell of its pink deodorizing cake she felt her head was inside a wreath.

Next morning before Mary was awake, Georgia had talked to Frank, to Dr. Gorbin, and to a local doctor ten miles away. Soon she was whispering above the pillow, "Mary? Mary? Can you wake up? Mary? How you feeling? You up to doing the exchange by yourself? Dr. McVeigh wants to see you before you eat any breakfast so he can run some blood tests. Just to be on the safe side?"

Mary stirred and stuck out a tongue that felt borrowed— dirty upholstery, dry, sour. Georgia said one drink of water was allowed, but she held it out in a Pyrex measuring cup.

"Four ounces, help me keep track. We'll take some ice cubes along with us. You still feel sick?"

"Tired."

"Christine thinks you ran a fever in the night."

Mary yawned to aerate her smelly mouth. "I didn't run it very fast."

LATE THAT AFTERNOON, Georgia parked the camper again outside the trailer and watched Christine run from it to tug at Mary's door, her open mouth between smile and laughter. "Oh, I was so relieved to get that phone call! And I finally reached Frank and got him calmed down." She pressed her smile briefly to the place where Mary's hair was parted while making gestures beyond to Georgia at the steering wheel. "Were they hard on you, baby? You're feeling better? Is she better, Mama?"

Georgia put the keys in her purse. "They decided not to keep her in the hospital, but we're to start home tonight. When it's cooler."

"But Mary's all right? Is it the flu?"

"Oh, there might be some kind of infection. She's taking antibiotics against—what, Mary?"

"Strep." Mary moved very slowly on the seat to dangle her feet outside.

"But her blood pressure's up and she's anemic so they want her regular doctors to see her. Virgil still here?"

"Rode into town with Nolo."

Leaning across the seat, straight into Christine's face, Georgia said, "The doctors say stress alone will raise blood pressure."

Christine, her smile dropping to a straight line, reached for Mary's arm to help her down but recoiled from tape and gauze.

"I got a transfusion," Mary explained, sliding out as if limp.

"Ugh." Christine took hold of her fingers. "I hope they checked it for AIDS, you know?"

By sliding across the front seat, Georgia was able to move her frown and headshake closer.

Then Christine said heartily, "You sure do *look* better, baby, but did you miss lunch? I've got some clam chowder, OK?"

Mary, tired and numb, plodded past her toward the trailer door.

"That's liquid! Christ!" said Georgia, irritated. "Chowder is *liquid*. She's had to use up lots of her fluid allowance just swallowing pills."

"But this is thick, real thick." Still talking, Christine followed them both. "I'll carry it to you at the TV, baby, OK? And what about crackers? Can you eat crackers?"

Flesh of my flesh, Georgia thought. Too old to whip. And Virgil? He'll be drunk when I see him next, and I would be, too, if I didn't have to drive this thing home.

Christine said on the front stoop, "It's in the microwave already."

Inside Georgia found Mary, pale, had curled up on one of the love seats watching a soap opera. "Time for another exchange yet, Mary?"

"I want my chowder first."

No wonder Mary whined. Georgia sank against a bar stool. "I'd hate to tell you how long it took every time just getting a needle in her vein."

"Then don't tell me." Reaching into the microwave, Christine stirred each bowl and pressed the power button for more time.

While it hummed and blew hot air and the TV raised its voice for a commercial, Georgia said softly, "You've got to donate your kidney right away, Christine, don't think about it, just do it; go right ahead and do it. Now. Get it over with and . . ."

The covering noises faded. Christine set Mary's hot bowl on a tray and carried it to the glass coffee table. She set spoons and the other two bowls on the serving bar in silence.

"Christine? Hello?" By reflex, Georgia's words grew hard, took on corners and edges. "Yo, Christine? Anybody home in there?" She thumped her own head.

Face turned away, Christine lined up their two napkins just so, saying softly, "From what I can find out, it's never a sure thing for either, ah, party."

"Party my ass. You're not a natural mother, that's all there is to it. And I'm not a goddamned bit hungry."

After taking a few lethargic sips, Mary said, "I can't hear TV."

Georgia muted her voice to a low growl. "Them Thompsons have always thought us Broomes was trash. Don't you go proving them right, you hear me?" She snatched her napkin and crumpled it back inside the box, then dropped her clean soup-spoon into the drawer. "Look at me when I'm talking!"

But the full sight of Christine's wide eyes, as fearful as they had ever been from childhood nightmares long ago, from thunderstorms, made Georgia blow hard into midair. "Shoo, Christine." She fell silent, watching her daughter move about the small kitchenette on tiptoe, acting as if even knives, spoons, and forks were breakable. The fact was: Christine *was* childish; she had stopped paying attention to any of Life's hard lessons in her early teens, as if menstruation had proved as much unpleasantness as she could ever bear. Thereafter any experience, if it had not come straight from movies or television, Christine had sent back to Life to be repaired. The prince she had married turned out to live through weeks and months of being only a frog at heart. She had not seen beyond Frank's tall uniform, and now could not see Nolo beyond his, either. To Christine, pregnancy and birth had been tortures endured and repressed. But denial had not worked; in time the bridegroom as well as the baby daughter who had seemed so cute and talcum sweet turned into two great sucking blobs of constant need.

Georgia could remember the first tense days of that marriage, then the jittery ones of parenthood, then the day Christine waved her hands overhead, saying, "Frank puts it into me and Mary drains it out and I'm just disappearing in the middle. If I was to die it wouldn't even leave much of a space now."

And the day came when Christine did go. Leaving a space, Georgia supposed, that had not been large, had quickly healed over.

Georgia snapped her head toward Mary, as if the look on that face would either confirm or reject any healing. But Mary seemed to have been deboned and dropped from a great height, eyes half-closed, chowder half-eaten, all her limbs half bent.

Georgia drew her daughter against the back door to say with soft emphasis, "Think about how you'll feel if you keep your living kidney, but Mary dies."

Christine pulled free. To give her credit, the sudden tears were real. To be honest, though, Christine could always cry on demand, had wrapped herself in bedspreads and practiced the feat in mirrors. "You know it hasn't come to that yet."

"No. I *don't* know."

"It's just like you and Frank to push, push, push. When the doctors have all these other things to try first."

"What other things?"

"I'm keeping in touch with Dr. Seagroves, and he's the one I'll answer to, OK?" Without warning she suddenly snapped her head forward and bit Georgia on the shoulder, efficiently, the way a dog has a duty to nip the slowest sheep. "Now let me alone," she said when Georgia jumped back. Christine whirled out of the kitchen and hurried to Mary, who was drowsing on the love seat. "I could warm up that chowder? Maybe some milk would be good? I guess to hear your grandma talk you'll have to eat dry milk by the spoonful or something. Oh, you like 'General Hospital'? My favorite is 'The Young and the Restless,' or it was when I was home every afternoon."

Mary said something short that Georgia couldn't hear.

"I was just talking to your grandmother Georgia about getting my palm read so I can really know the future."

"I've quit reading palms," Georgia said.

Abruptly, as if she had just noticed that Mary was slumped exhausted beside her, Christine sank into the love seat murmuring, and took her in her arms. She began stroking Mary's red hair, not with her hand but with an awkward fist that had crumpled the lines of her unread future out of sight; and beyond her moving arm past Mary's moving head, she fixed her defiant gaze on Georgia's face as she rocked Mary back and forth, letting her mother drink in this full example of another natural mother in natural action.

Mary seemed sleepy, almost drugged.

"I'd think your grandma Georgia would read palms now of all times, wouldn't you? Unless"—she made a face—"unless she's finally admitting there's nothing to it."

"There's plenty to it. I've lost interest, that's all." Georgia set her uneaten chowder in the sink. "Besides, who could ever tell you anything about where you was headed? I'd as soon tell a rock about gravel."

"But what do you read in my hand, really? The sure thing or not? Or is it in—" She stopped; she had almost said "Mary's hand"; Georgia could see the shape of each word come up her throat and fill her mouth. Even when Georgia flung both her own hands in the air, motionless, to stop her, Christine let risk hang in the room that the words might speak themselves and insist on being answered.

"In the stars?" she finished. "I never could take astrology seriously, though, could you, baby?"

Mary shook her head.

AFTERWARD, as that implacable summer wore out first one day and then another, Mary's frequent minor crises began to seem manageable; they shifted toward normal, and Tacey Thompson hardly noticed her scale of measurement decline until any mild ailment appeared almost healthy. Since every chemical fluctuation recorded in Mary's thickening medical file was relative, judged only better or worse than its counterpart two days before, Tacey found herself living the way villagers must live on the slope of an old volcano, keeping busy, inured to occasional rumbles or puffs of ineffective smoke.

Even her rage at Christine faded first to anger, then to a paler disapproval. Thoughts of Christine might risk diverting her energy from Mary. Besides, Christine's delay, added to the fact that doctors had set no deadline for transplant surgery, combined to reassure them all. Gradually it almost seemed that Christine's indecision was even preventive, that postponement kept Mary in some form of remission. There was no hurry, no emergency. It would be unlucky to think so.

With relief, Tacey rushed forward into new routines: from 6:00 to 8:00 a.m. she did her own housework very fast, left Dandy a sandwich, then went to Frank's apartment, cleaned and did laundry, froze main dishes and desserts geared to Mary's diet. (Frank had decided to save money by letting Rosa go. Tacey would never forget the way Rosa had embraced Mary before she left, so tight that it felt like a last-time embrace, and even across the room Tacey had felt her own ribs squeezed and held until the breath rushed out.)

On each summer day Tacey gauged Mary up or down a few degrees compared with her condition yesterday—poor appetite and headache Monday, but on Tuesday willing to baby-sit the two-year-old next door.

Tacey saw nothing wrong with Mary keeping little Warren Bailey, since Frank had forgotten to tell her the absent Mr. Bailey had robbed a Quik-Mart at gunpoint last April. But she did ask if it would bother Mary to be back in Miss Torrido's apartment.

"I've already been, Grandma. It's repainted and everything. Besides, Miss Torrido is doing just fine now."

"What?"

Mary said quickly, "I'll be home about ten. You going to stay that late?"

"Till Frank gets home." Tacey gave her a hug. "But what did you mean about Miss Torrido?"

"Nothing." Mary examined her fingernails. "Just Heaven, I guess." She slung a handbag over one shoulder as she hurried outside, then straddled the iron railing on her own front stoop, stepped with a long stretch onto the next concrete landing, and swung a leg over that one, too. She was certain it was good luck to move from one household to another without even touching the earth.

The door was opened by the older Mrs. Bailey, Warren's grandmother, who was tall and skinny and nothing like Tacey Thompson. The Great *un*-grandmother, Mary thought, because everything about Mrs. Bailey was "un." Her bony gray face looked *un*healthy; she always snatched her own body back from Mary and even from little Warren—*un*touchable. *Un*friendly. She never looked rested or calm, and her *un*smiling mouth turned down. Arthritis in both knees made her walk *un*evenly. Mary supposed any mother whose only son had ended up in jail would be *un*happy, but Mrs. Bailey always looked as if she might, any minute, lean against one of these walls and press her face hard into its new paint.

Talking to her was hard. "Both of you don't usually go out at night," Mary said with a smile as she watched Mrs. Bailey gather keys and a purse.

"Why do you say that?"

"Well—daytimes, maybe, but—"

"There's nothing wrong with Karen and me both going out one evening for a change."

"No, ma'am. I told my grandmother ten o'clock, is that right?"

"We can't be sure to the exact minute. I'm meeting Karen at work."

"OK. Where's Warren?" But she could hear from Warren's bedroom—the one that used to be Miss Lila's—his tape of Mother Goose rhymes to tinkly music. "I'll go in."

Behind her Mrs. Bailey raised her voice. "Just Karen and me. We're eating out. Then a movie?"

Mary nodded. Warren's mother always posted details and phone numbers and Warren's doctor right by the kitchen phone. She had to brace in Warren's doorway, letting the image of a sprawled dead Miss Lila overlay part of the room and then swirl into a scattering of blue clowns and balloons as Warren came to hug her.

But after more nursery songs and blocks and top spinning, when she went to microwave Warren's supper she saw neither a schedule nor the usual phone numbers had been posted after all. Mary got down to see if the note had fluttered off the corkboard and under the refrigerator or table. No.

She fed Warren, gave him a bath, and put him to bed. When he had finally fallen asleep, she dashed next door to grab a fresh bag for her fluid exchange. By now casual about the process, she hung it on a cabinet doorknob in the Bailey's kitchen, glad at least to get paid while these boring minutes ticked by; and sat at their counter with a stack of *People* magazines.

The Bailey women were not home by ten. Nor by ten-twenty when Tacey telephoned.

"They said *around* ten, Grandma. You can go on home. Well, why not? Of course the doors are locked. You can reach over and test them yourself. . . . Dinner and a movie, she said. Some last till eleven. I will."

By eleven-ten she had talked with Tacey twice more. During the second call the rattly Bailey pickup truck arrived. Mary was surprised when only the grandmother limped inside, sagging with weariness, looking as if she'd endured an *un*movie after an *un*nourishing meal.

"Is something wrong?"

"I'm just tired. Karen wants to know if she can pay you tomorrow?"

"Sure." Mary stared at the closed front door. "Isn't she here?"

"She's riding with friends, so I came ahead."

"You? I didn't know you could drive that truck!"

Mrs. Bailey took off her glasses and slumped into a chair, pinching the bridge of her nose. "You can do what you have to, I guess."

Carrying her straw purse and dialysis case, Mary waited in the open door. "He ate part of his supper but drank all the milk, and he's been asleep since seven-thirty." They always asked for this report.

"Good, good." *Un*interested.

This time Mary walked down the concrete steps, glancing at the truck parked crooked in its space, and climbed her adjoining steps and let herself in with the key she kept strung around her neck. Tacey was snoring in the recliner in spite of war whoops from an Indian fight on TV. The snap of the off button woke her.

"There you are." She snuffled a few times. "They ought not keep you so late."

Mary shrugged. She was thinking she would rather have had her pay tonight.

"I'm sleeping here tonight anyway," said Tacey with a loud yawn.

"Sorry."

"It's not that—Frank has to work past his shift. Somebody escaped from the prison unit, he said. They had a late announcement on the TV news."

"Which prison?"

"Lord, I don't know. In Frank's district somewhere. The patrol called, said he'd be on a roadblock." She motioned Mary to help unfold the couch.

Since both were tired, they made up the daybed in silence,

though Mary wanted to ask if maybe the next-door apartment could be unlucky—maybe this one, too; maybe this very street or the whole west end of town. But she was feeling the lethargy that signaled she was late on the day's final dialysis, so she hurried through top sheet and pillowcase to get to her own room, even dozed off during the exchange. After she woke and while she was groggily putting her unit away, Mary froze at the sound of a man's low voice just beyond her bedroom wall. For an instant she thought Miss Lila's killer had come back, the way Miss Lila herself kept coming back in Mary's dreams with one hand spread over the crater in her chest, the right hand always beckoning. But now the adjoining apartment went silent. Mary touched the wall over her bed, even pressed her ear against its grainy texture to hear the man again. Not a word.

Imagining things, she thought with a stretch and yawn. Half-asleep.

Next morning Frank was still not home, and Tacey said he and a local cop were next door at the Baileys. Mr. Bailey was one of three who had broken out of prison overnight, and Karen Bailey was missing, too. "You're to stay right here, since after the man's mother he wants to talk to you."

Mary shivered. What came to her mind was the Bible story about Israelites marking their doors in Egypt so the Angel of Death would pass by. "Grandma," she began, "I wonder why some people or some places . . ."

But Tacey was hanging her dishrags on the sunny back porch and couldn't hear.

Or wouldn't hear. For some time it had seemed to Mary that a conspiracy of good cheer surrounded her, that her entrance into a room tugged the mouth of every adult present into a broad, unconvincing grin, that General Franco's frown marks between both eyebrows never went away no matter how many teeth he showed her. Deep down they knew what she knew— one time when Miss Torrido beckoned in the night, Mary would go away with her, taking along her sac of yellow urine the way Miss Lila had retained her final wounds. Wherever they went would not be like Tacey's storybook Heaven at all, since everyone over there would be frozen in his terminal condition— broken in car wrecks, charred when their houses burned, gaping open where doctors had made a last try to restart their bloody hearts. But the majority would be very old, Mary thought. Thin. Crooked and pale. What, for eternity, would she talk about to all those old people?

A week after Karen Bailey drove the getaway car for her prisoner husband and disappeared, and after the *un*-grandmother had taken Warren back to Conover without ever settling the baby-sitting bill, Mary began practicing the conversations that might be required in Heaven, where she would likely be surrounded by the very old. She followed Tacey around her yard, helping drag the garden hose, asking about azaleas. Her sudden interest seemed to make Tacey nervous. She switched to encouraging Dandy to reminisce, and in her own room at night Mary recorded notes in her five-year diary about old people's gardening, about plow mules, and even the industry shift from making uppers of shoe leather to making them from shoe plastic. When she resumed attendance at Damascus Church, she chose to sit with Tacey's widowed friends, whose face powder ended, like high tide, at the jawline. Here she eavesdropped on their blood pressures, grandbabies, slipcovers.

During regular checkups, Mary nodded politely when nurses told how easy she would find school this fall, how she could make only one midday exchange instead of joining classmates in the cafeteria. The doctors and nurses would stretch their mouths into the toothy, optimistic smiles Mary knew so well while she forced a matching one of her own. She told no one that this August Miss Lila Torrido was coming to her bedside more often at night, that she had begun to speak more clearly.

In spite of all Mary did not say, despite how much Tacey

and Frank and doctors omitted from what they did say, Mary knew that her illness had become a great one-way drainpipe down which everything else poured.

One night Frank came home exhausted after an hour trying on foot to catch a crazy man who kept running across I-40 in front of speeding cars to kill himself. Several drivers were forced off the road or struck cars in another lane, trying to miss the screaming man. When finally Frank and Elmo got him subdued and secured in their locked backseat, he kept moaning that his hands were on backward.

What gave Mary the creeps, even as she snatched both wrists, was her instant flash of understanding just how that would feel.

It was a shock when Christine called a few days later to say she'd been in Chapel Hill and had done blood and tissue tests at U.N.C. Memorial Hospital, "just in case, OK?"

"You're here? Mama, why didn't you let me know?" Mary was furious at her throat for clogging up, at her eyes for running over. "Where are you? How long can you stay?"

"Oh, I can't stay, baby. I'm on my way from the Hairdressers Convention in Winston-Salem, and I only taped three days ahead, you know? And Nolo has to get back, too. But you get Frank off my back now—I've done the preliminaries and I want him to quit pestering me. He fills up my whole answering machine with his phone calls, and who knows how many other calls I've missed while he was saying the same thing over and over? Now how are you feeling, baby? Better?"

"Didn't you get my letter?"

"Of course, but how are you feeling right this minute?"

Mary had to swallow, say, "I'm OK," and then breathe through her mouth. During stress she still felt as if she might simultaneously pee in her pants and tube. "Are you coming by? Or I can come uptown? You're at the hospital?"

"Actually, I *was* in Chapel Hill, but your line was busy and Nolo's got to report, so we drove on. I'm supposed to do some other tests sometime. What's an arteriogram?"

"I don't know."

"Well, there's no rush. Anyway there wasn't time today. We're just beyond Raleigh headed east."

"Raleigh." I hate you, Mary thought. "When are you coming back?" I hate Nolo. "Did the doctor set a day?"

"I didn't talk much to this fat little nurse taking blood, and she couldn't find my veins without bruising both arms."

"They've already run my PRA percent so they can cross-match us." Mary thought briefly of Indian braves mixing their blood as a sign of brotherhood. Some old movie on television. Shirley Temple. "The antibodies and stuff?"

Christine said, "Did you know that people that give kidneys can get blood clots and high blood pressure? Somebody donating blood told me that today. But chances are you'll never need me if you're taking care of yourself. You think about your mother and take care of yourself, OK?"

"Did they say anything about me getting transfusions from you in advance?"

"I think that's outdated. Aren't you glad they keep learning new things? I'm *coming*, Nolo! Here you are on the cutting edge of . . . ha, ha. Well, you know what I mean, baby. Got to run. You keep writing me, OK?"

The telephone emptied except for a hum in Mary's ear. She stared at it as she hung up, then at her fingers, which often felt numb and twitchy, and along her arm with its yellowish suntan that was no suntan at all, but some uremic glow beneath the skin. Probably Christine stocked a dozen skin products she could prescribe, instead of the vinegar-water soaks. And what would Christine say about Mary's gain in weight? Though some of it, she knew, was the heaviness of her usually distended abdomen, which she carried before her like an early pregnancy. Pressure inside her belly had made trotting or cantering Chancy a threat to hemorrhoids or hernia, though she could still ride him in slow trail walks along woodland paths north of Chapel Hill.

Today, Frank's day off, she had planned just such a trail ride with him, to demonstrate that horses could be calm and safe. Jill had promised to put Frank on the oldest and slowest mare in her barn. While she waited for him on their front steps in jodhpurs and hard hat, carrying a backpack with extra dialysate, Mary decided not to mention her mother's call until after the ride.

Driving them to the stables, Frank bared all his tooth enamel making cheerful talk. The bombardment pressed Mary against the car door. Lately General Franco seemed able to say only unimportant but madly irritating things. Then he would blame Mary for being so touchy, and worry Tacey in whispers about her mood swings. Often he would urge on her an extra dialysate exchange, as if she could drain out her bad temper by gravity and have her whole nature sweetened by liquid dextrose.

At the hitching post, Jill already had their horses brushed down and saddled. Jill's smile, too, had been stretched to a width to fit dental posters. They were not dating now, Mary had been told, because of their hectic schedules. But it's really me, she thought.

She dropped a few yes-nos before riding ahead and then walking Chancy downhill from the barn under spotty shade. The wavering patterns of light/dark cast through the leaves made her hands look underwater. She decided to keep Christine's phone call altogether to herself. Some doctor would notify Frank that Christine had finally begun the tests—they were always taking off their smiles to talk soberly to Frank behind Mary's back.

He rode up beside her, ramrod straight, his legs forked over the horse's back like a pair of tongs. They turned onto a former railroad bed with young pines on either side. In spite of herself, the creaking leather and rhythmic motion began to calm her.

Frank said, "You down today? Another headache?"

She shook her head, beginning to dampen a ring of sweat under her riding hat.

"Did I tell you they've moved up your name on the UNOS computer in case a donor kidney comes up with the right antigens?"

He always said "donor," not "cadaver." Never "corpse." Mary, on the other hand, had roamed the hospital until she found the Health Sciences Library that medical students used. She had learned to speak Nephrology. She said, "Mama's going to come through."

"It's not an either/or choice, though, Mary. You could use somebody else's kidney for a few years and still get hers later."

"If I didn't reject. One rejection means you'll probably reject the second time." She didn't want to talk about it. "Is that a snake?"

While Frank reined in, saying "Where?" she walked Chancy steadily ahead. "Any news about the Baileys?"

"Probably in Mexico by now."

"Let's try this path." She turned into woods despite his complaint that the way was too narrow, probably just a game trail. Humming, she rode faster. Maybe it was the music from—yes—some science fiction film about a time tunnel through which history could break loose into the present and St. Paul show up to gape at the Suez Canal. Maybe she could ride back to be adored by Robin Hood or even Ben Franklin, who had probably been kind of cute when he was young. Or maybe there was some weak spot in the world's wall that let crime and death leak into Ramshead Chateaux apartments. And become a spreading stain. Maybe they ought to move away.

Troubled by her silence, Frank raised his voice. "They took me yesterday to see a transplant surgery. I feel a lot better about it. They bring in this little blue pump with a plastic box on top, and the kidney's in that. They don't even have to take out your old kidneys, just sew the new one in. Took about thirty minutes to get it in just so, and right away it starts working." Mary said "Um," and he went on, sounding more relaxed. "After the operation, those doctors and nurses acted like the

Carolina Tar Heels when they win. Laughing? They couldn't slap each other on the backs because of the sterile gloves, so they did it with elbows. Clapping with elbows!"

Riding ahead, feeling her steady side-to-side pelvic motion and the matching shift of fluid above, Mary wondered where she had bodily room for a kidney implant. She felt bloated, bulbous. "With your weak stomach," she said, "you must have been pretty worried about me to watch any operation without fainting."

"Nobody's worried, Mary. I'm getting prepared is all." When she said "Um" again, he added, "I want to understand."

She shook her head, imagining how her moving black hat would look to him from behind. Then she couldn't stop shaking it. In silence they rode out of the pines and under hickories and oaks while she kept on like a metronome.

"Mary?" He pulled his horse too close until Chancy took a little skip so he could threaten with one hind hoof.

By setting her jaw she was able to steady herself. "I'm worse than I was," she said through her teeth. "Everybody can see that."

"The doctors warned you'd have good days and bad days."

"Half and half?"

He waited, dodged a small limb that twanged back off her shoulder, then said, "They want us to consider going ahead. Without waiting for Christine."

"Even if she's started the tests?"

"Started is right. They gave her the list of all she has to be checked for, Mary, from hepatitis to AIDS, and the other tests she has to be in the hospital to take. She forgot and left it in the waiting room. Somebody had to run over the bridge and catch her in the parking deck."

"So?"

Now they were on the edge of a farmer's hayfield and frowning against the hot glare. In one corner was a fenced rectangle around a magnolia tree above eight or ten gravestones. Mary looked for the site of the original cabin—probably there, where the fallen rocks had once been part foundation, part chimney. Now the grandchildren had pulled away from the farm's center to its edge and lived by the roadside in trailers or fiberboard houses.

Mary turned Chancy with the reins so they need not pass the family graveyard.

"We need to be ready to take a kidney if it comes, Mary. Just the option of it. Maybe your mother will be ready long before then."

"Of course she will."

"But I have to tell the doctors now, that if they get any kidney with a good antigen match? That we want to be called?"

"Daddy, how can we pay for one operation, much less two?"

"We've had some help on that. Not just Medicare and the Kidney Foundation but people have started a fund for you."

"I'm tax deductible?"

His laugh seemed to rattle, and his tone still sounded urgent, "I've got to tell the hospital that we want the first suitable kidney."

"All right. Tell them. But it won't matter. By then I'll have my mother's and we'll both be home from the hospital and I'll have at least three boyfriends and you'll get promoted to first sergeant and—"

"And I'll grow new hair on my head and we'll be rich?"

"And you'll marry Jill." With a grin Mary glanced over her shoulder, but instead of Frank's face, she felt her gaze magnetize toward the burial plot and fix on its green, poor-man's privet and dusty periwinkle, the leaning stones crusted with dirt and lichens.

And you'll have more children, she didn't say.

"AND ALL FOR THE WANT of a horseshoe nail" goes the nursery rhyme about how great battles may be affected by small events; but for Mary the reverse was true. Surely Iraq's invasion of Kuwait early in August 1990, could have no effect on one kidney operation in Chapel Hill, North Carolina? Mary was continuing to eat poorly, lose weight, sometimes vomit, receive an occasional transfusion of red blood cells. There was talk of scheduling surgery soon so she would miss less of the eighth grade.

When her bad days seemed to come more often than the good, Frank decided he'd use Mary's upcoming birthday as a reason to call Christine and insist she proceed with preparations to donate her kidney. He spoke to her answering machine— then twice, a third, five times in all, without ever hearing anything but a recorded voice—before a package of nonallergenic sunscreen, skin creams, depilatories, antiperspirants, shampoos, and nail-care products arrived for Mary in the nick of time.

On August 12 they celebrated Mary's thirteenth birthday— Tacey, Dandy, Frank, Georgia, Virgil—with cupcakes (small) and ice cream served in her hospital room. She had overheated her dialysate above 98.6 in the microwave and given herself a high fever.

There were still cupcakes left when Cindy Scofield came by with a crossword puzzle magazine and two book-tapes Mary could hear on her portable player. "But one's poetry," she said, "and you might hate poetry."

"If I don't, it's not the fault of the seventh grade," Mary answered.

"They're by African-American women. People who've been through hard times." Cindy showed her the names: Lucille Clifton, Maya Angelou, Nikki Giovanni, Alice Walker, Gwendolyn Brooks. "Black poetry just reads aloud so well," she added nervously.

"They got rhythm," Dandy said in spite of her frown.

Mary flipped pages of the small accompanying pamphlet, letting words break loose from the printed poems: "My mother is jelly-hearted and she has a brain of jelly . . ." "Hope is a crushed stalk . . . ." The absence of optimism cheered her up instantly.

Later Jill came with a pink bouquet bought downstairs from the hospital's floral refrigerator.

Frank followed her into the hall. "I miss seeing you."

She nodded. Within their rings of makeup, her eyes looked tired. He walked beside her to the elevator, across the lobby, over the concrete bridge to the top floor of the parking deck, and then slid into the passenger seat of her car. She said wryly, "I feel like you've come to me for treatment."

Maybe he had.

She waited for a minute, then started the car. "Hell," she said. "Come on."

But in bed, every movement seemed marred by effort. She was just slightly too dry, or out of synch; his elbow almost assaulted her body; he finished far too soon, but his fingers had suddenly become too fast or rough or clumsy to bring her after him. They lay listening to each other's rapid breathing, then to how easily it slowed.

After a while she said, "You're not asleep."

"It's hard to unwind."

Screw, she thought. Wind, unwind. She turned onto her side.

He said, "It's not like Mary to be so careless."

Jill lay staring off the mattress into some small abyss. Her body was feeling more devoured than loved. "I know," she murmured into the dark.

"Her hospital counselor says maybe it's a defeatist action."

"What did Mary say?"

"Just that she pressed the wrong numerals on the microwave."

"Could happen."

"But unconsciously she maybe wanted to. One boy who was getting machine dialysis had one of those external shunts, you know, where the tube is on the outside of the body between vein and artery so they can hook up the machine."

Jill said she had seen one.

"And one day he just got tired, and he went home and got in a tub full of hot water and took his mother's pruning shears and just cut through it and let all his blood out. People get tired."

She was tired herself. Jill reached back to rub his shoulder. "Was that here in this hospital?"

"It was somewhere. I *heard* it at this hospital. Probably was."

"Tales get started, you know."

"Mary won't admit she's tired out."

"She takes after her father. He's not big on admitting, either." Jill felt the bed shift as he sat up.

"I smile and she smiles," he began, and then swung his feet to the floor. "I'll call Christine right now. Surely she's home in the middle of the night. Mary's in the hospital, and she can get her ass up here."

Jill closed her eyes. It was almost 2:00 a.m.; she heard him dial wrong, hang up, and dial again.

Just as the ringing began, Jill's cat brushed by his naked leg and almost made Frank drop the phone.

Jill mumbled, "Don't cuss before she even picks up."

But Frank, pushing the cat aside with one bony foot, braced himself in silence to hear Nolo's sleepy voice. This time a different female voice came from the machine after four rings. "If you want to speak to Amanda Cook, leave a message at the beep. If your message is for Christine Thompson, contact Mrs. Georgia Broome in Durham at 919-555-1435."

Frank pulled the receiver off his ear as if burned.

"What now?" grumbled Jill, seeing him rigid in the dark with one arm extended. He told her. "So call," she said. He found Georgia's number in his own book, and when it rang Virgil croaked, "What?"

"It's Frank Thompson. Put Georgia on."

"Is she worse? Georgia? It's Frank. What happened?"

"No. Georgia? She's all right. Yes, she likes your present. Christine's answering machine says to call you?"

A cleared throat, a silence. Maybe Georgia was feeling the lines of her own palm in the dark. "Frank? What's this about Christine?"

Very slowly he went over the message. "So I guess Amanda Cook is a friend or a sublet, who knows; but where's Christine?"

"I don't know."

"You're *bound* to know or else it wouldn't say to call you in Durham and give the number and—"

"I heard you." More silence while perhaps Georgia read her own palm. "Maybe Christine has sent me a letter or something that hasn't come, but I don't know a thing about this. Nothing."

"Don't cover up for her while Mary's in the hospital! Did you know my mama found her passed out on the floor? So don't you save Christine's goddamn skin with me. I had to hear on the radio at headquarters that the rescue squad had gone to my own apartment number—*code three*—that's the way I heard about it!" He almost shouted over her denials. "So we might need to move on this transplant business any minute, and Christine knows that. So where is she? Don't lie to me."

For a minute, hearing him so fierce about his daughter, Jill was sorry she had never been able to tell Frank that she, too, had a child somewhere. Would that have drawn them together? Frank would probably think that giving birth and letting go were insignificant, compared with thirteen years of Mary Grace Thompson and how they might end. She remembered her mother's advice: "When the next man comes along, don't ever tell him. Men can't forget it. They'll throw it up to you years afterward."

But by not telling him she had nothing to offer the size of what Frank was feeling now. Sometimes he saw her as an adolescent girl still playing with animal pets.

She heard Frank say, shocked, "But I don't understand it! She knows we need to call on her at a minute's notice! Even if she didn't listen to me, the doctors told her!"

The fear in his voice drove Jill out of bed into the bathroom, where the mirror showed her lank hair and discontented face. She blew bad breath in a fog against the glass, then sank onto the commode seat. For the first time she put words to the heaviness that had lately dragged her body down. It's too hard. *Loving Frank Thompson right now at this time and in this place is just too hard.*

The white case that held her diaphragm lay empty on the counter. She still kept both diaphragm and pills, sometimes used both. If I was in that business, I'd pick the trade name Pandora, she thought, too tired to cry. In the other room Frank's anger and bewilderment rose and fell. I wonder where Sonny is, but I don't much care, Jill thought.

Next day Georgia's mail from Christine—a postcard—said: "Nolo has to go overseas to Germany and then can't tell, so we're getting married. It'll be my only chance to see Europe while I'm a marine wife—isn't that great? Will send new address soon. Tell Mary I love her and give Frank the news and to quit worrying so much. OXOXOX. Love, Christine Broome Thompson Overcash.(!)"

THERE FOLLOWED during August a long-distance telephone chase of Christine across Germany. After Nolo's unit was moved somewhere in the Middle East with Operation Desert Shield, Christine turned into Europe's leading American tourist. She dropped an occasional postcard home criticizing the primitive hair permanents inflicted by prehistoric salons in West Germany; these cards would continue to trickle to North Carolina for weeks to come. Nolo—finally summoned to a field telephone by the Red Cross—told Frank she had planned a sight-seeing trip to castles on the Rhine.

Frank doubted it. He thought Christine was probably twirling her way from one *biergarten* polka to the next, while Mary's blood pressure rose and got reduced by pills, while she developed signs of thinning bone fought by extra calcium and vitamin D, while her iron loss from dialysis caused a slow drop in her hemoglobin, while a cloudy drain fluid indicated an infection that had to be treated by antibiotics, and so on. The counterattack moves and stalemates went on and on.

Where once his work hours filled with speed chases and traffic accidents had been relieved by the contrast of normalcy at home, Frank now seemed to shift back and forth from public to private crisis. Even attempted time off could turn surreal.

When next he called Jill and she wouldn't go out and they quarreled, he telephoned Cindy to go to dinner at Angus Steakhouse in Raleigh. Awkward at first, they filled the drive with talk about local news, the district court, the upcoming fall elections. But then they began laughing when Cindy pointed to where the *G* in the restaurant's sign had been painted out by vandals. An hour later they were still smiling, even talking easily over their salads, when a truck driver dozed off and drove his eighteen-wheeler over that same lighted sign and through one corner of the restaurant. Frank wound up giving CPR, breathing Italian dressing deep into a diner with cardiac arrest. During the rhythmic count he tried not to consider the victim as the owner of two healthy kidneys that might outlive this heart attack.

Another time Tacey was taking her turn with the overseas operators seeking Christine when a summer thunderstorm spawned a small local tornado that sliced across Chapel Hill and dropped half a pine tree through her kitchen ceiling. The roar, the snap of trunk, and the crash all came so quickly that she remained holding the dead phone in one hand—the air before her singing from the twang and scent of evergreen needles. She closed her eyes and waited for this odd bad dream to fade. But the sound of raindrops spilling onto Formica became too real to disbelieve. Dandy ran in from the dining room and fell face first into a treetop.

A few days after the local paper ran a photo of the Thompsons' broken house, Georgia Broome made the news herself. One of the numerous Durham addicts, hoping to fund his coke habit out of Georgia's pocketbook, snatched it as he rushed past outside South Square Mall but hung up its leather strap on her meaty shoulder, and before he could jerk it free she had grabbed up a brick and beaten him on the head—not once, but a number of times. The brick had been lying in the center of the parking lot as if divinely placed. There was some speculation that Georgia might be charged with assault, and considerable risk that she might commit it on anybody who dared say so. While the thief recuperated in Duke Hospital, her fury had to pass through layer upon layer of Frank's calmer translations that finally led to charges being filed against the addict, not Georgia, and his trial set for September. Meantime, Georgia and a neighborhood conjur woman collaborated by laying on the thief a curse or two—just as backup for the court system, Georgia said.

Frank seemed to be watching these events of dog days through a long and badly focused lens. Jill seemed smaller, receding, preoccupied as she was with the coming fall semester at the vet school in Raleigh. He sometimes stopped by Centaur Stable. She came to his apartment a few times to watch videos. Marriage was not discussed.

Only Mary's illness seemed a constant. Constantly present. Gradually but steadily worse.

Frank was calm, unsurprised, when the phone rang in the middle of one late August night and a nurse's voice offered their first chance at a cadaver kidney. He reached absently to unstick a dozen Post-it notes from the wall above the phone, fruitless efforts to trace Christine, while the nurse told him where to come.

Outside Mary's bedroom door he wondered briefly where

Christine might be sleeping tonight; then he went in and woke their daughter with the news.

He called Tacey. While Mary dressed, he carried the suitcase they had packed weeks before, along with her dialysis supplies, downstairs. Then he threw on his own clothes, stuffing in his shirt while he waited outside Mary's door. At this hour he could hear everything through its wood: the buzz of a zipper, a rasp of one button shoved into its hole, all this against the thud of his own heart.

Mary came out. She asked with a catch in her voice, "Who is it, was it?"

"Some guy that drove into the Rocky River." Did she care to know the dead man's age or race? He decided not. He wondered if both kidneys had been busy filtering out alcohol or crack. "You're ready?"

"I guess." She walked ahead of him, Frank noticing how thin her arms were. Better this gamble than nothing, he thought. At least it's a try.

At the hospital they hurried her out of his hug and left Frank to call the Broomes. As soon as she recognized his voice, Georgia said numbly, "Yes, I tried again today to reach"—but he broke in.

"Forget it, forget her." He made the news fast and terse. Then he hung up on all she was adding about the Red Cross, the U.S. Embassy in Berlin, whatever.

In the waiting room he sat rehearsing in his mind what might be happening to Mary now. He knew there would be a switch—the man's left kidney would go into her lower right abdomen, but would they move two if both of hers proved to be destroyed as doctors believed? Or did they gamble fifty-fifty, one kidney per person? He tried to read the faces of other people waiting, to see if they had come at this hour to claim the second kidney.

For the past month Mary's dentist had treated every cavity

to eliminate sources of infection. Even so he supposed they were checking her white blood count again for any new suspicions of illness, repeating the routine cardiogram, taking her blood pressure, feeding her liquids so her veins would be plump with the fluid that would force a stranger's kidney to restart.

Frank caught himself pacing figure eights around the plastic chairs. The windows were turning gray with dawn. He forced himself downstairs for coffee, came back, could get no news from the busy nurses. Read magazines. Tried to decide what this carpet smelled like. Mildew? Sweat? Vinegar?

Mistake or not he decided to telephone Jill at her barn office.

The phone rang so long he knew she was in the paddock working horses before the day heated up. "Hello?" she finally said in an irritable voice.

"I'm sorry I've called you inside. They've found Mary a kidney."

"Found," she repeated. "Then that's good. The operation's today? You'll call me? I'll come by the hospital after I feed tonight."

Something down his throat hurt for a minute and then quit. "You don't have to. She knows we broke up, she's accepted that."

"That's not quite right," Jill said, "broke up."

"Broke down."

"Wore out. With school starting next week, I just didn't have the energy—well, I've said all that and it never got through. I needed some breathing room, that's all."

"I said I understood, Jill. I just wanted you to know."

"When's the surgery?"

"As early in the afternoon as they can get everything ready."

"Call me when you know anything."

He left the phone and then came back and rang Cindy, woke her up. Her little wasp of a dog was barking behind her sleepy voice.

"Oh good—isn't it good? How did Mary feel? Was she excited?"

"She looked more long-suffering than anything else."

"That's how you sound, too. Who's there with you? You want me to come? You want Elmo?"

"Not a bit," he said, and added quickly, "I don't mean you."

"Elmo's all right. Did he tell you about putting up Mary's name?" No, Frank said. "In the back of Elmo's church they've got a—well, a wall hanging, I guess, a prayer shawl, fabric that Elmo's wife put a cross on with needlepoint, and people stop by and pin little slips of paper on it, prayers they want. Some are anonymous. And Mary's on there, for healing."

It seemed too much like magic.

She said into his silence, "I wouldn't knock it if I were you."

"All right."

"I'll go by the paper early, then I'll come."

"I doubt they take her in the operating room before two or three."

"But you're there, aren't you? Now what about Christine— does she know?" When his *"Hell, no!"* exploded, she said, "Send her word, Frank. She could still get here in case this one doesn't take."

"Of course it's going to take!"

But he knew she referred to their conversation at the Angus Steakhouse; she had urged him not to lay on Christine the helplessness of future guilt. She deserves it, Frank had said. "I doubt anybody does," Cindy answered.

"Think about Mary," said Cindy now. "If she ends up needing Christine and there was any way to have her standing by, you'll hope you tried."

But he was tight-lipped and tight-chested when he left the phone. Christine had given up Mary twice. No more chances. If Georgia was back on the phone to Germany—fine.

Frank left word at the nurses' station, crossed on the overhead bridge to level three of the hospital's concrete parking deck, and sat where he felt most at home—in the car. Its odors he understood, the way his own familiar blood and sweat and shit set the right standard for how these things ought to smell if they were not to be repugnant. One of Elmo's postcards was on the dashboard under his sunglasses. He threw it out, waited. If his own name was stuck to a yard of cloth inside that church, he doubted Cindy would tell him. He waited some more, trying not to scratch the tingly surface of both arms.

Not far away was the elevator that carried people from every level to this bridge that crossed the busy street to the main hospital entrance. Relatives who had been awake all night were straggling out from it, trying to remember where they had left their cars.

Before long Tacey and Dandy Thompson stepped out. Losing weight, both of them. Under both chins the skin, wrung out, sagged around their necks in twists and folds. He rolled down his window to call, knowing both would straighten themselves and light up their eyes by willpower. But he kept silent while their true selves limped out of sight. Probably Georgia would be coming next; Virgil not until his afternoon beers had settled. Christine, he supposed, must be eating bratwurst sausages in Cologne or Hamburg.

For some reason he suddenly felt late, overdue, and panic without cause made him hurry back into the hospital. Perhaps he was psychic? But the receptionists said no O.R. had yet been assigned for Mary. Before he went upstairs, Frank stopped at the hospital chapel and prayed through gritted teeth the only honest words that were in him: *Don't you dare let her die.*

At 2:00 p.m., in O.R. 3, the blue-robed surgeon (while lecturing aside about the operation to a class of medical students in matching suits) made a short incision in flesh that had been dyed by antiseptic and so draped with sterile sheets that what was visible had become an isolated specimen, belonging to no one in particular. His electric scalpel cauterized small blood vessels as it sliced down through layers of fat and muscle, while his calm voice, almost electrical itself, stated the age and sex and an abbreviated medical history of both donor and recipient. Once the retractors were in place, a collection of internal organs looked artificial, like plastic imitations removable for classroom study. Only the doctor's gloved fingers seemed alive as they pulled back the web of unreal peritoneum, then tied off false vessels that seemed imperfectly colored, until he had made a nest below the appendix. There was surprisingly little blood.

During the deft movements of both sheathed hands, steady reports on anesthesia and vital signs came in a flat monotone from far off, where the tanks and gauges kept busy, where the patient's head must be located.

Then, from the perfusion machine, an assistant loosed catheters from the veins and arteries attached to the donated kidney, and two doctors rinsed its dull surface in a sterile bowl before slowly lowering it in place. The cool object seemed to float on what was already present in the abdomen, lightly, like something made of papier-mâché. The doctor's rubberized fingers settled the organ in.

With great care, then, the surgeon began joining veins, arteries, and ducts with sutures as thin as spider strands. The connections seemed to take a long time. Some had to be done over. Nobody spoke, except for the regular reports about respiration and blood pressure.

After forty minutes of delicate needlework, several medical students were motioned closer to the table to view close-up the systematic removal of vascular clamps so living blood could rush for the first time into a dead man's kidney. As these came off and clattered one by one into a tray, the organ seemed almost to bloom. Its color lightened, then turned pink. But what flowed into the borrowed organ was not just red blood but poisoned blood, blood bearing bodily wastes and by-products and cast-off chemicals. Now the kidney seemed swollen with them, engorged, so pink as to be overripe with virulence. The doctor slid his gloved finger under the ureter, which still lay open and unattached inside the body cavity.

They waited. Finally one yellow drop welled slowly at its end; then the ureter jerked before throwing out its first small splatter of urine onto the stained sheets. The masked heads nodded, and in silence the doctors knocked their elbows against one another like awkward, celebrating penguins. The anesthesiologist said something quickly. At that the doctors bent forward again to open the waiting bladder, sew the ureter well inside with great care, stitch up the bladder again. Their wrists were tiring, their eyelids scratching when these raked against their concentrated stares. The surgeon had to focus closely on careful attachment to the interior membrane. He fought any inclination to hurry through this last connection, or to slacken his skill for the final closing of the main incision.

The whole wall of blue bodies now drew slightly back, as if until the last stitch tightened, all members of the surgical team had been literally inside the patient and had slowly withdrawn their whole selves backward until, in unison, they had backed up to the patient's epidermis and outside for the last surface staples. Now they were able to see the room, the glaring light, the tired eyes blinking above each surgical mask. Now the table would be wheeled into recovery for an hour, but their completed work lay deep inside the sleeping patient, where it would recover out of sight. Someone of lesser rank would henceforth keep watch for external signs of that process.

An assistant was dispatched to the surgical waiting room to notify someone—

(Who?

Thompson)

that the kidney transplant operation had gone well.

NEXT MORNING in her regular private room, nurses made Mary sit to press a rolled blanket against her incision and cough, blow, inhale, and otherwise clear her lungs. She told Tacey later the pain made her cry.

But fresh urine was collecting in her bottle like some priceless golden elixir. Everyone remarked on it, held it to the light the way a vintner might, promised that soon the bladder catheter would be removed. Already the drugs to prevent rejection of the kidney were beginning to drip into her bloodstream: aza-thioprine first, then prednisone in descending doses, with cy-closporine to be phased in for maintenance. All were toxic. Each dosage had to be monitored for side effects and steadily adjusted.

So many medicines? Frank demanded of a doctor when he could catch one, "Is Mary some kind of guinea pig? Doctor, is she being used . . ."

"Of course not," said the boy (who looked as if weekly shaving would be too frequent). "And I'm an intern."

That morning before her dressage pupils arrived, Jill came to the hospital with two Polaroid snapshots of Chancy with his saddle blanket turned into a get-well card. On one side: SPACE RESERVED FOR MARY! On the other: HURRY HOME!

Cindy came by, too, with food and a thermos for Frank, but Mary was asleep and did not see her.

Frank stayed in the room while Georgia and Tacey, like lionesses with disputed territory, stalked in and out. Georgia had still not spoken with Christine but was following some leads. She complained that Mary couldn't get enough rest even to heal. When she wasn't being bathed or walked or medicated, her blood was being drawn, or a renal scan was double-checking blood flow into the new kidney, or dressings were being changed or a drainage tube was being removed from the incision. Tacey agreed with a vigorous shake of the head. Someone was palpating the kidney for swelling or tenderness, or a thermometer was in Mary's mouth or a blood-pressure cuff on her arm, or ultrasound was being ordered just to check on abdominal fluids. "And people come in and out with the same questions all the time!"

"It's a teaching hospital!" Frank told them both. "That's the price you pay for getting the latest treatments." He hoped he sounded more confident and optimistic than he felt. He hung around outside Mary's door while doctors took students inside on regular rounds, but he hated to hear Mary become the impersonal topic of class discussion. Most of all he hated their disagreements. Should they be using monoclonal antibodies? But these might produce chills and fever. The lower platelet count was to be expected. Preventive antibiotics? What were the pros and cons? Bowel motility could be better, but the patient's BUN and creatinine levels were good.

Frank found he was making a loud speech to Cindy while his mouth was full of her chicken salad. In a rising and rapid voice he swore that modern medicine had gone backward instead of forward. "When the old witch doctors burned feathers, nobody knew the reasons why or what effect all that dancing might have, and this stuff is just the same. Mystery—they trade on it, Cindy! The doctors have got away from us! It's still all smoke and chanting. The big words are the smoke. So they can know the true names of the evil spirits that we aren't wise enough to know and—"

She nodded and passed the tea.

On the third post-op day (while the prednisone dose was being lowered and they were preparing to introduce intravenous cyclosporine continuously for twenty-four hours), Christine herself placed an overseas call directly to the hospital, and the phone rang right by Mary's bed. Someone had finally located Mary's mother with the news. In France, not Germany.

She cried in Mary's ear, her voice as clear as if she had been next door. "And I feel terrible that I didn't know, baby. That I wasn't there."

You knew plenty, Mary thought. "It's over and I'm all right."

"But how wonderful they found you a kidney so soon. Have you met the family? Won't they be glad it could do some good after all?"

"No, I haven't. I don't know."

"Soon as I can get a flight I'm coming to see you, OK? God knows where they've sent Nolo these days, and things are very expensive here. But I've got you a stein from the Black Forest and a piece of the Berlin Wall and all kinds of postcards, OK? You still make scrapbooks, don't you?"

"Not much, Mama."

"Well, you don't have much to say, do you? I guess you're not feeling good yet. Is Frank there? Grandma Georgia?"

"No." She thought the new kidney might be aching.

A pause. "Grandma Tacey, then?"

Mary handed over the phone and pulled the sheet up to her cheekbones. Where the secret of lasting beauty lay, according to Christine.

Her grandmother's monotone described the surgery, the recovery, the prospect of taking Mary home Friday if there was no fever, no complication, if she maintained what was called "stable renal function." The latex staples would still remain in her wound but would come out during her first clinic visit. By then Mary would be taking all her medications by mouth.

"More medicine," said Tacey in her firm but chilly way, "than she might have needed if she'd got her mother's kidney."

Even from her pillow, Mary could tell when the phone went silent in Tacey's hand. Then her answers began to drone on in rhythm. "Of course I'll be with her. . . . No, it's usually easier to reach Frank at this hospital number; this is where he stays when he's off work. But he may not talk to you, not now. . . . Well, I don't know where Georgia was, but she's been here at the hospital a lot. . . . They've only done dialysis once and don't expect to—what? It can be rejected anytime. That's right. It's a little late for that now, isn't it, Christine?" Her neck began to mottle, then a red flush rose over her jaw and into her face. "No, I don't. I never will. Here's Mary." As if it had turned poisonous, she thrust the phone away and walked to the window, back turned.

While she had waited her turn at listening, with her fingers lightly touching the bandage on her flank, Mary had been wondering if Christine, at twenty, pregnant, had felt something strange as a borrowed tumor had been grafted inside her. When she lifted her hand off the incision her fingers surprised her by taking easy possession of the phone. She put the plastic against her ear, checking herself. She could almost feel her longtime yearning for Christine's love and affection evaporating.

"I'm here, Mama." Where were you? Mary took a deep breath. The memory of three years' accumulated needs and disappointments still swam around her in the air, like humidity, but thinning.

"Baby, I hope you're not letting Frank's family talk against me all the time."

"They don't mention you much."

"To get back to better days, then, how was your birthday? I guess you filled up your makeup kit with all that new stuff? Grandma Georgia says you've thinned down—I bet Elizabeth Taylor wishes she had your problem!"

"I'll trade," Mary said, to stop Christine's nervous giggle into the receiver.

"Write down this number now, OK? Because I don't want to be waking you up all the time, with the time difference and all, you know? So Frank can call me? Especially if there's any change. And I'll give him my travel plans as soon as I can work out a schedule. Have you got a pencil or do you want Tacey to take it down?"

Mary turned over a flowered card from Kay Linda (who was now crowning her summer vacation at Atlantic Beach) and listened without moving to Christine's careful enunciation of each numeral. Then she doodled above the Hallmark imprint with her ballpoint pen. She wrote a large "NO" in flowing script.

Christine said, "Want to read that back?"

"Just repeat it." Mary extended the blue *N* into a curling vine and drew petals around the *O*. "Fine. I'll tell him."

"And you'll have more energy soon, I just know that. I love you, baby. You know that?"

After Mary hung up, Tacey bent to find her embroidery hoop that had fallen on the floor. She had been cross-stitching horses on a cushion cover for Mary's room. "If God had asked my advice, I'd have made horses square," she complained as she seated herself by the bed, but she lifted the needle so she could thread the floss and watch Mary's face at the same time.

Mary kept swallowing in case the lump in her throat should turn crying size but, no, this was anger.

"So Christine's coming home?" asked Tacey.

"Don't hold your breath." With a clink, Mary dropped the pen into her bedside pitcher and watched the slow blue tint drift upward through the ice water.

"You wrote down her phone number?"

"I couldn't hear it," Mary said. "She was too far away."

ON DAY FOUR, Elmo carried into Mary's room a giant vase of yellow flowers from the State Troopers' Association and laid on her pillow one of the stuffed bears patrolmen had been handing out to child wreck victims. "Even teenagers like teddy bears, don't they?" His voice dropped as he leaned over the chair in which Frank, still in uniform, was crumpled on his left side, and he asked more softly, "Your daddy sleep here all night?"

"I guess so," Mary said. "I wish he wouldn't."

Elmo stretched as if the sight of Frank had cramped his own muscles. "I ought to see some eye specialist while I'm here. They say using those older radar units can gradually burn out an eye. Frank probably needs glasses himself."

Mary knew Frank wouldn't even have an annual physical exam if it weren't required. "You just getting off?"

"Headed home. I stopped this one old woman for speeding, and she claimed it was because her husband's car had high-test gas in it and she just didn't know how to handle high-test."

Laughing stirred up an ache low in Mary's pelvis, and she tensed, fearing she might overflow and leak into the bed. The new kidney lacked brakes; it seemed to generate urine by bucketfuls. She thought of it as thirstily soaking up old wastes that had settled in remote swampy cells of her body. A starved, fat kidney poorly matched to her small and overworked bladder.

Frank stirred and began unfolding himself in the chair. Even in sleep he had heard her shift on the hard bed and press both legs together. "What's the matter?" he mumbled.

"Elmo's here and I'm fine."

He reached overhead so Elmo could find his hand in midair. "What did they do with the Silver Man?"

"Sent him up to Butner." The Silver Man had been stopped near Hillsborough for erratic driving and was found to be wrapped from head to toe in aluminum foil to ward off rays from outer space. "I see Mary's off the IV?"

"They've got her walking up and down the halls."

Mary said suddenly, "I don't know why they won't tell me who I got the kidney from."

"Because it doesn't matter, that's why," said Frank.

"People get funny ideas," Elmo offered. "This guy at my church wouldn't sign the organ donor card because he thinks you can't get into Heaven unless you got all your parts. I asked him what about people with fingers and legs cut off, and he said at least those didn't get mixed up inside other people." He met Frank's frown and changed the subject. "Is the food any good?"

"I'm still on liquids. I think they gave me a fat man's kidney. I'd just like to know, that's all. Was Miss Torrido an organ donor?"

Frank didn't know. Elmo said anyway hers would have been too old.

"This is a young one," Mary said. "And I'm pretty sure it's a man." When her doctor had talked to the medical students about rejection he meant that *she* might reject *it*; but Mary had begun to think of this borrowed kidney as a puzzled orphan that would do the rejection itself, trying to run away and get back to where it belonged.

Tacey came in to admire the flowers and the fuzzy bear and then announce that Christine's plane had landed in New York; she'd be here tomorrow. She shot a glance at Mary over the yellow chrysanthemums.

"I don't want her," Mary said. "I don't want her now."

"Well, she's your mother," Tacey said without much conviction.

"Now she is," Mary said.

"People are different—why, some can't even stand to give blood transfusions," Elmo said. Mary could see that he was moving into what Frank called his New Testament Phase, and wanted to persuade her to turn the other cheek. To turn the other kidney. His hands palms up, he said, "I've known people after a wreck just to drop dead without any injury at all, from shock—they've just got a different body system. And somebody else cut to ribbons not hardly complaining?"

"So everything's luck," Tacey said, pulling her mouth into a puckered ring like a drawstring bag. "Nobody's brave, nobody gets blame or credit."

"I wouldn't say that." Elmo frowned. "People can make the most or the least of what they get born with. But with Christine, the operation's over and Mary's getting along so well. Doesn't Christine feel bad enough as it is?"

"Probably not," Frank said.

Elmo drew closer to the bed and said earnestly, "You got your whole life ahead of you, Mary, so don't you dwell on what your mama wasn't or what your mama didn't do."

Tacey edged up to the other side. "I never said not to forgive her. We all know our Christian duty, Elmo. It's not just you Methodists that can read Scripture."

Mary looked from one to the other, then closed her eyes. She could hear Frank saying, "We've tired her out," and Tacey insisting that she'd stay for a while; she'd brought her Sunday-school book to read and it probably explained just as much about forgiveness as Elmo's did.

Forgive us our trespasses, Mary thought, as we forgive those who trespass against us. About this petition she had once felt safe, since she never invaded others' property marked with NO TRESPASSING signs. Now she was using—indeed, over-using—a strange man's kidney; other strangers had trespassed deeply into her own body.

Elmo's voice came from near the door, ". . . the future, that's what's important. You and Mr. Thompson need to take a vacation, go up to the mountains where it's cool. And Frank ought to marry that girl, let Christine come to the wedding; who cares? Let her be the matron of honor—what difference does it make?"

Lead us not into temptation, Mary thought, imagining Christine flinging flowers ahead of the bridal procession.

Out of nowhere she felt her father's dry lips pressed against her forehead, then again at the edge of her hair. "Take a nap then," he said. "Mama, does she feel warm to you?"

The sounds of footsteps, closing door, Tacey settling into the bedside chair. She was sleepy. Our Mother, who art in New York, hollow be thy name.

BUT WHEN CHRISTINE ARRIVED on Day Five, Mary's temperature was elevated, and she had been moved into isolation while doctors made alternate wagers that she was experiencing an episode of rejection or an unknown infection.

Jill said wearily, "You're so negative, Frank. Try to remember you and the doctors are on the same side."

"Well, why didn't they tell us that even flowers might bring germs in on them?"

"Nobody blames the flowers, Frank. You pick up these notions in the waiting room, but you skip over any optimistic word that gets said." She leaned back in the chair and closed her eyes against the ever-present television programs that droned and flickered from a high shelf. "I'm glad I'll only have to treat animals. Animals butt out."

"After they bite you or kick you," Frank said, pacing.

Jill barely glanced at the woman who had come to the door just long enough to decide that her hair was too blond to be natural.

But Frank stopped in midstride, slowly lowered that foot. "Christine?"

"I know it's too light," said the woman with a small, tentative smile while making a quick pass at her curls with a row of red fingernails, "but it's still an improvement, don't you think? How's Mary? At the desk they didn't know."

"She's worse," said Frank. Jill had gotten to her feet and now explained: the fever, a reduction in urine output, other symptoms that might mean a reaction to her medicines or an infection or even rejection of the new kidney itself. She put out her hand. "I'm Jillian Peters," she added. "Mary's riding teacher."

"Among other things. I met you at the picnic but I was redheaded then." Christine, avoiding the handshake, had the gall to lift her chin and nose while frowning with superiority. Surprised, Jill waited for Frank to defend her.

He said bitterly, "I guess if this kidney fails you'll get a second chance."

Around the edges of her rouge, Christine's face paled. She sank into a chair. "Can I go in?"

"The doctors are there right now," said Jill. "Until today she's been walking around and everything. Eating solid foods."

"But her blood pressure's been up."

"Again, that's from the medicine," Jill said.

"They have to give more medicine when it's a dead man's kidney," said Frank in a harsh voice.

"Stop, stop," whispered Christine. Her tears were dark with mascara.

Jill made a helpless movement with both hands and waited for Frank to do something. His own hands had compressed into fists and lay lightly on both thighs like coiled springs. He said, "Notice, Jill, how the dress almost matches the hair. I guess she was out shopping all the times we tried to find her."

Jill finally said, "Everybody's tired."

"Well, so am I after being on that airplane without even lunch. OK? There's no point talking to you, Frank. I just want to see Mary."

Jill murmured something about the cafeteria downstairs.

"I just talked to her on the telephone and she was getting along fine!" Christine sniffled. "Why isn't Mama here? Where's Tacey?"

As she stood, Jill said, "I need to leave you two to talk—" and ignored Frank's shake of the head. "Besides, we've got to worm all those horses today, and I need to be there when the vet comes."

"You'll get more conversation out of a horse than out of Frank Thompson!" Christine exclaimed.

A man in white appeared, drew Frank aside, and began discussing a possible kidney biopsy for which he'd have to sign. It might settle the cause of Mary's fever and white blood count.

"She's been through so much already," Frank said.

Christine came closer to peer at the clipboard. "They're not going to cut on her again, are they?"

Frank pivoted away, holding the pen waist-high, where it could not agree to anything too quickly. From the doorway Jill was saying that if she wasn't needed, then, she'd call in later? Nobody answered. The doctor mumbled more explanations.

Christine's voice rose. "I'm her mother!"

"She's never had custody," Frank said. He hardly noticed Jill disappearing down the hall.

"Mrs. Thompson?" The doctor or whoever it was shook Christine's hand while Frank braced the clipboard on one knee and signed. "Please don't hurt her," he said.

"Can't I see her first? I've been running ever since the plane landed."

"We'll be very careful."

In the hospital room a few minutes later, one of the smiling nurses told Mary what her daddy had said, and she supposed they *were* very careful. She felt too tired and limp to care.

They had told her she could watch preparations on the ultrasound screen, the same one that would later guide her doctor in making his accurate trespass onto the new renal cortex. But she didn't care to watch anything. Something thick was in her head, under her ribs. She wanted to sleep.

"Your parents are in the waiting room," somebody told her through a mask. That word, "parents," made her briefly imagine them paired as they once had been in car seats, at the movies, posed for photographs. She laid a forearm against her eyes to turn such images into sparks and flashes. They flew like tiny fireworks under her hot eyelids.

Afterward she had to lie for hours without moving while some kind of weighted pillow was kept pressed against the biopsy site. She tried not to cough, though her chest also felt weighted down; she was surprised to find nothing heavier there than her own feverish skin.

Through fog she saw nurses tiptoe in and out every few minutes to check her blood pressure and pulse. It seemed to her that no time passed before the next one was murmuring her name, making her open her eyes. When Mary dozed, sometimes Miss Lila Torrido took their place, would pump up the cuff and read the gauge herself: "It's a thousand and one." Miss Torrido's appearance was improving, Mary noticed, now that she had made an adjustment to death. The bruises were gone from her neck, and deep in the center of the hole where her breast had been removed, a new one was slowly growing. Probably a transplant. Probably a transplant from an adolescent girl, with a pink nipple that would never quite match in size or color.

During Miss Torrido's visitations Mary often found herself alert but speechless, so she only pointed with a smile to the new growth. Miss Torrido nodded without looking down. Mary wanted to ask if the developing breast had been patchworked in, if Heaven was actually full of people dressed up in spare human parts after all. Or maybe Heaven was the place where everything would be restored; maybe this breast had been kept in God's storage and was actually the same one, now healed by Jesus, that a younger Lila Torrido had forfeited in surgery. Perhaps an old man might, in eternity, have returned to him the pudgy fingers he had lost as a boy to the wood saw. But there was no way to get all these questions into pantomime while Miss Lila was saying "One thousand and two," and making gestures as if Mary might get up and come away with her. Mary was too hot to come away, hot enough for Hell, where the wicked amputees and the cremated sinners went.

She woke to a sensation of wet smothering. Somebody's face and yellow hair were in her way. Though the hair was the color of mustard, even as her hands flew out reflexively to push the stranger away, Mary recognized the smell of Christine's perfume. She sneezed and it hurt.

"I'm right here, baby, don't you catch a cold now!"

The light above the bed had been turned to dim. It must be nighttime. Hanging in midair, Christine was only a blurred face within a cloud of bright hair.

"I hated to wake you up, but it's now or never. I can't stay but a minute."

For answer Mary worked a small grunt out of her dry throat. Already she could tell how tired it would make her to talk.

"No matter what Frank may think, there's not a thing wrong with your new kidney, and you could still have come down with pneumonia if you'd got mine or his just the same. Now that they know what's wrong they can treat it. And then you can change into this!" She took from a paper bag and held up a rosy nightgown suitable for a honeymoon. "Cheer you right up, baby!"

Christine's size, no doubt. Mary found it hard to nod, lying down, so she said, "Pretty," and coughed. Surely they had shifted the weight onto her ribs? She touched her chest; no.

"Look at this lace," said Christine, spreading her fingers inside the gown's transparent bodice. "I should maybe buy you a bed jacket? With all the visitors you'll be having? A boyfriend, maybe?"

A nurse opened the room door and waited just inside.

"Yes, ma'am, I know it's time," said Christine sharply. "I'm leaving this right in your bottom drawer, OK? You feel like reading? Well, you will when the fever's down, and I've brought all my flyers and guidebooks. I've got a map marked with everywhere I went. You can use it in school, OK?" At the door she asked the nurse, "Wouldn't she sleep better if her bed was level? I know I would. I'm Mary's mother." They went into the hall.

That night the Broomes and Thompsons and Christine went home, relieved to carry with them the word "pneumonia," something specific that dozens of kin and friends had already recovered from.

If she hadn't been short of money, Christine would have chosen any hotel rather than sleep in the cluttered, dirty Durham house on Cromwell Street, where in every room hung the odor of something undone—garbage and sour dishcloths in the kitchen, mildew deep in closet corners, urine and sweat and dirty-feet smells near the beds and toilets. She threw up the living room windows, holding her "Pew!" to a whisper.

"That screen's out; you'll let in bugs."

"Doesn't Virgil ever fix anything?" She'd have to sleep on that uneven brown couch, its upholstery scented by Virgil's behind.

Georgia said, "Catch the sheet on your end," and tucked hers under the cushion. "Did you fall out with Nolo or just get tired of him?"

"I'm tired of every man that lives," muttered Christine.

Georgia's flat voice disagreed. "Is that so?"

"I used to think it was just Frank, but every one of them—" Breaking off, she made a face when she pulled from inside the couch a comb, a Popsicle stick, coins, a glob of sticky crumbs. "They every one expect you to come when you're called? There they are in front of TV, maybe, changing channels because that's something they do the best; and they call to ask you something? And *they* call *you*—oh, no, *they'd* never come to find *you*. You've all the time got to stop what you're doing and come."

Virgil, who had been parking the car in the backyard, came in now and threw his red baseball cap onto a chair where it lay—open as hibiscus—exuding hair-oil musk into the room.

"Pick that up," Georgia said without looking at her daughter.

He moved it to a table. "Ya'll want a beer?"

Both shook their heads while Christine cleaned trash off her hand into a wastebasket. When he had gone into the kitchen she said, "You know it's so, Mama. And men don't take care of themselves, so they break down while women are still young. They get fat and they snore and they catch diseases." She went back to the couch and got the top sheet spread neatly. "If I could afford it, I'd live like all those women movie stars—I'd take in a younger man for a year or so and then buy him off and get his kid brother."

"He'd run around on you," said Georgia, sliding a pillow inside its slightly yellowed case.

Christine reached out to feel it. "This hasn't been in mothballs, has it?"

"Lord, no!"

Christine wondered how moths that had died of old age might smell, in there with the mildew. Taking the pillow, she dropped her chin against it. "Mary's got hollow eyes, those dark circles. I don't know."

From the door, between swallows, Virgil said, "I bet she got. A nigger. Kidney." He waved the can left and right. "Them young bucks are always shooting each other down in the projects. Drive by and shoot anybody. Die young. Nobody claims 'em. No telling what he was high on when he died. Mary's caught something from that kidney."

Christine said angrily to her mother, "I won't listen to any of that, it's depressing, I've already told you."

"This would have been low-life. This wasn't no General Colin Powell."

"Shut up, Virgil. I've left you a counterpane."

Counter*pin*, she pronounced it. Virgil sometimes said a fireplace had a chimbley. Christine was glad she had moved on to a different, higher life. "Where's my suitcases?"

Virgil dragged three from the hall while Georgia gave her a quick hug. "They'll call if Mary gets worse, so you might as well sleep."

"Frank, they'll call *Frank*."

"They've got this number, too," Virgil said. He held out the beer can as if it were a flashlight. "You leave that window up, somebody's gonna come on in and cut you. I'm telling you, Durham is Crime City these days, Christine—" He was still talking as Georgia moved him out with jabs and small pushes. "Somebody throwed a rock from the highway overpass, went right through the windshield, didn't leave nothing left of this schoolteacher but a greasy spot. This boy took a pistol to the fifth grade—"

But Christine couldn't sleep, and not from fear that crack addicts were hiding in the unpruned yard bushes. Automatically she undressed and put on gown and robe, hardly noticing that they didn't match, for she was seeing Mary's bruised eyes, the oxygen tube in her nose; remembering her cheek hot as a coffee cup, her breath that seemed fast and uneven with a weak voice blotted up by the effort of it. Maybe pneumonia germs had been alive in that dead man's kidney. Or maybe AIDS—didn't the queers that had it finally drop like flies from pneumonia in the end?

Christine rummaged in her makeup kit until she found a tube of Erase, the beige cream she smoothed onto shadows below her own eyes; but then she carried it inside one fist, forgotten, onto the front porch. She sat in the rocker and pushed herself forward and back while watching the crescent moon not move at all. Once Mary had suggested—was she eight? nine?—that a narrow moon was God's clipped fingernail; He didn't cut much or often. By the time He worked all the way around both hands, it would be Christmas at least. "So what's the big fat round moon, then?" Frank had asked. "Hush, Frank," Christine said, "that's sweet." He said, "That's Grandma Tacey."

Christine whispered now, "That's sweet," and decided to let herself cry out here in the dark for her little girl, and because people blamed her for not giving her own kidney months ago —they all did; she knew it; Frank, of course, but the nurses, too, and even her own family. And whatever went wrong now would be Christine's fault! Mary could get run over by a truck or drown in the river, and Christine knew where the fingers would point.

She cried harder.

Even Nolo, who knew Christine couldn't even bring herself to get breast implants, even Nolo had shrugged off her explanations. "You got two and Mary needs one," he'd said with a shrug, as if explaining a grade-school problem in subtraction. And Nolo hated the broken home he came from (broken to *smithereens*, he said), and what was he? Some steady Red Cross blood donor? No, he was not. Would he even read that magazine article on vasectomy? No, he would not.

The sound of voices made Christine remember Virgil's warnings, and she slid the rocker deeper into the porch shadows and held it still. Four black teenagers were passing under a street-light: male, tall, and lean, the one in front with both ears wired to his portable radio, the other three laughing, talking in high party voices with theatrical emphasis. Probably they lived nearby; the neighborhood was mixed now. They had been to the movies? Or a club, had a beer, whether they were old enough or not. No car—not unless they were to ease into the backyard now and steal Virgil's. She doubted they would consider the Buick worth stealing.

Or come on this porch! For a gang bang. Oh, she was afraid of the dark and angry men; they would all burn Watts and Detroit and Los Angeles if they could, even those black marines in uniform in Jacksonville who called her ma'am politely when she knew what they were really thinking.

The four came bouncing, half dancing, along the sidewalk and past the Broome house while she tried to shrink in her chair. One reason Christine supported women's free choice for abortion was that otherwise the white race would be swamped by the colored birthrate, swamped, and then—awash in a tide of black babies—would go down under the rhythmic waves that would roar what had always been meant by "We shall overcome."

But the young blacks were moving away now, and from behind they looked too thin to be much threat. It was the hospital—not Virgil's ravings—that had made Christine think like a Nazi. She had been doing it all day, watching hospital patients rolled this way and that like small broken machines. They would even be fixed (or experimented with) by insertion of plastic joints, with metal pins through bone and wounds stapled shut. Had they not stapled the layers of Mary's stomach as if they had been paper pages? And the sight of so many sick and hurt patients reminded Christine of watching those two men die as if in her own living room, that Barney Clark and William Schroeder, men who got saved from heart failure with an artificial Jarvik machine, but then no battery could keep their bodies from clotting up everywhere else while television cameras rolled. Nobody could stop the strokes and the pain with a wall plug. In the hospital today she had felt that behind every wall doctors were saving some sickly newborn baby whose future children would inherit double trouble and cost everybody a fortune. Why, when Virgil had pickled his particular liver, somebody would stick in a fresh young one and send him home crippled and mean so she and Georgia would be expected to spoon-feed him twenty years.

Well, I won't, Christine thought, watching the four young men turn at the corner downhill toward public housing units. UPPER GARDENS, said the sign at the top of the hill where the stark apartment buildings began, then LOWER GARDENS halfway down, though nothing much grew in those clay yards but clotheslines and broken tricycles. There were dogs. African-Americans plus their dogs, the Canine-Americans. They've about taken over Durham the way Virgil says.

When Mary gets on her feet and goes to school with them, the teachers will have to protect her, Christine thought. There can't be any pushing in the halls or on the school bus. Maybe it's good that Frank's a state trooper, after all; people will be afraid of her daddy. That's one good thing.

She tore down the MADAME GEORGETTE sign before she went inside to sleep, sniffling in fast, shallow inhalations to dilute the odors. Tomorrow at the hospital there would be alcohol and medicine smells, thick as a mudpack, to clean out her nostrils; and before she left Durham she would spread perfumed gel between her breasts where her own heart would pulsate it forth, and she could breathe the sweet fragrance of no one but herself.

CINDY SCOFIELD had been writing a series of newspaper articles on rescue squad volunteers in Orange and Chatham counties, following first a whole class as it took the EMT training course, then focusing a personality piece on one woman volunteer, and tonight (post-op Day Six for Mary) she rode with the squad to document a typical eight-hour shift with the crew performing on-site emergency treatment that used to be delayed until arrival at the hospital. Cindy was used to monitoring the 10-50 calls on her scanner that had directed her to many car wrecks, where often she had admired Frank Thompson calmly at work, but it was different to hover near the gurney inside an ambulance while a victim lay choking on blood and pieces of her tongue.

Now she waited another hour in the noisy emergency waiting room for the closing paragraph of her story to be revealed—that the woman will recover, had died, was drunk, would be paralyzed.

Most of the crowd waiting with her were women of all ages—largely black, a few white, one Hispanic—which meant that most of the night's emergency patients were men, men who'd been fighting or speeding or claiming their heart attacks were only indigestion. These women wasted no energy by pacing. None of them touched a magazine. They solidified themselves in the first chairs they had taken some time ago, and waited like stones for something external to make them move.

By stepping into the back hall, Cindy could watch new injury and illness being rolled onto the loading platform: pill takers, wrist cutters, an old man who had at last rested to death at a nearby rest home. Two deputies wrestled one hysterical man past her to an orderly who helped get him into leather restraints. He was high on something. He had cut off the end of one thumb because it did not really belong to his own hand, he cried—*they* had grafted it on while he slept; it was separately alive and filthy.

Cindy edged into the parking lot for fresh air mixed with exhaust. How do they stand it? Sent to clean Hell with a dust cloth.

When she asked again at the desk about the wreck victim

and showed her ID for the third time to the same weary man, he said that the patient would live, that her ruptured spleen and broken hip and ribs and all those bloody lacerations could be treated. Cindy made a note of the hospital room number, since there were weeks of recuperation to come, and her editor might want a follow-up. "And can you tell me anything about a regular patient, Mary Grace Thompson? Kidney transplant? I didn't get a chance to call today."

He didn't have those records but showed how she could telephone the nurses' station nearest Mary's room. To Cindy, the nurse who answered sounded reticent. Still serious, she said. No, not critical.

Not yet, her tone implied.

"Is any of her family still there? I'm an old friend. I could sit with them."

The nurse went away, then said, "Her father's still here. I thought he'd come back—he usually does."

In the sprawling hospital, Cindy got lost several times trying to follow directions and read the signs posted in different colors down the many turning corridors. When at last she looked into the correct waiting room, Frank was folded up, asleep between two chairs, part of his body sagging into the gap. At sight of him her whole head instantly swelled, and both eyes stung. It must be the entire night's stress just waiting in my throat, she decided—and gulped hard. She eased into another chair to watch. He needed a shave, a bath, a vacation, a goddamn miracle.

And where was this precious Jillian Peters, this girl who would stay up all night with a mare in foal when Frank needed her? Cindy had kept her distance, unwilling to intrude; she had steadily telephoned the desk and checked with Elmo for details. It was Elmo who'd said Christine had finally been able to work motherhood into her busy schedule.

He also told her, "This is killing Frank."

She saw firsthand that it was. The few tears that got past her

willpower and slid down her face were for Frank—not Mary—
for Cindy's hopes for Mary's future had always been compro-
mised. At best, she'd decided months ago, they might with a
substitute kidney keep her a member of the chronically ill. She
had learned close-up the price such survival exacted from the
rest of the family. But she'd never said such things to Frank,
and he'd never once connected Mary's case to what he'd always
called Cindy's morbid pessimism. *Earned* pessimism, she'd say
to correct him.

Now he is earning his own, she thought.

As Frank jerked in his sleep one bent knee slid aside. The
air-conditioning was too cold. Cindy went to ask a nurse for a
blanket.

"At least he's sleeping," said the nurse as she handed one
out of a storage closet. "He's hardly been home."

"He loves her," Cindy said, hugging the folded blanket to
her chest. She looked down the empty hall. "He'd give his life
for her."

"Too bad it doesn't work that way." The nurse took off her
eyeglasses and wiped them. "And too bad there's no system
that trades off criminals instead of sick children. I think about
all those killers on death row."

"Without even a headache." When the nurse turned aside,
Cindy—reluctant to see her go—said, "I've just spent hours in
emergency and I don't know how you people stand it."

"I'm too old for code-three duty anymore," the nurse said.
MURDOCK was the name on her plastic pin. "No more trauma
team for me. And emergency wears you down, too. One night
this man brought a dog in here, a *dog*, mind you, said his kids
had fed it Drano! And at the time we had everything from
women in labor to perforated ulcers."

"But you still work with crisis patients. Aren't all these
people"—Cindy nodded up and down the hall—"seriously ill?"
She would not say *critically* ill.

"Here it's the families that get worn down," said Nurse

Murdock softly. "At first they all try to learn our names and they'll bring in little presents. Like candy? Hand cream. They want us to like them. They have the feeling if we like them that guarantees we'll be extra careful, extra nice, to the one that's sick. Of course we're nice to everybody. And after a while families smile less and criticize more. They fuss with each other. They get tired, you see."

Cindy saw. How many times could you count the acoustical tile overhead or the vinyl tile underfoot or watch Vanna White flip alphabet cards?

In the waiting room she covered Frank and watched the touch of the blanket bring him awake. For a minute he smiled as sleepily at her as he had when waking many mornings in her own bed. Then his body remembered where it was and thrashed until both chairs slid apart and he dropped to the brown tile floor. He looked rumpled and silly, folded into a wide V.

"Everything's OK," said Cindy quickly. He was in jeans and a T-shirt. "I was just passing by."

"Mary?"

"Everything. Fine. Let me help you."

He got to his feet with a grunt. "Time is it?"

"Little after three." When he frowned she added, "Three a.m. I was covering a wreck."

Frank pushed both chairs against the wall. "Nowadays I only think about wrecks in terms of kidneys and livers."

Cindy nodded as she refolded the blanket. A man came to the door and went away. There was a silence. She finally said, "Editors like my series on the rescue squad. I'm getting some offers."

"What series?"

Of course Frank had no time to read the local feature pages. She decided right then she'd move on, take the job at the *Charlotte Observer*, or now that Dow Jones had bought out the Chapel Hill paper, perhaps even try the *Wall Street Journal*. "So how's Christine—you able to be civil to her?"

Yawning, he shook his head. "Only to Mary. Too tired for anybody else."

"It's pneumonia?"

"They call it one of those funny pneumonias, whatever that means. She's very sick."

Cindy could see cigarette butts in an ashtray; she thought he'd quit. "You here all the time?"

"I'm on leave till Mary's condition"—he hesitated—"settles down."

Down, down, down, thought Cindy, more and more depressed. "I'll leave the blanket here, then." She stepped forward; he ducked; their hug was awkward and the light kiss meant for Frank's cheek landed instead on his scratchy neck. She stayed off balance for a moment, breathing in his weariness and old shaving cream, then whispered, "I'll stay in touch," and hurried into the hall to the elevator.

Its doors separated immediately. The floor buttons were controlled by the heat of the fingers, as she knew from having once tried to punch them through leather gloves. She tried now to remember if she wanted the first or ground or basement floor. Down, down, and down.

When she got outdoors, the helicopter, like a nervous hen, was clacking its way between buildings and electrical wires to land in its concrete nest in front of the hospital. At the edge a trauma team stood ready, shielding their eyes with forearms against the whip of flung grit.

Cindy had already ridden once in this chopper, pushed aside against hard knobs of metal, because there was really no space or time for observers, so her presence had been very much resented.

People in white uniforms raced for the sliding door while the noisy rotors were still turning.

She imagined that nurses and interns had come running out to the curb the night her mother went into premature labor after she fell downstairs. She pictured obstetricians rushing her onto the medical table and getting both feet into stirrups so they could catch the baby boy when he came—too small, too blue.

But alive—alive even today.

Cindy crossed the bridge to the parking deck and took its dirty elevator down.

"I WASN'T EXPECTING YOU," said Mary very softly, surprised she could speak at all.

It must have been her turn to talk instead of Miss Lila Torrido's, who only smiled and beckoned with her left hand. She was holding something white in her other hand.

"I'm tired of this hospital," said Mary while Miss Torrido nodded. Even when she sat up in bed she could not recognize what Miss Torrido was carrying. It looked lumpy. She almost slapped her own abdomen to find out what had cured it since her last medication. Powerful stuff, that must have been! There was no pain. And it was easy to breathe? Mary started to push aside the plastic tent, but her hand passed right through so she dropped both feet off the bed to see if the rest of her could follow. Nothing to it.

Miss Torrido backed away toward the door. She seemed entirely healed and normal, although one of her peachy breasts was as inflated as a balloon. She watched Miss Torrido turn to display it, as if showing her best side to a mirror. "What have you got with you?" No answer. The floor was not cold; in fact, her bare feet were not quite touching.

"Mary?" Who did that sound like? Grandmother Tacey Thompson.

Mary bobbed past her and across the room like a tumbleweed.

They were into the long, long hospital hall. Miss Torrido had emptied it out for them. Not a nurse, not a wheelchair. After a while there were not even any doors. It was wonderful to be able to move the way astronauts did in space. She did not weigh as much as the seed globe of one dandelion. Nor did Miss Torrido, still turned to face her, still drifting backward down the hall.

From behind, below, somewhere, came the call "Mary!" And there were loud noises in the room she had left: thumps and talking, a scream, rattles; the bell noises of bottles sliding against one another—but she could not go back just to listen to that. It was a very long corridor with its double doors open to sunlight at the far end.

She almost turned back because Tacey sounded as if somebody were hurting her.

But now she could see that Miss Lila Torrido in her white nightgown was carrying a white plate piled high with squares of fudge—white fudge!—and waving a white napkin over the candy as she drew them farther and farther down the hall.

So Mary laughed and went forward toward that light and that sweetness.

NOBODY, of course, was in the right place when on Day Seven the heart screen above Mary's bed changed sound and picture, and Tacey ran screaming for the nurse, who was already racing toward her.

The Broomes—en route to the hospital—were just driving up the long slope of Franklin Street into Chapel Hill with Georgia at the wheel. Virgil was reading aloud as he and Christine revised together the locksmith ad he planned to put in the newspaper. Georgia listened to neither of them but hummed happily along with the radio, which was coming in very strong since they had just passed the WCHL station. Because she was psychic and knew intuition would warn her if Mary should get sicker, Georgia was certain today would be Mary's turning point, when all the benefits of surgery came true. After all, it was the seventh day, that magic number seven from Genesis; seven—which was 3 + 4, the spirit plus human body, seven for wholeness; and Mary's mother had come, and the moon was full.

Over Georgia's singing Virgil read in a loud voice, *"Thieves come back!* Robbery victim? Change your locks! Protect your children, your privacy, your new renters—"

"Tenants," Christine corrected from the backseat. "Has anybody emptied these ashtrays since World War Two?"

At the same time Dandy was out in his backyard watering Tacey's new row of chrysanthemums so she could take the early morning shift at the hospital and send Frank home to rest. Though she had shown him exactly how to pinch back each plant so it would grow bushier, he soon got tired of that and began using his pocketknife just to snap off each main stem while the hose ran at the roots. He was pleased by the evenness of the row—a ten-inch hedge. The task had left him free to plan what cheerful things he would say to Mary if she were awake this afternoon. "You know what would happen if you swallowed a spoon? Why you wouldn't be able to stir!" Maybe at least she would smile? And then he'd say, "It won't be long till you're back riding that Chancy horse. You know what horse sees as much in the rear as he does in the front? You don't? Give up? A blind horse!"

At that moment Frank was actually in Chancy's stall. Last week the gelding had gone down with colic so the vet had come and forced mineral oil into his stomach through a long tube. Now no one could tell he'd ever been sick. Mary's fever was lower then, though, and she'd had enough energy to worry. Frank bent to lay one ear against the horse's side and listen to intestinal gurgles. Gurgles were good; silence could mean impaction.

Over the stall door Jill said, "I didn't hear you come in."

"You were finishing up a class. Did he worm this horse, too?"

"Yes, we both thought the colic was brought on by parasites. And he seems fine."

"You didn't call."

"I got swamped, Frank. Somebody brought in a new horse for me to board. The vet was late, I was late for my chem lab. How's Mary?"

"About the same. I wanted to be able to tell her about Chancy."

"I can get the Polaroid camera."

"All right." While she was gone and he wiped his shoes of the greenish balls of fresh manure, he kept wondering if too much money got spent on animal health, if vet schools should all be research centers into human disease, but he was too tired to care very much. He rubbed a kink of pain between his neck and shoulder blade where he'd slept on it wrong.

After Chancy's picture, Jill took another of rumpled Frank alongside, so in the future he could always see for himself what worry did to him. He did see. In the print he was middle-aged and disheartened. He looked from it to her carefully made-up face, the long blond plait. He thought about the butterfly permanently alight on her silky shoulder.

"Are you going straight back to that hospital?" He nodded. "Without any lunch?"

"Can you get away?"

"I was only able to get the farrier this afternoon, and there's a show coming up. I'm sorry."

One of her students, a chubby girl in velvet riding hat and jeans, could barely hoist nose and eyes over the edge of Chancy's stall door to gasp, "Ralph's loose, Miss Peters! I couldn't help it! Brenda Jean can't catch him and he's running toward the road!"

Jill made an exaggerated shrug before unlatching the door. Still she stood there another moment, as if one of them might say something that would surprise the other. Then she passed the stall door to Frank's hand, and as he fastened it carefully behind them, she began trotting gracefully down the aisle to the wide barn door.

He left more slowly, examining the two photographs. The sight of Chancy's long head slightly turned and gazing toward the camera reminded him of something Cindy had said once about the eyes of animals, something from one of her English-major poems. That the creature world "beholds the open," while humans have their looking restricted by what they know. Animals were free of any knowledge of mortality, she'd said, and the openness showed in their open gaze. He could hear her reciting: "the free animal / has its decease perpetually behind it / and God in front, and when it moves, it moves / into eternity, like running springs." Of course she had only been talking about that goddamned little Pomeranian at the time, holding its oddly distorted head between two hands, and the occasion had been long before Mary's illness and unimportant. He had not thought of it since and was surprised to find the words embedded in him like a row of buckshot.

Frank walked past the barn bulletin board with its different photographs: horse-show winners with ribbons, young Jill with young girls and boys.

She was right about one thing—he ought to eat if only to substitute for lost sleep—and Tacey was there in Mary's room. Frank pulled into McDonald's and took his bag of food through the car window, decided to eat it at Gimghoul Castle, an ivy-covered stone tower not many blocks away from where Tacey was watching Mary sleep and regain her strength. From its top, he could see the top of the hospital buildings but not the side on which Mary's room was located. College boys played King Arthur here; maybe some future frat boy would bring Mary to show her the rock with eternal bloodstains where some college boy from the last century had dueled and died for love.

Frank ate his hamburger on that rock, where the stains were really iron oxide, and the weak coffee tasted as if it had been strained through many newspapers. There were wrens, cardinals, and on the edge of the clearing one squirrel waited for his leftovers.

He felt as if he had benefited from a good nap. The picture of himself he stuck in his wallet, but Mary would like the one of Chancy with his dark and bottomless eyes.

Christine was the first of the Broomes to arrive at Mary's hospital room. Virgil had let the women out at the main entrance and gone to park the Buick; Georgia then stopped downstairs to find something cheerful that she could afford at the gift shop.

As soon as Christine left the elevator, the nurses who had been clustered near the station broke apart, and the one with round glasses put down the telephone and hurried toward her. Immediately Christine saw that something had gone wrong with her twisted mouth in that awful pearlized lipstick. Perhaps she had just come from the dentist. Perhaps her jaw felt puffy and numb.

The nurse said rapidly, "We've been trying to call everybody."

They had certainly given her too much novocaine. Christine shook off her hand. The hand came back and became an arm around her shoulder.

The nurse said very softly, "Everything was tried, everything was done. I am so very sorry."

"No," said Christine in a loud voice, dodging. She was near Mary's door, but she did not touch it.

"The doctor's been waiting to talk with you; I'll get him."

"No!" Christine broke loose again. In her awkward high-heeled shoes she trotted past that door and turned and ran back by again. "No! No!"

Another nurse reached out for her. "Mrs. Thompson?"

She screamed it. *"No!"*

Down the hall a doctor was running toward her—if he was a doctor; how could you tell in this place? He could be a janitor in somebody else's clothes.

But he turned out to be a doctor she'd met yesterday. He

tried to hold both her arms, saying things like "quick . . . unexpected . . . did not suffer . . . could not revive . . ."

Something volcanic was happening inside Christine. It burst out in sobs and shivers and broken, gasping screams. "I'll do it. OK? Yes! She can have it! Take the goddamn kidney! Hurry up!" They were dragging her into a different room. "Oh, please! Hurry up! Take it now!"

As soon as the elevator door opened Georgia heard her screaming and knew.

KIDNAPPING. It was a kidnapping by Death, Frank was finally able to say, but not until the next summer or fall. Today he said nothing. Saw little. Heard less. Something else—not his own joints; they had melted—moved him out of the hospital, into somebody's car where he sat between silent old people said to be his parents.

He'd walked stiffly away from the shriek of Christine's hysterics. They gave her a shot. She kept babbling that this was an injection for anesthesia, soon the operation would start, these doctors could do wonders now, OK?

Christine grew smaller and smaller and less and less loud, so he must have walked away.

Tacey took him home. He had grown up in a different house out from town, but that was no reason for him to look around her present kitchen as if he had never seen it.

"Here's where the tree came through. You can't tell it," she said. She led him to their bedroom. Into the old sleigh bed she got him by gentle pressure, as if pushing stubborn fabric underwater. First he was sitting but lifted both hands. She lowered them. Raised his stiff leg and worked off that shoe. When his foot floated off again, she laid them both—shoe and all—on the bed and then eased, smoothed, and rubbed his long, rigid self down onto mattress and pillow. "Lie still."

She waited. His pale face looked cold and hard as glass. He

was staring. There was nothing to see on the ceiling but an ugly brass fixture, disconnected now. "Don't you get up!" she ordered.

Dandy had come no deeper into the house than the first kitchen chair. From the door she said to him almost angrily, "You just can't have a heart attack now. Have you got your nitro?" He straightened and nodded. She went to sit (to drop, not sit), at the hall telephone. She weighed a ton. Lists, she thought. People to call. Arrangements.

She placed a hand on her face, almost struck herself. Underneath, her mouth kept struggling. But she could not allow it to wail, not yet. And in the dim hallway there was no one to confide in, to tell how easily and quickly Mary had gone away even while Tacey was bending over the hospital bed— just the sudden fixity of both eyes, so that Tacey had then half turned to see on whom her stare had frozen, and then the flat line and alarm from bedside machines. Uniformed people ran in. They had thrust Tacey from the room while the team tried everything to bring her back, but no; Mary had all at once evaporated from that body, gone out as small as one breath, as fast as a wink of her wide eye pupils.

Tacey opened the telephone book, but its type was too small, too blurred.

She did not know what all the doctors had tried to restart that vacant body, and she did not want to know. Sometimes doctors cut open dying people and shook their cooling hearts by hand the way you might shake a cheap pocket watch to set it ticking. She hoped Frank would never let the doctors tell him all that they had done.

Tacey swallowed then and began to make the calls Frank was not able to do. A funeral home. Her preacher, Mr. Ware. She wrote down: Mary's clothes. Grave site? Jill. Elmo. Cindy. Pallbearers. *Raleigh News and Observer. Chapel Hill Newspaper. Durham Herald.* Memorial gift. Flowers. Mary's teacher and classmates. She wrote down names of her kinfolks and Dandy's

who could be trusted to call those farther out on the circumference of the family circle. Georgia can handle the Broomes,
she decided, and for one moment dreaded the white trash who
might come, then quit caring.

For all of that day and the next Tacey had to keep breathing
in and out, moving the right hand and the left, only because
there was so much to do. The first night Frank kept lying fully
dressed (except for one discarded shoe) on her bedspread. She
and Dandy slept in the second small bedroom, the one Mary
had used when she came to stay. Except that neither one slept
very much. Tacey wanted badly for Mary, who had stopped
living the way a turned-off lamp stops shining, to come back
now on some ghostly visit and say to them something comforting, some word that would linger. Nothing happened. She
said a few automatic prayers. A need to cry had filled like cement
that small place where Tacey's voice and breath and swallowing
had too little room. But she could only do one thing at a time,
so she lay in the dark and breathed in and out.

Next morning Dandy said, "We better make Frank move
around. People that don't move have been known to lock up."

So that morning they got Frank on his feet and fed him toast.
Tacey tried to ask him about funeral plans and could tell when
he finally tried to listen and answer, but words were like faraway
smoke to him. Nods. Headshakes. He would wave one hand.
It seemed to Tacey his mechanical chewing kept time with his
eye blinks. Drove her crazy.

She sat Frank in the living room where Dandy put an electric
razor in his hand. Then she cleaned house between interrupted
buzzes and long silences from that room, where the shaving
took a very long time.

In an hour Jill came to sit by him on the couch, murmuring.
He didn't seem to say much. When Tacey passed going back
and forth to answer the front doorbell she thought that up to
now Jill was too young to have had anyone important die yet.

Not that you could practice up for it. Once after several people had come through with food Jill tried to coax him back to another room, the bedroom, but he got sidetracked by some family photographs on the mantelpiece. Tacey thought Frank would cry then—good!—because of the way his shoulders jerked. He didn't. After a while Jill came to the kitchen, crying herself.

"I might as well go. I'm not helping."

"Too soon for that," Tacey said.

"Tell him I've been here; it's hard to tell if he's even noticed. And I'll be back. Or you can call if?"

Tacey said she would.

When Cindy came she did not sit with Frank at all. She walked by and squeezed his shoulder once, and then took over part of the doorbells and phone calls and visitors. She made a list of those who'd brought casseroles and meats and salads and desserts. She put cut flowers into bowls. Every time she went through the living room she gave the same clutch to Frank's shoulder and kept moving.

Tacey was surprised, almost felt guilty, that she could still wipe crumbs off a table when Mary was dead, as if a clean table mattered, as if anything at all mattered, really; and she stepped back to look into the damp dishcloth and marvel at these speckles of toast that were taking up her time.

When Cindy said she had to go to work she added, "Maybe Frank could sit in the backyard awhile."

"He doesn't seem to notice people coming in and out."

"He does, though. All those busy people without a thing wrong with them."

The funeral home had already put up a sign by the curb DEATH IN FAMILY / DRIVE SLOW, but it was true that every fast car with rock music playing had raised Tacey's blood pressure fifty points.

So Dandy took Frank out under the red oak where the lounge

chairs were and the crepe myrtle hung full of bees. Tacey could see the two men sitting there, Dandy pretending to read the morning paper, Frank not even doing that.

Maybe thirty minutes later, when she was still staring at the cloth, Dandy called from the back door, "You hurt your hand?" When Tacey could not answer he came to hold her clumsily around her middle, where once she'd had a narrow waist. She tried to dwell on how she would get older and fatter without Mary there to tease her about calories, and hoped she could cry at last. She was dry as a dune. He kept his arms around her while they both looked out the kitchen window at Frank. No, still she could not cry.

And so the next busy day passed, with Tacey cleaning and organizing and finding places to locate all the food and display the potted plants, passed with Frank's emptied face sleeping or looking half-alive when he would wander through her house (he couldn't bring himself to go to the apartment where Mary's possessions were), passed with Dandy wishing he could help them both. The mailman brought sympathy cards and a free spa membership Dandy had won from the local dry cleaner.

Though the house filled up with food, Frank ate very little. He seemed unnaturally thirsty. In the night she heard him drinking straight from the bathroom faucet, or sometimes thrashing in the old crackly bed. He stayed in it a lot—ten hours, twelve.

On the night before the funeral, she and Dandy were pretending to watch television in the living room when Frank ran in half asleep in his underwear. He said, "I thought I heard Mary's voice?" Tacey led him by one clammy arm back to bed. He was muttering, "If we'd just kept her on dialysis. She was doing fine. We didn't need to run that risk of an operation."

"She wasn't doing fine. The doctors said—"

"The doctors said the transplant was successful."

Thinking it would do Frank good to spew out whatever guilt or rage he felt, she asked, "Do you really think anybody's at fault here?" When she looked deeply into his twisted face, head-on, the sight made her blurt, "And don't say God; don't do that! It's a sin!"

Frank closed his eyes. They were sunken. "Takes one to know one," he said softly and lay down and rolled so his back was turned. "Must be on your mind."

"It's not." Tacey shook her head until the gray curls of her permanent flew in and out of her peripheral vision. "Absolutely not. That's untrue. Frank?"

He said no more. Almost blindly she felt her way back to her TV chair and lowered herself in place. Girls not much older than Mary with pink hair pulled up into spikes were doing a dance in black fringed costumes. Bouncing their skinny little pelvises forward to have sex with the air.

Over the throbbing music she could hear the rain that had been falling since sundown. She prayed silently, "Get this rain stopped before the funeral," then wondered what kind of God might fix the weather but let a girl die so young you would never see her wear a wedding dress.

Tacey started crying then. She made very little noise. Hard, hurtful sucks of breath made her whole body writhe but were nearly soundless. The few anguished gasps and grunts seemed to tear muscle as they came.

Dandy ran to her. She pushed him back. When she kept fending him off, hoping Frank could not hear her moan, Dandy finally sat on the carpet by her feet. She wondered if he could remember the night Frank had been born and knew how similar the wrenching groans of labor seemed to these. And the body spasms felt just as involuntary, but now these came from her chest and throat. She felt his hand go tentatively round her ankle. That touch grounded her. The convulsions eased. She heard him ask if she wanted aspirin or brandy. No. She wanted the explanations Job had wanted.

She shook her head. TV programs came and went while he kept hold of her ankle. Occasionally he would ask, "You OK,

Tacey? What can I do?" If she'd had the strength, she would have stroked his thin gray hair in thanks. Sometime later she napped, and when she woke he had turned off the set and covered her with an afghan and was watching from across the dark room.

"It's late?" She could still hear the rain.

He said it was.

Clumsily she got up, full of dread, nauseated. "Hard day tomorrow. We better go to bed."

But as Tacey led the way down the hall to the room Mary would never sleep in again she was silently lecturing herself:

This isn't the first time—Tacey Thompson—you felt like giving up on God. This is like stomach flu; you've come down again with the Atheist Stomach Flu. Sick as a dog. Sick as the Devil, even. You didn't catch it from Frank, either. It's always waiting. The germ, it's always there, it's there anytime your resistance drops. No wonder you know the symptoms—you've had it before, you've got it again. This time you're going to be real sick for a while. Real pukey sick. You'll throw up everything, Tacey Thompson. But you got over it before? Last time you knew it was all a lie and we die like the lizards and bumblebees, but you got over it, didn't you? But this is the worst case ever. It's just coming on, but already you can tell it's the worst. You'll be the sickest this time that you've ever been. So you can't do anything now but hang on and be altogether sick and survive it if you can. That's all.

It wasn't like Tacey to throw her soiled clothes over a chair and fall into bed in her petticoat.

Amen, she thought.

SINCE FRANK would remember very little about the funeral, Dandy tried to pay attention so he could answer questions if they ever came. After her one episode of racking sobs, Tacey had become almost as withdrawn as their son. She moved very slowly as if sore all over, inside and out.

Her preacher, whose name Dandy always forgot, seemed a

fool when he spoke as himself, but his personal nature dissolved while he was reading the old words most of the congregation could have read for him, without even using a Bible.

". . . in my father's house are many mansions . . . neither can they die anymore, for they are equal until the angels; and are the children of God, being the children of the resurrection . . . that whosoever believeth in him should not perish but have eternal life . . . God so loved the world . . . and whosoever liveth and believeth in me shall never die . . . ."

Not that Dandy believed these things, but he thought it proper that the weaker women and children should be consoled by stories. He waited dreamily for the Twenty-third Psalm to be said, for its rhythms were still in his own childhood memory and Tacey had made him say it in the hospital. When? In June? A hundred years. They had said it over his dead mother, over his dead father. He didn't know anybody underground who had gone down without it.

". . . Christ, the first fruits of them that slept . . . sown a natural body, it is raised a spiritual body . . . we shall not all sleep, but we shall all be changed in a moment, in the twinkling of an eye . . . ."

At the front of the church, directly below the pulpit, was the white coffin. Some would say casket, a container of jewels. Jewel. The casket lid was closed under a blanket of pink flowers.

They had gone together earlier to the funeral home to see inside. Truly the deserted shell of Mary's face was beautiful, more than it had ever been in life, so beautiful that not he nor Tacey nor especially Frank could bear it. Nor did any of them mention the yellowish tinge just rising under the surface of that beautiful skin. Dandy wanted to cry then, but the other two had hardened their grief past crying, and now he no longer had the urge. They had hurried out of the viewing room into false opulence, down the wide hall with its wine-colored carpet, velvet chairs, those hidden lights too low to see by. High-class violin music could barely be heard.

"At the funeral, you agree we should leave it closed?" Tacey asked. Dandy nodded, but Frank's mind was on something else. She touched his elbow.

"She used to sleepwalk," he said vaguely.

Tacey hoped Mary was still walking somewhere, during this deepest of all sleeps, but it didn't seem sensible to think so, not today. She stepped into another room to leave instructions with the far-too-polite man who had seen Mary's body unclothed, had taken things out of it, and put other things in. She could hardly bear speaking to him with any manners at all.

Dandy had followed, uneasy over her self-control. "You stay with Frank," she ordered. "Don't let him go back in there."

Now at the funeral Dandy longed to see inside the casket one more quick time. What if someday he forgot exactly how her unruly hair had curled? Someone had neatened it and spread a hank over the scar from the eleven stitches in her scalp.

He jumped as a loud, high bawl from Christine rose over the preacher's words. No, he would not even glance down the pew to where Georgia was holding on to her, hard. Frank, too, stared straight ahead. Not at the preacher, the flowers propped on metal stands, the white box Tacey had finally chosen without anybody's help, but into the tall and shining organ pipes he stared.

". . . but I would not have you to be ignorant, brethren," droned the voice, "concerning them which are asleep, that ye sorrow not, even as others which have no hope. For if we believe that Jesus died and rose again, even so them also which sleep in Jesus will God bring with him . . ."

Dandy supposed the eleven surviving disciples had honestly believed. Uneducated country men. Caught fish for a living. Sometimes, and especially right now, he wished he could believe as effortlessly as Tacey did. To apologize for this thought he took her hand, the fingers too thin, the veins too swollen, big freckles everywhere. Two years ago the jeweler had cut off her wedding ring and made it a bigger size. As he touched the

knuckle he could tell what a skeletal hand would be left someday. By reflex he jerked when pain suddenly howled in his
heart.

When he could look around again he realized every bench
was full. People he'd never seen before stood around the walls
under the Technicolor windows that showed Peter falling into
the water and Jesus with children at his feet. The glass children
were as pretty as those in TV commercials. Strangers who'd
given money to the fund and then read Cindy Scofield's obituary
article had come. That made him seek out Cindy, across the
aisle, sitting with Elmo and his wife. The women were crying
softly.

Men were also standing outside on the wide steps and in
clusters around the Damascus churchyard. When the noises from
Christine subsided he could hear schoolteachers and their pupils
crying. There was the stuck-up girl whose mother had brought
her by the house, Kay-Something. On one front bench the
pallbearers, all state troopers in uniform except for hats in laps,
sat at attention and examined—like Frank—the different
heights of the organ pipes and the gold cross on the center wall.

". . . let not your heart be troubled, neither let it be afraid."

He spotted Jill just two rows behind Cindy Scofield, also
crying. He wondered if she knew that the black woman beside
her, Rosa, was old-fashioned and had not been pleased to find
long blond hairs in Frank's sheets.

There was too much crying, now; Dandy was absorbing too
much of it.

At last came the Twenty-third Psalm in all its aching familiarity, and Dandy felt his mouth moving to every one of
those words he did not trust, words that after all these years
were still perfectly arranged in storage deep in his throat.

". . . and I will dwell in the house of the Lord for ever."

There was singing—but not from him or Tacey or Frank—
then they filed stiffly behind the troopers who carried the coffin,
the casket, the box; he could not let himself think they were

carrying Mary—no!—and he and Tacey had to take second place behind the Broomes, who were half dragging the wreck of a whimpering Christine between them, down those steps between rows and rows of dark Sunday suits, and over the still-wet grass behind the church where a sycamore dropped last night's rain and a green tent stood. Hundreds of people were moving behind them making a collective noise that sounded like a wind.

He knew they were moving because the uniforms in front of them kept moving, but his legs had little feeling. At the tent you could not see down into the muddy ground. That was good, Dandy thought, as he sat in a metal chair. He still held Tacey's hand; she, he saw, had taken Frank's but there was no grip. It must be like holding a fish.

All the red earth on either side had been carpeted somehow, and the green rug reached all the way to the silver rack on which the patrolmen set her—set *it*—down. Christine had dwindled into a moan.

Now the preacher said something more, but shorter and faster. Tacey's knobby fingers were almost hurting his; he looked across the lap of her black skirt to see they were gentle on Frank's. He was her baby still, as Mary—no. He stopped himself. Other heads bent low so this must be a prayer. Dandy got his eyes shut in time for it to end. Suddenly the preacher was moving down their row, shaking hands; he had to unwind Frank's and Tacey's and his own so he could shake all of the Thompsons', then he was moving past and murmuring to relatives who sat in the other rows. Dandy felt wrung-out but dazed. Is that all?

Tacey pulled till he stood up; they each took one of Frank's arms. Nobody was making as much noise as Christine. Virgil held her back from the white coffin until Georgia could lead her away. As Dandy crossed the muddy cemetery behind her he noticed for the first time her black hat and veil.

Yes. Cover your face.

Then they were climbing into the long rented car. When Frank turned abruptly Tacey grabbed his coattail in case he might run back to the tent and tear off the blanket of flowers, but he only stood motionless by the car to let Jill embrace him, then Elmo, then others whom Dandy did not know, then Cindy, who grabbed him awkwardly around the waist and almost shook him, then men who yanked Frank forward very quickly, eyes averted, so that their bodies banged.

At last Tacey pulled him into the limousine. They seemed to sit waiting silently for a long time. The driver must have been called away. Dandy put his hand on Frank's knee—too bony; he had lost weight—but Frank, having had all the touching he could stand, shuddered away.

THREE DAYS after the funeral, Dandy began to wonder if Frank was ever going to move back to his own apartment. He had refused leave time, went to work, ate very little supper, went early to bed. He never mentioned future plans.

Dandy waited until Tacey had sent the last thank-you note before he told her Frank had gotten morbid. He shouldn't put things off.

"I guess." Tacey sighed. That afternoon she had bought from the ABC Liquor Store a stack of cardboard boxes for a nickel apiece. On the fourth morning after the funeral she carried these into the Ramshead Chateaux apartment. After tiptoeing through the rooms, already musty smelling with no air-conditioning, she marched into Mary's. She began folding and packing clothes. This shirt had been a Christmas gift. She laid in the outgrown jeans, the bikini underwear that had never been on a decent-sized hip, but had fit neatly just below the dialysis tube. The sneakers she found must have rotted in the closet. Into a different box went stuffed animals, souvenirs. Though she had expected to cry, the task was mechanical. Items like scrapbooks and diaries, school papers, piano recital programs, photographs, she stored on a high shelf. She took down posters of half-naked actors and singers whose names she did not know and whose navels seemed to her surgically improved. Tapes and CDs went into one box; into another was all the stuff that had come home from the hospital—even the plastic basin and a Styrofoam water pitcher. When Tacey was through, it almost looked like a motel room.

That emptiness made Tacey drag down the box of photograph albums and unstick from the pages an assortment of snapshots to place in a random border around the frame of the bedroom mirror: Mary with Kay Linda, on Chancy, when she was a Brownie Scout, in Halloween costume (purple tights with attached purple balloons—she had gone trick-or-treating dressed as a bunch of grapes), in Easter clothes between Tacey and Dandy wearing her first pair of real panty hose, on her bike, sunbathing by the pool—so thin!—and one with Frank and, in a brief flare-up of justice, one with Christine in Jacksonville.

Within that wreath of smiling Marys, she looked at the reflection of her own tired face with its old pale skin draped under her tense mouth and below her chin. Whew. Tacey shook her head. What she hoped was that Frank, in time, could stand at this same mirror and glimpse in his image the first fleeting signs that even grief might have an end. Or a brief remission. In her own face there were no such clues.

The next day she asked Rosa to come help her with one massive housecleaning. At its end the rooms and both women smelled of pine oil and Lysol and soap and wax and polish.

"That's as ready as we can make it," Tacey said.

"Ready to move out of," said Rosa.

The next week Frank was persuaded to move back. Tacey left the apartment wide open to air out the chemical smells, and when she arrived early to close windows, lock doors, and leave groceries, she found the refrigerator already stocked. Jill or Cindy? Cindy, she decided. But how did she know? Unless she's been riding by a lot and today saw every window wide. Tacey carried her own groceries home.

Now that he was out of her own house, Tacey had no way to check Frank's symptoms. Was he still sleeping too much? Eating at all? She telephoned Elmo, who said he'd been by and noticed Frank kept the door closed to Mary's room. Sure he was tense, he was blue, at work he didn't have much to say. What did she expect? Give him time.

As if she, Tacey, could give anyone time or take time away.

She found she was not yet ready to go back to church. How could she concentrate on prayer knowing that just outdoors, in the very backyard of God's house, were the rows upon rows of graves, and a new one? She would not even be able to park in the lot without seeing the place where the earth was still raw. The stone she had ordered had not been delivered. (Frank had barely glanced at its inscription, had not asked the size or price.)

But perhaps once the headstone was in place, she would go? Perhaps.

Nor could Tacey drive her car within sight of N.C. Memorial Hospital—its old name—or U.N.C. Hospitals as they were now calling it, the way Jill's boss had recently renamed the place she leased from him Centaur Farms and Riding Stables. One hospital was too much, and too much was aplenty, Tacey thought. One of the women at Damascus Church was always saying that, "and too much is aplenty." The same woman had once told her the old folks made cocklebur tea for kidney trouble, which women didn't even get back in the days when they wore hoopskirts.

No, she couldn't go to church, and she wiped the whole complex of brick medical buildings off her mental map. Sometimes the tallest and most intrusive roof would stick up into view with its satellite dish on top. It's only a dormitory, Tacey would insist to herself. She turned her back to the whole university and drove east to Durham to shop.

I'm not getting over this, she sometimes admitted while she was driving the long way round. But she tried to pretend to recovery for Dandy's sake, and especially for Frank's.

Dandy sent out feeble jokes into her world the way Noah once sent out doves to check the floodwaters. "I got the giant bottle of vitamins," he announced on returning from the drugstore, "because I'm getting so fat I plan to spill these on the floor and pick them up twice a day."

Nothing. He tried again, "I've decided to quit entering contests and get rich writing this book called *How to Get out of Doing It Yourself.*"

Nothing.

One day Tacey found herself in the same line with Jill Peters in the Chapel Hill post office.

"This is silly," Tacey said, indicating the aluminum posts and velveteen ropes that made patrons corkscrew forward in a neat arrangement.

"They learned it from airports," Jill said, but Tacey had never been on a plane in her life. "How's Frank doing now?"

"Fair. I thought you might know more than I did."

Jill shook her very curly head; the long plait was gone. She lifted her wide envelope. "These are my summer grades from Carolina; I'm in vet school now and our schedules didn't mesh. We tried going out, but it didn't work."

"What about your riding lessons?"

"I'm down to a few pupils at night." They edged forward, made a right turn in the artificial barrier, and waited again. "He sold Chancy."

Tacey was relieved that Frank had been able to make at least that decision. "Your own child," she began and stopped. "There's nothing harder."

"I know that." Again they moved sideways, forward, and back in a parallel row toward the clerk who was working on a money order.

Jill said, "He seemed pretty depressed. Every job, every

drunk, every arrest, even the TV news got on his nerves. I used to complain that he wouldn't talk about his feelings, but I ended up wishing he'd quit."

"Did he talk about Mary?"

"Only if he'd dreamed about her."

Tacey felt envious. She longed to dream of Mary but never could.

It was Jill's turn with the clerk who was weighing her first-class mail. "He dreams he visits her in funny places, tourist places. He said it was like reading the *National Geographic* all night. She's with the Japanese or she's riding a camel."

"How strange." Not at all the dreams Tacey wanted. They waved, and it was her turn to mail Dandy's latest sweepstakes entry and buy some stamps.

But then one day when Tacey carried him supper, she found Frank awake in midafternoon, dressed, shaved, with an appetite for her tuna fish salad right away. Lately she herself could not stomach meat at all. Flesh. Animals that had recently been alive. She could not even walk near that part of the grocery store and see the price of veal. But tuna came in a can; it did not look like the living creature it used to be.

Eating, he said, "You people ought to keep that church locked." Tacey stared. "People don't care anymore that it's a church. They'll steal the collection plates and the communion service and sell 'em for dope."

"You were out at Damascus Church?"

"And the main door was unlocked and the fellowship hall, too."

"I think that's so anybody can go in that wants to pray." She wondered: Did you go in?

"One Sunday morning you'll all go in, and that gold cross won't be hanging on the wall."

He went in; at the funeral he'd noticed nothing.

As if re-creating other visual details about the sanctuary Frank stopped chewing and absently turned the empty fork in his hand. His color had improved. But into his silence she said, "Is it too salty?" This prompted nothing. After clearing her throat she asked uneasily, "Did you notice if they've put up— if Mary's stone is there?"

His face almost shrank for a minute, then he shook his head. He ate more salad, some lettuce. "But the grass has grown."

To Tacey it seemed sad that Mary's final resting place was marked only by a rectangle of greener grass. "I better call them."

She spooned him a little more tuna. Mary Grace Thompson. When the baby was born, Christine had wanted to name her Candy or Debbie or Meryl. In a compromise with the latter, Frank had prevailed with Mary. And Tacey had suggested Grace in remembrance of a favorite dead aunt, Grace Alexander, a woman she had made up on the spot. It was "Grace, Amazing" that she really had in mind.

Shocking Grace, she corrected now. Disappointing Grace.

She'd asked the tombstone people to carve under the name and dates that verse from Psalm 30: "Weeping may endure for a night, but joy cometh in the morning."

She hoped it was true.

"This is good," Frank murmured, showing more appetite than she'd seen in a long time. "Mama, have you been on a diet? I've just noticed that you've lost a lot of weight."

"Dandy throws down these vitamin pills twice a day, and I have to bend over to—oh, never mind," she said, but the smile was there. She slid the plate of crackers closer to his hand. "Ah, were you out there by yourself?" Perhaps he had even spoken downward through that fresh grass; people did talk to the dead, she knew. One of her best friends, the widow of a serious basketball fan, came out to the cemetery every time Carolina beat Duke and told her husband's tombstone what the score had been.

"I just happened to be in the area."

While he was eating, she stepped away from the persistent odor that mayonnaise could not mask—the smell of meat, of flesh, dead animals—and went down the hall to open wide the door to Mary's room. This apartment was much too quiet now. Frank couldn't forever keep this room closed off like a morgue. She saw that around the mirror the snapshots had curled, their edges like drying leaves in a wreath.

Tacey did not go in but called back, "You need to air out these rooms!"

"What?"

She said no more, just pushed that door back against the wall, propped it wide open with a chair.

Over the next slow weeks she watched Frank avidly for the smallest symptoms of healing. Sometimes when she let herself into the apartment in his absence, Mary's door would be standing open, sometimes closed. She always left it open. She would check inside the closet to see if Frank had opened any boxes of Mary's mementos. Occasionally she tempted him by leaving open the closet door also.

On one visit she thought there was a light odor in the living room, Jergens hand lotion, or even Pond's cream. On another morning, when he was still sleeping off the night shift he now preferred, she was shocked to find—instead of *T.V. Guide*— the Bible she had given Mary open on the table by Frank's chair. Tacey checked the cover; yes, in gold lettering, MARY GRACE THOMPSON. The Bible had been opened between chapters six and seven of the Book of Revelation.

Oh, don't head in that direction! Tacey thought, dismayed. Maybe Elmo had come visiting, quoting Scripture. Elmo had gone all the way to Greenville, South Carolina, one summer to take a course on witnessing and had been a pest ever since. The truth was that as a young man Elmo had got religion about five minutes after he got the mumps, and Tacey just couldn't take seriously a case of conversion by the testicles.

She gave a quick skim of the Bible pages open to verses about seals and horsemen and stars falling from Heaven like figs off a tree. Quickly she thumbed back to the Gospels, knowing that

John was usually assigned to potential converts, but stopping instead at Luke, which she preferred because it had more women and Gentiles in it. She sank into Frank's chair, trying to select a chapter. It would be too much to leave the New Testament set like a bear trap wide open to the raising of the daughter of Jairus, but just before that came the widow's son called off his funeral bier at the gates of Nain. Actually, as she ran through the chapter headings, none of these stories seemed tailor-made for Frank. She had expected better of the Holy Spirit. In fact, she had to suppress her own irritation when leprosy disappeared so easily on one page, and mud alone restored eyesight on the next.

She settled on sticking a pencil like a bookmark so if Frank ever did open to Luke his eye would fall straightaway on the story of the Prodigal Son. As good as anything. A lot better than the Great Tribulation.

Then it seemed too much to leave the Bible faceup with Mary's naked name shining on the front. She turned the whole book over, stepped back. She relocated Frank's chair a little closer, a comfortable arm's length, and edged the lamp in place.

But these little tricks: photographs, open door, the Bible turned upside down—these probably would not help Frank; they were certainly not helping Tacey. Driving home on a wide loop beyond Carrboro so she would not pass the hospital, Tacey thought she understood too well the phrase "a heavy heart." Its burdensome weight and pressure were physical. Daily she buckled her seat belt over the cage of her chest in which it hung like a sandbag.

I'm not getting over Mary's death at all, she had to admit. A silent admission, but her teeth were locked as if the truth had been dragged out between them. She counted the others: my mother, my father, my grandparents—but they had lived long, and her father's slow cannibal-cancer needed a death instead of morphine to stop him from screaming. They were so much older then. I was younger and stronger.

Surely this spiritual flu, like the physical kind, became harder to fight off when the patient was older. Recovery used up more strength. Took longer. Was prone to complications. Might cause implosion of a heavier, older heart.

When she crossed onto Estes Drive and passed a school with its playground and bicycle racks, she got bloated with unshed tears. But to cry them out would take too much energy, would fog her glasses; driving was hard work enough these long, gray days.

And if Dandy or Frank saw her crying, they might suspect that her faith had undergone so serious an infection it might not recover. For Frank's sake, at least, she had to pretend that with autumn the days were slowly getting better.

I have to pretend, she thought, that the Prodigal Son is more than a bedtime story and that the Heavenly Father who ran out to meet him is real.

AT 10:00 P.M. SATURDAY, between thundershowers, Frank stopped by the patrol station to swap cars; his was overheating. With sixty-five thousand miles it would soon be replaced anyway.

Elmo was already there, complaining because he'd given so few tickets lately that his current evaluation sheet might look bad. "Nobody's speeding these days with all this rain."

"I hear they closed the Deep River Bridge."

"They need to replace that old bridge anyway. Morgan Creek's out of its banks, and there's standing water on a lot of roads and a new front moving in, so we'll have a busy night."

Frank noticed that Elmo had laid his paperwork atop something thick, and he pushed the sheets aside. A Sunday-school quarterly lay underneath. He had to laugh. "Everybody else reads porno. You're a disgrace to the reputation of law enforcement."

Elmo got red. "I got to teach tomorrow."

High lightning made the station windows brighten and then go dark; after a pause the thunder grumbled at a distance. "Maybe you better do Noah," Frank said. He put a red tag on his car key, signifying the need for repairs, hung it on the board, and took down another.

"You want to call Cindy?" asked Elmo, the old matchmaker. "When she called to get the wreck reports, she didn't sound like herself."

"I talked to her," Frank said. "It's that ugly little dog of hers. Heartworms. They'll have to drip arsenic into the blood system or something."

"Something serious like that, I'd take the dog over to the vet school. How's Jill getting along in her studies, by the way?"

"Don't know, haven't seen her."

Elmo followed him outdoors to the substitute car, where they stood in a misty drizzle making a quick check of its radio, electronic siren, and P.A. system, activated the blue light, then ran through the list of standard equipment. Frank read while Elmo checked items in the front seat and trunk.

"Cindy ought to have children," Elmo said. "She's got this dog thing out of all proportion."

Frank only kept calling items on the list: shotgun and ammo, ax, booster cables, crowbar, first-aid kit, steel tape, broom, wrench, and so on. The sky lit up and they waited for thunder. "The main storm is where, about Greensboro?"

Elmo said he hadn't heard a recent weather report. "So you've been seeing Cindy again?"

"Some. Not much."

"I thought she was talking about moving on to a bigger newspaper."

"She still talks about it sometimes. I don't know."

Elmo closed the trunk. "Ruby saw your mama uptown yesterday, said she looked bad."

"Mama? No, she's fine, she's solid as a rock."

"That's good to hear." Elmo looked hard at Frank while he

rubbed on one elbow the metal diamond insignia that gleamed on the front crown of his hat. "Ruby asked me how old she was and I didn't know."

"She's fine," Frank insisted. "Which way you headed?"

"This side of Durham. You're on Sixty-four?"

"Siler City to Pittsboro." They parted to their cars with a nod, Frank to spend east/west time on what had once been the longest straight stretch in North Carolina, still became a some-time racetrack for soldiers roaring back from Greensboro to Fort Bragg, with a convenient observation point—Midway Hill—on which he could park with a good view on both sides for drivers who were too fast, too slow, too wavery.

Around midnight Frank had made the sweep all the way from Siler City (and checked the Rocky River, high and fast but not flooding), had swung through Pittsboro and north, and was eating a doughnut while he drove through light rain when the radio call came in about a wreck fewer than five miles ahead on 15-501. There was a buzz of tension in the careful enunciation of the broadcast voice. It hinted at the gathering swarm of helpers who would soon home in on the site: rescue squads and deputies and volunteer firemen from Orange and Chatham counties. But he was the closest. Two vehicles involved. At the Haw River. One driver not located.

He gave his location and E.T.A., threw the doughnut into the rain, accelerated, and flipped on his light.

Frank braked his speeding cruiser on the wet pavement when the Haw River bridge came into sight, a truck turned sideways and leaning, an unexpected gap in the concrete rail, a cluster of people pointing—*oh shit!*—down to the rushing water. He radioed quickly for more help as his car slewed sideways and then stopped.

When he leaped out he could see a large chunk of cement wall had been knocked by the truck into the river, but a small car had been tossed on the sloping bank and had then cut a swath downhill through black willow and honeysuckle before falling into the current, where its hood had been stopped by one of the rock ledges that made the muddy river foam after rains like these.

From the bridge people were screaming and pointing to the half-submerged car. He threw himself down the muddy shore toward it. The flashlight wasn't much help—moon and stars were too far beyond the dark clouds, he thought, as he floundered through the path of crushed underbrush the car had made. One man ran from the bridge after him.

The driver's door was caved in. Water was splashing through that broken window. When Frank got close enough to shine his light over the crumpled roof he knew the car had rolled, rolled hard. The front seat was empty. He yelled over his shoulder, "How many?"

"Don't know!" The fat man was blowing hard. "Somebody said two."

Nobody visible. On the floor maybe? No seat belt fastened, maybe loose in the fast river. Frank ran straight into the rushing water, which was cold but stopped just below his holster. No car doors would open. The swift water felt grainy with silt and stung his hand. The other man tried to help him jerk the doors but only knocked Frank's flashlight into the muddy river.

He stretched inside to the front seat, now displaced backward, but not even a hand or shoe could be felt.

Above the backseat a twisted dark shape had been shoved onto the high side out of the water, crammed into a narrow space as into a vise and clamped there by the broken metal roof. Frank pushed through the window, crawled over a tangle of broken seat through glass crumbs until he could grope and touch hair, long hair; a girl, wet hair, not wet with water. His fingertips slid into either a mouth or a wound. She groaned.

Just getting her out would require prizing apart the crushed automobile using the Jaws-of-Life equipment. Though he didn't believe it, he said softly, "You're going to be fine," while feeling for the sharpest edges that enclosed what he hoped was a very small person and not a full body crushed now to jelly. "Help's here and we'll get you right to a hospital, you're going to be OK, just fine," and on and on, murmuring between her low whimpers while he made sure there was no easier way. On the bridge, someone had located a car so its headlights could try to shine through the rain toward him, but still Frank could not tell if the dark hair belonged to a small child or an older girl. The face was turned away at a painful angle. Perhaps her neck was broken.

He wriggled backward. For a minute he thought the victim was crying out, "Christ! Jesus Christ!" but those words came from the fat man standing behind him in the cold water, now able to see where the headlights shone.

"I'll be right back, you're going to be fine," Frank kept saying to the trapped girl as he slid back toward the window. "You hang on till the doctor comes, just a minute or two, we'll get you right out of there." He dropped into the torrent. Both his hands were cut.

"Here," said the fat man, and handed him the wet flashlight. It still worked, but faded bright and dim and back to bright. Frank began calling out while passing the uncertain beam in a regular pattern across the rapid river, then along both shorelines. There had to be a driver somewhere.

"I'll be back for you!" Frank shouted over the noise of water hitting rock and metal.

Behind him the fat man panted as they sloshed to shore. "We just came around the curve, and that truck flipped sideways—it might have been a blowout—and hit the bridge, and then this car behind went right over it like it had bounced." He waited for a pause in Frank's yelling to find a second victim. "Can't we get that one out?"

"No. Was there one or two in the car?"

"Two?"

For some reason Frank was certain there had been two, a child and her father, perhaps, the child asleep, driving home late and it raining all the way; he could almost see them driving downhill to the bridge and the taillights of the truck just ahead going crazy off to one side.

"You search upriver toward the bridge. Keep calling." Frank shook the flashlight sharply as he pointed with it, then worked his way by breaking blackberry canes downstream where it was more likely the driver had been thrown. He called back, "Who's in the truck?"

"One man. He's unconscious."

Shit and damn and hell, Frank said repeatedly, while he struggled against the green tangle and sought for some lighter patch of color along the river's swampy edge. The rainwater was warmer than the river water. As soon as the rescue squad arrived, those people on the bridge would see that the truck driver got help. But the crushed girl in the wrecked car would take much longer, and meanwhile a third victim might be drowning or bleeding to death.

A trio of sirens could be heard, grew louder. First a fire truck careened onto the bridge from the south in case gasoline had spilled. Then from the north two ambulances and more law enforcement. Somebody shouted; Frank waved him downhill toward the Haw. He had already seen a pocketbook floating in river water on the car's floorboard. The other troopers saw it, too. Soon their stronger flashlights were bobbing beside his wavery one through the dark.

"Have they got the girl out?" he yelled.

"Just getting started." Elmo added that it was raining hard now to the west so the river would rise even more.

"Shit."

"It's a woman we're looking for," Elmo said. "Mother and daughter."

"No, it's a man," Frank said with a shove through wet bushes.

"Woman," Elmo said. "They got two pocketbooks out and ID."

Frank finally nodded. Behind them came a shriek of rasping

metal as the rescue machinery set to work. In a wide cluster of lights a crowd of men were straining to tear open steel like paper. In their shiny slickers they looked like yellow aliens.

Surely a paramedic was staying inside with the girl, Frank thought. Talking quietly. Holding her hand if he could find a hand. Maybe they'd already been able to get in an IV, give her a shot against pain.

While they searched, one ambulance sped away from the bridge with its lights and siren on, the other had driven through mud and waited, back doors open, as close as possible to the battered car. Traffic had backed up on both downhill slopes to the river.

As other uniformed men spread out and moved past him through the thickets, a shout went up and they converged downriver. Frank found himself shoving his way back toward the screeching noise made by the workers under their bright lights. He slogged as fast as possible through wet sand toward the wreck. One man in a white suit passed him dragging a folded plastic carrier shaped like a shroud. Frank thought: They found him. Her. But he kept moving. Down the long Haw Valley, wind shook both wooded sides of the river as it blew toward them, and blew heavier rain into Frank's face.

With a scream, the vise grip of the jaws scraped loose from the car and had to be reset.

Frank plowed through mud and ran to the crazed back window where he would not be in the workers' way. Now he could clearly see the distorted face of the trapped girl shoved into the cracked glass. Her broken nose was pressed into one bloody cheek. The crooked jaw must be broken, too, but under the shading of blue—were they bruises or makeup?—her undamaged eyelids seemed intact. No child's face, then. Maybe fourteen, fifteen.

Suddenly those eyelids flew up and her wide blue eyes stared into the bright maze of fractured glass and right through him at God knew what, perhaps at some premonition that even now men were picking up her broken mother from among the river weeds.

Frank yelled, "Get her out of there! Get that girl out!" He would have beaten his fist on the car but for fear of causing the girl further pain. "Get her out!" he shouted over the crumpled roof to the startled crew, and then was afraid the slightest disturbance would send glass slivers into those wide blue eyes.

Harder rain blew into the upturned faces of the men, then they went back to prying off the next chunk of the warped back door. Over their metallic struggle he could feel his open mouth still yelling, "Get her out! Get her out!" but he could not even hear himself above all the noise. With a wrench they broke open the car; the back window held together; the workers instantly stumbled out of the way so the rescue team could reach and carefully extricate the girl without damaging her even more. The wind and rain were noisy, but all the men fell silent.

Frank, too, made himself stand still and be still. Forcing himself well away from the stretcher, he waited by the flattened rear tire and picked glass splinters and briers out of one hand. When they carried her by ("Still alive?" "Still alive.") he moved too quickly on the slick hill and slid almost to his knees.

Elmo helped him up, holding out the two soggy pocketbooks. Whatever their color had been they were wet and dark now.

"Somebody's got to carry in the ID to the hospital. And call the father," Elmo said, waiting, since Frank had been the first on the scene. "You're wet to the bone."

"So's everybody else. I can do it," Frank said. Now the shape of the dead driver, for whom there was no hurry, was being carried past them.

On gusts of wind, cold rain slapped into Frank's eyes and ran down. "I wonder if she'll live. Or what'll be left of her if she does."

Elmo gave a helpless shrug. "They got her out pretty quick."

"It was a long time. A long time."

"No, it was quick. They did a good job. Everybody did a good job. You've lost your hat."

"It's in the river, I guess." Frank took from him the wet handbags, leather and denim, he saw.

"They're Catholics," Elmo said as if that mattered. Maybe it mattered to him; he'd been heard to say the Catholic religion was just one decoration after another.

Frank said how in the world did Elmo know that.

"St. Christopher was on the dashboard, and the mother had stuff in her pocketbook." Beads and medals, Frank supposed. "So you could get the local priest to call the family?"

"Maybe I will." With both bags hung on one arm, Frank leaned through rain and climbed to the bridge. As if it had been pulled downstream by the current, thunder had rolled in from the west and tumbled past, and lightning kept cracking the sky well below the wreck, maybe beyond Jordan Lake by now.

A crowd of lawmen was handling the work on the bridge and highway, getting tire tracks measured, handling witnesses, paperwork. The Highway Department had someone en route to inspect the bridge. He kept himself from thinking about the stranger whose telephone would ring with terrible news tonight.

Later—tired, sore, smelling of sweat and wet cloth, with both eyes scratchy, Frank drove through the waning storm north toward Chapel Hill, toward U.N.C. Hospitals, where the trauma team must even now be working to save the girl. Her name would be in the denim pocketbook. The rain was still thick enough to obscure the road except in moments when crooked lightning from the east broke the sky and ran down its curve to ground. On such a night he missed the cigarettes Mary had hated him to smoke. This rain that his windshield wipers tried to shove aside must be soaking down to where—*Oh Mary! Mary!*

He struck the steering wheel sharply, and the blow opened

the nicks and scratches in his palm. When Cole Park Shopping
Plaza, dark and empty, came into view he entered its broad
parking lot and drove in wide and wider circles front and back
until he felt calmer, turning the wheel smoothly with hands
that felt sticky and cold. The parallel lines made by his tires
on the rainy pavement swirled into giant rings and then were
erased by rain.

Back on the highway, he made himself concentrate on the
living though badly injured girl, then on her parents—one
dead, but one living. The dead mother made him think of
Christine, now back at the River Haven Mobile Park, who
sometimes called Frank late at night, sometimes drunk. At first
he had hung up on her. He knew that another mother, Georgia,
turned off her own phone every night when the clock struck
twelve to keep from hearing Christine cry. Some nights now,
he let Christine talk and cry—especially if Cindy was with him
and he could move one foot over the sheet and just touch the
edge of her body anywhere at all while he kept the phone
propped on one shoulder. And while he was thinking of mothers, how about Tacey? Elmo was wrong; Tacey had borne up
better than any of them. She was quieter, maybe. Even a faith
as serene as Tacey's couldn't keep parents from worrying; she
must be as helplessly worried over Frank's state of mind as he
had for so long been helplessly worried over Mary's state of
health.

He glanced at the glow of his watch and, late as it was, on
impulse, swung his car off Columbia Street and drove along
narrow winding streets climbing toward his parents' home. The
town and its university had been built on a hill, and the older
suburbs followed the ridges with house basements cut into the
slope. He turned onto his own street under dripping trees briefly
ashine when the faraway lightning flared once. What had Tacey
told Mary the first time an electrical storm scared her? "It's just
lighting up to see to rain."

He thought of ringing the Thompson doorbell, even at 2:00

a.m., for no particular reason but the thought that he and his mother might talk about Mary, that's all, just talk about her; but through the mist saw from the curb as he slowed that the house was black. Deep in the house, like a pilot flame on a cookstove, glowed the small night-light Tacey kept shining in the hall; that was all.

Frank smiled at the certainty that hours ago Tacey had said her prayers (for him, no doubt) and then had gone easily to sleep. The storm must have blown a transformer, he suddenly realized, for the whole wet street was dark behind him. Ahead was only the narrow path cut by his headlights through a mist thin enough now to shine.

I'll see her early tomorrow, he thought, before she goes to church. But now he had to go to the hospital, check on the girl, look up a suitable Catholic priest in the telephone book. Possibly call the girl's father himself.

A NOTE ON THE TYPE

The text of this book is set in Garamond No. 3. It is not a true copy of any of the designs of Claude Garamond (1480–1561), but an adaptation of his types, which set the European standard for two centuries. It probably owes as much to the designs of Jean Jannon, a Protestant printer working in Sedan in the early seventeenth century, who had worked with Garamond's romans earlier, in Paris, and who was denied their use because of the Catholic censorship. Jannon's matrices came into the possession of the Imprimerie Nationale, where they were thought to be by Garamond himself, and were so described when the Imprimerie revived the type in 1900. This particular version is based on an adaptation by Morris Fuller Benton.

Composed by PennSet, Bloomsburg, Pennsylvania
Printed and bound by Arcata Graphics,
Fairfield, Pennsylvania
Designed by Peter A. Andersen